KU-305-324

A WINTER WARMER AT THE LITTLE CORNISH KITCHEN

JANE LINFOOT

One More Chapter
a division of HarperCollins*Publishers* Ltd
1 London Bridge Street
London SE1 9GF
www.harpercollins.co.uk

HarperCollins*Publishers*
1st Floor, Watermarque Building, Ringsend Road
Dublin 4, Ireland

This paperback edition 2022
1
First published in Great Britain in ebook format
by HarperCollins*Publishers* 2022

Copyright © Jane Linfoot 2022

Jane Linfoot asserts the moral right to
be identified as the author of this work

A catalogue record of this book is available from the British Library

ISBN: 978-0-00-853704-3

This novel is entirely a work of fiction. The names, characters and incidents portrayed in it are the work of the author's imagination. Any resemblance to actual persons, living or dead, events or localities is entirely coincidental.

Printed and bound in the UK using 100% Renewable Electricity
by CPI Group (UK) Ltd

All rights reserved. No part of this publication may be reproduced, stored in a retrieval system, or transmitted, in any form or by any means, electronic, mechanical, photocopying, recording or otherwise, without the prior permission of the publishers.

Five years ago we waited for you through a long rainy August. The morning you were born the sun came out – and it's been shining ever since.

For Eric, with love xx

To appreciate the beauty of a snowflake it's necessary to stand out in the cold.

Anonymous

SEPTEMBER

Stargazey Cottage, St Aidan, Cornwall
Glass eyes and party walls
Wednesday

'So this is it – Stargazey Cottage, St Aidan!'
We made it! What's more, the larger-than-life pottery Stargazey pie that fascinated Ella and me all those years ago as kids is still firmly stuck to the doorstep.

I stoop and put my fingers out to touch the fish heads poking out of the pastry crust. The shiver slithering down my back is exactly the same feeling I had when we used to race up the hill for the thrill of being horrified by those glassy fish-eye stares the last time we were here together, the summer I was seven. Ella was two years older and like a gazelle, so it was a given she got here first every time.

Ella's family lived next door to ours, and as kids in a Highland village Ella and I were inseparable. My family was just my dad, my brother and me – I was so young when my mum died I can't remember her ever being there. I mostly know her as someone with a face just like mine, who smiles out from the TV screen on the family videos with a toddler who was me, and Ned, who was always bigger.

But Ella's mum, Merry, was always there to help Dad out, especially when he struggled with the girlie stuff, which he always did. I also got to go on holiday with Ella and her mum and dad, because as well as Ella and me loving it, it gave Dad a break. The year I was seven was the last time we came to Cornwall. After that we went to Suffolk or Wales, then Merry got a taste for Spain and later Greece.

But some things stick in your head forever. The fish-head shivers and clay-baked pie at Stargazey Cottage are right up there along with the time I fell off the donkey on Santorini as a teenager and my boobs popped out of my bikini top.

This time round in Cornwall, twenty-five years after the first, Ella and I left her sleek car and my less smart van by the harbour and wound our way up the narrow, cobbled street side by side. And this time we were here for a lot more than just a holiday. As a Cornish devotee, Ella would have been happy to rush past the familiar geranium-filled window-boxes with tumbling lobelia, bushy from a summer's growth. But I was stopping to point at each new brightly painted cottage door, gasping when gaps between the buildings opened to reveal glimpses over the dark slate cascade of rooftops that tumbled down to deep turquoise flashes of the sea far below. Nodding as we dragged in deep breaths of salty air and silently agreed, *this is a great move we're making here.*

Ella's legs are still miles longer than mine, but my lung capacity has been boosted because I spent most of my twenties in the Alps. She's also been here enough times to know each cobble by heart. St Aidan wasn't a random choice to move to either; we're here because the bustling village is set against a backdrop of picturesque idyll. In the end, excitement overtook her, and she hurried me up the last hundred yards to the bend in the narrow road and the rental cottage we're about to move into.

As I straighten up again, she's still getting her breath back, and gazing at the random stone facade with its small-paned sash windows repeating either side of the front door and the tangle of clematis over the name plate. 'It's exactly as it was when I was here in January.' There's a beat of silence when she must be thinking back to the last holiday she had with Taylor, shortly before they separated. Then she pulls herself together, and a smile spreads across her face. 'We're so lucky they chose us as tenants, Gwen.'

'It really was meant to be.' I grin back at her. It's the first time she's been without a frown in ages. And I know recently I've headed abroad in autumn, but she's helped me so much in the last four years since I lost my brother, Ned. If I can be here to help her kick-start her brand-new life, it's the least I can do in return.

In reality, us landing the lease on this cottage was less about serendipity and more about Ella's dogged determination. Moving to a Cornish village by the sea had been Ella and her ex, Taylor's, dream for ages.

As best friends who'd been together since the first week at uni, they seemed so solid as a couple. They were the ones who'd done the grown-up stuff when the rest of us were still messing about. I mean, I'm thirty-two, and since I moved on from being a perennial chalet host, I still don't properly know what I want to be yet. They'd married, moved around, done up houses, had successful careers for so long that Taylor had even moved on to a new one. They'd been to Cornwall so often their holiday-let bookings rolled from one year to the next. Pretty much all they had left to do was to have kids and get some monogrammed towels saying 'The Simpson-Ramsays'.

And then Taylor fell in love with the Head of Sport at the school where he was doing his probationary teaching year, and Ella's whole world imploded.

Ella's an interior designer, and as she picked up the pieces of her life her London-based office landed a contract with a developer building luxury holiday homes in the Southwest. This was the opportunity she'd been longing for – a job she could walk into, for the firm she already worked for – and she was galvanised to make the move to Cornwall. With Cornish rents going through the ceiling, the living options weren't looking great for a single person, but she didn't give up. She spent more time on the St Aidan Facebook page than the residents so when the rental ad for Stargazey Cottage popped up one afternoon, she jumped on it within seconds of it appearing.

Trenowden, Trenowden and Trenowden Solicitors, Harbourside, St Aidan.

On behalf of an esteemed but absent client, we are offering the tenancy of:

Stargazey Cottage, Whelk Row, St Aidan

(Sound but slightly tired, 3 bedrooms, would benefit from TLC)

Prospective tenants should be willing to carry out minor renovations and redecoration while in residence. A suitable sum has been allocated to pay for work and materials. A below-market rental figure will reflect the practical contribution the tenants will be making to improve the property.

Would suit friends sharing or a couple, DIY/handy-person skills an advantage.

Full-time residents only please.

On successful completion of the works, the tenancy will be re-offered at the same rate should the tenants wish to extend.

Please apply in the first instance to George Trenowden.

Talk about good luck! If they'd written their ideal tenant description, it would be Ella down to a T. Not only is she an interior designer; she and Taylor have renovated so many homes together she can do it in her sleep. She had to be the perfect choice. Knowing the cottage so well too, she was already a jump ahead of the opposition.

Two seconds after she spotted the ad, Ella was on the phone to me at my temporary job at a summer language school near Brighton, which was officially in housekeeping but basically consisted of ferrying kids to and from the airport. I was actually on the M25 heading towards Heathrow when she suggested we join forces and I move to Cornwall with her. I'm flexible about where I go so long as there aren't any mountains, so by the time I reached the Arrivals Hall, I was 100 per cent on board, and Ella swung into action.

She fired off those first phone calls and emails so fast we assumed Stargazey Cottage *had* to be ours. But with a deal this good, there wasn't just a lot of interest – *there was a stampede.*

We ended up sending dossiers and having a series of Zoom interviews which were then viewed by a committee. I mostly left the talking to Ella and hoped no one would realise what a rookie I was. We thought Ella's local work confirmation would be our golden card, but that still wasn't enough so we moved onto blind blags and wild claims, always trying to second-guess what they were looking for, so we could go one better than the opposition.

We never knew exactly what swung it for us. Like all the tensest interviews, we both had brain freeze after every one, so we're hazy about what promises we *actually* made. But when we've just signed the lease for a cottage as close to our hearts as this one, in one of Cornwall's prettiest villages, with the promise of a forever tenancy, we're not going to look back.

And the rest – as they say – is history. Ella is all set to start her new job and I'm hoping to find some temporary work now I'm here. Obviously for me, with my perennially itchy feet, the move is less of a whole-lifetime commitment than it is for Ella. But I won't be moving on until the cottage is done and Ella's completely rooted; by then I'll have set her on her way to her brand-new future.

I shiver again as a gust of September wind whips down the lane, and slices through my T-shirt. It feels a good twenty degrees cooler than the endless summer Ella described to me that day as Heathrow's Terminal Three loomed into view, but I'm not about to grumble.

Since I lost my brother in a mountain accident, I've learned the trick is to only talk about good things. And lately, Ella has embraced that tactic too. Let's face it, no one wants to hear about internationally renowned relatives getting buried in freak avalanches or husbands breaking your heart and going off to live the life that should have been yours with someone else. So we're the happy women; to look at us, there's no clue that we have anything other than perfect lives.

Ella dips into her bag, pulls out the key we just picked up

from George Trenowden at the solicitors' office by the harbour and grins at me again. 'Selfie to capture the moment?'

We flick back our almost matching blonde hair, lean into the door and beam at my phone like life couldn't be better. 'Got it!'

She wriggles the key in the lock, but the door moves before she turns it. 'How sweet, they left it open for us. That's the kind of village this is, no one locks their doors. Honestly, you're going to love it here, Gwen. Come on in, I can't wait to see inside.'

I'm with her on that. Taking the tenancy without an official viewing in the flesh wasn't ideal but the solicitors' involvement reassured us it was above board, and I knew the house enough from the outside to know we'd love it. There are times in life when you have to take a gamble, because if you didn't, you'd regret it forever. Even so, as I follow the swish of Ella's smooth blonde hair into the hall I'm holding my breath, and have my fingers tightly crossed.

'Oka-a-a-a-a-y...' Ella's hesitant tone is unsettling.

The room we're in is wide, and bright enough to make me blink. I'm guessing the pile of plasterboards and the bare wires hanging from the ceiling are a surprise we weren't expecting.

The vibe's definitely building-site rather than the tired cottage we've been promised, but the up-side is staring me in the face. 'Look at that view!' The gigantic floor-to-ceiling windows still have their manufacturer's tape on and open straight out onto the vista of the ocean in the distance. 'If you lean out far enough, you'd almost feel the sea spray splashing up off the rocks down below.' I'm exaggerating, as usual, but whatever. If it's this size downstairs, repeated on three floors, I'm also thinking that's a whole lot of decorating to do. It's not as if I've done any before.

Ella's eyes are brightening as she assesses the space. 'It's been extended since I was here, but we can definitely work with this.' She pushes through the next door into a wide room with a double bed that's already made up and a pile of books on a crate. 'It's amazing what people leave behind.'

I drop into the tub chair in the corner of the room and peer over the side. 'It's a complete welcome pack. There's even a mug and a kettle!' As I wrap my arms around me, I'm wishing my cardi was here rather than in the parking area with the rest of the luggage.

Ella's one of those people who notices every nuance, and she's straight onto my goosebumps. 'Are you cold?' She's also a problem solver, and she doesn't hold back when it comes to telling people what to do. A second later she's shaking out a neatly folded hoodie from a stack by the bed. 'Take one of these then we'll look at the rest. Some places you get complimentary bath robes, at Stargazey Cottage it's over-sized outerwear. They're probably left over from when it was a holiday rental.'

As I pull it over my head, I'm breathing in the delicious scent of fabric conditioner. Instantly warmer, I stare down at the logo and grin because you have to love the bullshit signage you get on clothing. 'Team GB Sailing? That's as fabulously inappropriate for me as my Harvard University one.' Much to Ned and Dad's dismay, growing up I was as uncoordinated and wimpy as they were athletic and brave. And I've never been anywhere near America *or* higher education.

Ella laughs. 'We should probably get our own team sweatshirts to wear around the village.'

I'm not entirely keeping up with her. 'Sorry?'

'Star Sisters Styling – so exclusive we aren't even on Instagram. I *might* have mentioned it in our pitch.' She looks a lot less sheepish than she should.

I let out a groan. 'Let's hope no one finds out I can't design to save my life.'

She half closes one eye. 'You have a lot more talent than you know, you just haven't discovered it yet. Until you do, I'm happy to provide the expertise for both of us.'

Ella's always been great at wriggling to get her own way, while I'm the one who watches in shock with my jaw on the floor. On reflection though, well done to Ella, because the space will be great when Merry comes to stay, which could be more often than not once she's back from her autumn in Spain.

Ella flops back onto the bed and spreads out her arms. 'Don't stress. We're here now and we've landed ourselves a humdinger of a house. This bed is like a dream; the rest will all fall into place too.'

Right on cue as she says the word 'fall', there's a clatter from the main room. Even for Ella, that's too good to have arranged herself. We're exchanging puzzled glances when a guy saunters into view in the doorway.

'Ladies. Good afternoon.'

I try to ignore it, but his voice is so low those three tiny words have brought my goosebumps back.

Ella props herself up on her elbows, but to my surprise I'm the one who jumps in. 'Actually, first things first – we're women, not ladies.' This is usually Ella's line, due to her spending so much time on building sites. I can only think I've rushed in with it myself because I'm so taken aback by this guy crashing in looking so entitled. I hate reacting to guys at all because it makes me feel weak and powerless. And if I'm even more honest, it's not something I do, because when I lost Ned, my insides froze and the numbness hasn't ever gone away.

Our first visitor appears to be amazing to look at, which is not something I'd ever bother to pick up on either. Since my last relationship fizzled out it's been easier on my own. Obviously I've heard people dish out the 'drop dead gorgeous' label, and I never really knew what they meant before. But when I look more closely, backlit by the sun, this guy's like a composite of all the men I've ever swooned over in pictures – except that those *Vogue* models and rock stars always had a negative, like their mouth being too straight or their jaw being a bit weak, whereas right now I can't see anything I'd change about this one. He's so damned perfect it's actually making me feel a bit sick.

Working in customer slash domestic service, I'm used to handling unexpected situations. 'We aren't local, we've literally just walked into our brand-new place, so you'll have to bear with us.' Unless he has a good explanation for why he's just strolled into our welcome-pack room like he owns the place, this is going to be really embarrassing for him. Even so, I harden my tone, because I'm not prepared to let anyone derail Ella's arrival. 'Can we help you?'

I'm taking in long, strong legs covered in denims even more faded than mine, dark, messy hair and hazel eyes that are gleaming with challenge.

If Ella's ordered us a 'welcome to our new home' strip-o-gram it's over the top even for her. In any case, Dial-a-Naked-Man-Islington probably don't stretch as far as Cornwall. On the other hand, if he's brought us some of those bake boxes she's always sending me links for off the St Aidan Facebook page, I might need to put the kettle on.

When I look again his hands are rough in a rugged kind of way, but they're definitely empty, so that dashes my brownie hopes straightaway.

He's also rude enough to be leaning a shoulder against the wall. 'What's this about your new place?'

There's a little bit more involuntary melting on my part, then I come to my senses with a jolt. It's the twenty-first century! Women don't fancy the pants off men *or* objectify any more. Liquefying into a little pool on the floor is *so* uncool; I need to woman up. 'Watch your metal buttons on the wall, please! That plaster looks new, and we'd rather not have chunks taken out of it.'

The guy jumps to attention, steps away from the wall, then turns to me again. 'Do you have a house name – for your new address?'

So maybe he is a delivery driver after all. I'm hating that my stomach flipped when he rounded on me so suddenly there, but he can't catch me out with this. 'Absolutely. Stargazey Cottage.'

The furrows in his forehead disappear. 'I'm not local either, I've hardly even visited the property I own here. But I know enough to guess what's happened.'

Ella rolls her eyes at me; it's a pet hate we share. Living in a Scottish village since we were kids, we've seen the cottages picked off one by one by incomers who turned them into holiday homes, then rarely came, and priced the locals out of existence. I have nothing but derision for guys like him, and I'm not afraid to call him out on it.

Just to prove what little effect he's having on me, I'll pass on that thought. 'Absentee home owners kill communities, I hope you appreciate that.'

He shakes his head and turns back to me. 'I'll definitely bear that in mind. But first let's clear up where we *actually* are.'

I'm so certain of this, I allow myself an ironic smile. 'Apart from the fact that *you're* standing in *our* future living room, I'm not sure how that's going to help.'

He gives a little cough. 'From where *I'm* standing, the problem is *you* being in *my* temporary bedroom, not the other way around.' He sounds horribly sure of himself. 'Just to make things clear, *this isn't Stargazey Cottage.*'

Ella sits up abruptly. 'What the actual eff?'

I'm not giving up on Ella's dream without a fight. 'We've been visiting this place for over twenty-five years, *so believe me, we know!* We've just let ourselves in.' As Ella shakes the keys at him, I remember we didn't, because the door was open. But I'm not showing weakness now. 'The Stargazey pie on the porch *might* be the giveaway!'

The guy winces. 'I'm really sorry about the confusion. And I'm really sorry to disappoint you. But this is Stargazey *House.* And it's *definitely mine.*' He pauses to let it sink in. 'Stargazey *Cottage* is the next door along, up the hill.'

I open my mouth because my stomach feels like it left my body. But I force myself to speak. 'So you're telling us we're currently not lounging on the bed *at ours* – we're actually a hundred per cent *at yours?*'

He nods. 'An easy mistake to make; it could've happened to any of us.'

It absolutely wouldn't, this is totally our stuff-up. And whereas Ella moves on from her mistakes, mine haunt me forever. A blunder this big will keep me awake at night literally until I die. 'In that case, we'll move to the other side of the wall and leave you to get on with your day.' And I know he said he's hardly here, but even if he's the worst absentee owner in the world, I'm dying all over again remembering he'll be our neighbour.

I don't often boss Ella around, but this time I'm on my feet. 'Come on, Ells, time to go.'

She's way taller than me, but as she gets up off the bed, I manage to spin her round and propel her through the space-with-so-much-potential that was almost our living room. Even her wriggliest counter-arguments aren't going to change this. I get her all the way to the front door, and I'm a nanosecond away from shoving her onto the street, when she digs in her heels and turns around.

I hiss at her. 'Truly, don't argue. We have to pass his door *every* time we go down to the village.'

She nods frantically and hisses back. 'All the more reason to return the sweatshirt we borrowed before we leave.'

I let out a sigh and die all over again before I turn back to the guy. 'So, not only have I accidentally misappropriated your top, but in my hurry to go I'm now about to steal it.'

He waves his hand. 'No worries, I'd hate you to be cold. Drop it back some other time.'

Like I'd ever be able to face him again to do that. I'd actually rather freeze. 'Best do it now.'

I grab the hem, peel it off, and hold it out to him, just wanting to get this over as soon as I can. But instead of leaping forward to get it, he's standing rigid, his mouth open, as if he's about to say something, but nothing's coming out.

Ella coughs. 'Gwen, your T-shirt. You've taken it off with…'

When I look down, sure enough, I'm standing there in my jeans and bra, and my T-shirt is fully embedded in the hoodie hanging from my hand.

'I've got this.' Ella grabs the bundle and starts to free my T-shirt. Which in some ways is a worst-case scenario, because it leaves me standing like a contestant in a beauty pageant, wobbling my shoulders and waggling my boobs and bare midriff at Mr Drop Dead Gorgeous like there's no tomorrow.

Every embarrassment in my life to this point pales to nothing.

If only I'd worn my sports bra – I know I'm not sporty, but I still own one. Instead, due to a last-minute rush to catch up on laundry before we left, I'm standing here in my skimpy, see-through lacy number that leaves zilch to the imagination, bought light-years ago when I once had the semblance of a love life. It's one of those times when bad follows worse. Not only have I fully flashed my boobs at the man, now if he thinks this is my everyday wear, he'll also think I'm…

I'm thankfully spared from going there when Ella passes me my T-shirt. My freezing nipples being fully visible through the T-shirt fabric seems like nothing after what came earlier.

I hold out the hoodie. 'And now we really are leaving.'

He gives a low laugh and puts out his hand, but instead of taking the sweatshirt he grasps my fingers. 'Ollie Lancaster. Good to meet you – is it Gwen?'

Except there's nothing good about it at all, because the seismic quakes running up my arm and down my back make the fish shivers seem like they didn't exist. And his hand is big enough to wrap mine up.

Ella's jumping forward. 'Gweneira. She's Gweneira Starkey. It's Gwen when you know her better. And I'm Ella Simpson.'

For some reason Ollie is still holding my hand. Then he blinks, takes the sweatshirt and turns briefly to Ella.

'Tell me, Ollie, do you ever go to village events?' This is Ella, and why she's asking this is beyond me. Ollie's a million miles away from the type of guy she'd go for and he's just told her he's never around. 'I've heard the singles club is very good. They do everything from cocktail evenings to sky dives.'

I grab my chance to move the subject on. 'Ella is *the* Ella Simpson who won the *Small Building Designer of the Year* award in 2019.' I've started so I'll say it all. 'She won it for a tiny but innovative conversion of a public convenience in Leighton Buzzard.' I'm not making it up; her stunning upmarket decor converted a toilet into a superb home. Usually when I pull this out in public it's a total showstopper. 'She actually got to touch Kevin McCloud at the reception.'

That's how I know who Ella's type is apart from Taylor. She was wobbly for days after that whenever we FaceTimed. Hopefully that will be the image that sticks in Mr More-beautiful-than-anyone-deserves-to-be's head, rather than any of me in my barely-there bra.

As we finally pass the pottery pie and arrive on the cobbles outside the cottage, I'm shaking my finger at the name plate on the wall. 'If you'd cut back the plant around the sign, this fiasco would never have happened.'

Mr Lancaster raises one sardonic eyebrow. 'Not at all, I'm pleased you dropped by. If you specialise in small, you should be fine next door.'

We have no idea at all what he means by that. But with just a few steps further up the hill to go, we're about to find out.

2

Stargazey Cottage, St Aidan, Cornwall
Small potatoes and great expectations
Wednesday

'Don't worry, Ells, we're fine to narrow our horizons.' Who knew there would ever be a time when I'd say those words, but as we step out onto the lane, I do.

The next door we come to a few yards up the hill has paint that's peeling. There's one small-paned window beside it, then the rendered wall cranks round following the twist in the lane, and a vertical line marks the abrupt change to a pristine white painted part belonging to a whole other, sharper cottage. The teensy frontage we're standing outside is barely wider than our shoulders.

I rub at the name sign as Ella finds the lock. 'It *might* say Stargazey Cottage under the salt crust.'

She raises her eyebrows hopefully. 'At least the key fits this time. Shall we try another selfie?'

'Totally.' I pull a paint flake out of her hair, fight back the feeling of *déja vu*, and beam at my phone. 'Our first house together.' This time round there's more opportunity to reflect. It's the first lease I've ever signed my name on, which is why I was relieved that George the solicitor whizzed us through it super-fast before I lost my nerve. I was way too on-edge to take in most of what he said.

Don't get me wrong – I'm just as much in love with cosy cottages and lovely homes as Ella is, but as a designer she's involved with creating them every day. I've stayed in some wonderful places with my work and made them very comfy for other people, but me making or having an actual home of my own has never been more than a fleeting dream; I've never felt like I was worth the trouble. I was actually more wrapped up in keeping Ned safe, but I managed to fail at that.

Ella frowns as she turns the knob and pushes the door open. 'This has to be the skinniest house in the world.'

I'm pleased she's giving this a positive spin because I'm not the kind of person who'd get hung up on how much wider everyone else's houses are. 'That's great news for whoever is decorating.' With the whirlwind of the move and not really knowing what was here, we haven't fully finalised who is doing what yet.

I follow her into a room that's approximately the size of the worn-out doormat, with walls a similar colour. Even as an amateur, I can see anything we do here can only make it better. 'As a hallway, it's bursting with potential.'

Ella coughs. 'As the stairs are going out of it, this *might* be the living room. But on the upside, there are two more floors above.'

I'm squinting at the walls. 'Does it feel wonky to you?'

When Ella puts out her arms with her back to the front door her fingers are almost grazing the side walls, but at the other end of the room she has more to spare. 'It's shaped like a wedge.'

I grin at her. 'Small is beautiful. Think what we'll save on furniture if we can't fit any in.' So long as Merry leaves her biggest pieces of jewellery at home when she comes to stay, it'll be great. Every year that she's been without Ella's dad, her beloved Hugh, Merry's beads and earrings have grown more massive. It's as if she's poured all her grief out of her heart and into stonking jewellery. That's what we tell ourselves every time we see her with a string of beads the size of tennis balls round her neck.

This is already hard enough for Ella. Even without next door blowing our expectations out of the water, I'm kicking myself for storming past the bakery on our way up the hill. 'Seeing as we forgot chocolate eclairs, how about some music?' I wave my phone at her.

Ella rolls her eyes. 'If we're singing along to your happy-teenager playlist, please let it be "Pure Shores".'

It used to be our favourite as teenagers, miming with our hairbrushes in front of the mirror-wall of fitted wardrobes in her bedroom. That one song somehow captured all our hopes for the wild beauty (mine) and freedom and choices (Ella's) our future lives were going to deliver. And in many ways, at first, we weren't disappointed; it's only lately that things have gone downhill.

As I take an old flowery curtain off the windowsill and pull it around me to stop the shivers, Ella's lips are twitching into a smile. 'Great wrap you've got there.'

I laugh. 'It's less cosy than next-door's hoodie, but at least it's not committing me to a yacht race.' As we start to sway to the music it already feels more like *our* place than someone else's. And it's important we get our priorities right. 'Let's take a quick look around, then we'll go for cake.'

But first I turn up the sound, and even though we have to limit our arm waving, we're singing along to the chorus like we're fourteen again. We're on our way to the stairs, halfway through a spectacularly enthusiastic 'out of r-e-e-e-each' when we realise there's someone at the window, peering past the cobwebs and knocking.

When I sway forward far enough to ease the door open there's a sandy-haired woman, in chinos and a checked shirt, holding a box.

She's got her head on one side, listening, then a beam spreads across her face. 'Don't tell me – it's All Saints!'

I grin at her and turn down the volume. 'How many years since you heard it?'

The woman gives a grimace. 'It was actually only last week. St Aidan's big on retro discos. But you'll find that out for yourselves soon enough.' Then her smile broadens again. 'I'm Nell, George Trenowden's partner. I hope I'm not rushing you, but I've come to say hello and welcome. I take it you're the Star Sisters?'

My mouth drops open as I hear the childhood label we reinvented to help our cottage application rolled out in real life. 'Lovely to meet you, Nell, I'm Gwen *Star*key, and this is Ella Simpson, *supernova* of the design world. Now you know where the starry part comes from, why not come in?'

As I close the door behind Nell, Ella carries on. 'We're honorary sisters rather than real ones.'

That's a typical example of an Ella line, but I back her up anyway. 'As kids that's what we pretended, we've been besties for ever.' I grab Ella's head and squeeze it next to mine. 'So long as you overlook that Ella's a foot taller and the same amount slimmer than me, we do look quite alike.'

Ella's carrying on the theme. 'If Gwen stands on a chair and I do my hair in wild corkscrew curls like hers, you literally can't tell us apart.'

Nell laughs. 'Your secret's safe with me. I've got some besties in St Aidan who are very much the same, we call ourselves the mermaids.' She holds out the box. 'Some of my mermaid friends made the cakes in here.'

As I squint at the label, I can't believe I'm seeing this in the flesh. 'A Little Cornish Kitchen cake box! I've been drooling over these on Facebook.'

Ella clutches the carton. 'I can smell the chocolate through the box. Better still, tell me which of the bakers baked them?'

Nell nods. 'They're Clemmie's brownies, and Cressy's double chocolate chip cookies.'

Ella smiles. 'I see all their posts on Insta.' She will have too as she was living here vicariously for years before the cottage came up.

Nell shuffles. 'As for the house – it's seen better days, so we hoped cake would help.'

I'd hate anyone to think we're disappointed. 'It's little but that's what makes it manageable. And rough edges were part of the deal.' Without either of those things, we wouldn't have been able to afford it.

Nell gives a knowing glance. 'It's obvious you're a design duo. Half an hour after you've picked up the key, you're already got the measure of the place.'

Star Sisters Design Duo was another ironic joke between Ells and me that somehow escaped into the application ether. Who knew it would come back to bite us so fast? 'I'm not sure what you've heard – Ella's the real deal, but I'm more of an apprentice.'

Nell purses her lips. 'My George is usually like a clam with his clients, but he was instructed to consult with the community for this tenancy, so our inner circle saw your Zoom calls.' She wiggles her eyebrows. 'We loved that you were *so* willing to join in.'

It's unnerving to be hearing about this from the other side.

Ella's beaming her reassurance. 'We won't be disappointing you. We'll be embracing all the community activities – alongside the renovations and the day jobs.' She gives me a shove. 'Won't we, Gwen?'

I shrink further inside my curtain, because the holiday cottage cleaning I'm banking on isn't actually arranged yet. And I definitely hadn't anticipated socialising. Left to myself, I'd rather stay home with a book or go for a solitary walk, although with the kind of work I do I've never had many days off. But I need to say something authentic.

'We'll be painting and partying for all we're worth. Woohoo!' Then I realise what I've said. '*Obviously* the parties will be in town, due to no more than three people fitting in here.'

Nell gives a chortle. 'It's St Aidan's most slender cottage as they squeezed it into the gap between the buildings either side. That's why it's narrower at the front than the back.'

As I look around, that explains a lot. 'This room is all we need; we'll be fabulously cosy in here.'

Nell's frowning at us. 'You have seen the kitchen with the views of the sea? And the little secret shed at the top of the garden? And those lovely sloping ceilings up in the attic?'

I'd hate anyone to know we were in the wrong place earlier and haven't had time to catch up. 'We haven't seen *everywhere* yet. We actually got chatting to the neighbour from Stargazey House.'

Nell's eyes open wide. 'That's a first! It's impossible to keep a low profile here, but that man's completely under the St Aidan radar. People have barely glimpsed him, let alone spoken to him.'

Ella's not the type to melt, but her expression goes all mushy. 'He's very nice.'

I don't want to be negative, but what planet is she living on? 'He was pretty reluctant when you mentioned activities earlier.' Working so long in hospitality, I can spot the aloof ones as easily as the party animals. Whatever it said on that hoodie, I doubt he's a team player.

Nell laughs. 'All the more reason we're lucky to have you two. I'm not just here with cake, I've also come to invite you to the singles club events.'

I exchange glances with Ella. As well as the St Aidan cake porn, Ella's made me fully aware of every fixture in St Aidan, and the singles club was one thing we clashed over. She's convinced it's right up my street, which is complete rubbish, because I'm fully committed to being on my own. And obviously she desperately needs to move on, but she just can't see that. What we did agree on is, it *would* be good for Merry. So long as she didn't know what she was going to, obviously.

I nod. 'Singles events sound perfect for Ella's widowed mum; we'd love her to meet someone so we'll point her in the right direction when she comes to stay.' Here's hoping her extended trip to the Balearic Islands doesn't go on for too long.

Nell chortles again. 'Sorry for letting you get the wrong end of the stick! Singles club events are open to everyone in St Aidan, regardless of relationship status. The only rule is: the more the merrier.' She pauses for a second, then brings out the big guns. 'We're counting on you to come! That's what you're here for!'

'Fabulous!' says Ella in her stony voice. Which is exactly what she says when it's totally not.

I can't see any way out of this without massively blowing our credibility, but there's no need to panic. By the time an event comes round in a few weeks' or even a few months' time, no doubt wriggly Ella will have thought of a way to get us out of it. 'We'll look forward to that.' I'm going the extra mile here. 'Will that be around Bonfire Night?'

This time Nell's laugh explodes. 'November? You don't have to wait that long! We've got breakfast club tomorrow if you're really keen. Otherwise, it's Friday at eight. The Little Cornish Kitchen are doing a barbie and beers in the garden at Seaspray Cottage, along the beach path beyond the harbour.' She hands me a flyer then squeezes past me back to the door.

I fix my smile so it doesn't slip. 'Lovely. Anything else we should know?'

Nell slams her hand to her head. 'It's fancy dress! How did I forget to say that?'

My heart has plummeted as far as my flip flops, but my mouth's still in the happy position. 'Better and better!'

Nell's halfway onto the cobbles. 'And if you ever need any eggs, give me a shout. They're free range, fresh from my mum and dad's farm, I'll most likely be able to tell you the names of the hens who laid them.'

Ella takes the paper from my hand and waves it at Nell. 'Brill. We'll be sure to tell our neighbour about the barbie too.'

I press the door closed behind Nell and turn to Ella. '*Why* would we ask him?'

Quite apart from everything else, after flashing him my underwear I was counting on never seeing him again. Ever.

Ella just looks at me. 'You might have forgotten, but neighbourly relationships are very important in small places.'

'What about the neighbours on the other side, then? I don't see you rushing to invite *them*.' I've got her there. She might wriggle with other people, but there's a lot less squirming with me.

She flicks back her hair. 'Honestly, Gwen, you can spot a mile off that one's a holiday cottage.'

As for Mr Stargazey House, I hope she's not set her heart on moving on with him. I'm quite good at reading people, and he's truly not the type to go for a village barbie. Add in fancy dress, and he's more likely to fly to the moon. On the bright side, that does mean one less thing for *me* to worry about.

When I grin at Ella, this time it's real. 'So what shall we do first? Eat brownies, or find this kitchen with the ocean view?'

She's already prising the lid off the bake box and her grin is as wide as the bay. 'Star Sisters multi-tasking lesson one: whatever you're doing, you can eat cake at the same time.'

3

Stargazey Cottage, St Aidan, Cornwall
Miniaturists and masquerades
Thursday

Nell was right – there *was* more cottage to come, but I suspect that *every* bit of it is less than Ella was expecting. The back room has a sink and not much else, the bathroom is mainly a corner bath, and the three bedrooms are each approximately the size of a suitcase – that's the teensy hand-luggage kind. As we unload our cars Ella's trying to be optimistic, saying how promising the plank doors are, but from where I'm standing, a working kitchen might have been better than bits of wood. I keep that to myself though, and thank my lucky stars I travel light.

As far as the work goes, George made it clear that we can do as much or as little as we choose. The only rule is that we have to run our ideas and costs past him first, so he can check that his absent client is in agreement, and any work we begin must be completed before we end our tenancy.

We'd assumed the landlord's cash-pot was going to run to fancy wallpaper and accessories, but now we're here we can see it's there to pay for the basics. But the mistake is all ours. If we hadn't had the unfortunate mix-up over house names, we'd have viewed and seen it for ourselves. As it is, we're determined to put the mistake behind us, and make the best of what's here.

The most amazing feature of the cottage is the sea view from the back, and nothing can take away from that. The kitchen door opens out onto a minute area of wonky paving which also looks out over the sea, it's great so long as you don't suffer from vertigo. We can just about make out the shed Nell mentioned on the hillside high above, but for now the steps are too overgrown to reach it.

The lack of size will be a lot harder for Ella than it is for me. As a ski resort chalet host, which was my job right through my twenties up to the time I lost my brother, I'm used to shared rooms and cramped conditions. But the home Ella and Taylor sold when they split up was a gorgeous flat in Islington. They'd poured their hearts into making it beautiful, and it embodied everything Ella had been striving for her whole married life.

Until we turn things around here, it's going to be a lot like camping, and that's going to be harder for Ella than for me. As kids, Dad would take Ned and me off in our ancient camper to the most remote places he could find, so I'm used to roughing it. Ella came with us a couple of times, but she never really took to peeing outdoors, cooking on a fire or sleeping under the stars. The more I keep saying, in my cheeriest voice, 'It's going to "scrub up" nicely,' the quieter Ella gets.

Even after we've plugged in the microwave, made up our air-beds and sat on the bean bags we brought to eat fish and chips, the mood is still dismal. In the cold light of next morning, when I'm washing up our coffee cups on the floor because the plastic bowl we brought is too big to fit in the sink, I step in to cheer Ella up.

'First things first. We need to decide what to wear for the singles do!'

Ella watches as I put a mug on the wonky draining board, then catches it as it slides off. 'Ideally I want to sort out a schedule of works for this place before my day job kicks in on Monday.'

Ella's working for the same company she was with in London, and their new contract is with a developer with four different holiday home sites across Devon and Cornwall. Her job is to guide the buyers on the layout and interior choices, all the way from purchase to hand-over. As it's at the luxury end of the market, making each humungous log cabin sold into an individual bespoke home is likely to be a very exacting task even when she's used to it. Picking it up from scratch she's going to be extra busy so, with that in mind, she's already offered to pay my share of the bills, to make up for me doing the lion's share of the household chores at the cottage.

We might as well start as we mean to go on. 'I'll grab the Flash and you get your notebook. We'll brainstorm fancy-dress outfits while we work.'

Ten minutes later I'm on my knees, scrubbing some cracked bathroom lino and trying to sort out Ella's costume. 'If you go as interior-designer Barbie you could just turn up as yourself?' Neither of us is prone to panic, but as it's tomorrow we can't hang around.

Ella looks up from her notebook and stares at the end of her ponytail instead. 'I'm not feeling swishy enough for that.'

As she's already rejected Batwoman and Dorothy from *The*

Wizard of Oz I have one last character to offer. 'Lara Croft, then!'

She lets out a cry. 'Jeez, Gwen, she kicks ass, and gives no fucks, I'm hardly in a place to carry *that* off.' Though we don't talk about it, I know how much Ella is aching inside. It's just easy to forget sometimes as she puts up a damn good front to the world.

I've always sidestepped fancy-dress parties myself, but I'm sure Ella's been to plenty. 'What do you usually go as?' As soon as the question is out, I know it's the wrong one.

Her lips go all wiggly and her voice is like someone else's. 'Taylor and I always go as surfers, in our board shorts and rash vests, with those super-expensive surf boards we bought but never use.' Her moan turns into a wail. 'Except it's … it's all in the past now. We'll never surf a-g-a-i-n.'

'Sweetie.' I'm mortified for upsetting her.

She stabs her pen at her pad so hard it flies into the air. As it clatters off the side of the outsized corner bath she sinks down to sit on the floor and rubs her fists in her eyes. 'It's fine.' The sob she lets out says it isn't. 'It's just *such* a bummer.'

It's hit me twenty times an hour since we arrived; I wouldn't be anywhere near here if it weren't for her and Taylor's split. But then neither would I be in France, where I had been right through my twenties, because when Ned died my life there broke too. It's a completely different scenario, but at least I have an idea how it feels for Ella when everything you rely on disappears from under you. The funny thing about pain and loss is you can't predict how they're going to hit you. For me, it's helped to avoid all things French, which has been hard as the Alps have been such a huge part of who I am.

My mum and dad were obsessed with climbing. They both had worldwide reputations and literally lived for the next rock face. Once they had us kids, they compromised by running a Highland climbing school, and took it in turns to go off on expeditions. When Mum died in the Alpine accident, I was too young to remember, but rather than staying away Dad actually took us kids to the Alps as often as he could. For him, the best way of keeping us close to Mum was to make sure we grew up loving the mountains, so we would understand what motivated her.

For Ned, that went hand in hand with the climbing genius he inherited from my mum, but for me, who couldn't ski or climb to save my life, there was still a deep affinity, which kept calling me back.

As soon as Ned was old enough, he went to join all the other climbers who worked the winters on the French ski slopes and spent the summers climbing. Obviously I wasn't into the sport, but the chalet hosting let me work in the places I'd grown to love so much. But at least remembering this reminds me of something that might take Ella's mind off Taylor.

'You've got your bike on your car roof and your blue and white stripy top. If we get you a beret you could come as a Breton onion seller?'

Her face is blotchy. 'You wouldn't mind how French it is?'

I pull a face. 'I'm going to have to face my demons sometime.' Since we lost Ned neither Dad nor I have been able to return to the Alps. Four years on, I still can't face melted Camembert or croissants. But seeing Ella as a French onion seller is a small sacrifice to make if it helps her. And it might be a small step for me on the very painful road back to normality, which is somewhere I never expect to get to anyway.

'Thanks, Gwen.' She blows her nose and pushes her hanky

into the pocket of her jeans. 'How about you? Who can we dress you up as?'

I'm straight back on that. 'I'm going as the paper bag princess.'

Ella shakes her head. 'This is why I love you so much, Gwen. You're full of surprises.'

'I'll make a sack out of brown paper and rub dirt on my face so I look like I'm smoke-damaged. Make a cardboard crown. I've got it all planned out.'

'But, *who is she*?'

I can't believe Ella's forgotten the heroine in my favourite book *ever*, the one that we used to read all the time in primary school. 'She's that princess who fights the dragon and saves the prince.'

Ella raises her eyebrows. 'Gotcha!'

'She ends up wearing a bag when her dress gets trashed, and when the ungrateful prince she's going to marry criticises her outfit she tells him to get stuffed. I need to be brave again like her.' I used to be so strong. But struggling to come to terms with living my life without Ned, all my strength has ebbed away.

Ella's eyebrows close together. 'It's certainly a *brave* choice.'

All my life, growing up as the one without a mum, even at home as a girl with my dad and Ned, I've been the one on the outside. It wasn't that I minded; what mattered was staying true to myself. So long as I quietly know who I am, and hold my course, I'm fine to be different.

Ella's trying to be helpful. 'Is a sack *really* what you want to wear the first time you meet everyone in St Aidan?'

I have another thought. 'When I did a *What's your Patronus?* quiz on Facebook, I got "sea horse". I wouldn't mind going as that.'

Ella's eyes hit the ceiling. 'We can't possibly make you into a sea horse by tomorrow.'

'That's decided then – let's go and get some paper and glue.'

'Before we do' – she's got her hanky out again – 'I may have made a terrible mistake.'

It's an emotional time for her, so I get that being indecisive goes with the territory. 'If you'd rather go as Lara, we can easily look for some black shorts?'

Her voice rises to a cry. 'Not with the fancy dress. *With the cottage!*'

I peer through the tiny square window and cling on to the shimmer of blue in the distance. 'Most people would give their left leg to have a view of waves breaking from the loo.'

Her mouth is going all wiggly again. 'I'm starting to realise how much Taylor and I synchronised our strengths with our home improvements.'

'Come again?'

Ella sniffs. 'My superpowers were sourcing and spaces, Taylor was the Black and Decker expert.'

I let out a groan. 'I'm not even sure what a Black and Decker *is*. Any problems at the chalets, we rang maintenance.' Actually, that's not entirely true. One time, I improvised with superglue and put up a shelf that had fallen down, but only because the guest was completely losing it. I'm ace at hammering in tent pegs and obviously, Dad taught me and Ned to climb, but fixing anchors into a rock face is light-years away from hanging kitchen cupboards. Climbing *without* ropes was more their thing anyway.

Ella sags as she sighs. 'We were such a team when it came to the DIY! Like two puzzle pieces that locked together to deliver perfection.' She gives a long moan, then she lets loose the killer punch. *'Now we're here, I'm not sure I can do this without him!'*

I'm not wanting to give up, but I have to stay real. 'As a renovation partner, I can't replace Taylor.'

I'm also thinking of how, when it was me at a loss with my life, Ella was the one who found my job as a mother's help in Milan and flew out to make sure I was okay. I know Ella's only crumbling now because she's so far been in denial about Taylor leaving, but I'm also dying inside to think we may have got the place under totally false pretences.

Ella sniffs into her tissue. 'I'm sorry I got carried away and misled everyone. We probably need to give the keys back.'

I breathe in the salt air leaking through the gaps in the window frame. As I stare at the distant patch of ocean, and the sun comes out and turns the surface to a mass of sparkling lights, a tiny part of me is reluctant to leave.

'Or we could stay and give it a go?' As I hear the words echo up off the cracked beige hand basin, I'm as surprised as she is to hear them.

Ella's shaking her head harder. 'How can we?'

In my job as a chalet host, I had to solve a hundred different problems a day, for ten winter seasons. Would I dare to use those skills to solve the problems at Stargazey Cottage? Gwen from a few years ago would have jumped right in and winged it.

I mean, I used to go parafoiling with Dad and Ned. That's how brave I was once. It wasn't my natural state, but when they encouraged me, I made the effort. But now I'm paralysed; I just can't do those gutsy, reckless things any more. If I could get up the courage to jump off a cliff and go soaring across the sky once, helping Ella to sort out this place should be possible too.

I'm imagining how much better I'd feel if I could pull this off, and Ella would be the same. It would be so good for her to know she didn't need Taylor. I need to make the leap for both of us.

I take a deep breath. 'We're the Star Sisters, we'll tackle this together and somehow we'll make it work.'

She's staring up at me. 'You truly think we can?'

I grit my teeth, tell myself to hold my nerve and my airy tone. 'Now we're here, what have we got to lose?' If we fail dismally, we can go back to London and pretend this never happened. I wouldn't ever have been able to do this for myself but doing it for Ella makes it easier. And we'll never know if we don't give it a go.

I just hope I can find enough courage to make it work. Because if I can't, we're going to be in so much trouble.

4

On the way to Seaspray Cottage, St Aidan
Blowing in the bag
Friday evening

'Are you sure you're okay, Gwen? If the wind blows any harder, we'll be in the water!'

It's Ella, and she's four strides ahead of me, pushing her onion-laden bike past the pink and white cottages along the harbourside.

While I've been wiping the kitchen walls and making my paper bag, she's been writing very fast and very neatly, noting down every defect in the place. The shower is only a trickle, but she's still managed perfectly varnished red nails, and her long plait is shining in the evening sun. Despite her androgynous costume, thanks to her lippy and the tight striped top accentuating her boobs, she looks a total knockout. She's not going out with any intentions, but if she doesn't accidentally pull tonight, I'll eat my crown.

Except actually I won't, because my crown is tonight's first

39

casualty. It was a total triumph of glue and gold foil, and it was firmly clipped to my hair when we set off. But managing to hold my dress in the gusts has taken all my attention. I've no idea where the crown went, but as we stopped at Crusty Cob's window to drool at the tarts, it wasn't on my head any more.

'I'm fine, Ells. Just trying not to catch my bag on any wing mirrors.' To look at my soot-covered skin you'd never know I'd been under the trickle in the bathroom too.

We pass Ella's shiny blue car and my workhorse van that used to belong to Ned, and as we finally get to the end of the car park she pauses and sighs. 'Not far now. Seaspray Cottage is the tall one that's practically on the beach with balconies along the front, and a walled garden round the back.' In spite of our pact to present happy faces to the world, after yesterday's realisation, Ella withdrew. I've tried everything from iced buns to millionaire's shortbread, but she's barely said a word all day.

As we make our way along the dune path towards the house, the waves are frilling up the beach, and over the sound of the sea and the crackle of my brown paper we catch voices drifting from the party. We follow the sound round the far end of the building, through an open picket gate, and turn into a walled garden edged with fairy lights that are swinging in the wind. As we start to cross the grass, a figure I recognise as Nell appears from under the apple trees.

'Hey, you made it!' She's wearing a pork-pie hat with straw sticking out and a jacket with rope around the waist, and she's clutching a live hen under her arm. Otherwise, she looks much the same as she did two days ago. 'Come and get a drink. Roaring Waves brewery are sponsoring tonight, so all the beers are locally made with surf-inspired names.'

We make our way past cowboys and what looks like the entire cast of *West Side Story* and arrive at the drinks table.

Ella picks up the first bottle she comes to, whereas I stand reading the names. 'Wipe-out, Goofy Foot, Hump Back. How exciting are these?' By the time I decide on a Kick Flip, Ella's already paid for our tickets and shoved the rest of our beer tokens into her money bag.

Nell's calling to a woman with wavy auburn hair and a baby on her hip. 'Clemmie, come and meet Ella and Gwen.'

The woman's pale-blue checked skirt is gathered and swishy, and as I spot her white ankle socks and glittery ruby-red courts, I murmur to Ella, 'Good thing we didn't go for Dorothy.' Then I smile at the woman. 'Loving the shoes.'

She beams back. 'They're great, aren't they? All I'm missing is a yellow brick road. You probably heard, I'm Clemmie, from the Little Cornish Kitchen, which is based here. And you must be the Star Sisters from Stargazey! So lovely you're here at last.'

I give a cough because it's wise to make this clear from the outset. 'That's the teensy Stargazey *Cottage*, not the much wider Stargazey *House*.'

Her eyes light up as she nods. 'The small places are the best. I began in a tiny flat here on the top floor, but we've moved downstairs now. This summer has been frantic; we've done afternoon teas and picnics and weddings all across the county.'

Nell smiles at the child, who has the same-coloured curls and sea-green eyes as her mum. 'All with a new-born too. This is Clem's baby, Bud, short for Buddleia.'

Clemmie smiles. 'I couldn't have done it on my own. Nell helped a lot, and Sophie and Plum, who are over by the barbie.'

Ella's looking at the crowds. 'Is Cressy Cupcake here

tonight? I came round and bought one of her bake boxes and a recipe book when I was in St Aidan last summer.'

Clemmie laughs. 'St Aidan's own internet celebrity promised to be along later. She and Ross are running residential courses up at their farm on High Hopes Hill now, but she still bakes for us.'

Nell joins in. 'If you want to know about raising rare breeds, you'll have to call in.'

A woman in paint-splattered overalls appears, wafting away the smoke from the barbie beyond the drinks. 'Did someone call?' She swishes a dark ponytail. 'I'm Plum, dressed as myself! I'm from The Deck Gallery, up the hill from Crusty Cobs bakery.' Her smile widens. 'I know who you are from your application, but it's great to see you in the flesh.'

As a blonde woman follows behind her, wiggling in a shimmery turquoise fish-tail skirt, I nudge Ella again. 'See, I *could have* been a sea horse!'

The woman smiles. 'I'm actually a mermaid.' She holds out her hand. 'I'm Sophie. I'm the only one in a tail tonight, but we all have them at home!'

Nell beams at us. 'These are the besties I mentioned the other day. We mermaids helped George choose the tenants for the cottage.'

Half a bottle of Kick Flip has relaxed me, but that nugget snaps me closed like a clam. If we're here thanks to them, we need to keep quiet about our temporary crisis of confidence.

Sophie's arm is round my shoulder. 'And look at you both! We knew you'd be the perfect choice!'

Plum's eyes are bright with interest. 'How are you settling in?'

Ella is taking a swig from a bottle labelled 'Ankle Slapper' and she chokes as she hears the question. Then she recovers. 'Fabulous. Thanks for picking us.'

I'm looking around, beaming, to make up for Ella's flat tone. 'We're not in any rush to start work. We're going to wait and let the cottage speak to us.' This should buy us the time we need to sort ourselves out. I might need to enrol in a DIY course.

Sophie's nodding in agreement. 'We're doing the same with the wreck of a castle we bought a few years ago; thinking while we save up.'

Plum's smiling too. 'Very wise. I can never understand these people who rip the guts out of places when they've barely spent a night in them.'

I'm cringing that we've hoodwinked such supportive people.

Nell gives a cough. 'We've got all the Stargazey residents tonight!' She gives me a nudge and looks over my shoulder. 'That *is* your neighbour coming now, isn't it?'

My gulp turns to horror as I turn and see him sauntering across the grass. I can't believe I called this so wrongly!

I'm opening my mouth to reply to Nell, but Ella gets in first. 'Ollie, lovely to see you again, great that you've made it.' I'm delighted she's leapt back to life, but I'm still not convinced he's her type.

Nell jumps in too. 'Grab a beer, Ollie, then come and meet everyone.'

As they remind us of their names a second time, we also discover that Nell's an accountant and Sophie has four kids, a husband called Nate and a multinational cosmetics company.

She puts her hand on my arm. 'I'll give you some Sophie May cleanser samples before you go. You can let me know how well they work on your grime.'

I'm cringing all over again as I see Ollie's wearing the exact same sweatshirt I peeled off myself the other day. I need to take charge of this conversation before he runs away with it first and tells the world about me flashing my bra. 'Good effort with the costume, Ollie. Great idea to come as the British sailing team.' I make my voice airy. 'Are the rest of them arriving later?'

He takes a sip of his Glassy Wave. 'They're on a training weekend in Abersoch; they send their apologies.'

That's a very slick, authentic-sounding answer for someone who's blatantly faking it.

Ollie stares at my arms. 'It must be a very impressive cosmetic range of yours, Sophie, if it'll remove dragon smoke.' His eyes narrow. 'That *is* what it's meant to be?'

Ella's smile is broad and real. 'She's *definitely* here as the paper bag princess, rather than just an ordinary sack. Well done for spotting the connection.'

Plum jumps in. 'Great choice, she was our heroine when we were kids too.'

I'm blinking at Ollie. 'The crown was the real clue until I accidentally misplaced it.'

As Ollie whips his hand out from behind his back there's a flash of gold. 'That's why I came! I was upstairs and I saw it blow off as you passed so I chased after it and followed you down.'

Ella's practically purring. 'That's so sweet of you.' She jabs me in the ribs. 'Isn't it, Gwen? Take it then!'

'Thanks, Ollie.' It's not that I'm ungrateful, but when I'm flying the flag for strong women it's somehow ironic that it was a man who had to save me. As I re-attach the hair clips, I'm also kicking myself that it was *my* carelessness that brought him here, when he makes my stomach so fluttery. 'Sorry to wreck your evening. Now you've made your delivery you're free to go.' I used my most regal voice to dismiss him. It's obvious from the way he's hovering that he's desperate to get away.

Nell puts up her hand. 'Hold on! No one can go anywhere until they've sampled the hot dogs. The sausages are from Artisan of St Austell; tonight we have apple with cider, stilton and leek, and cracked black pepper with sage.'

I mutter a silent curse that my golden goodbye has failed.

Clemmie turns to us. 'Nell's parents breed pigs. She's a great champion of pork.'

Nell's already shepherding us towards the barbies. 'The only reason to refuse is if you're veggie. But we also have vegan ones, so no one's exempt.'

My only hope of getting rid of Ollie now is if he's gluten intolerant and can't eat the submarine rolls. Though the way my luck is going, they've probably got that covered too.

5

In the garden at Seaspray Cottage, St Aidan
Rip curls and history repeating itself
Still Friday evening

In spite of the bad-news start to the evening, things do unexpectedly look up. The Artisan sausages are going down a storm and in the queue on the terrace area we're introduced to loads of people.

I have to come clean – away from my work, I'm not a natural party animal. Social gatherings of big groups are my nightmare scenario. For me, the ideal size for a get-together is two people, or, better still, one. But if I have to meet the village, a situation where there's only enough time to wave and smile before people move on to get their food works for me. At least this way there's no time for me to say anything wildly inappropriate, or, even worse, bring the conversation to a halt when my brain seizes up under the pressure.

Another lucky excuse to remove myself from the crowd is that I need to keep my dress away from the flames. So once we have napkins and a plate piled with hot dogs, I pick up more beers and steer Ella to one of the empty pale-green metal tables beyond the apple trees. Here, in the shadow of the garden wall, it's so blissfully quiet we could almost be the only ones here. Part of me feels guilty that I'm wasting an opportunity for Ella to get to know people but now she's broken the metaphorical ice of St Aidan's social scene, I'm sure there'll be many more nights like this she can come to. As the sea to the side of the house darkens, I'm hoping we can demolish our food and slip away quietly before anyone notices.

Whatever Nell said about the event being inclusive, as I watch Ella heading off to the terrace to fetch some more ketchup, I can't help but notice the flirty banter in the *West Side Story* group.

I know losing my brother is different from a relationship break-up, but they can both involve the kind of pain that takes away your logic. Looking in from the faraway place my emotional self is inhabiting now, as I watch those couples with their heads inclined, limbs brushing carelessly as they laugh their way towards new attachments, all I'm seeing is the potential for more hurt when things go wrong. It's as if I've become super-sensitised; every atom in my body is crying out and every last molecule of my survival instinct is in overdrive trying to steer me away from the potential danger.

If you want to avoid the train wreck, don't get on the train, Gwen.

I catch my breath as Ollie's profile slides into view beyond a black leather jacket and have to blink three times before I can prise my gaze away from him.

I have no idea how my dad has coped with losing my mum, then Ned, too. He's a very down-to-earth kind of guy, but these days he uses his words more sparingly. Talks about choices not motivation. When we call each other, the comfort comes from the silences not the conversation. Like me, he's shifting and unsettled. Unreconciled. For now, he's in New Zealand, helping a friend who's documenting rare mosses at high altitude.

'I saw you watching Ollie just now.' Ella swings in and slaps a bottle of squirty mustard down on the table.

Who, me? 'I don't think so.'

She gives a low laugh. 'You know the biggest giveaway that you fancy someone?' She's not waiting for an answer. 'If they sent you a dick pic, you'd look.'

'Ella!' My protest is a yell.

Her eyes are bright. 'You would, wouldn't you? It's written all over your face! *You definitely would!*'

This is the downside to hanging out with someone who knows me better than I know myself. I dive for cover and pick up the serviettes that just blew away in another freak gust. As I rub away the goosebumps on my arms and pop my head up from under the table my stomach goes into freefall again.

'Ollie!' However he found us, I need to send him straight back to wherever he's come from. Immediately. 'This corner is committed singles only. If you're looking to pull or find in-depth conversation, there's no point hanging round here.'

After an hour without a hint of a lip twitch, Ella's suddenly reconnected with her smile again. 'Don't listen to her, Gwen's a lot more ready for a relationship than she lets on.'

I scowl at her and aim a hard kick under the table as I slide back onto my chair. But instead of finding Ella's ankle my trainer collides with the table legs and the beers are wobbling horribly.

Ollie leans over to steady the bottles. 'Solo-and-staying-that-way is a good fit for me.'

It's not lost on me. Ella just outed me as available, and he closed her down flat. Obviously, he's the last person I'd ever consider, even if he does have spectacularly beautiful wrists now he's pushed his sleeves up, but there are politer ways of declining.

He turns to me. 'I noticed you shivering. Would you like to borrow my top?' The corners of his mouth twist. 'After all, we already know it fits.'

I may be on the verge of hypothermia, but truly, I'm not going there again. I push my chin up and lie through my teeth. 'I've spent a lot of my life at high altitude, I don't actually feel the cold.' Since Ned died, I try never to mention the mountains at all, and I wouldn't have done now if I wasn't so flustered.

Ella's smiling at him again. 'Thanks for that. Why not have a beer while you're here? We opened them at the bar.' Even for Ella that's taking the 'be nice to your neighbour' thing to extremes, but next thing we know he's pulled up a green curly metal chair and he's swigging pale ale like there's no tomorrow.

Ella's still going. 'And don't mind Gwen, she's always been stubborn and fiercely independent. It comes from growing up around older kids – she'd rather jump in the sea than admit she needs help.'

Far from being derogatory, Ella's summed me up exactly, all without mentioning Ned, too. It's best that it's out in the open, then people will know not to waste their time fussing in future.

Ollie lets out a sigh. 'I have sisters. That's how I know to offer my hoodie even if it's turned down – and never to act like a Ronald.' He's back to my costume again and even named the prince in the book who was a complete arse.

If I was being true to my fancy-dress character, this is where

I'd mention I used to have a brother, which is why I'm currently not completely able to say what I feel for myself. Obviously if I could do that, I'd be able to politely refuse his sweatshirt too. But instead, I steal Ella's line and say, 'Fabulous. At least we all know where we stand now.'

Ella's really going for it here. 'Great you've had a chance to meet people now, Ollie. St Aidan's social scene is one of its big attractions.'

He pulls a face. 'I'm not in St Aidan to enjoy myself, I'm here because I have to be.'

'If you've had enough, please don't feel you have to stay for us.' I'd be a lot more comfortable if he left.

It's Ella's turn to scowl at me, then she turns her smile back on for Ollie. 'Renovations can take their toll, especially a large one with extensions like Stargazey House.' She said that with a bit too much feeling.

I should keep my mouth shut, but for some reason I can't. 'Lucky you've almost finished, Ollie. You won't have to endure St Aidan for too much longer.' I'm not a house expert or a signed-up member of the Cornish fan club like Ella, but given what he's got I can't understand why he isn't more appreciative. If *we* had his house, believe me, we would *not* be grumbling or ungrateful. Just saying.

I'm limbering up to tell him that, but I'm saved when Clemmie dips under the nearest tree bough. As she comes to the table Bud stretches her hand towards my crown.

I've looked after quite a few babies in my working life and seeing this one reminds me how much I like them. So long as you can pass them back to their carers after a couple of hours, they're fascinating to be with. Let's face it, conversation with a non-verbal human like Bud is so much more interesting than with a killjoy like Ollie. Better still, when I grin at her, she smiles straight back.

Clemmie watches me untangle Bud's sticky fingers from my hair. 'We'll get you a tiara when you're older, Bud.'

I wrinkle my nose. 'It's funny how some of us are wired to love anything pink or glittery.' I know I was. Still am, really. And that's despite Dad bringing me up as a second Ned. Luckily, I got all Ella's hand-me-downs; all the pink stuff Merry showered on Ella was barely worn because Ella was more of a rainbow girl.

Clemmie's looking down at Bud, who is holding out her arms to me. 'Looks like you've made a friend for life there, Gwen.'

It's an instinctive reaction. I hold up my hands slightly, and a moment later the weight of a baby lands in my lap. 'I'm not very comfy to sit on, Bud, my dress is all crackly.' But Bud doesn't care, so I pull the crown off my head and she starts to play with that.

Clemmie laughs. 'While she's quiet, I'll tell you all about the breakfast club.'

'Lovely.' As Ella and I murmur together we both know this isn't anything we'll be doing – Ella will be setting off to work so early she'll hardly be going to bed as it is.

Clemmie's pushing on. 'It's another singles club thing that everyone joins in. People drop in here before work three mornings a week.' She turns to Ollie. 'Not that I'm stereotyping, but the guys mostly come for the pastries. And on Thursdays we do pancakes too.'

My mouth's watering at the thought, but it's still a 'no' from me. Unless I'm working, I'd rather be on my own in the mornings. And from Ollie's expression, the baking isn't tempting him. Not that I'm biased, but I'm *so* done with those sporty guys who live on protein shakes and avoid calories.

Clemmie turns to me. 'You're welcome to come and use the internet until you get yours sorted.'

That's something I've overlooked. It's going to be another couple of weeks before we get a proper connection ourselves. 'That would be great. So far, we've managed with our mobiles but at times we have to go all the way to the attic before our messages come in.'

Clemmie's eyes light up. 'Thanks to my geek partner, Charlie, we have the fastest broadband for miles around, so a lot of people work over breakfast.' She grins. 'If you come in your crown and keep Bud *this* quiet, I'll throw in free coffee too.'

We're all so busy laughing at that, by the time I notice Bud's hand reaching towards the bottles, it's too late. One swipe skittles them all and a second later a river of beer is glugging over both of us.

'Bud!' Clemmie jumps forward to grab her, but Bud clings on to my chest, her fist tightly closed. As Clemmie scoops Bud up there's a ripping sound, and as she steps back an entire strip of my bag-dress disappears with her.

Ella jumps in front of me and shoots her arms out sideways. 'The plus side of paper clothes is they're easily mended! A roll of parcel tape and you'll be good as new!'

I'm peering downwards, assessing the damage. 'It's *really* not a problem. Unlike the princess in the book, I've got shorts and a T-shirt on underneath.'

That's a big exaggeration. For T-shirt read skimpy lace vest, which for some reason known only to Primark is totally see-through now it's drenched in beer.

Ollie steps over, his top already off and hanging from his finger. 'Ready to change your mind on the hoodie?'

I'm weighing up the shame of backing down against how ice-cold and excruciating it will be walking the whole way up the hill with my boobs on show but before I come to a decision, he bundles it into my hands.

'No arguing. Have it. I'm going now anyway.'

I give a silent cheer and punch the air in my head.

'Return it any time. You know where to find me.' He's backing across the grass. 'Thanks for a great evening, every-one.' Obviously, he's being ironic there.

As I pull the fabric over my face and breathe in his scent my head spins. Then, as I thrust my arms into the sleeves and the warmth encloses my body, I push out my head and smile at Clemmie and Ella. 'Brilliant! For the first time all evening I'm toasty. How about we get more drinks?'

Clemmie nods. 'Puddings will be out soon.'

Ella and I are hanging on every word. 'There are *afters*?'

She laughs at us. 'Nothing fancy. Just a few meringues and some baked Alaska.'

For two women relying on a microwave, she has no idea how good that sounds. And I know I'm hopeless at casual chat, but if there's ice cream and sponge involved, it's worth the risk.

I know I've got to face Ollie again to return the hoodie. And as far as lasting first impressions go, tonight has been a disas-ter. But for now, I'm going to concentrate on the sound of the waves rushing up the beach, and the upcoming sugar hit.

Clemmie's laughing. 'It'll be a good chance for more people to chat to you too. Since word got out you'll be running Design Duo workshops for the locals, everyone's been desperate to meet you.'

'Design Duo *what*?' My shrieking question is cut short as Ella's trainer thumps down on mine.

'The sudden inspiration *we* suggested to George the day your Zoom call kept freezing, Gwen, remember?' From her smile there's no clue how hard she's grinding my toes into the lawn. 'We hoped us offering to run workshops might help if the tenancy came to a tie-break, remember?'

Clemmie's eyes are shining. 'Limited numbers, with trade secrets and hot tips! Who wouldn't want a piece of that?' Then she winks. 'The Star Sisters were miles ahead of the competition. No one else was even close.'

It's hard to believe what I'm hearing, but I'm straight in there to present a united front. 'Workshops are our favourite, aren't they, Ella?'

Remind me never to think things couldn't be any worse. Because however bad they were, they just went so far downhill even baked Alaska can't save me now.

6

The Little Cornish Kitchen at Seaspray Cottage, St Aidan, Cornwall
Gongs, colour charts and sticky endings
Early Thursday morning, six days later

Me helping run design workshops? Some things in life are so disturbing, the only way to handle them is to put them to one side and not think about them at all. I'm desperately hoping that's the last wild promise that's lurking to trip us up, but there's no point me asking Ella. I suspect we both made so many there's no way either of us can remember them all.

Once we set that challenge to one side, the week flew by with me doing anything I could to avoid taking the borrowed hoodie back to Ollie. Flashing my chest once, we might have moved on from, but twice is unforgivable.

But it isn't only the man himself I'm reluctant to face. I also hate the way my stomach turns cartwheels whenever I'm anywhere near him. How desperately weak it makes me feel knowing how fast he makes my heart beat. It's not just about him being the most miserable guy we've yet met in St Aidan. If relationships are off my table for ever, I shouldn't even be looking at him. When I can't take my eyes off him, I'm disgusted with myself. More so, because every time he opens his mouth there's something new to disagree with. But at least that keeps the whole jaw-dropping beauty of the guy in perspective. So long as I keep a garden-length away from him and look the other way I'm telling myself I should be fine.

Ella had her first day at work on Monday and drove off to some far-flung corner of North Devon to work her magic at a site meeting. Since then, she's been working all-the-hours on the day job, while I've been scrubbing every inch of the cottage. Not that it's dirty; I simply want to make it smell like it's ours. Then, when I finally screwed up my courage to return the hoodie, I found it smelled like a brewery so that meant a trip to the launderette down on the quayside. By the time the hoodie was washed, dried, folded, and dust-free enough to return, it was Wednesday, but I put it off again.

During spare moments, like when I was sitting warming my back against the quayside launderette tumble drier and staring at the brightly coloured boats bobbing in the harbour, I've been looking into improving my house-renovation skills. It takes an entire year at the local beginners' woodwork class to make a stool, a weekend residential course costs an arm and a leg and at the end I'd only come away with a spatula. So, I turn to videos on YouTube instead, but then I hit problems with buffering. Which is why, in desperation, I head down to Clemmie's place on Thursday morning for breakfast and some decent Wi-Fi. And as I can't put it off any longer, I'm planning to return the hoodie on the way.

As I rap on the door of Stargazey House the fish eyes in the pottery pie on the step stare up at me accusingly. After knocking four times, I finally decide Ollie's not home, so I run all the way down the cobbles and past the harbour, which leaves no time to be nervous as I cross the terrace towards the sign saying, 'The Little Cornish Kitchen'. Through the small-paned windows I can see Clemmie wiping tables, an apron tied round her flowery dress.

She smiles as I push through the door. 'Gwen, you've made it!'

I step over a large hairy dog, and stare round at a rainbow explosion of colour, with apple-green shelves against a pale-pink wall, a dark-blue serving counter, and a long, magenta crushed-velvet sofa piled high with bright patchwork cushions. There are low tables surrounded by easy chairs, upholstered in blue and green checks or red and pink stripes, while the chairs at the higher tables are painted in pops of blue and pink and yellow. And on two sides, there are windows looking straight out across the shining wet sand, and the turquoise-blue shimmer of the water beyond.

I beam at Clemmie. 'What a place – it's amazing!'

She looks pleased. 'It's extra nice hearing that from a professional like you.'

After Zoom performances worthy of an Academy Award, it's unsurprising they're attributing me talents I don't have, but I'd rather be straight now I'm here. 'Ella's the one with design qualifications, I'm more instinctive.'

'Any heartfelt compliment works for me!' Clemmie's smile widens again. 'The Little Cornish Kitchen style and the recipes are down to my late grandmother; the inspiration came from her flat upstairs.'

'Brill.' I could do with moving this firmly away from design. 'I love your dog too, he's very well behaved.'

As she looks down, the enormous hound lying at her feet

lets out a gentle snore. 'That's Diesel, he's flat out because Charlie walked him right round the bay earlier.'

I wrinkle my nose. 'I'm with Diesel. Mornings aren't my greatest time.' Ella, Dad and Ned were always up at the crack, raring to go, and invariably I'd get dragged along too, and doing ski-chalet breakfasts always meant an early start. Left to myself, I like to wake up more slowly. If I hadn't been desperate to watch the videos, I'd never have come here at seven-thirty.

It takes me a while to work past the smell of warm pastries to notice the customers sitting in corners, drinking their coffee from mismatched vintage china. The whole place is so cosy, it drives away the chill of the early morning air. After a week in St Aidan's most basic cottage, it actually feels like heaven.

Bud's here too, kicking in a blue-painted highchair by the counter, a board-book in one hand, pushing pieces of pancake into her mouth with the other.

Clemmie puts down her tray and thrusts a menu towards me across the counter. 'Why not join Bud and me over here? What can I get you?'

The piles of Danishes are already making me drool as I clamber onto a high stool. From my seat I've got a view out across the sea and around the room. As I read down the menu I come to a must-have. 'Pancakes with berries and vanilla cream.' I skim down the drinks, wanting to save my caffeine hit for later in the morning. 'With an extra-large strawberry milkshake, please.'

Bud and I watch as Clemmie builds the pancake stack, dribbles on maple syrup and adds the fruit. As she puts the dish down in front of me, Bud stretches out her hand, opening and closing her fingers.

I put down my spoon. 'If you want to share, we'll have to ask Mum first.'

Clemmie laughs. 'You can't *always* eat other people's food, Bud.' She wipes her hands on her tea towel. 'When she was smaller she stayed upstairs with Charlie, but lately she loves the company down here.'

I slide some berries onto Bud's tray, and she dives in. 'Strawberries are my favourite too.' I can't help laughing as I fill my mouth with pancake. 'One for me, one for you, then?'

I'm not forgetting what I'm here for, so I set up my laptop next to my plate, slide in one ear bud, and type in the broadband code from the menu. Within moments I'm watching a time-lapse video of someone knocking a hole in their house wall and installing patio doors.

I laugh at Bud's curious frown and tilt my screen towards her. 'Do you want to look too?' I was hoping to get an understanding of what's to come, but the demolition and reconstruction scenes playing out in front of me are so terrifying, they're giving me indigestion. This food is way too good to spoil, so I type in 'decorating for beginners' and turn to Bud. 'A woman with a paint roller – that's more our level.'

I'm concentrating so hard on the instructions of how to pour the paint from the tin to the tray, I block everything else out. When we get to the part about how to transfer the paint onto the wall, it looks so tricky I actually forget to chew. I'm watching, amazed at how the on-screen woman is zigzagging across the wall and still keeping her dungarees and ponytail pristine when there's a cough beside me and I realise Clemmie's looking over my shoulder.

I choke on the last mouthful of pancake and try to cover up. ' "Wall painting with sponge things". I thought Bud might like it.' When I came here to watch the videos, I'd overlooked how

61

easily I might out myself as a beginner when I'm supposed to be a pro.

Clemmie nods. 'You've picked a winner there! I'm not being nosey, I just wondered what she was looking at so intently.' She watches with us for a few more moments, then takes my empty plate. 'Is there anything else I can get you?'

I'm sucking up the last of the milkshake, wishing I was starting not finishing. 'I may need to order the same again' – I grin at her – 'seeing as the videos are going down so well.' I am sharing with Bud after all.

Clemmie does her biggest smile yet. 'Coming right up.'

Obviously, I won't be doing this *every* visit, but I'm happy to spoil myself this first time. Note how in my head my one-off trip has already morphed into something more regular. Look at it this way; after a week rushing up and down the hill, and all the ripping up of old carpet I did yesterday, I'm due a serious calorie intake. After all, I was brought up on Dad's portions; I'm not the kind of woman who picks at my food, I get straight in there and demolish it.

Half an hour later, as I come to the end of round two, and Bud and I have soaked up every paint-rolling clip I could find, Clemmie slides in beside me, puts an elbow on the counter and props her chin on her hand. 'So…'

I take it she's here for my reaction. 'That was my most delicious breakfast in ages, if not ever. And thanks to Bud for being a great TV buddy.' I know a lot more about paint and rollers than I did before. Although on balance I've decided it's all way too scary for me to tackle without a hands-on professional in the room to do it for me. Not great news for the cottage, but at least I know.

Clemmie's smile widens. 'Thanks for the compliment, but that wasn't what I was leading up to. I was actually wondering if you'd be interested in some paid hours at these early-morning sessions?'

It's so unexpected it leaves me speechless at first. And it's also confusing, because unlike Ella, I haven't got loads of cash in reserve or a salary, so I should be grabbing any work that comes my way. It's just that I've always avoided café work because I hate the idea of strangers watching me while I work.

I can avoid sharing that and still tell the truth. 'I'd hoped to look for a cleaning job.'

Clemmie tilts her head. 'Dainty Dusters have the St Aidan market stitched up. You could try them.' She's still smiling. 'If not, the work here would be clearing tables, stacking the dishwasher, making sure Bud's happy. I'm really just looking for an extra pair of hands.' She's watching for my reaction. 'We could throw in free cake?'

Even that last bit doesn't make me think again. 'I wouldn't mind it but my first priority has to be the cottage, so I don't want to over-commit.' I got my BTEC in Childcare, but the rest is *way* too scary.

Clemmie smiles. 'If you ever fancy a trial run, give me a shout.' Then, as the door clicks open, she turns round. 'Two Stargazey residents for the price of one! Ollie! Take a menu and find yourself a seat.'

After two helpings of pancake stacks, it's not ideal for my stomach to suddenly be going round like a windmill. I swallow my shock and dive down into my bag. 'While you're here, let me return this.' Two seconds later, his hoodie is back in his hands, and I never need to speak to him again.

He looks pleased without actually breaking out a smile. 'Thanks for that, it's very old but I'd still hate to lose it.'

I'm looking from his face to the logo and back again when

it dawns. 'Oh my, it's not fake at all! You *are* on the GB sailing team!'

He gives a grimace. 'It was a few years ago now.'

I've seen that exact same flinty hunger and drive in Ned's eyes. That chilling desire to succeed. To be better than everyone else, whatever the cost.

I don't even need to ask because I know he will have, but the words escape me anyway. 'I suppose you've got Olympic medals?' At least we were saved that; climbing didn't become an Olympic event until after Ned's accident.

Ollie pulls a face. 'I may have one or two. It was a very obscure class; it wasn't hard to be the best.' He's watching my reaction. 'Nothing like as many as Laura Trott, obviously. We were world champions ten years running though.'

I knew it! That explains the super-confidence – the way he looks like he owns wherever he is. Knowing they're the best in the world must twist something in their heads. I knew the way into Ned's shell, but for the rest of the world he was impenetrable. It was part of his armour. Part of his secret to success.

I give a sigh. 'Congratulations. Are you still involved?'

There's a barely perceptible twitch of his cheek. 'I'm a sport ambassador, so they still give me a car. And I run a racing yacht design consultancy from where I live, further up the coast.'

'Nice one.' I'm thinking of the four by four in the harbour car park that's so big it takes up two spaces. He was never going to be one of us, but this has removed him to a whole new plane.

He pulls out the stool next to mine. 'A large black coffee please, Clemmie. Is this seat free?'

He's so close to me I can see the pores in his skin and it's not just feeling sick that's the problem. The hammering on my chest wall is so hard, if I stay here I'm likely to have a heart attack. For now, there's so much adrenalin coursing round my system, I'm on emergency alert.

A second later I land on the floor. 'I might give Clemmie a hand.' It's the last thing I'd intended, but the alternative is so much worse. I turn to Clemmie. 'If that's okay?' If I have to stay here rubbing elbows with Ollie, I'll either expire or turn to stone from the chill in his soul.

'Absolutely.' Clemmie's eyebrows shoot up, but her voice is steady. 'I'll make Ollie's coffee, how about you clear the tables?'

Ollie's blinking. 'But you've barely touched your milk-shake, Gwen.'

I grin at him and grab a tray from behind the counter. 'It's hardly going to get cold, is it?' Then I remember he's a customer, and I'm the worker, so I reset. 'Thanks all the same, I'll finish it later.'

When I got a job in the local hotel as a teenager, I opted to be a chambermaid rather than a waitress because it meant I had to talk to fewer people. By the time I was eighteen I was working in the ski resorts, being where I wanted to be, and able to hang out with Ned and his mates, which propelled me forward more than my shyness held me back.

As a chalet host, I've cooked and served thousands of evening meals and breakfasts and clearing up after them was part of the job too. But the good thing was, I only had one new group to meet every week, and mostly they were too busy having fun to notice me. It was way less terrifying than working in a bar or restaurant and being faced with hundreds of new people I'd have to make conversation with every night.

My heart is galloping due to being next to Ollie, but seeing all the faces in the room, it races even faster. For a moment, as

Clemmie pushes a cloth across to me, the room spins and I feel as if I might need to run for the door. But if I tear off up the hill now, everyone will write me off as loopy, and I can't possibly let Ella down so soon after we've arrived. So, I close my eyes tightly and take a deep breath.

The only thing that makes this different from what I usually do is the strangers. In the chalets we'd look after the same one for a whole season, so I always managed to smile and feel at home as I worked. At breakfast the guests were often still so hungover from the night before I'd have got more reaction serving porridge to zombies, and when it came to the evening, they were flat out after a day on the slopes, or busy sharing stories with each other.

I just need to persuade my legs to walk around the room here now and do the stuff I used to do every day. I tell myself this is business as usual. And take a step. Then another. As I inch my way from table to table, wiping and clearing, at first I'm doing it very slowly. But by the time I've done every table, I'm getting better at blocking out the white noise of nerves crackling in my ears.

The whole thing is, since I lost Ned, I've tried to do different things in new places, so I'm never reminded of that other life. But this is feeling uncomfortably close to everything I've been trying to distance myself from.

An hour and a half later, as I stumble round the last of the tables then head for the sanctuary of the kitchen, I'm proud that I've made myself do it. As the last but one customer leaves, it feels like I've been here for a lifetime. It's still only ten o' clock, but at least I haven't dropped a tray or spilled anything on anyone. And there's a comfort in knowing I'll never have to do this again.

As I come out after loading the last tray of crockery into the dishwasher, wouldn't you just know it, the last man still here is Ollie. I left him to Clemmie, but I suspect he's still only on his second coffee, which is a flaming cheek, as he's barely looked up from his laptop. He must be literally melting their broadband.

Clemmie's lifting Bud out of her chair by the counter. 'Well done for keeping up there, that was a bumper morning, Gwen!'

I know she's just being kind. 'All thanks to your delicious pancakes.'

Ollie coughs, which is something I wouldn't have done in his position, because it reminds us all he's outstayed his welcome.

I can't help but comment. 'You're still here?'

He looks up from his screen for a nanosecond. 'Special dispensation from management, the builders dropped a sack of plaster on my router and wiped out my internet. I'm almost done.' He's still staring. 'You never came back for your milkshake.'

Clemmie puts a glass on the counter in front of me. 'I made you a fresh one anyway.'

'You didn't need to do that.' There's a terrible feeling of being back where I started.

Ollie pulls out the high stool between us. 'There you go, that's settled then.'

Clemmie looks at Bud, sitting on the countertop, her legs out in front of her. 'You can't expect "decorating for beginners" again, Gwen will have other things she needs to catch up with.'

Ollie frowns without looking up. 'Who's learning to decorate?'

Clemmie and I exchange glances, but I seize the chance to

get this out there. 'We're watching them for the comedy not the instruction. Some of them are hilarious.'

My chest is constricting all over again at the thought of having to stay and drink my milkshake now. Heart attacks apart, I'm simply not up for another ten minutes of conversation dodging the truth. I'm staring round, trying to find a way out without being rude to Clemmie, when I spot the answer on the shelf and look pointedly at my phone. 'Could I possibly have this to take out?'

Clemmie smiles. 'Not a problem, I'm sorry if I've made you late.'

I step towards the counter and put my hand out to keep Bud safe while Clemmie goes to the shelf for a tall cardboard cup. Obviously, there's no explanation for why my eyes are glued to the stubble shadow on Ollie's jaw when I should be fully focused on the squirming baby. It's literally only for a nanosecond, but what I miss is Bud's outstretched arm heading for my glass. When I finally wrench my eyes to where they should be Bud's arm is doing a perfect forehand sweep, then her fist hits the milkshake.

It's as if I'm watching in slow motion. The thick pink liquid flies forwards as the glass tilts and travels through the air like a giant splat of ectoplasm. Unfortunately, I'm the first solid object in its way. It collides with my front, and a moment later my sweatshirt is covered, there's milkshake dripping from my hair, and the floor is a milk lake.

Ollie coughs again. 'Nice shot, Bud.' Then he looks at me. 'It missed the laptops. Nothing else matters.'

I'm calling to Clemmie. 'I've got Bud safe, can you bring cloths?'

Ollie's mopping the counter with serviettes. 'Seems like I'm destined *not* to have my hoodie back.'

Clemmie comes back and swaps an armful of towels for Bud. 'I'm so sorry.'

As I stare at Clemmie, I'm dying inside. 'It's not your fault, I'm supposed to be helping, and look at the mess I've caused!' My attention was in entirely the wrong place. Which also underlines that despite my ancient childcare qualification, I wouldn't be up to looking after Bud. 'I'll peel off my top and keep as much of the milkshake as I can on the inside.' Obviously being careful not to strip off any more clothes than I intend this time.

I drop my sodden sweatshirt onto the counter and grab another towel.

Ollie's still mopping. 'Seems I'm destined to see your underwear *yet* again, Gwen. I'm definitely not looking, by the way.'

I roll my eyes. 'It's a crop top, Ollie.'

He gives a shrug. 'There's a difference?' If he really has all those sisters he was boasting about the other evening, he should know. It also shows that medals indicate a high level of skill in a very narrow area. A specialist can be a superstar, with an ego to match, but still can't tell the difference between a bra and a vest. Sure, I need to stay well clear, but there's no need to be intimidated.

I scrape the worst of the milkshake off my hands and hair and drop the towels to mop the floor. There's no coming back from this for me, which is a bit of a relief.

Ollie's holding out the hoodie. 'Good to have you back on the team again.' He waits until I dry my arms and take it from him. 'If you're going to be working here, I'll no doubt be seeing a lot more of you.'

Had I been wavering – which I'm definitely not – that

would have been the decider. I turn to Clemmie. 'About the job, thanks for the offer, but I'll stick to cleaning if I can.'

Clemmie's smile is rueful. 'You know where we are if you change your mind.'

I pull the hoodie over my head then sweep my laptop into my basket before swinging it onto my shoulder. 'I'll return the hoodie as soon as, Ollie.' Maybe this time I'll send it through the post.

At least that's cleared one thing up – if Clemmie's job was the last one in St Aidan, I wouldn't want it. As I drop a note on the table to pay for my breakfast, and remember how fast my money is going, I have my fingers tightly crossed that some alternative work turns up soon.

7

On the way to Seaspray Cottage, St Aidan
Gin shacks and awkward questions
Early Sunday morning

When I was small it was always Ned and Ella out in front with me running to keep up. It wasn't deliberate; they simply had longer legs and bigger, better ideas than mine because they were older. While sheer enthusiasm propelled Ella forward, Ned was single-minded and driven. He climbed compulsively; any surface with a handhold, he was on it. Even then, there was no doubt in anyone's mind that he was going on to greater things. They'd been taught to be patient with me, so mostly they'd turn round and wait for me to catch them before they tore off again.

This Sunday morning, ten days later, as Ella bounds ahead of me across the sand, this is what I'm remembering. Except this time round I have no wish to chase after her.

When Ella publicly announced my stubborn streak to most of St Aidan at the barbie, she was right; the times when I dig

71

my heels in, I *am* completely immovable. But it doesn't happen very often. The rest of the time I'm malleable and persuadable, because that's how I learned to be to fit in.

She's been so busy her first two weeks on the new sites we've barely seen each other. Whenever we have coincided, I've tried to ask what we're going to do with the cottage, but every time she's looked at me with a rabbit-caught-in-the-headlights expression and started talking about something else. I'd hoped I could pin her down this weekend, but on Friday night she came home with a stack of client folders. While she worked yesterday, I padded around the cottage cleaning windows because that was next up on the list we'd agreed on. By the time I managed a thumbs-up from Ella I'd polished every pane three times inside and out, and it was bedtime, and I was still no wiser about the cottage.

I guess this highlights another difference between us. I like to bash on and get things done, while she homes in on the finer detail and demands complete perfection. Let's hope it's a winning combination rather than a disaster waiting to happen.

Usually, we fit together fine because I'm happy to go with the flow. When Ella decides for both of us, we don't waste energy on argument and discussion. She's got more drive than me, so it's an advantage for me to be pushed. Me doing what someone else wants, safe in the knowledge that I have enough guts to refuse at any point if I feel strongly enough – most days that sounds like the best of both worlds.

So straight after our breakfast had settled, we came down to the beach for Ella's substitute park run. Apparently, she and Taylor would always join in a local 5k at the weekend. We only got past that wobble by diverting down a side alley so steep that we both ended up on our bottoms. But at least it made her forget that Taylor will be belting round Highbury Fields watching someone else's bum not hers.

Once we get onto the firmer part of the beach Ella reconnects with her mojo. She's running backwards in her Lycra leggings, the wind catching her high ponytail as she tells me what's happening next. 'We'll head round the bay to Comet Cove and Cockle Shell Castle, Gwen. I'll do sprints and come back for you.' With her super-lightweight trainers and yellow T-shirt saying 'Running Woman', she definitely looks the part.

'Great.' I've relented and borrowed her '"Beach Run St Aidan 2015' T-shirt so I don't wreck her image. 'Is that the place with the distillery? We could call in for gin tasting while we're there.'

Ella shakes her head as she speeds away. 'There's no time for gin today. We'll catch their next organised event.'

As an adult I draw the line at actual running on the beach. I can hike for miles, but it has to be at a pace that allows me to look around and, ideally, I do it on my own. So, Ella disappearing into the distance then coming back again is fine by me. It's actually a lot like having a dog again. Ned and I used to have one called Spangle when we were kids; he'd scamper off up the glens, but he never went too far away. He was also the perfect warmer on my bed at night, snuggling in the crook of my knees.

Every time Ella bounces back to me her brain's run on to a new place.

'We're so lucky with this amazing weather, Gwen. Have you brought any sunscreen with you?'

She should know I won't have. Unlike her, I'm not constantly reaching for the factor 50. 'I've got my baseball cap. And when we get to a café, I'll find a parasol.' The sun is shining from a cobalt blue sky every time it pops out from behind the cottonwool clouds, but since we arrived there hasn't ever been what I'd call a *proper* hot day. 'When you said St Aidan had as many hours of sunshine as Marseilles, you forgot to mention the hurricane blowing through all year too.'

Ella stops in mid-turn. 'What I *actually* said was, if you're in the UK, and wanting to avoid winter, Cornwall's your best bet. I still stand by that. At least it's properly different from you-know-where.'

She whips around, and a second later I'm staring at her back disappearing into the distance again.

We both know she bigged up the hot Caribbean air being pulled straight into Cornwall by the gulf stream. But she's right about the last bit. As I look out at the waves cutting the glassy surface like furrows in a field, so long as I don't think how much like spindrift the water is when it crashes on the cliffs out towards that place down the coast called Oyster Point, there's nothing in the blue-green plateau of water in front of me that would remotely remind me of the Alps in winter. And that was my main ask.

And in spite of never particularly being a fan of the beach, I've been loving my solitary walks along the water's edge too. I stop and pick up yet another cockle shell, because however many I collect, there's always one more begging me to take it home. It's amazing how a simple line of shells along the bathroom windowsill at the cottage takes your eye away from the stained beige wash basin and instantly makes the room more homely.

'By the way, did any of those cleaning firms get back to you, Gwen?'

How did Ella come back again so fast? She's standing, hands on hips, one foot back, dipping her knee and doing her mid-run stretches, impatient for an answer.

I blink and try to focus. 'A couple rang to say they'd put me on their reserve list but not to hold out any hope.'

'Damn.' She hitches up her leggings and speeds off again.

The last couple of weeks I've been job hunting. Once I found that St Aidan's Dainty Dusters have more staff than they need I rang every other cleaning firm and holiday cottage rental company in a thirty-mile radius, and the answer was always the same – if I want to clean cottages, I need to turn up in spring, not autumn.

This time when Ella arrives back, she turns on the run. 'You do know Ollie next door hasn't been near the place for two weeks now.' She rubs her nose. 'The castle's coming up soon, by the way.'

I can just make out some turrets sticking out above the distant treetops. By the time I meet Ella again the lawns in front of the towers are coming into view.

'It's actually a week and three days since our neighbour left.' The builders have been there, but there's been no sign of him, which means his freshly laundered hoodie has practically taken root on the bedroom floor. If he doesn't come back soon, I'll be at the damn laundrette again.

Ella pursues her lips. 'You discounted the job at Clemmie's because you didn't want to bump into him.'

I shrug. 'It wasn't only that. I'm still reliving the shame of causing mayhem. I seriously doubt I'll enjoy a milkshake ever again.' My other dream job would be putting books back on the shelves in a library, but when I rang the council, they were cutting staff not recruiting. And none of the hotels I tried were hiring housekeeping staff either.

Ella sniffs. 'If he's not going to be here, you can think again. If the cleaning companies aren't coming through, you can serve breakfasts in your sleep.'

'I suppose.' Even without Ollie, it's my nightmare job. But I have to pay my way, and if there's nothing else around, I'll have to suck it up.

She claps her hands. 'That's decided then! We'll head round to Clemmie's straight after the run.'

I hadn't planned to move quite that fast. 'I thought we were calling in at the place that looks like a heap of planks for ice cream?'

She pulls a face. 'That's the Surf Shack. Let's wait until Clemmie takes you on, then there will be more to celebrate.'

As we approach the painted sign on the edge of the beach, the rose gold gin label reminds me how much I love the chink of ice in a G&T. 'The distillery is right here. I've got my card in my pocket – if I nip in, I can easily carry a bottle back.'

Ella gives a horrified gasp. 'We can't stop now, it'll ruin my intervals! And what's the point me running then hitting the gin?' She tosses her ponytail and checks her fitness watch. 'This is where we turn round.'

As I automatically turn and follow her back along the beach, I can't help noticing something. She's always been proud of her strong personality, and that the guys at work refer to her as a 'force of nature'. But when she insists on her own way with *every single* thing, the line between compelling and domineering is very fine. It's possible that Taylor's unquestioning dedication to her needs may have given her so much of her own way it's become a habit.

I love Ella, we're here for each other, and we don't shy away from the truth, so as her oldest friend, I'm the one who should raise this with her before it gets completely out of control. I just hope I'm not too late!

I know I love a quiet life, but something tells me that if I don't stand up to her, it's only going to get worse. However hard and unnatural it is for me, I'm going to have to challenge her on a more regular basis. If I'm going to go head-to-head with Ella so she wakes up to what's happening, it won't be over anything as insignificant as ice cream or gin.

But for now, I'd be a fool to let her think I'm limbering up to flex my muscles. The next time she comes towards me I shout, 'Next stop, Seaspray Cottage?'

She sticks her thumb up. 'Right answer, Gwen.'

8

Outside at the Surf Shack
Sundaes and desperate measures
Later on Sunday

'Eating ice-cream cones in the sun, with the waves practically lapping at our feet. You won't get much nearer to the sea than this.' This is Ella, leaning back in her shiny metal chair at one of the hewn wooden tables out on the Surf Shack's front deck. As the tide is coming in, the strip of sand we're looking down on is getting narrower and narrower as each wave pushes higher up the beach.

I have to agree. 'Any closer, we'd be in the water. Unless we were on a pier, of course.'

Ella sniffs. 'Projecting platforms don't count.' She takes a long, lingering lick of her cone. Apparently dark chocolate chip and mint doesn't count as ice cream in her book either, due to being bean-and-leaf based. Which is why it's fine to have a double scoop of that straight after her run when she wouldn't entertain the idea of gin. But whatever. At least, so far, we've managed to skirt around this being one of her and Taylor's favourite hangouts.

You can tell I'm less in practice at this than she is. I inhale my strawberries-and-cream and vanilla-and-white-chocolate scoops so fast I get brain freeze. With ice cream this delicious, I'm grateful she's momentarily developed selective relationship amnesia. No man on earth, whatever they'd done, would be worth giving up this place for.

As for Ella ordering me around, now I've properly woken up to it, I'm pouncing on every instance. Since we turned at the distillery, Ella overruled me fifty-four times – and then I stopped counting. This might be an even bigger issue than I'd first imagined. Funnily enough, in the end she over-ruled herself too and decided we'd call at the café first as Clemmie's is on the way home from here. So, as I watch the figures and family groups jumping out of the way of the tide along the water's edge in the distance, instead of being totally relaxed I'm screwing up my courage for what's coming next – begging Clemmie to give me the job I majorly stuffed up the trial for and told her I wasn't interested in. I'm staring so hard towards Seaspray Cottage, I actually miss the little crowd gathering at the bottom of the steps until I hear their shouts.

'Hey, it's our starry designers. How are you doing, Gwen and Ella?'

I take in Clemmie's red hair and dress blowing in the wind, Nell in shorts, carrying Bud in a backpack, and Sophie surrounded by blonde-haired kids of all sizes carrying so many buckets, spades and fishing nets it's like a page from the Seasalt blog.

I swallow the last of my sugary cone. 'Just out for a walk and a cornet.' As Clemmie adjusts Bud's floppy sun hat, I'm psyching myself up. I don't want to miss my chance here, but I don't want to intrude on her private time either.

Nell laughs. 'If you've had cones rather than sundaes, that's good. You'll still have room for cake with us.'

Clemmie joins in. 'We're just off to the top floor at Seaspray Cottage to check out some new recipes. Why not come and join in, you can have a look at the flat at the same time.'

I heave a sigh of relief that she's invited us, then I remember her saying it's tiny. 'If there's room for all of us, we'd love that.'

Sophie's nodding. 'Clemmie can never have too many tasters! It's small, but we've squeezed in a lot more.'

If Ella's staring pointedly at her watch it's carb intake rather than time she's worried about, but I'm guessing she won't mind if it means I get my significant chat to Clemmie. 'If you run the hundred yards from here to there, Ells, you'll burn off the calories in advance.'

Nell chortles. 'It's four flights up, the stairs will do that for you.'

A moment later we're down on the sand and ambling along with them.

Sophie falls into step with us. 'Clemmie and Charlie have flats on the same floor. They met when they shared the balcony.'

Clemmie overhears. 'You're welcome to see both. Mine is a tiny patchwork of vintage colour, and Charlie's is huge, white, and fifty shades of opulent. We shuttle between the two.'

Nell's laughing as we reach the wall and she opens the picket gate and lets Diesel the dog through first. 'To look at their flats, you'd never think they'd get on. Opposites must attract.'

Clemmie laughs as we walk across the lawn. 'We did clash

to start with. But once he stopped being obnoxious and started teaching me to bake, he was actually quite hot.'

Ella gives me a shove with her elbow. 'I guess some guys next door *are* worth the trouble.'

I'm about to tell her she's welcome to Ollie, but knowing what we know now, we'll both do best to keep our distance. We're pushing through the door, into a hallway smelling of beeswax and thyme, and then we're straight onto some winding dark wood stairs. By the time we've clattered up four floors, there's no breath left for anything but gasping.

We follow the crowd along the landing, Diesel the dog bumping against our thighs, and glimpse the view across the bay from a tall window as Clemmie pushes through a door on the right. We might be breathless, but as we move through into a lofty room that's approximately the size of a football pitch, Ella's still got enough air left in her lungs to let out a long, satisfied groan of appreciation.

'Oh yes, I see what you mean by luxurious. It's the perfect use of the space.' Her eyes are all dreamy, and she's already crossed the living room and the bit beyond. As she runs her hands over the polished work surface adjoining the distant dining area, she gives a little shiver. 'If I lived next door to a single man with a kitchen island like this, I'd move in with him whether he wanted me to or not.'

I roll my eyes. 'You'll have to forgive Ella; she has her head turned every day with the high-end projects she works on.' I smile round at Clemmie and Sophie. 'It's a beautiful flat. But some of us are more in touch with the real world.'

Clemmie laughs. 'You two sound like Charlie and me. Come through to my side and you'll see. In case you're wavering, Ella, that's where the cake is, and Nell's already got the kettle on.'

Everyone's filing out again, following Diesel and Clemmie across the hall, but Ella's lingering. I stare up at the impossibly high sloping ceiling as I hold the door to the landing open for her. As she finally hurries across the grey wool rug to join me, she pauses for one very long last look.

'We can't do anything this up-market, but all-white empty spaces would work perfectly for the cottage.'

I'm taken aback. 'I thought you weren't ready to talk about it?'

She frowns. 'You're right. I've had no idea what to do up to now but seeing this has suddenly crystallised it.' Her expression relaxes to a smile. 'This is how the best design works – just when you think it's never going to happen, the answer hits you like a thunderbolt.'

It's my turn to frown, because nothing I see here feels as if it would fit at the cottage. 'It's just – very surgical.'

'Trust me, you'll love it when it's done.' Ella squeezes my hand. 'That's the other thing I've realised. My day job's taking up so much more of my time than I'd anticipated. We'll need to keep the cottage schedule as minimal as we can.'

I'm opening my mouth to ask what she means, when a shout comes from across the landing.

'Tea's ready.'

As I hurry Ella past the ocean view and towards the door across the hall I can't quite believe what she's just said. And then I completely forget, because beyond the crowd of children there's a fuchsia velvet sofa against a peacock blue and lime green wall, and a riot of brilliant silk cushions that blasts every thought out of my mind other than how beautiful it all is.

I'm staring around. 'It's like the Little Cornish Kitchen downstairs, only way more miniature and multi-layered.'

Clemmie's smiling. 'This is the original. Downstairs is done in the same spirit, with a lot more practicality.'

As I run my hand over a rainbow of mismatched wallpaper I've got the feeling that I want to embrace it all in the same way it's wrapping itself around me. 'It's quirky but so comfy and interesting and welcoming.' In a way it's a bit the same with the women too. Their warmth is so immediate, I almost feel as if I've known them forever.

Once I look past the cluster of easy chairs and side tables, it's probably not much bigger than the cottage. But that's the clever bit; there's so much colour and interest layered into the tiny space, size is the last thing that I think about. I lean to peer out of the French windows that are flooding the room with light, and look past a balcony, then straight out to sea.

I turn to Ella to see if she's enjoying it too. 'Isn't it lovely?'

'Fabulous.' The way she blinks and pulls herself back into the room, I suspect she hasn't looked at any of it. 'Very eclectic. I'm pleased I saw both sides.' And then she stares out across the bay again.

Nell appears at a door in the corner. 'Tea's in here, so we can give the cake our full attention.'

We all follow Clemmie into an even smaller kitchen, where the table, covered with a pink spotted cloth, is surrounded by the same brightly coloured wooden chairs as downstairs. The shelves on the apple green dresser are covered in mismatched china and piles of cookery books, and the windows beyond look out around the bay too. My mouth waters as I squeeze in between Ella and Bud in her highchair. Then Nell slides a platter piled with cake slabs onto the table.

Clemmie hands round mismatched flowery plates and clears her throat. 'Okay, today we have three types of brownies – blueberry, red velvet, and Mars bar.' She looks at

Bud. 'And there are some of your favourite carrot sticks for you.'

Sophie nods as she passes out the mugs of tea. 'Every day is good for Little Cornish Kitchen taste tests, but Sundays are our favourites.'

Nell takes a bite of her first piece. 'It's a matter of pride that nothing new reaches the public before it gets the thumbs-up from us.'

There's the sound of a distant door closing, and Plum arrives by the dresser, adjusting the strap of her paint-splattered dungarees. 'Hi, everyone, I managed to slip away from the gallery.' She smiles at Ella and me as we bite into cake slices the size of our heads. 'All we have to do here is check they're delicious.'

Sophie's waving a Mars bar piece at us. 'And while we're doing that you can tell us how you're getting on at Stargazey.'

I smile, remembering yesterday. 'I'm pleased to say the windows are sparkling now.' As much as the misty glass will allow.

Ella's looking triumphant too. 'And we've firmed up on our scheme of works too. We're going for Farrow and Ball No 2002 throughout.' She ignores the underwhelming hush. 'White Tie. It's a yellow-based neutral.'

Plum's frowning. 'Is that for starters?'

Ella narrows her eyes. 'No, for speed and simplicity. A quick refit in the kitchen and bathroom, and we'll leave the rest alone as much as we can. It's what we call in the trade a light-handed approach.'

I'm so shocked now I'm hearing it out loud I swallow my second bite of red velvet brownie whole and don't get to taste it. As if we'd palm off Stargazey with anything *that* boring after seeing Clemmie's place. I can't let this go, so I give a cough. 'Or...' I wait until Ella's properly looking at me. I hadn't planned to go head-to-head with her so fast, but she's left me with no alternative. '...there *is* a rival order of service – I mean, scheme of works. The *heavy-handed* approach.'

'*What?*' Ella screws up her face in incomprehension.

I'm making this up as I go, desperately thinking back to the YouTube clips for inspiration. Anything has to be better than wall-to-wall operating theatre. 'In my version – *which is straight from the heart* – first off we'll knock a stonking hole in the kitchen wall and put in massive doors opening out onto the terrace facing towards the sea.'

Ella narrows her eyes. 'But we haven't got a terrace!'

'Our patch of concrete then.' I'm suddenly feeling very territorial and defensive. What's more, I'm looking at Clemmie's balcony thinking how a railing would make that perilous outside space at the cottage useable. I hate to mention the mountains, but after so many years of hanging round in chalets, I know how hard a balcony can work for you.

Sophie and Plum's eyes are bright as they nod. 'That would be amazing.'

I ignore the hard kick from Ella that lands on my shin. 'And the corner bath needs to come out too, and I definitely want one of us to wake up to the view from the bathroom window from a bed, rather than only getting to see it from the shower.' I'm thinking out loud here. 'So that means knocking through to the second bedroom to make a huge one and moving the bathroom into the bedroom on the other side of the cottage.'

When I say huge, it's all relative, but whatever. Another chorus of excited shouts from around the table is really spurring me on.

'And I'd like to make the little window in the attic into a door too, with some rails across that, and a window-box.

Because I've always wanted my very own room with a balcony.' I'm guessing if Ella's obsession is white emptiness, my own motto has to be *You can never have enough balconies*. 'And we'll have window-boxes at the other windows too.'

Ella's rolling her eyes. 'Obviously my version has window-boxes. *And* a fridge with an ice-maker.' From the way her jaw is jutting, she's bringing out the big guns here. 'In fact, with my no-frills scheme we could afford to make the entire street elevation into a planted vertical garden to offset our carbon footprint.'

I grin at her, because that's such an over-the-top, Ella-thing to suggest. 'That's wonderfully eco-friendly, but if I'm going to be the one doing the watering, maybe we should start small. We can move onto the wall when I've learned how to keep the plants in the boxes alive.' I need to move this to a place where we're presenting a united front, so I beam round at the others. 'Of the two of us, I've spent a lot more time at the cottage. That's why I've had more of a chance to assimilate.' I hope *someone* understands this explanation, because I'm not sure I do. 'And I'm happy to paint *some* walls white, but I'd definitely add other colours too.'

As Dad was more obsessed with rock faces than home decor I never had the chance to paint my room at home, and since then I've only ever been passing through. I know I'm not planning on staying here forever but when I wake and see the dawn light seeping across the sloping ceiling of the attic where I've taken to sleeping the last couple of days, I've imagined how it would look if it were pink. Nothing too dark, nothing too dusky. Just a colour that made the peachy morning light even more amazing.

'And a free-standing bath. For sure.' I've truly got no idea where that come from. Other than how wonderful they always looked in the chalet master-suites.

Sophie's eyes have narrowed. 'It's great that you're considering two really different approaches.' A smile spreads across her face. 'Two designers competing makes it even *more* interesting!'

Plum looks as if she's going to burst. 'This is the perfect opportunity to let more people from the singles club get to know you better. Let's put up a poll on the Facebook page, then they can all join in the discussion.'

Nell laughs. 'Have *your* say about what the Star Sisters do with Stargazey Cottage! Everyone here always wants to be involved in everything so that's a great way of satisfying village curiosity too! Send us some options, and we'll get it going!'

My heart is sinking. I hope I haven't inadvertently started something I can't handle. It was bad enough leading people to believe I had talents that I didn't. It feels as if I've made that a hundred times worse and there's no going back.

Clemmie smiles at me. 'Don't worry. You two will always have the final say. This is just a bit of fun to raise your profile. Homemaking is on a lot of their minds; this way they get to join in from a safe distance.'

Ella looks up from her Fitbit. 'Fabulous. That's just what we always hoped for.' Which means it's not. 'Great cakes, by the way. They were definitely worth blowing my calorie budget for.'

I send her an apologetic smile. When I started this, I truly didn't expect it to end here. 'We can run all the way home.' I've eaten all three pieces of mine. 'They were all spectacularly delish, but the Mars bar one was literally to die for.' The others somehow got inhaled in the stress of the moment. I definitely loved them, I just can't remember the exact taste.

I'm so flustered by how out of hand this has got so fast, the next thing I know I'm accidentally on my default setting, going round the table, collecting the plates and mugs. I'm at the sink before I remember it's not my place.

Clemmie arrives at my elbow and puts another handful of plates on the work surface. 'You did that without thinking.'

I hope I haven't rushed them. 'Sorry if you weren't ready. Give me a table and plates that are finished with, I can't help clearing.'

She gives me a searching stare. 'Are you *sure* you can't spare me an hour tomorrow morning?'

I can't believe that I haven't had to beg. 'What if I spray the place with milkshake again? Or beer? Or pancake batter?' Even thinking about it I'm panicking 'I get so nervous with so many customers I don't know. Honestly, anything could happen.'

Her hand lands on mine. 'You'll soon find your feet. But until you do, keep to the kitchen or talk to me and Bud.'

Ella's calling from the table. 'Gwen's the queen of breakfasts.'

Clemmie's smile widens. 'Better and better! Shall we say seven o'clock tomorrow morning then? And take it from there?'

I manage a squeak. 'Great.' Now isn't the time to explain that cooking mass breakfasts is so close to the life I'm trying to forget, doing it would probably make my head implode. And after that, there's no chance of saying anything more, because I'm hyperventilating with the worry. But after the other developments this afternoon, a job I'll hate that I'm likely to stuff up hugely is likely to be the smallest problem on my horizon.

9

On the way home
Tight corners and lightbulb moments
Sunday afternoon

'So what happened back there? Since when have you had *plans for the cottage*?'

At least Ella waits until we get across the harbourside before she fires the question at me, so I've had a few minutes to think about it. But before I answer I need to tackle her about the rest.

I take a deep breath. 'There's something else I need to mention first.'

She gives a sniff. 'Can't it wait? Surely this is more important?'

Which only goes to show how much we need *my* chat. 'You know how sometimes you have a tendency to get over-dogmatic?'

'Yeah...'

I don't give her time to say more. 'Well – that.'

Her eyes widen and her voice rises. 'It's happening now? I've turned into a steamroller again. *Why didn't you tell me?*'

I'm feeling like I should have done this, ages ago. 'Sorry, but I'm late to the party. I only just noticed.'

'Damn.' She slaps her thigh and closes her eyes. 'It's always worse when I'm feeling insecure – I over-compensate.'

I pull her into a hug because we both know how hard she was hit by Taylor walking out. 'It hasn't been an easy time at home.'

She's shaking her head. 'It's not only that. When I'm on these building sites, if I'm not forceful I won't get a word in at all. The only way is to interrupt and talk over everyone. Anywhere else it would be super-rude, but as a lone woman in a workforce of men, it's the only way to survive. But it's hard to switch that off at home time.'

I do sympathise with her situation and I want to bolster her. 'You've got where you are because you can power through. Just cut the rest of us a little more slack outside work, that's all.'

Her expression is even more anxious. 'You will tell me if I do it again?'

'Too right, I will.'

We pause for a breather and a drool by the shop window of Crusty Cobs, and her elbow lands in my ribs. 'So are you ready to tell me what was going on back at Seaspray Cottage?'

This is going to put her flexibility to the test straightaway. 'I was so at home in Clemmie's tiny flat, and then when you sprung your whole bright-white Colgate-smile scheme it felt unfair – like we were short-changing Stargazey Cottage by not giving it a chance.' It's ironic that the same building that opened my eyes to the possibilities of the cottage has made Ella have such a different reaction. 'I don't get how you can feel comfortable with clinical. For me, cluttered and cosy means safe and happy.' With my tiny bedroom squeezed under the eaves in our Highland cottage, that's all I've ever known. But it was useful because afterwards I never minded the tiny bunk rooms staff have to share at the alpine resorts.

Ella pulls a face. 'I blame all those holidays you spent in a camper van the size of a sardine tin.' She lets out a sigh. 'I can't help that my childhood influences were more upmarket. Remember how my dad loved his classy hotels?' He worked on the oil rigs out of Aberdeen and when he wasn't toughing it out offshore he could afford the best. Ella rolls her eyes. 'I'm sorry, Gwen. My day job is huge, and my whole future here depends on me making a success of it. If I take on too much with the cottage, I'll sell everyone short. Doing the minimum is the only way I can make it work.'

I'm not giving up on this without a fight. 'Opening the cottage up at the back could turn things around at Stargazey. I pulled that idea out at random, but it might be the answer.' In my head I'm already seeing doors with chairs and a table beyond, tumblers of gin. It's so real, I can practically hear the tonic's fizz and the chink of ice cubes melting in the evening sun. 'It would bring the wide open space of the ocean into the house and make it ours. And we could do you a mirror wall in the bedroom like you had as a kid.' I'm sure that's a hundred per cent what got her hooked on spaces like Charlie's flat in the first place as much as her dad Hugh's obsession with five-star accommodation.

Ella's striding ahead of me up the cobbled hill. 'Even if the budget *did* stretch that far, *and* there were builders on hand to do it, there really aren't enough spare hours in my day for me to organise and keep it on track.'

Now it's my turn to toss my head. 'Then I'll have to do it myself.'

Her mouth falls open. 'You?'

I bring in a sweetener. 'With your help, obviously. But I'm here, I have the time. So that's decided.' I don't know how the hell I'm going to do it, or even why. But there's a tiny voice inside my head telling me Stargazey deserves a chance to shine. If I can do that before my feet start to itch and I have to head off on my travels again, I will.

Ella's frowning at me. 'Are you sure you know what you're taking on?'

As we finally stagger up the hill past Stargazey House, I deliberately turn my head away from next door's frontage, and there's still a part of me that's wanting to prove her wrong. 'I'll be fine.' Or maybe ignorance is bliss.

She's raising her eyebrows. 'You're going to need engineer's calculations and building regs and planning approval before you even start.'

I take a deep breath and hold my course. 'Which is why it's good you'll be around to direct me.'

And then she pushes open our front door, and we both see the reality of what's inside. We let the door slam behind us, move through the cottage, and peer through the scratched panes of the kitchen window to the cracked pieces of concrete collapsing down the hill outside. The only bit that looks anything like okay is the sea in the distance.

I let out a groan. 'It's so far away from the pictures floating round in my head when we were at Clemmie's.'

She nods and squeezes my hand. 'The important thing is,

you've had your vision, just like I had mine. That's what's going to help you carry it through.'

I'm wanting to be nice back. 'If you really want your plant wall…'

She looks at me as if I'm losing it. 'Hell no, we'll never afford that *and* a free-standing bath. Not with all the knocking down you'll be doing.'

I have to remind her. 'We don't know that. We'll have to see what the Facebook poll says.'

She pulls me into a hug. 'Those walls will be going, I guarantee. And well done on getting the job with Clemmie. You've been on fire today – that's good to see again.'

She's right. I can't remember the last time I was fired up about anything. I'm not a hundred per cent sure my flash of enthusiasm was well placed. But after I've spent so long drowning in apathy and despair, anything positive has to be an improvement.

I look at the box that Clemmie's sent me home with. 'Working at the Little Cornish Kitchen is going to mean lots of cake.'

Ella rolls her eyes. 'So long as it has fruit in, my Fitbit will probably turn a blind eye.'

'You lie to your Fitbit?' It's a valid question.

Even as I ask, I know the answer. Of course, she does. It's very Ella. Waving her watch around, haring up and down the beach then eating her bodyweight in brownies and ice cream.

She's clearing her throat. 'Changing the subject, did you notice there's a light on next door?'

My stomach drops then does a somersault. 'Probably just the builders.'

Ella looks at me. 'If *you* manage to get *your* construction team on site on a Sunday afternoon, you'll be a better woman than me.' She pauses to let that sink in. 'It's much more likely to be someone else.'

As if an awful new job and holes in walls aren't enough to worry about, without adding in another impossible complication.

10

At the Little Cornish Kitchen
Omelettes and broken eggs
Thursday, four days later

I'd barely slept on Sunday night, but in the end I needn't have worried. When I'd crept through the garden and into the Little Cornish Kitchen at five to seven on Monday morning Bud was already wide awake, bashing a spoon on her highchair tray, so I'd sat with her behind the main counter and played and looked at books. Then, as the early morning customers came in on their way to work, Clemmie had served, and I'd helped by making drinks.

She'd been doing these breakfasts for ages before Bud arrived, so she was used to running the place on her own. I was mainly on hand to sort out Bud if she got tetchy while Clemmie was busy with the other jobs.

Everyone had stopped to make a fuss of Bud on their way to their tables and most of them had introduced themselves to me while they were chatting to her. I have to say, meeting people with the buffer of a baby between you is a lot easier than meeting them without. With less stress I'd even managed to put some names to faces from the fancy-dress evening.

Then, once everyone had gone, I'd taken over the clearing and tidied up in the kitchen. As I said to Clemmie, compared to some of the manic chalet breakfast times I've dealt with, it had been a quiet morning. And right at the end, Nell had dropped in with some home-cured bacon and eggs from her parents' farm, so as a thank you for the morning I'd made bacon and egg cobs for the three of us. Then I'd left with a cake box loaded with goodies, which Clemmie pressed into my hands as I was about to go.

Obviously, for the entire three and a half hours, I'd had a quarter of an eye on who was walking in. When I was also looking after a baby breakfasting on Rice Krispies, sloppy Greek yogurt and sliced peach, me watching out for flying projectiles had to take priority over the door.

But I needn't have worried. In fact, I'd been the only Stargazey resident in the place for all three mornings this week, so I was starting to think I must have been right about it being the builders we'd heard next door on Sunday afternoon.

So now, browning the bacon and flipping the eggs for our cobs at the end of Thursday's session, I'm wondering what there was to feel so jumpy about. As I stand over the frying pan, I'm inhaling deeply, smiling at Nell as she stands jiggling Bud on her hip in the doorway. 'I've cooked some tasty rashers in my time, Nell, but yours beat them all.'

Clemmie's unloading a dishwasher, stacking plates onto the worktop. 'We've enjoyed your bacon cobs so much, Gwen, I wondered if you'd mind cooking a few for customers next week? We could get them to order in advance so you wouldn't be overwhelmed.'

My stomach drops like a lift. It's such a shock that my tongue completely disconnects from my thinking brain. Even as I hear the words come out, I know I shouldn't be saying them. 'Since my brother was killed in the mountains, I've never been able to face proper catering. Cooking breakfasts for large numbers of people would be too much of a throwback. I'm not sure I'd be able to.'

As they're looking at me, their faces are sympathetic, but I'm kicking myself too much to stop. I let out a wail. 'And I'm not supposed to tell anyone about Ned dying, because once they know, no one knows what to say or how to cope. If they know, everyone will cross the road to avoid me, or else they'll forget and say something insensitive, and then I have to watch them look like they want the ground to open up and swallow them.' Now I've started I just can't stop. 'And just when I wasn't doing too badly here, now you'll be the same.'

The tears running down my face show why this was such a bad idea. 'I should have stayed away. I'm sorry, it's been four years now but I'm still a mess. No one should have to watch this.'

Clemmie's coming towards me, and her arms close around me, and she's patting my back with her hand. 'It's okay. We're completely used to grief, and how wobbly it makes you. We understand.'

Nell's beside me too, squeezing my arm. 'No one's judging. We're all here to help you feel better.'

Clemmie lets me go and pulls up a chair at the table. 'My partner Charlie's fiancée died, so we understand it takes a long time to learn to live again. But don't ever give up hope – you *will* get there.'

Nell puts a tissue box down on the table and sits down too.

'When Charlie was in pieces after losing Faye, teaching his sister Cressy to bake helped him through the worst times.'

Clemmie joins in. 'And then, years later, he taught me the same recipes all over again. And that was what finally helped him to mend enough to move on to a new relationship. Cooking can be very healing – the simple steps, concentrating on the recipes.'

Nell joins in. 'Eating the food at the end.'

I scrape a tear away from under my eyelashes. 'I'm not doing very well with the mending. When Ned died, I was working as a chalet host. If Ned was nearby, he used to drop in every day for leftovers; he was always hungry. There are still so many things I can't bear to make because I'm scared it'll break my heart all over again. Cooking for strangers is one of those things too.'

Now I'm saying it out loud it feels more of a relief to have told someone than it does painful. And even when it comes to the surface there are different levels of hurt. What I'm crying for here is more in frustration at myself for doing so badly than for the loss itself.

Nell's folding her arms. 'No one wants you to do more than you want to. But you might find that if you try things now, a little bit at a time, it might help.' She gives me a nudge. 'And I'm not only saying that because your bacon butties are so delectable either. But it would be a shame if other people didn't get to enjoy them too.'

'Maybe.' I'm half laughing, half crying, because Nell loves her bacon so much.

Clemmie's squeezing my fingers. 'Everyone is here for you; we'll help as much as we can. St Aidan's a very healing place.'

Nell's nodding in agreement. 'With the sea and the village,

a lot of people feel better for spending time here. But you must only do what you feel comfortable with.'

I'm seeing if I can talk myself through this. 'It's not that big a deal. It might only be a couple of sandwiches more than I've been making for you.'

Nell smiles at me. 'We could limit it to four to begin with? You could see how you got on and do more only if you felt you could.'

Clemmie sounds so encouraging. 'You're just so much better at this than me, which is why I always stick to making sweet things. But if you find you can't do it, I promise I'll step in and take over.'

Clemmie's being so considerate, making sure nothing there is outside my comfort zone.

'Okay. Let's start with four. I'll try that and see how I go.'

Nell's eyes are lighting up. 'Great, I'll put them on the singles page on Facebook. "Gwen's bacon cobs" has a very nice ring to it! Order in advance as numbers are limited.'

My stomach clenches again. 'Do you *have* to mention me by name?'

Clemmie drops her arm onto my shoulder. 'Everyone knows I stick to pastries and puddings, and I only stretch to cucumber sandwiches and sausage rolls for my afternoon teas. But if you aren't okay with it, we won't do it.'

Nell laughs as she pats my hand. 'It would help to avoid the entire village assuming that Clemmie's taste buds have gone haywire because she's pregnant again when she's not. It would be round the village faster than you can say "Clearblue rapid results".'

I'm shocked. 'Would that really happen?'

Nell inclines her head. 'People in St Aidan know what

you're thinking before you've thought it. What's more, they never hold back on sharing what they *think* they know.'

Clemmie gives an indulgent smile. 'Always with the best of intentions. It's only because they care.'

'As it's for such a good cause, go ahead, use my name.' At the same time, it's another gentle wake-up call for me; Ella and I need to guard our secrets even more carefully than we already do if the village is onto everything. But cooking Little Cornish Kitchen breakfasts is a big step forward. If I actually managed that, I'd be more than pleased.

11

In the garden at Stargazey Cottage
Seashells and a stairway to heaven
Later the same day

Half an hour later, I've got my first week's cash-in-hand wages safely tucked into my jeans pocket, and as I head off in search of a shop called Hardware Haven, I've practically forgotten all about my name being in proverbial breakfast lights.

Thanks to growing up with Dad, I always like to spend my money on things that are worthwhile. Buying tools to use in the garden at the cottage seems like a good way to celebrate my first week of work in St Aidan, even if it has only been for a handful of hours. Investing time in cutting back the garden feels worthwhile too now our plans for the cottage have more shape to them.

In spite of Ella's initial reluctance, we decided to put ourselves out there and see what the locals think of our different ideas. Ella and I each did a brief outline of our thoughts on the hole in the back wall, I took a couple of photos of the front of the cottage and the sea view framed in the bathroom window, and by Tuesday visitors are flocking to the singles club page to add their weight to the *'What shall we do with Stargazey Cottage?'* poll, with a finish date at the weekend. When I also set up a 'Sisters at Stargazey Cottage' profile for Facebook and Insta and added the same pictures it felt like we were properly official.

I know there are a lot of hoops to jump through before work actually begins on the building but going out to work has given me a new-found energy; chopping a way through the hillside wilderness at the back will put that to good use and get some outside work underway too.

I find Hardware Haven in a tiny side street above Iron Maiden cleaners and the Hungry Shark pub. It has a hundred different brooms, buckets, shovels and bird tables stacked across the pavement frontage, and when I step inside the fluorescent-lit interior it has the same peaty smell as the hardware shop Dad used to take Ned and me to as kids to buy our oil-lamp wicks. This one is bursting with every random household item you can think of from scissors and soap to screws and marrow seeds and budgerigar cages. There's also a mind-boggling cabinet filled with dishes and plates and ornaments all saying 'A present from St Aidan'.

When I ask for secateurs the woman in the green-checked nylon overall calls me 'my lovely' in a way that actually makes me feel I am, then goes in the back and brings out a choice of five, and some shears. Then, when I've chosen, she kindly asks if I need lawn trimmers too, and when I tell her I'm actually trying to tame a cliff face we both laugh about that. In the end she persuades me to buy a souvenir from her selection, so I also come home with a miniature lighthouse with a diamond for the light that says 'St Aidan on the Rocks' around the base.

When I actually get out onto the broken paving slabs and find the bottom of the steps that lead up the hillside at the back of the cottage I'm almost blown away by a gust from the sea. From here the only visible part of the famous little shed everyone talks about is the rooftop, sticking out high above me through an almost vertical curtain of scrubby vegetation.

'Ella could have this as her plant wall. I'm not sure brambles count though,' I mutter to myself. The slope the steps are cutting across is steep. There are patches of sea holly and burdock, and dried hogweed seedheads sticking up above the bramble clumps.

As I make my first cut and snag my shirt then rip open my finger I'm reminded – brambles have thorns. I dash back down to Hardware Haven and come back armed with two pairs of full-strength gardening gloves, and also get talked into buying a plate with a picture of St Aidan Bay and 'Wish you were here' in curly gold writing. Between us, I'm more likely to swim the channel than get Ella out in the garden wearing the gloves, but Janice-in-the-green-overall seems to know how many of us live here and wouldn't hear of me only taking one pair. She also whispered that she's voting for my idea not Ella's in the poll so after that I wasn't going to argue.

As someone who constantly moves on, I can easily reel off the names of the wild plants, but what I know about garden plants and maintenance would fit on a very small leaf. But once I'm back outside the cottage I start on the bottom step, making cuts along the plant stems, and stack my clippings into a pile by the side. At first, I get hand ache, but each time I clear another little platform it takes me a few inches further up the hill.

When I've done ten steps, I nip back into the kitchen for some of Clemmie's cake. The flight is so steep, it's almost like climbing a rocky ladder, but when I sit at the top munching my slice of lemon drizzle, the view of the sea, pale-blue and shimmering in the distance, spurs me on. I promise myself a cup of tea when I've done twenty more.

As I sit on the thirtieth step, I look up from dunking my custard cream blondie reward and it hits me. From here I'm looking straight down on next door's terrace, and thanks to the steps winding around the hillside as well as upwards I'm getting a bird's-eye view of the extension across the back of the cottage. From outside it's even huger than we imagined when we were in it. I scan the walls for movement inside, but all I can see is the zigzag of builder's tape on the expanses of glass, so I go back to my tea.

Sometime in mid-afternoon I forget all about counting the steps, because the sun has come out. It's warm on my back, and as I peel off my over-shirt all I care about is getting to the top. As I spring up and down the flights, feeding my twig piles, I'm blocking out how much it reminds me of running up and down the hillside path where we used to stay as kids in a little stone Alpine shepherd's shelter that belonged to a friend of Dad's.

And then suddenly I'm clipping back the last brambles and grappling with a clump of elderberry branches, and I'm stepping onto an uneven stone platform leading to an ancient timber shed, hoping it's not going to collapse under my weight.

As I pull armfuls of sticky bud strands away from the weathered shed frontage, I'm talking to myself again. 'A little window . . . it's not *that* much smaller than the cottage.' As I grasp a doorknob, it turns. 'Another St Aidan front door that's been left unlocked.'

I push my way in to find a rough plank table up against the wall. The way the wooden chair with arms is pushed back at an angle, it feels as if whoever left it like that was meaning to come back. The air inside is warm, and there are dust particles flickering in a sun shaft. Beyond the chair there's a stove with a metal flue pipe going straight up through the wriggly metal roof.

I perch on the chair edge and find it's perfectly placed for a view across the bay, but when I look through the open door and see the hillside and its dizzying drop, framed by the planks of the shed wall, my heart does a somersault and lands in my throat.

I let out a groan. 'How can it be so like the mountains?'

How could anything as small as bacon sandwiches have been a problem when everything I came here to avoid has been waiting for me at the top of the garden? As pictures of Ned flash though my brain the hurt in my chest explodes and my throat constricts. I put my hands over my ears and curl up in a ball trying to make it all go away again.

Pushing it down, keeping it locked away. Trying not to let anything reminding me of Ned anywhere into my current life. It's the only way I've found to deal with the anguish. The rawness. The awful, devastating jolt of realisation I get over and over again every time I remember that he's gone. That he won't ever be there again to coax me along a rock face I'd really rather not be on, or handing out horribly burned sausages from the back of his van, with disgusting amounts of mustard, because he can't see how you could possibly enjoy them any other way. Or messaging me pictures of a dog in Chicago sitting on fire hydrants all around the city. Or making me drink hot chocolate out of a baked bean tin. He won't ever be shouting at me from his selfie-videos on Instagram, halfway up a Himalayan peak. Ned who was amazing at everything, Ned who was always there, Ned who never stood still and never let me down. Ned, whom I spent the whole of my twenties worrying about and watching over. That next time he wakes me in the middle of the night with a call just to check I'm okay, it will only ever be in a dream.

I'm dragging air in through my nose, blowing out through my lips, counting as I go. One, two, three, four, five, one, two, three, four, five.

Tranquillity workshops for very small groups used to be my second string in summer. Back then, being calm and strong enough to pass that to other people was part of who I was. Who'd have thought I'd be the one desperately counting just so I could get oxygen into my lungs?

There's a reason people learn the counting. As a technique, even though it feels impossible at first, it hasn't ever failed me. It sounds crazy, but the important thing about a panic attack is – trying not to panic. A few minutes later the constriction in my chest is easing and my breathing is regular enough for me to try to stand up again. Once my legs feel strong enough to hold me, I walk back outside, hoping the sunshine and a blast of salty air will bring me round faster.

I'm wavering in front of the shed, tugging further along the curtain of sticky bud strands, when a sudden shout from nearby sends me lurching.

'Gwen!'

It's a man's voice somewhere near my feet, and it's so unexpected I jump sideways like a startled pony. Except I'm so close to the edge of the platform that as I lunge to find a foothold, instead of my trainer landing on stone, all it hits is thin air where the hillside is falling away.

As I wave my arms wildly, trying to save myself, my scream is growing. I'm horizontal, gravity wrenching my body backwards in an arc. I'm pretty much off the edge, the sky above me is sliding in slow motion, and then there's a lurch, a pain in my shoulders, and suddenly I'm not falling backwards any more.

Instead, I'm staggering forwards and hitting the hard planes of chest beneath a very soft T-shirt. And thanks to my desperation to survive, I've flung my arms around the torso in front of me, and my nails are digging into this person's back. I couldn't be clinging on any harder if I was on a plank floating next to the *Titanic* without a life jacket. And in turn, they're grasping me just as hard. I say person, but as my racing heart steadies, the muscles rippling under my fingers tell me it's definitely a man. And as he clears his throat and I hear a familiar gravelly tone my stomach plummets. I know I should be showering him with thanks, but my self-protection instinct kicks in and overrides it.

'Ollie! What the hell are *you* doing here?'

His tone is incredulous. 'Stopping you from falling, for starters. Don't you know to stay away from the edge?'

I was perfectly safe until he startled me! 'Don't *you* know not to creep up on people on narrow ledges?' As I give a snort of disgust my nose fills with the scent of laundry and pure guy and reminds me I might need to let go of him. Resume the conversation at a distance so my blood isn't fizzing in my veins. 'Thanks for catching me. If you let me squeeze past you, I can take it from here.'

I push him away to arm's length, but to get to the other side of him without falling down the hill again I end up grinding my pelvis against his jeans' zipper, then dragging my boobs across his arms. I have to leap all the way to the shed door before I'm far enough away to feel comfortable.

'So, great to see you' – it really isn't – 'how can I help?'

He shrugs. 'I saw you from the window and thought I'd come up for a chat.'

My out-of-control pulse is still racing. 'I didn't even know there was a path from yours.'

'There isn't. I had to climb an overhang. But someone's done a great job clearing the steps on your side.' The way he slides his thumbs into his pockets he looks like he owns the place, even though this bit is very definitely ours. As he props one shoulder against the shed, he looks alarmingly comfortable, and disgustingly hot. 'I hear you've got big plans for the cottage too.'

I shut out that last thought and deal with the rest. 'You saw the Stargazey Cottage poll on Facebook?' I give a grimace. If he came across that, he'll likely have seen my breakfast advert too, which is bad, bad news.

He shuffles. 'Not exactly. But it's good you've found this place' – he nods to the shed – 'it'll make someone a great home-office.'

I roll my eyes. 'Have you *seen* inside?' I don't want to remind myself again how much like an Alpine hideaway it is, so I try to concentrate on the old, beaten-up bits. 'It's definitely not for me, and I can't see Ella clambering up steps this steep.'

He gives a grimace. 'I'm sure once Snow White gets going with her broom she'll work the same magic as she's doing in the cottage.' He pauses for a second, then carries on. 'They're great ideas, by the way. It's good to know the place is in the hands of someone with such a great combination of vision and empathy.'

I'm still picking my jaw up off the floor. 'Snow White?'

He frowns. 'She *is* the one who stays at home all day and cleans? I've never seen your friend rolling *her* sleeves up, that's all.' He blinks and starts again. 'The little cabin that would suit smaller-than-average people was a reference too. I did see you come out of here just before?'

I let out a sigh and kick myself again for being weak enough to give in to emotions I'd thought I was keeping at a distance. One of the awful things about losing someone is that the grief is so unpredictable. It never strikes you when you're feeling strong and able to cope; it sneaks up and fells you when you're least ready. Just when you feel you might be making progress, it comes hurtling out of left field, and knocks your legs from under you. Strikes you down and reminds you that you never will be better because this is you forever. Bacon sandwiches earlier, and now this. It's not been the best of days.

Dragging in a breath feels like a luxury. 'I tried out the chair and stayed longer than I intended.'

He laughs. 'At least you didn't do a Goldilocks and break it.'

I groan inwardly. 'What's with the fairy tales? Before you ask, I didn't see any bears *or* porridge.' Even for a child-centric bookworm like me, it's a bit much.

He's looking at me sideways. 'You have to admit, it's very *Hansel and Gretel* up here.'

I'm arguing before I can stop myself. '*They* got lost in a forest, there's not a tree in sight.'

He wrinkles his nose and stares up at the shed. 'That triangular gable and the over-hanging eaves *could* be straight out of *Little Red Riding Hood*.'

I'm shaking my head. 'As her dad was a lumberjack, I'm guessing that was in a forest too.'

Ollie sniffs. 'Lumberjacks are Canadian. Her dad was a *woodcutter*.'

I'm not here to discuss the finer points of chainsaws and axes, I'm trying to close this down. 'Whatever. I've seen all I need to. If I'd known what was up here, I wouldn't have bothered buying the shears. I definitely won't be visiting again.'

He gives me another disbelieving sideways glance. 'I like the feel up here. For me, it's a lot nicer than down at the house.'

I could roll my eyes at every second sentence of his, if not all of them. Another unbelievably throwaway statement from a guy who has it all. This time I'm not holding back. 'It's *a shed*. How can it *possibly* be better than your mansion with a huge glass box on the back?'

He's shaking his head. 'Mansion is an exaggeration. It's just my personal reaction, that's all.'

I can't let him get away with this. 'From the person who told the builders what to build and spent a bomb, I find that hard to believe.'

He gives a deep sigh and pulls a face. Then he brightens again. 'The shed has a stove, of course it's better.'

I'm onto him. 'How can you possibly know that when you haven't been inside?'

He cranes his neck sideways. 'The chimney pipe sticking out of the roof might be the giveaway.'

So he's a show-off as well as not appreciating what he's got and never visiting. I glance at my phone to check the time. 'If that's everything, I'd better be getting back down.'

His brow creases into a frown. 'Please tell me you're not rushing off to cook her tea?'

As it happens, Ella – she does have a name – will probably

be back too late to eat with me, but I'm not telling him that. 'Would it matter if I was?'

'I just hate to think of you slaving, that's all.'

There's no point explaining that Ella still hasn't mastered lighting the gas on my camping rings even to boil a kettle, or that she calls into the Nando's lookalike in Falmouth for dinner often enough to be on first-name terms with the drive-through assistants, and that she's more than covering my cooking hours with her share of the bills. But all the same, he might want to butt out. '*Not* living in the cottage next door doesn't give you any right to judge our domestic arrangements.'

'Okay. Point taken. A couple of other quick things while I'm here – how would you feel about helping with the interiors for next door?'

If I hadn't been leaning against the shed, I might have collapsed with the shock. Luckily, I'm still up to thinking on my feet. 'Ella's got so much on at work she barely has time to come home as it is.'

There's another slow sideways glance at me. 'Which still leaves the other half of the Star Sisters free?'

Why do people always assume that the talent is equally distributed between us instead of fully weighted to one side? I can't draw any more attention to my job at Clemmie's either. 'I anticipate I'll have my hands overflowing with the work here.' I don't want to completely count my chickens. If we're sticking to a bird theme for our clichés, there's still a lot of ducks to find before we even *start* getting them in a row.

'So that's an unconditional no?'

There's no point pretending. 'It definitely is.' I couldn't do it even if I wasn't already over-run and completely without skills. I'm about to put my foot on the top step.

'One last question—'

As I pull myself back, I'm staring at his chest. Thinking about how it felt to have those arms around me. How long it is since anyone male pulled me into a hug. Properly wrapped me up like they meant it. It creeps up on you; time passes while you're looking the other way.

I look up, take in the stubble shadow on his jaw. The smile lines at the corners of his eyes that make my insides disappear a little more every time they crinkle. And as I look at his dark hazel eyes behind his long lashes, it's not just that he's dangerous to tangle with because of his achievement levels. It pulls my own particular situation into focus again too.

I'm wary. I'm on watch. Every time I find myself inadvertently glancing at Ollie, with each unwelcome stomach clench, my protection walls push upwards. Now I know how deep despair can be, I'll never willingly lay myself open to that again.

Even if Ollie's personality did match his awesome looks – if he wasn't flinty and driven, if he was someone else entirely, in other words – even in the unlikely event that he wanted to – I would have to walk away.

'Have you got a cat?'

As I zone back in to hear Ollie's voice, it sounds like a trick question. 'That's random. But again, no. Sorry to be so disappointing.' Then it hits me. 'On the up side, I do have your hoodie. I'll bring it round to the front of the house for you now.'

His smile is a lot wearier than it should be for someone so fortunate and full of themselves. 'The door's always open, as you know. Just drop it inside.'

I make sure my smile stretches all the way to my eyes. 'Will do.'

And then I run all the way down the steps, and only stop when I burst back into the kitchen

Living life on my own is how I have to be. Self-reliance and staying single are a small price to pay if it keeps me safe from pain like I've learned to live with because of Ned. One other thing is certain too – that's the last time I'll be venturing to the top of the Stargazey Cottage garden.

Now all I have to do is work out where to find an engineer. And someone who's good at making holes in walls. And then calculate how I'm going to get all the way through to Monday when I've eaten all Clemmie's cake this afternoon.

OCTOBER

12

At the Deck Gallery
Trick or treat?
Sunday

'I t's not that I mind losing – I'm thinking of the disruption!'
We're at the Deck Gallery and for the last ten minutes
Ella's been entertaining us talking about large, detached lodges
and unique locations. Then Nell unexpectedly moved the
conversation on to the landslide victory for the major-work
option in the Stargazey Facebook poll.

It's Sunday, ten days later, which means we've been on our
calorie-busting substitute park run, and now we've moved on
to a completely contradictory activity – a weekend tasting for
Clemmie's autumn recipes. From Ella's neatly braided bunches
and her pale complexion, you'd never know she'd spent the
last ninety minutes tearing up and down the beach. And it's
not that she means to moan – but second place isn't anywhere
she's used to.

I need to explain the wail. 'Ella's never come second

before.' I turn to her. 'You did those lovely sketches to show off my ideas, so you're on the winning team too.'

Ella sends me an apologetic smile. 'I'm sorry, Gwen. I know your plans are the ones that maximise the potential and it's brilliant the village has recognised that.' She gives my hand a squeeze. 'I'm very grateful to you for taking on the challenge.'

We're gathered round the table at Plum's because her usual assistant is off and she didn't want to miss out. As the clouds are stacking up in billowing grey layers outside, we're sitting with the glass doors open at the end of the light, white, airy gallery space. After that surprisingly gracious climb-down from Ella, it's a relief to see Clemmie arriving with a pile of cake boxes, followed by Sophie's three girls who deliver everyone a plate and a cake fork.

Sophie peels the lid off the nearest container. 'What's in this one, Clemmie?'

Clemmie leans to look. 'Spooky cupcakes – dark chocolate sponge topped with white marshmallow icing ghosts, and cobweb brownies in the other.'

Ella's licking her lips. 'Ghosts weigh nothing at all, I'll go with two of those please.' She catches my eye and gives me a wink. 'Cakes *are* why we run, after all.'

Clemmie passes the second box around. 'Dig in, everyone, and see what you think.'

Believe it or not, we're here as a 'thank you' for how many bacon cobs we've sold with the breakfasts this last week. On Monday I was shaky even making four, but by Tuesday I got in the swing and made a couple of extras. By Thursday we sold so many we ran out of bacon. I know they're only sandwiches, but for me it's quite a breakthrough. And after pitching in at a mums-and-bumps lunch and helping at a birthday afternoon tea for a group of people from the care home, I'm starting to feel more at ease with the mermaids too.

I pull back the floral bun case and sink my teeth into a brownie. 'Mmmm, the orange cream cheese spider web is amazing.'

Sophie's son Marcus is pushing a ghost into his mouth whole, the other kids are running around making banshee screams and listening to the echoes, and everyone else is chewing and nodding their appreciation.

Nell's waving her ghost at Ella and me. 'So, any more news from the cottage?'

After Ella contacted the solicitors to ask how much work we were allowed to do, Nell's partner, George, sent an engineer round. And I know I'd said I'd never go to the top of the garden again, but I crept up one day just to clean the dust off the windows. Apart from that, I'm ashamed to say, we're still very much where we were.

I need to manage their expectations. 'There's a long way to go. We haven't even begun to look for a builder yet.'

Ella cuts in with a sigh. 'I'm afraid that's my fault, not Gwen's. I've been waiting for my workload to ease, but it seems to be ever-growing.'

I have to sympathise; with clients who pay more for a kitchen sink than footballers pay for engagement rings, she's under a lot of pressure. On the other hand, if we don't have a builder there won't ever be any holes in walls. It's not that I'm being negative or mean, but I'm truly hoping the delays aren't a long-game tactic so we do less on the cottage.

Nell gives me a sideways glance. 'There's an easy way to find a builder! We'll ask for recommendations on the singles page.'

Plum's nodding. 'Then you can take your pick!'

Sophie folds up her bun case and sighs. 'Think yourself lucky you've got the funds to begin.'

That's another sticking point I won't be picking up. We won't know how far our cash is going to stretch until we get some prices in. Ella's already warned me that's the stage where a lot of projects get cut back.

I smile at Ella. 'Thanks, Nell, that's one less thing for Ella to do. I'll message you a photo to go with the post.'

Clemmie laughs. 'Lucky for us, plenty of people are finding your bacon cobs are even tastier than they look in the pictures.'

Plum's resting her chin on her hand. 'Do you have any other breakfast specialities?'

Ella gives me a sideways stare. 'Gwen's got lots of tricks up her sleeve. It's time she brought them out again.'

I'm going to have to give them something. 'My own-mix muesli, topped with yogurt and honey, is photogenic.' Ned was always in too much of a hurry to chew muesli, so it isn't painful to remember that.

Ella's eyebrows go up. 'Don't forget your Eggs Benedict.' The trouble is, since Ella heard I'm doing bacon butties, she assumes I can do things I can't.

Sophie smiles. 'The smoked salmon version is my favourite.'

My tummy unclenches. 'Smoked salmon and scrambled egg on toasted bagel. That's popular.' And easier too because Ned hated fish unless it was in batter.

Nell's eyes are shining. 'Any you'd like to add to the menu, Gwen, give me a nod. It's very fortunate you've arrived.' She turns to Clemmie. 'We've been wanting to expand the breakfast club for ages, haven't we? The way things are going, we may need to open Monday to Friday!'

Ella gives me a sharp nudge under the table. 'Gwen would love to do that – wouldn't you?'

She's right in a way. Once I get my head around it and stop ducking out, there's nothing I can't handle. But they're being so kind, I can't deceive them.

I brace myself for the shame of admitting I'm less permanent than they think. 'I'm not sure how much longer I'll be around once the cottage is done.' The tenancy we signed was for an initial six months, then renewable; everyone else here seems to have very permanent roots in comparison. I take in their shocked expressions, and hurry to explain. 'Saying I'll stay for ever feels like a very long time.'

Clemmie's surprise softens to amusement. 'Someone else with itchy feet? I can sympathise with that.'

Ella's got a ' tip-toeing diplomat' look on her face. 'Gwen's come to help me settle in. Beyond that depends on her commitments elsewhere.'

Sophie gives me a knowing smile. 'You sound a lot like Clemmie used to. She was determined to get as far away from Cornwall as she could, as fast as she could. And look what happened to her!'

It's a relief they're taking this so lightly. Some people would have been cross we'd got the cottage when only one of us wants to be here for a lifetime.

Plum puts her hand on my arm. 'We aren't trying to undermine your ambition or wreck your plans, Gwen. St Aidan has a funny way of making people want to stay, that's all.'

Nell's chortling to herself. 'But we completely understand. Gorgeous hillside cottages and endless beaches aren't for everyone.'

They definitely aren't for me. My trouble is that when I try to think about where I *do* feel comfortable, nowhere springs to mind any more.

Clemmie's pushing lumps of cream cheese into Bud's mouth. 'We'll just be pleased to have you for as long as you want to stay.'

Nell backs her up. 'Why not take it a week at a time? Then the pressure's off.'

Sophie jumps in. 'In that case, smoked salmon and scrambled eggs has to be first on the new breakfast menu. If you're likely to get called away at short notice, I refuse to miss out on that.'

Ella's grinning at me. 'Free to leave at any time. Even you should be able to work with that, Gwen.' She shakes her head. '*And* you've forgotten to mention your porridge. And what about your smashed avocado with pine nuts on sourdough?'

Sometimes I wonder whose side she's on. To think there was a time when having to make bacon cobs seemed to be my biggest problem. It's funny how things happen here – I'm ending up doing things I never intended to at all. I just can't imagine what's going to happen next to push me out of my comfort zone. But on the plus side, we've got through another meet-up with no mention of the workshops we volunteered for, so I'm putting this down as a win.

Clemmie's waving a cupcake at me, 'I know we've promised not to tie you down' – she makes a shamefaced grimace – 'but knowing what stars you both are, please say you'll still be around to help with the Halloween deccies!'

I'm opening and closing my mouth in shock. But before I can form the words to say they've completely misunderstood the meaning of interior decoration, Ella cuts in.

'Parties are what we Star Sisters love best.' She's smiling as hard as she's lying. 'Gwen's not going anywhere, she's got this!'

Whatever I said about winning, take it back. On the plus side, nothing about Halloween makes me feel like I'm going to fall apart.

Nell's flapping her hands. 'It's not only for Seaspray Cottage either. The singles club are having a Scare Yourself Silly evening at Cockle Shell Castle. You'll be able to have fun with that one too, Gwen!'

I let out a groan as I count on my fingers. 'But that's less than two weeks away!'

Ella winks at me. 'Not too much longer to stick around, then.'

Nell chortles. 'Is that too much notice? Things in St Aidan are very immediate!'

Clemmie reaches across the table and squeezes my hand. 'Don't worry, Gwen. There will be gin!'

Ella's nodding, wiggling her eyebrows at me. 'We'll have to get Ollie to help. His big strong arms will be ideal for lugging pumpkins around.'

Now I've heard everything. I may just crawl under the table and not come out.

13

At the Little Cornish Kitchen
Looking for Mr Right
Friday, five days later

'Great breakfast, thanks, Gwen.'

This is Ollie. He's sitting on his usual high stool at the counter of the Little Cornish Kitchen, laptop open in front of him, scratching Diesel's head with one hand, and jingling Bud's multi-sensory moose rattle with the other. Who said men couldn't multi-task?

As the sunshine clock on the wall shows it's almost twelve, I have to ask. 'Do you mean breakfast, or brunch?'

He pulls a face. 'Actually both. I had porridge when I arrived, and I've just had two bacon and tomato cobs to see me through until teatime.'

As he's been here the best part of four hours, it's a relief I've mostly been in the kitchen and avoided the worst tummy churning.

He leans into his keyboard, then turns back to me as I come

in for his empty plate. 'It's great to see someone really working at the top of their game.'

I swoop his plate onto my tray and shake my head at Clemmie as she follows me into the kitchen. 'Could he *be* any more patronising?'

She's trying to hold back her smile and failing. 'He probably just *really* enjoyed the food.' Her smile widens. 'Like everyone else, he's loving the new variations.' She pulls me into a hug. 'We're so proud of you for everything you're trying!'

Nell's popped into the kitchen for her usual early lunch break, and her fork of scrambled egg stops halfway to her mouth. 'He's been here every day this week. At this rate, he'll be getting his top-fan badge.'

Once we realised how enthusiastic everyone was about a wider menu, a few clicks on the keyboard were all it took to extend the breakfast club hours and add Tuesday and Friday in too. And even though it's pretty full-on for the time I'm here, it's not like at the chalets, where breakfast was followed by cleaning, baking afternoon cake and then prepping and delivering a four-course evening meal. At the moment it still feels like a rest by comparison, although obviously I mostly try not to think of the past too much to compare. I might feel differently if work ever starts at the cottage.

I'm stacking the cups on the shelves behind the counter as Clemmie arrives with another tray-load for me. 'Any luck with finding a builder yet?'

I roll my eyes at her. 'We had loads of recommendations, but we're not *entirely* there.'

Clemmie laughs. 'Finding the perfect person to knock holes in your house is a lot like finding Mr Right. He *does* exist, but he doesn't always arrive when you'd like him to.'

Ollie's fully engrossed at his screen, but from the widening of his eyes I'd say he definitely heard that.

'That's one search I won't be starting personally, thank you very much!' I let out a loud laugh because I want to make my point clear.

Clemmie winks at me. 'You're *so* like I used to be.' She stares fondly at Bud. 'I wouldn't swap what I've got now though!'

I'm still laughing. 'Ella's seeing the builders too. She's very picky, don't forget.'

I've rung everyone who got a shout-out in the comments on Nell's looking-for-a-builder post, and most arrived at the door quite fast. All week we've watched them walk round the cottage sucking their breath through their teeth. Some said it was easy and got as far as giving prices, but when we saw the figures, they didn't just make our eyes water, they made me want to weep.

Getting so close to my doorway in the wall, then always falling at the final fence, it's been a rollercoaster few days. But even without the jaw-dropping prices, Ella found reasons to give the thumbs-down to all of them.

Clemmie's looking at me sideways as she wipes the counter. 'So no one's made the grade yet?'

'Nope.' I reach to put some plates on the next shelf up. 'The good news is they all liked our heating and wiring and said the pipes are well placed, and there's no problem making holes where we want them.' I'm pausing so I cover everything. 'In the meantime, we need to strip the paper off the walls and ceilings right through before anyone begins. That'll be my job, obviously.' I'm making it sound as if I have a clue when I don't at all – other than knowing it's a gargantuan task.

The smile fades from Clemmie's face. 'I'd hoped you could

do a few extra afternoons for us here next week. Here I am, piling work on you when you should be pushing ahead at the cottage.'

I have to be realistic. 'Paid hours for you are my priority.' I give a sigh. 'I'll have to fit the stripping in around that.' There are Halloween preparations too, but I'm leaving them out for now.

Clemmie's brow furrows. 'You know those up-the-sleeve talents of yours Ella mentioned – can you cook suppers?'

'Suppers?' I try not to hyperventilate straightaway. I'm cooking breakfasts when I never thought I could. Maybe I'll go with this and see where it leads. 'I have some tried and tested dinner menus.' I made them for so long I *should* be able to pretty much produce them without thinking – so long as I choose the right one. It's not only the menu limitations. I also need to put this firmly in perspective in case she gets her expectations up. 'It's not gourmet cooking. They're tasty but satisfying dishes that are easy to make, like shepherd's pie and chicken and roasties.' Except probably not the roasties, as Ned was always trying to snaffle those if he had half a chance.

'They sound just the job.' Her smile's spreading across her face again. 'So that's the answer! You can put on a work party at the cottage. Have people round for a day to help with your stripping and give them supper and wine at the end.'

I can hardly believe what I'm hearing. 'But who would want to come and do that?'

Nell's come through from the kitchen. 'We do stuff like this all the time for the singles club. People usually pay for the privilege too.'

Clemmie laughs. 'The Little Cornish Kitchen began with sorbet parties in the flat upstairs when I needed to find money fast for renovations.'

'You're kidding?'

'A lot of people are desperate to do something different at the weekends. People already know the Stars at Stargazey Cottage, they'll be falling over themselves to come.'

As Ella sometimes says, when I'm daydreaming, which I've admittedly done a lot of over the years, I simply zone out the sound. But I'm picking this up loud and clear and I'm seizing the opportunity. 'Maybe this could work as one of the Star Sister workshop events we promised?'

Nell's punching the air. 'Good thinking, Gwen! I'd forgotten all about those.'

I'm kicking myself for reminding her, but whatever. I'm thinking back to the YouTube clips. 'Bring your own bucket, sponge and a scraper! Followed by spag bol, a glass of red, and cheesecake.'

Nell's nodding. 'Work at Stargazey with the Stars!' She's looking at her phone. 'Saturday's free next weekend. We can move on to preps for the Halloween event straight after. Let's do it then!'

'Totally! How many people are you thinking?'

Nell and Clemmie look at each other.

Clemmie says, 'Fifteen?'

'That many?'

Nell nods. 'Our events always work best when they're crowded.'

Numbers like that, they'd probably be sitting in the street, but what do I know? I'm blinking, working out where the catch is, then it hits me. 'Spot the deliberate mistake! Stargazey Cottage doesn't have a kitchen.' I curse silently. 'That's the end of that then. It won't work without supper.'

Clemmie's smiling. 'Not so fast! You could use this kitchen

then take dinner up the hill. Or everyone could come down here to eat?'

'Or…' There's a cough from the other side of the counter. The sudden silence that follows is only broken by the jingle of Bud's moose.

As I turn to Ollie, I'm only saying what we're all thinking. 'What's this got to do with *you*?' He might have Olympic medals, but no one asked for his opinion on our stripping party.

He gives a shamefaced shrug. 'I couldn't help overhearing. You could always use the kitchen at mine.'

Clemmie brings her fist down on the worktop. 'Brilliant! It's so handy, too.'

This is the worst idea in the world, and I'm on it. 'Wasn't your kitchen in boxes when we last saw it?' As I relive the horror of standing there in my bra the last time, I'm wanting the ground to open up and swallow me.

Ollie looks straight at me. 'That's the *main* kitchen. There's a fully functioning utility version that should be more than adequate. You're welcome to use it.'

If our weeks in St Aidan were a rollercoaster, this is where the car plunges right to the bottom then crashes off the rails completely.

It's a good thing I can think on my feet. 'You'll already be in there, cooking *your* Saturday night dinner. There won't be room for both of us.'

I swear he's looking right down his nose at me. 'Easily solved. If I join in the scrape-off, you'll be cooking for me anyway.'

Spending all day with Ollie in the confines of the cottage would be the equivalent of being trapped in a lift with him for eight hours. Like, would I willingly step into a wardrobe with him and close the door? *I absolutely wouldn't.* I'm looking for *any* escape. 'I'm sorry, with so little space we won't have room for beginners.'

His superior expression cracks a little as he raises one quizzical eyebrow. 'Who said I'm a beginner?'

What *am* I hearing? 'Spending so long at sea, you can't possibly have had any time for decorating.' I'm on very firm ground here. If he got good enough at sailing to be world class, he absolutely won't have.

His eyes are sparking the same way they were the first day we met him. 'As a teenager I worked for my uncle doing painting and decorating in the holidays. That's how I bought my first boat.'

The nosedive my heart makes takes my breath away. 'Fabulous to hear your life history but being over-qualified is worse than not knowing anything at all. You'll undermine people's confidence. You joining in is *out of the question!*' My voice is going all high with the panic. Worse still, if his expert eye catches me in action, he's sure to see I'm faking it.

Nell's got her hands over her face, but eventually she stifles what sounds like a choking laugh and clears her throat. 'Our singles events are completely non-discriminatory. You'll be fine to come, Ollie. And thanks for the offer of the kitchen, that sounds like a very practical solution.' She turns to me. 'Send me a photo or two. So long as Ella's free and agrees, we'll get the event up on the Facebook page.'

I thought my heart had plunged as low as it could go, but that sends it lurching even further down. 'Sponges and buckets aren't Ella's thing.' I'm actually thinking if she's as picky as she was with my window cleaning, she'll definitely upset everyone. 'She may have to spend the day shopping in Falmouth.' It'll be better for all of us in the long run.

I'm looking from Nell to Clemmie and then to Ollie. Together, their lips form the word, and when it comes out all at once it's huge. *'No! Ella's not ducking out of this!'*

I hurry across to check that Bud's not upset by their shout. 'Fine. Message received. I'll let her know.' Bud's kicking, oblivious and still chewing on the sleeve of Ollie's Team GB hoodie that she's pulled off the worktop.

Ollie's leaning forward, his head tilted, one eyebrow raised expectantly. 'Did someone mention Halloween?'

I'm blinking at him. 'What's *that* got to do with anything?'

It's rare to see someone so confident looking taken aback. 'If you need a hand carving lanterns, give me a shout.'

If he was the last person on a desert island, and I had to hollow out a pumpkin boat to escape in, I *still* wouldn't ask him. 'I've only ordered a hundred and fifty. We'll totally handle those on our own, thanks all the same.'

Clemmie's laughing. 'Or it might be a case of the more the merrier. We'll let you know.'

As if things weren't bad enough already! There are some excruciating days to live through before we even get to pumpkins.

14

In the garden at Stargazey Cottage
Dead ends and rocky roads
Monday afternoon, three days later

Pumpkins? There was no point fighting, Halloween had to be done. Blitzing the place with my favourite lanterns felt like a way to give maximum impact for minimum effort. Luckily, I'm used to dealing with suppliers for chalet shopping, so that's Halloween sorted for now.

As for next weekend's work party, twelve people have signed up, which makes eighteen when we add in Ella, Nell and the gang. For me it's a bit like when I first went to work in the ski villages; I was beside myself with nerves, but I wanted to be there so much, I was prepared to overcome them. It's the same with cooking supper – there are so many positives if we get the cottage stripped out, I'm going to have to woman up and do it.

I've worked out the menu and the shopping, made a list of equipment I need to borrow from Clemmie, and I'm putting the rest – negotiations with next door, in other words – on hold for as long as I can.

With everything else so well in hand, when I come back from this morning's shift at Clemmie's, I grab a cup of tea and drink it in the sun on the back doorstep. It's the first sit down I've had since I got up, but a few minutes later, without really thinking, I'm winding my way up the steps behind the cottage.

My first visit to the little shed in the sky was so upsetting I was determined I'd never come back again. But then I came up once to wipe the windows, so they didn't look so sad when I caught sight of them from my little attic room. And a few days later I found myself up here again, brushing the dead leaves off the floor. It's never a conscious decision, but in the last week something has drawn me back most days. By setting myself a short task each time, and directing all my focus onto that, I've so far always managed to breathe. And every day feels like another small step forward on my journey.

It's completely different up at the shed from down in the cottage and it's not just because it's empty. Everything's clearer – the air, the light, the sound of the seagulls as they wheel across the sky, racing the wind.

Today my task is to clean a small patch on the inside of one of the shed walls. As I rub the horizontal planks with their curving grain, they feel warm and regular and reassuring. By the time I lean on the door frame to look out half an hour later, I'm calmer than I've been for a long time. It's so rare, I don't want to jinx it by noticing or staying too long, so I pull the door closed behind me and begin to make my way down the garden again.

Okay, I may be craning my neck to see down onto next door's patio rather than looking where I'm going. Straining to see if I can spot any sign of life behind the windows, but I can't. Then a flash of white on the terrace catches my eye – there's a bird, hopping around in front of the extension. I stand and watch it in case it takes off, but it doesn't. Maybe it's hit the glass and stunned itself?

Me being ready to spring into action and help anything damaged is a recurring theme in my life. Half-dead mice the cat brought in, puppies on the internet needing operations, kids in the supermarket who have lost their mum. I may not be the world's most confident person in other situations, but for anything or anyone pathetic and in need of rescue, I'm your woman. Wounded birds most of all. If it's hurt, I have to check on it. A second later I'm down the steps and clambering across the rocky outcrop of the garden, trying to find the best way onto next door's terrace.

To see me now, inching forward on my bottom, you'd never think I came from a family of climbers. This was always my trouble. When it comes to rocks, I have as little natural ability as the rest of them had in spades. I'm creeping towards the overhang, trying to see if there's a way to get down other than jumping. And then gravity takes over, I slither off the edge, and next thing I know I land with a thud on the gravel below.

I can picture the headline. 'Girl going to save stranded gull falls off cliff herself.' As I scramble to my feet, I'm kicking myself for being so stupid.

But what do you know? Now I'm here, with the terrace stretching out in front of me, there is no damn bird. And what's worse, there's no way off the terrace either.

Beyond the sweep of the railings there's a sheer drop. Behind me there's the wall of Stargazey House. When I peer past my reflection in the tall plate-glass windows, the lights are all off and there's obviously no one there. The only way back to our cliff of a garden is up the overhanging rock face I just fell off.

It's going to be *so* embarrassing ringing Ella to tell her I'm stuck on next door's patio. I push my hand into the pocket of my jeans and let out a silent curse as I remember – my mobile's on the windowsill next to the kettle.

The rock I slid down from is towering, tantalisingly out of reach, and I'm hammering my fists on my head in frustration when I hear a click from above. As I look up, one of the little sash windows in the eaves slides open and a head pokes out.

'Gwen? What are you doing down there?'

'Ollie!' It had to be. Me being here to save a bird that flew away sounds ridiculous, so I improvise. 'I came round to check out the kitchen.' It's the last thing I want to do but it's the only reason I can think of for me being here. 'So long as you've got time, that is?'

'Give me a second, I'll be down.'

A few minutes later, as the plate-glass door swings open, I'm staring at the dust patches on the knees of my jeans, knowing there's more work to do here.

'I'd have come round to the front, but I was on my way down from the shed.' I hope he can't tell how much I'm making this up as I go along. 'As I didn't have anything else on, it made sense to drop by.'

Ollie steps out onto the gravel and stares up into our garden. 'Lucky I was in, it's quite a pull getting back up to yours, even for me. We're a level down from you here because we've done a basement.' He gives me a sideways glance. 'But if you're as good a climber as you are a cook, it might not faze you.'

I shrug in a way that doesn't confirm or deny. Even if I were two feet taller, I'd still have no chance of reaching it because my muscles simply don't work that way. 'If the kitchen's at street level it probably makes sense to leave by the front instead.' I make my tone throwaway to hide that it's my only option. It's also the same way I left when I stripped off my T-shirt. However much I feel like I'm going to die of embarrassment every time I think of it, if I'm coming in and out to cook, I'm going to have to get over it.

He leads me into a light, echoey space that goes all the way up to the roof, then up an open staircase that comes up into the room we were in on the first day. He pushes through another door and waves his hand. 'So this is the working kitchen. The shinier, on-show version will be going into the next room very soon.'

I'm staring at a floor-to-ceiling wall of cupboards with four eye-level ovens and a worktop with a six-ring hob. As Ollie goes around opening and closing doors, I catch flashes of fridges and freezers and dishwashers.

'Very impressive, Ollie. Whoever chose this knew what they were doing.' It's definitely a cook's kitchen, and from the makes I recognise from my more exclusive placements, it must have cost a bomb.

Ollie narrows his eyes. 'Nothing in here is down to me, I'm simply finishing the work a friend of mine began.'

I look around admiringly. 'A friend with great taste then.'

Ollie tilts his head and gives a sigh. 'One who pushed every opportunity to the limit.'

'It's a great way to be.' I wish I could be more like that myself.

His frown is doubtful. 'It's just not really…'

There he goes again. 'Don't knock it! It's so much more than anything we'll ever have next door.' I force myself to open the ovens, even though I already know they'll be bigger than anything I'll need. I peer into the fridge, run my fingers over a pristine white sink and brace myself to make a run for it. 'That covers everything, thanks. I'll be round early Saturday, time to be confirmed.' If I make a dash for the front door I'll be out of this mess with the bonus of not having to come round again until the weekend.

Ollie's hovering as we move back into the living area. 'Before you go…'

He stops so suddenly I crash into the back of him. 'Sorry. I do need to run.'

He gives me another sideways glance. 'I thought you said you were free all afternoon?'

The sideways glance, the crashing into the back of him. They're all things I could do without. The truth is, when I'm this close to him, anything could happen. I'm torn between wanting to run away as far as I can as fast as I can, and this equally out-of-control feeling of wanting to tear my clothes off and rub my naked body all over him. Obviously, that's not something I'd ever do. It's more a figurative way of describing the push and pull that's tearing me apart whenever I'm around him. Which is why I definitely want to fast-forward past reliving *the* most excruciating moment of my life that happened in his hall.

I'm cursing that he's caught me out. 'Can it be quick?'

'There's someone you should meet while you're here.' He leans and calls up the staircase. 'Jago!'

A few minutes later, when a huge blonde Viking of a man comes into view, I'm already smiling because he looks familiar. 'Don't tell me! You're the friend with an appetite for the finer things in life. Lovely to meet you, I'm just leaving.' If Ella had been born a man, this is what she'd look like.

He winces. 'It's not *quite* like that. I'm Jago – the builder.'

Ollie's searching my face. 'You *are* looking for one of those?' He looks from Jago to me and back again. 'Gwen, Jago, Jago, Gwen.'

Jago holds out his hand. 'Good to meet you. I was across the garden at the fancy-dress barbie. You were with the drop-dead-gorgeous onion seller?'

As his hand closes around mine, it's not just his Cornish burr that's making me smile. 'That was my housemate, Ella.' Even though I ended up with half a dress, she's the one who stuck in his mind, which is fine by me. 'We live next door.'

He nods enthusiastically. 'I've seen her going past.'

Ella's always been the same. She has the hip-waist-boob combo that makes guys go weak at the knees; in bars they literally used to queue round the block to talk to her. For anyone else on a building site, people looking at your boobs first could be a drawback, but Ella somehow twists it to her advantage even there.

Ollie coughs. 'If you're looking for someone to do your work, Jago's the best in St Aidan.'

I've exhausted all the other options, so I should be grateful that Ollie's throwing another possibility into the mix. But as I stare across the vast expanse of polished concrete floor and sparkling down-lighters, I already know. 'Very unspectacular builders have given us crippling quotes. *You'll* be *way* out of our league.'

He grins. 'Not necessarily. The others *may* have been quoting you incomer prices rather than the local rate.'

I pick my jaw up off the floor. 'There are *two price scales*? But that's *awful!*'

He laughs and gives a grimace. 'It's a well-guarded secret. The higher rate subsidises the people who live here, which sounds fair to me. You'd be on the lower one, obviously. Just like Ollie is.'

Ollie, who's apparently the biggest offending incomer of them all – or at least his friend is. Ollie, who's rubbing his chin with his thumb as he joins in again. 'Jago will do you a top job for half the price.'

The only catch is that it's coming from Ollie.

Jago's eyes narrow. 'With an extra ten per cent off because of Ella.'

My eyes open wide, and my voice goes high with shock. 'Dropping your price to get the job because you fancy someone is *hugely* inappropriate.'

Jago rolls his eyes. 'Ella's in the trade locally. Her knowing what she's asking for will make our job ten per cent easier, hence the discount.'

'Right.' Yet another moment when I want the floor to open up and swallow me. I won't bother telling him Ella will barely be there and instead he's going to be dealing with Gwen, the customer who hasn't a clue.

However hard Jago protests or denies having the hots for Ella, there are times you can just tell; feelings of attraction can happen, and the people involved have no control over them. It's nature's way of making sure we humans don't die out. Taylor may have fallen by the wayside, but Ella will not be short of volunteers to take his place.

Ollie's frowning. 'At least let him have a look?'

Whatever I say about attraction, my insides clenching as they do when I see Ollie's Adam's apple bob when he swallows is something else entirely.

Jago's smile is wider still. 'That's decided then. When shall I come round?'

All in all, this will be better without Ella home. And at

least that way, we'll get to see some local prices. If there really is such a thing, we might just get the chance to put an affordable job together. I also need to do it fast before Ella banishes him like she has every other builder. Obviously, I'd rather not be beholden to Ollie. But Jago might be my last chance, so for the sake of Stargazey Cottage, I've got to give him a go.

Ollie's eyebrows go up. 'Why not do it now? I'll come too, see the plans on the ground.'

That's the worst idea I've heard this week. 'There's definitely no need for you to waste *your* day, Ollie.'

He's shaking his head. 'Not a problem. It'll be a chance to see the size of Saturday's job too. I might even have suggestions to add.'

Suggestions? How arrogant can you get?

Jago gives a cough. 'Is that Saturday's work party? My name's down for that too.'

I can't believe what I'm hearing. I let out a sigh. 'If you're coming to show off your building skills to Ella, you do know it's just wallpaper stripping?'

Jago laughs. 'I'm not coming for the work, or Ella, I'm coming for the Malteser cheesecake.'

There's really no answer to that.

I might have started the afternoon in free fall, but it's ended with a builder promising a cut-price work rate so maybe things are looking up, at least for the cottage.

And as far as Ollie being the one who unknowingly came to my rescue again today, I'm definitely not comfortable with that. I promise myself I won't have any more unscripted damsel-in-distress moments in future. As for the way my body's betraying me whenever Ollie's around, I may have to spend Friday night sleeping in the deep freeze if I'm going to keep my cool on Saturday. But if that's what it takes, that's what I'll do.

What do they say about every cloud having a silver lining? Ours is back to front. If Saturday's work party is the silver lining for the cottage, Ollie coming is definitely the cloud. But pulling this work party off is all down to me. I can't let anything get in the way of its success.

15

The work party at Stargazey Cottage
Bubble wrap and celestial ambition
Saturday afternoon, five days later

'We can't possibly afford Jago. You do know that?'
We're an hour into our 'Work with the Stars at Stargazey' afternoon, and Ella's hissing at me outside on the street. I haven't mentioned Jago's promises for price slashing because I wasn't sure if they were real. This way, if they do come through, it'll be a surprise in a good way.

I can't resist teasing her. 'He would be an asset. Those lovely big forearms would knock through the walls in no time.' He also whispered when I passed him earlier at the top of the stairs that he'll have figures to run past us sometime soon, so I can't wait for those. He must have murmured something in Ella's ear too, because there's no other reason why she should shove me out of the front door for this urgent heart-to-heart slash site meeting.

She clutches her clipboard even closer to her chest. 'However much of a hottie he is, human resources do *not* approve of objectifying, Gwen.'

I grin at her. 'So you *do* like him?'

She gives a grimace. 'I can see he's attractive. The trouble is, in my head I'm still married.'

Her quickie decree absolute came through in August, but I can see what she means. I'd just hoped Jago's rugged looks and easy banter would have helped her past that. That the scorching come-to-bed sideways glances I saw him giving her as he arrived would help her make a quantum leap to the bit where she remembered that moving-on sex was an activity not a song theme.

She taps her pen on her teeth. 'I must go in, it's time for people to swap rooms, I need to tell them who goes where.' She looks at her phone. 'We're still good for tea and cookies at three?'

Before I can reply she's hitched up her belt, pulled her overalls tight over her boobs, and disappeared back into the cottage. If poor Jago gets an eyeful of *that*, his mind's not going to be on wallpaper removal *or* our estimate.

In the end we decided a one o'clock start today would give us a good working window without the need to supply lunch as well. Luckily Ella and I are still living minimally, so it didn't take us long to stack our stuff in the centre of the rooms and throw dust sheets over the piles.

The irony of me finally having a key to next door wasn't lost on me as I tiptoed in before dawn. I'd planned to start work in the kitchen at seven to avoid Ollie and get a head start in case of emergencies. But as I was awake way earlier I decided I might just as well be peeling potatoes and making cheesecake bases as lying in bed worrying. And once I got going, I did feel much better.

When Nell and George came round mid-morning with the wine supplies, my shepherd's pies were all done. By the time Jago arrived in his pick-up piled high with trestle tables and folding chairs borrowed from Plum's gallery, I was sliding the last of the finished cheesecakes into the fridge, and the M&M cookies were steaming on the cooling rack.

It only took a nanosecond to work out that the tables he heaved off the pick-up weren't going to come within a country mile of fitting in next door. Jago called Ollie, I called Nell, and half a dozen hastily eaten cookies later, supper was relocated to Ollie's future dining area.

The floor surface isn't down yet so there's nothing to spoil, the lights looped up overhead look on-trend rather than makeshift, and there's a cloakroom next to the kitchen I'm cooking in. What's not to like?

Jago had the tables and chairs set out and was off to deliver stepladders to next door before I could say dimpled cheeks and rippling six-packs.

As I said to Ella as I swapped my apron for the dark-pink dungarees I bought in the Cats' Protection shop, this way we'll avoid lumps of soggy wallpaper in the cider punch appetiser I've added in to make up for not having a starter. Okay, I know that wasn't in the plan, but I'm not about doing the minimum. Making people have the best time is programmed into my DNA; I want everyone to enjoy this to the max.

As people began to arrive at the cottage earlier, Ella stood at the door to welcome them, and directed them through to the kitchen. Then I filled their buckets with soapy water, and offered them an impromptu beer and a sandwich, because I couldn't send people off to strip our walls without a welcome snack. It did lead to a bit of a log jam, but hopefully it didn't throw Ella's minute-by-minute schedule out too much. The happy soundtrack coming from the mini speaker on the landing was making the house thrum from top to bottom and felt perfect for the laid-back but purposeful mood of the afternoon.

The big advantage of having a kitchen with no units is there's more floor space to shuffle around in. As Des and Miranda and Josie, Pete, Arthur, Madison and Morgan from the breakfast club arrived, I realised I already knew a lot of today's guests anyway. Nell was certainly right about crowds being good socially; I have to say, after you've eaten a vegan cheese and pickle roll with someone's elbow in your ear, there's no need for ice breakers. And thanks to Madison arriving in her shiny Lycra gym tights and leotard and demanding everyone watch her body combat and barre class moves, making conversation was the last thing I had to worry about.

There was certainly no room to feel shy or awkward as I handed out bin bags, then sent everyone back to Ella, whose tick-chart-spreadsheet looked more suited to a housing estate than a cottage the size of a matchbox. As people moved to their allocated places upstairs the crowd in the kitchen thinned. Plum arrived with another set of stepladders, and once I'd done a run through the house to check everyone knew what they were doing, I joined Clemmie and Sophie in the room next to the kitchen.

I watched what they were doing with their sponges and buckets and did the same. 'I hope it's okay to ask, but where are the children?' As they have five between them that's quite a lot to lose.

Sophie smiled as she slid her scraper up the wall. 'Nate and Charlie are great at stepping in. We couldn't have missed today! Since we mermaids did such a good job selecting the tenants, it feels like we're invested.'

Clemmie peeled a ribbon of damp paper off her scraper. 'We all helped Sophie strip out her ten-bedroom castle. This is a lot less daunting.' She passed me her dripping sponge. 'Use this to soften it up. A lot of Sophie's paper came off in whole pieces but they've used more paste here, so it's harder to get off.'

As Nell came down the stairs with a cluster of buckets in her hands, I jumped up. 'Do you want me to fill them for you?'

Nell laughed. 'You carry on there. They're for the first floor, but with the tiddling excuse for a bath tap upstairs, it would have taken all day.' She looked around. 'Where's Ella?'

I smiled. 'She's mingling and talking to the guests about design.' I was happy to go down for working alongside the pros, because I'm hoping to pick up all the moves.

Nell came in closer and lowered her voice. 'A word about Madison.'

I nodded. 'I love that choppy bob she's got, she looks *so* like Julianne Hough off *Dancing with the Stars*.' I give a sigh. 'Her body's like a professional dancer's too.'

Nell rolled her eyes. 'It should be with all the time she spends at the gym. But, be warned, she's our resident man-eater, and she hasn't met the lovely Jago before.'

I gave a cough. 'Ella's site rules: appraising men by their exterior physical attributes definitely isn't allowed. Just saying.'

Nell let out a guffaw. 'I was actually referring to Jago being lovely on the inside. But anyone new and hunky, our Maddie's likely to go in for the kill.'

My eyes snapped wide open. 'That bad?'

Clemmie winced. 'Nell tries to welcome everyone.'

Nell came even closer. 'Madison is a very enthusiastic, long-standing member. But if Ella wants a prior claim, we'll need to be very proactive with the seating plans.' And then she turned and disappeared into the kitchen.

Clemmie rolled a damp paper bundle off the floor and into the bin bag. 'Nell loves couples who get together through singles events, so her attraction antennae are super-charged, but we've all noticed the way Jago looks at Ella. If you're busy in the kitchen later, we'll cover for you with this one.'

And then Ella clattered downstairs too, and the next thing I knew, I was outside in the street.

Between then and teatime, I manage to scrape a teensy area on the living room wall – being careful not to take the plaster along with the paper, as it reminded me on YouTube. It's taken me so long to do so little and for the first time ever I'm wishing the cottage were smaller not larger. Ollie's not here yet – if he didn't turn up until after supper, that would be a win for me – so me watching the door so he doesn't take me by surprise is my excuse for my slow progress.

We all cram into the living room for tea at three, and luckily everyone is asking me about the biscuit recipe rather than design tips, so another hour goes by without my cover being blown. I'm just on my way back from loading the mugs into one of next door's many dishwashers when Ollie breezes in behind me.

I'm happy to give him a free pass. 'If you haven't brought a bucket, why don't we see you at suppertime.'

However much he's helping us here, when he stares straight down at me as he's doing now, I wish he wouldn't. 'Jago brought my bucket round earlier. I'm not missing out; I want to see Ella getting stuck in.'

I let out a sigh. 'She's up to her ears directing and mingling.'

Ollie rolls his eyes. 'I bet she is.'

Nell's behind us. 'If we want to do these work parties again, it'll be good if she has a go with the scraping too.'

Sophie's leaning on the kitchen door frame. 'Successful bosses never mind getting their hands dirty. I'm Sophie May's most energetic tea maker!'

Clemmie's head pops into view beside Sophie. 'We can't keep all the fun bits for ourselves, can we, Gwen?'

There's no backing down on this. As I squeeze past the pile of full bin bags at the bottom of the stairs and reach the landing I can't help noticing how amazing the finished walls look, paper-free and all sponged down.

I call through to where Ella's in her bedroom sitting on a stepladder, still clutching her clipboard. 'Any chance you could come for a few action pics for the Stargazey pages?'

She smiles through to me. 'Great, I'll refresh my lippy and I'll be straight down.'

'I'll get some clean buckets of water ready.'

I'm still standing at the sink with the tap running when Ella arrives. She reaches past me, seizes the Fairy liquid bottle and squirts a mega amount into each bucket. Then, for the first time since we've moved into the cottage, she pulls on the Marigold washing-up gloves and swishes the water round with a sponge. 'Bubbles will look great in the photos.' She takes the two strides to the living room, swinging a bucket in each hand. 'We'll soon get this done. Have you got your phone?'

Plum leans forward as we reach a bit of wall with paper left on. 'Would you like me to take these so you can both be in them?'

'Please.' I hand Plum my phone and pass Ella a scraper. 'Sponge the paper first, then scrape once it's soft, remember.'

As I look around, Jago's leaning on the banister rail, his head tilted as he watches her. 'That's what she's been telling us all day.' He laughs. 'It's good to see you in action at last, Ella.'

She blanks Jago and hisses at me. 'If I break a nail here, I will not be happy. I need them perfect for Monday's meeting with head office.'

I can't help smiling. 'They're acrylic, I thought they were unbreakable?'

She eases up the corner of a piece of wallpaper, pulls it, and it comes off in a big piece. She turns to the crowd on the stairs. 'Beginner's luck?'

Clemmie wails. 'That's the biggest piece anyone's stripped off so far in here.' She holds out the bin bag. 'Try again.'

I scrape and pull and peel off a bit the size of a five pence piece. 'It's not fair, my bit must have been stuck on with superglue.'

Ella rips off another monster bit, then turns round to Jago. 'Watch and learn, Mister Cheeky.' Then she leans in and drops her arm over my shoulder. 'A couple more photos, Gwen, then you might need to go and get the ovens on.'

Ollie's shaking his head. 'How do you know that?'

She rips another huge slice off the wall. 'I've stared at my schedules so much today, they're imprinted on my retinas.' She picks up her sponge and turns to me. 'Honestly, Gwen, I can take this from here.'

Jago's grinning. 'Anything I can help with, Ms Simpson, or shall I just stand here with your clipboard and check the work?'

Ella tosses her head. 'There's one reason this job has gone like clockwork today.'

Jago's teasing her. 'What, you and your retractable pen?'

She rips off another piece of paper and bundles it into the bag. 'Actually, it's Gwen. But if you're planning to knock holes in our walls, you're going to have to get used to my spreadsheets.' The way she stares at him and tosses her plait over her shoulder, he's definitely touched a nerve. 'So what have you got to say about that?'

My heart is drifting slowly downwards as I watch her. The house has made such a leap forward with so many hands here the last few hours, and now our last hope for the job is about to get a taste of Ella's stroppy side and run for the hills.

But instead of running, he dips forward, scoops a palmful of bubbles out of my bucket, goes towards her with his outstretched palm level with her face, and blows. Then he laughs straight at her. 'I'd say – the designer specified too much Fairy liquid.'

Ella's eyes are flashing. As she scrapes the bubbles off her nose her jaw is set. 'And I'd say a certain builder is talking out of his butt.' She picks up a handful herself and blows it back at him. Then a second later, when it only reaches his chin, she scoops up a spongeful, and slaps it over his head.

Jago's laughing as the drips roll off his nose. 'That was below the belt.' He returns a spongeful over her head. 'But I give as good as I get.'

She swipes the water off her sodden hair. 'Not very imaginative.' Then she gets a sponge full of suds and water, and rams it onto the front of his T-shirt.

Jago puts his hands up. 'Okay, enough! Truce! You win!'

'Too late for that!' It's Madison, bursting through from the kitchen with a new bucket of suds and a move that's straight from her body combat class. In her red and black Lycra, she looks a lot like Superwoman. 'You asked for a foam fight, that's what you're going to get.'

I stare round the room and find Nell. 'Is this *normal*?'

Nell chortles. 'Singles events can get a bit over-exuberant. But don't worry, it's only soap, and they're all very good at tidying up.'

Madison looks round the room. 'Come on, ladies, what are we waiting for?'

As the first fistful of foam flies across the cottage, followed by a second, then another, my mouth is dropping open. Five seconds later, the air is a mass of bubbles, but a shove on my hip sends me sideways.

The next I know I'm outside on the cobbles standing next to Ollie.

I frown at him. 'What did you do that for?'

He shakes his head. 'I couldn't stay in there. Women against guys, they'd have scalped me.' He gives a sniff. 'In any case, I'm helping you with dinner.'

'What about starry solidarity, and me staying to defend Ella?'

Ollie looks at me as he opens his front door. 'Three words – oven, jam jars, cider punch.' Even I know that's way more than three. 'In any case, something tells me Ella's going to enjoy her foam fight right down to the very last bubble.'

I'm frowning. 'What do you mean by that?'

He gives me that awful sideways look that makes my tummy slither to my knees. 'You must have seen the way she looks at Jago?'

'Excuse me?'

Ollie shakes his head. 'He's a dead man walking.' He puts two fingers in the air and makes the noise of a gun. 'And I doubt he'll mind at all.'

I roll my eyes. 'You can't mean that.'

'Let's wait and see who's right.' He pulls in a breath. 'And whatever you put in those M&M cookies, be more careful next time. People in St Aidan are very easily excited.'

'You're excluding yourself from this?'

'I definitely am.' He sighs. 'I've already told you, I'm here to get a job done, not to enjoy myself.'

Could the poor guy sound any more pompous? 'Work and fun aren't completely exclusive. It's possible to have both.'

He sighs again. 'Not for me, I'm afraid.'

I can't believe he's so gloomy. Not that I'm ever expecting fun for myself again. But I'm completely resigned to a life without.

I also can't believe the hardest part of the day is yet to come. Or that with all the screams next door, I'm stuck out here with the fun police.

Then the door opens and Clemmie slips into the street. 'Hey, it's crazy time in there.' She smiles at me as she pulls the door closed behind her. 'I've come to give you a hand.'

Ollie shrugs. 'We've probably got this covered for now, if you'd like to get back to the party?'

Clemmie steps in beside me. 'Gwen and Ella are the Stargazeys, but we two are the Little Cornish Kitchen sisters. If Gwen's cooking for twenty, I'm here for her.'

And the hug she pulls me into is so big it warms me through to my heart.

16

Stargazey Cottage
Herbs in pots and desperate measures
Later on Saturday

It wasn't just Clemmie helping. A few minutes later Plum came too and with us three women running between the table and the kitchen, Ollie hung back, which was great news for my concentration.

As the sky darkened outside the huge windows, he busied himself adjusting the lighting. As he looped the hanging bulbs higher and stood back with his thumbs in his belt, looking up to appraise the result, he caught me running past. 'I've never had dinner here myself; will that be enough light for you?'

I stand back trying to think of an instant fix to make the table more inviting. 'If only we had the flicker of candlelight at table level, it would make the whole room come alive.'

Ollie raises his eyebrows. 'You're right! It's *so* obvious this interior stuff comes as easily to you as breathing.' He sniffs the air. 'And your cooking smells amazing too.'

I beam at him to cover the pretence. 'We aim to please.' I hesitate, then decide to go for it. 'You don't happen to have any lanterns lying around?'

He pats his back pockets. 'Sorry, I don't seem to have any on me today.'

Plum bustles through. 'If you're looking for tea-light lanterns, I've got some you can borrow at the gallery.' She nods at Ollie. 'Come and help me, they're only two minutes down the road.'

'Brill.' I tweak into position a hastily home-made newspaper place mat that I cut from a copy of *The Cornish Gazette* I found under the sink, and hope it looks authentically 'eco' rather than plain old rubbish. 'And while you're away we'll bring the drinking jam jars in and fill the punch jugs. And as soon as the guests come through for the punch, I'll get the veggies on.'

Clemmie pulls me into another hug. 'Our little Gwen. Fifteen minutes away from serving food for twenty, how can you be cool as a cucumber?'

I give a shrug and grin back at her. 'The hard work happened earlier. So long as there's enough oven, fridge space and ice buckets the rest is simple.' I laugh. 'I do have a lot more helpers than I'm used to too. And it wouldn't be happening at all without all the stuff I've borrowed from you, not to mention Ollie's kitchen.' All the recipes I'm using are new variations, but even though I haven't done them for four years, the old routines are still there in my muscle memory.

Plum smiles. 'Even so, it's a great trick you're pulling off here.'

I pull a face. 'It's definitely a one-off. I can't ever see four-course home-cooked suppers catching on in St Aidan, can you?' As for an afternoon that ended in a foam fight, I'm guessing that's the end of the work parties too.

'Never say never, Gwen! St Aidan has a habit of surprising people if they stay long enough.' Plum gives Ollie a nudge towards the door. 'We'll be back in five. I'll give them a shout next door, tell them it's almost time.'

One thing's for sure. Even if I stay a year, it's hardly going to be long enough for anything to surprise me. I space out the zinc buckets of cutlery wrapped in napkins, then head off to find the cider.

17

Stargazey House
Highs and lows
Even later on Saturday

When I get back to the table with my full punch jugs Ollie and Plum are lighting the last of the lanterns. A few moments after that there's a half-knock on the door, a brief cry, and then the hammering of feet on the oak floorboards in the hall and suddenly everyone is there. Except now they've got room to spread out they feel like so much more of a crowd.

If you'd left the music choice to me, I'd have begun the evening with a few Meat Loaf-type driving rock tracks, and then mellowed down to Coldplay and Adele. Ollie's gone for something more jazz-and-bluesy, but halfway down the first jar of cider the noise of the voices rises so much that the up-himself playlist stops mattering.

After that it was as if someone pressed the fast-forward button. For a while people milled around with their jam jars, sipping their sparkling punch while Ollie pointed out the line of the lights around the bay in the distance. Ella kicked things off properly with a welcome speech and a jar wave, and then as she moved to her place at the centre of the table a stampede of guys all tried to sit next to her. Nell shouldered her way in there first, bagged a seat, and then chivalrously gave it up to Jago once the scuffle had subsided.

As I came out with my second load of plated shepherd's pie portions, I heaved a sigh of relief to see Madison was sitting at the opposite end of the table, a long way from the Jago-action. Then I realised she was actually sitting on top of some poor man. When it hit me the head she was cradling in the crook of her elbow was actually Ollie's I damned near lost my tray completely. In ten years on the ski circuit, I never came that close to dropping anything, so it just shows how out of practice I am.

Ollie must have got himself out of the headlock somehow because by the time I was refilling the veggie bowls, he was in the fridge looking for more dry white.

By the time the desserts have been demolished Ella's done three more impromptu speeches. As I pass her chair, handing out the chocolate mints and coffees, she leaps to her feet, then clings onto my hand and starts again telling everyone how great I am at looking after people, her especially.

An hour later, prompted by Nell, most of the guests move on to a karaoke night at the Hungry Shark. Then Ollie and Jago pack up the tables and chairs while Clemmie and Plum help me pack her plates and glasses into boxes. When they go off down the hill too, Ella and I are left looking out across the bay, ready to head back home.

Jago sidles over to us. 'The workers did a great job there. Next door's ready to go now.'

Ella tightens the belt on her overalls and beams at him. 'As soon as we decide on a builder, it'll be full speed ahead.' She's conveniently glossing over that we haven't yet had an estimate that's anywhere close to what we can afford, but whatever.

Jago fumbles in the inside pocket of his denim jacket and pulls out an envelope. 'I'm hoping this might help you with that.'

He's holding it out to both of us, but before I can react Ella leaps forward and seizes it.

Jago shakes his head. 'It's been a long day. Don't feel you have to look at it now.'

But Ella's already ripped the envelope open. 'As it's unlikely to be within our budget, I suspect we'll be giving you a very quick one-word answer.'

Jago laughs. 'I'm hoping that will be yes!'

I can't help smiling at how Jago's caught her out there. But she's pretty much confirmed my fears; as far as Ella and our build is concerned, there's only ever been one word and that's 'no'.

As she flicks through the pages her brows furrow to a frown. She looks up at Jago. 'But I don't understand. This has cut the other estimates we had in half.'

Jago's laughing again. 'Some jobs are more attractive than others. The price reflects that.'

I'm shocked yet happy to find that the residents' rate is real rather than fiction, but I need to give Ella more of a clue. As for Jago and his ambiguous statement, he's walking on very thin ice. However low his price and good his work is, with a laugh that flirty, Ella's likely to turn him down flat.

I clear my throat and prepare to fight for what's right. 'We're getting a good rate because we're local, Ells.' I really feel like a fraud saying this when I think I'm not committing forever. 'This way we'll be able to afford it.'

Ella's shaking her head as she looks down the page. 'I'm sorry, Gwen, because I know how much you want this.' There's a very long pause. 'Even with Jago's great price, it's still a lot more than George has allocated for us to spend.'

I'm so determined not to give up, my voice is rising. 'We can cut back in other areas!' Since I've had more of an interest, I've been watching back-to-back episodes of Kirsty and Phil. This bit I know! 'We can manage without kitchen units! I'll buy second-hand furniture!'

Ella winces. 'This doesn't include furniture.' She gives a sigh. 'It's a labour-intensive job. The bottom line is, on Jago's estimate we can afford the materials and about a quarter of the labour.'

Jago blows out a breath. 'I cut that quote to the bone. There's nothing in there for me. That's how much I want you to be able to do the work.'

Ella shrugs. 'I'm sorry if we've wasted your time, Jago, but we can't go ahead with the work as it stands. And cutting bits out would make the whole job meaningless. It's very much an all-or-nothing situation for us.'

I blow out a loud breath because I'm so frustrated. 'It's back to white all over.'

Ella frowns at me. 'I'm sure you can have pink in your bedroom. And we can run to a new shower and kitchen sink. Whatever you think, this isn't the outcome I wanted.'

Ollie's nodding. 'At least you've got all your wallpaper off now. That's one less thing to worry about.'

Ella's suddenly being all helpful. 'For any small things we do decide to go ahead with, Jago, we'll obviously come straight to you.'

Jago looks as crestfallen and disappointed as me. He pulls a face. 'You know where to find me. I'm only next door!'

I'm straight in there because there's no point prolonging this. 'Which is where we're going now! Thanks to you both for all your help today. I'm sorry the rest hasn't worked out.'

A quote cut to the bone from a builder who's desperate for the job, and we still can't afford it. I may have to accept that my vision for Stargazey was never any more than a dream. One thing's for sure, unless there's a miracle, it isn't going to happen.

As we head out onto the street, walk two steps and turn into our own door, I give a sigh.

Ella hears and pulls me into a hug. 'Don't be too disappointed. There were so many compliments about your cooking. You've had an amazing day today.'

I'm not taking all the credit. 'So have you! People were so interested in what you had to say. What were you talking to them about?'

She wrinkles her nose. 'Design, interiors, trying to deliver low-carbon solutions while still staying stylish.' She squeezes me harder. 'You did so well. I'm sorry it isn't working out here at the cottage.'

I pull a face. 'It's fine. At least I tried.' I blow again. 'Let's go ahead and order that paint.'

18

The Little Cornish Kitchen, Seaspray Cottage
Vegetables and desert islands
Friday

'I may have over-stretched myself with the pumpkins…'

It's lunchtime at the Little Cornish Kitchen on the Friday following the work party when my crisis of confidence finally hits.

Nell's biting into her third bacon cob and she waves her hand at the window. 'Your lantern overkill is brilliant. It's the best-dressed Halloween garden Clemmie's had yet.'

Clemmie's coming to join us. 'Charlie and I light the lanterns every night and it looks amazing. The kids are going to love it when they have their party; it'll last until Bonfire Night too.' She frowns. 'Is there a problem?'

I slide my phone across to show her the very orange photo that just popped up on Cockle Shell Castle's Insta along with the caption *'Preps going well for Saturday's Singles Get Spooky*

Cocktail evening! Let the scary shivers beGIN!! Here come the pumpkins!'

Clemmie's eyes go wide. 'How many are there?'

The wall of pumpkins in the picture looks ten times more enormous than I'd anticipated. 'We had thirty here, so there are a hundred and twenty at the castle.' I've only carved a couple of the Seaspray ones myself. Once the breakfast club customers spotted the pile on the terrace they were done in no time.

Nell's nodding. 'If we're decorating outside at the castle too, they'll all get used up. And my dad's collecting them to feed to the pigs afterwards. They'll be the treat that runs and runs.'

I know Halloween decorations were the last thing I wanted to get involved in, but since the work party, I've actually been pleased to have something to take my mind off the setbacks at the cottage. I went along to Comet Cove on Tuesday and met Ivy and Bill, who showed me round what they call the smallest castle in the world, and we worked out where to put the lanterns for biggest impact. They'll look amazing set against stony castle walls and lined up along the mantelpieces above the monumental fireplaces. We're hanging a cascade of skeletons in the entrance hall in front of the staircase, then lanterns on every windowsill, surrounded by candles in jars. Seeing this photo of the pumpkin pile is the first time I've started to waver.

Clemmie's wiping avocado off Bud's arms. 'Remind me when you're planning to carve those lanterns?'

'Tomorrow morning.' How can I possibly have thought that would work? But after seeing so much of Ollie last weekend, I've been determined not to open this up and have him involved too.

Nell nods again. 'And who's helping?'

Now it comes to it, it sounds crazy. 'Ella and I are doing it together, so long as she doesn't have too much day-job work to do.'

Nell always tells it like it is. 'So just you then.'

'They're really quick to do, it's something I love. But a hundred and twenty…' As I finally put my doubts into words my voice is a whisper. 'What if I run out of time and don't get them done?'

Nell rubs her hands. 'Leave this to me! If ever there was a job for the singles club, this is it!'

My groan was meant to be silent, but now it's out I have to explain. 'I just hate that whenever I'm rescued, it always involves men!' I make it generic, even though it's one man in particular.

Clemmie's laughing as she reties her hair into a ponytail. 'Good point, well made, Gwen.' She looks at Nell. 'How about we make this a women's morning?'

Nell lets out a cackle. 'I'll DM the coven! Calling all good witches! That's a date then.' She turns to me. 'You do know Ollie might be super disappointed to be missing out on this?'

I'm blinking. 'Why's that?'

Nell gives me a sideways glance. 'Just a feeling. Nothing more.'

I'm not going to feel guilty. 'If he wants to make lanterns, there's plenty of pumpkins in the veggie shop.'

Clemmie laughs. 'This has nothing to do with pumpkins. Remember what I was telling you about Nell and her attraction antennae?'

It takes a moment for the full horror to sink in. When it does, I let out a shriek. '*Attraction? Me and Ollie? Totally not!* If he was the last man on a desert island, I'd … I'd ride away on a turtle's back.' I'm not the greatest swimmer in the world.

Clemmie's laughing. 'Nice image there, Gwen. I'll remember that one.'

I'm looking for more ammunition. 'In any case, Ollie's not here to enjoy himself. He's always made that clear.'

Nell chortles. 'He certainly wasn't taking Madison up on her offer of fun the other night. He extracted himself from her clutches faster than any guy on record.'

I'm definitely not going to admit that I'm in any way pleased to hear that. And by way of changing the subject for good, I come to the other reason I'm confident that I'll be enjoying my ghostly cocktails without having to worry about Ollie. 'We've got our Halloween costumes sorted, so the pumpkins are all that's left for tomorrow.' Gin *and* fancy dress! That's two stops too far on the fun train for St Aidan's least fun-loving guy. I have to say this too. 'But thanks for helping me out here, I really appreciate it.'

Nell gives me a thumbs-up. 'It's the least we can do. Shall we meet at the castle at eight?'

A hundred and twenty pumpkin lanterns – what could possibly go wrong? But even so, it's great to know they've got my back and I'm not in this on my own.

19

Spooky Singles Gin Night at Cockle Shell Castle
A quiet night in
Saturday

There are times when woman power is exactly what is needed. Thanks to Ella, Nell and the women from this morning who came back to help light the four hundred tealights inside the carved pumpkins, the party rooms are literally glowing. And as far as this evening goes, by the time the castle has filled up with ghostly revellers all my boxes are getting ticked.

I couldn't have had any more compliments on the skeletons dangling in the hall, or the lanterns. The soundtrack is as awesome as the drinks – who doesn't love bopping around to 'There's a Ghost in my House' while throwing back Black Cat Martinis and Brainfreeze frozen-gin slushies?

We nailed our fancy dress with very little input too. I'm in a little black (T-shirt) dress topped off with a pink ombré wig, which was the kind of £2.50 bargain that proves Hardware

Haven really does deliver on *every* household need. I did also end up buying a 'Happy holidays in St Aidan' mini-schooner with real fabric sails too, but the way my collection is going, I might have wanted that anyway.

Ella's got an electric green version of the wig that looks fab against her super-sharp tux and her milky death-mask make-up. We had quite a discussion about whether her lippy should be black or plum but in the end she went with her signature red and she's working it like I knew she would.

The suit is one of Taylor's that she took intending to chop it up, but she stopped short when she saw the Armani label. The way she's throwing down bright green gin and absinthe Obituaries like there's no tomorrow, she might well be regretting the reprieve. Or the man. Or both. Whatever, it has to be a giant leap forward that she's wearing it at all without crying bucketfuls.

With everything going this well, there has to be a downside and there is. Contrary to all my predictions, my own particular nemesis is here, in his own tux, complete with Edward-Cullen-of-*Twilight* make-up, courtesy of Plum and Nell. He's helping to dish out Vampire Blood and Witches' Hearts at cocktail table number two.

Please don't ask me what the hell happened there. Ollie the party hater – not only dressed up in character, but also joining in like he's been in the St Aidan singles club his whole life and rocking it.

The final straw for me are his uber-subtle vampire tooth veneers. They make my stomach disintegrate in a way that completely defies explanation. There are no words. End of.

Add in that I may have been too worried to remember to eat today, and by the time I'm sipping my third Bloody Good G&T with a floating eyeball in, my legs are starting to wobble, and not in a good way. Across the room, in the flickering light of a thousand candles, Ella has moved on and is knocking back a lurid orange Hangman's Noose, surrounded by a sea of punters from last weekend who are hanging on her every word. Ella's the kind of woman who comes alive at a party and she's looking super-animated. As Jago's there too, I can't see her wanting to leave any time in the next four hours.

As for the others, Nell and George are resplendent in matching pumpkin outfits, Clemmie and Charlie are here as Mr and Mrs Spooky-Smith, and Sophie and Plum are in gorgeous ragged black sea-witch dresses that Plum's made.

I can't believe I've been banging on about gin for weeks, yet now I'm here drinking it, all I can think about is winding my way up the hill back to the cottage, and sliding under my duvet, with my sleep-easy playlist on.

But it's one of those things; once I've thought about it, my weary body won't accept anything less. I'm pretty sure once I'm outside, the gale off the sea will revive me enough for me to enjoy the wild walk home.

So I sidle across the floor to Ella, slide my cocktail vouchers into the pocket of her tux, push back her luminous green locks and shout into her ear. 'I fancy a walk along the beach, I'll see you back at the cottage.'

It's not the first time I've run out on a party, and she knows me too well to try to change my mind. She yells back at me, 'Shall I ring for a taxi?'

I shake my head.

She yells again. 'Will you be okay?'

I put up my thumbs.

Another yell in my ear. 'Text me when you're home.'

One more nod and I'm free to tiptoe out of the monumental

castle door. I'm halfway across the lawn heading towards the bay when I hear a voice behind me.

'Wait up, Gwen! If you're leaving, I'll walk back with you.'

As I turn round my heart drops as far as my clompy black boots, but at least I'm sober enough to give a fast reply. 'Edward, you've got a cape as well as your tux! How smart.' I'd be feeling the same resentment if Ella had run after me. Add in Ollie's attitude, and the prickles of annoyance are stabbing at my neck. 'I'm a strong independent woman, I'm quite capable of walking home myself.'

He falls into step beside me. 'Excuse me?'

If he isn't taking the hint, I'm going to have to be direct. 'My mum was a top mountaineer and I inherited her tenacity and her strength of character. I've heard she didn't take any bullshit either.' I've no idea why I brought this up now.

The moon comes out from behind a cloud and illuminates the shadows of his cheekbones. 'Does she still climb?'

I sniff. 'No, she died when I was small. I don't actually remember her. But sometimes it's good to say her name and remind myself how much of her there must be in me.'

'I'm sorry, Gwen. I had no idea.'

I shrug. 'No reason you should have. My point is, I don't need you or anyone else to rescue me.'

There's a shadow of a smile across his face. 'I didn't ever think you did.' He's in step beside me. 'If I'm the one who could use the company – is it okay to come with you then?'

He's thrown me right off here with that. 'Why not? Gwen is short for Gweneira. That was the closest name my mum could find to white snow. Not having her around might be why I have to look after everyone compulsively.'

This was the thing with Ned too. When we were kids he looked out for me, but by the time I went to the Alps to work, it wasn't only so I could be paid to live somewhere stunning. By then I was old enough to look out for him too. I felt better when I could check in on him, keep him topped up with cake. Then as we spent more time together there, I wasn't only around to fill his flapjack tin – more and more I was there to watch over him. It was as if me being close kept him safe. And even without me realising, me keeping him safe soon became the focus of my life.

Anyone else making the ascent by the routes he did would have been reckless and dangerous, but he'd been born to it. He knew his capabilities and he could assess the risks so well they disappeared. The more his ambition grew, the more I felt that so long as I was there on the horizon it would remind him he wasn't infallible. That so long as I stayed at the bottom of the mountain, he'd always remember to come back.

There was no concern at all for my own career progress or home making. We were simply locked into that pattern – Ned going off being invincible, me looking after chalets and the people who stayed in them. But mostly I was the keeper of Ned's soul – I was there as the talisman who made sure he came home.

And then one day he didn't.

And four years later, here we are. Watching the clouds race across the moon.

At times it's too easy to be so wrapped up in my own troubles that I forget about looking out to see anyone else's. Ollie's sudden rush of honesty is making me feel guilty for jumping to conclusions and causing my own gush too.

He gives a low laugh. 'Sometimes it's good to be looked after. Maybe Snow White wasn't such a bad name for you, after all?' He's giving me a hard stare as we cross the dunes and turn right along the soft sand towards the cluster of lights that is St Aidan. 'Great make-up, by the way. Your face really does look like it's been sliced apart then stitched back together.'

I was pleased with how it turned out for a first attempt. 'It's ironic.'

He raises an eyebrow. 'Isn't everything you do?'

I think for a few paces. 'My supper-night shepherd's pie wasn't.'

He pulls a face. 'It was vegan – I'd say making a plant-based pie without sheep in would be pretty ironic if you were a shepherd.'

What the actual eff? 'Do you have a smart answer to everything?'

'Your thing is irony. I like to search for the truth.'

Some of us might call that up himself with pedantic over-tones, but whatever. 'It wouldn't hurt to lighten up and let go sometimes, that's all.'

He shakes his head. 'Believe me, if you were me, you wouldn't find anything to joke about.'

The waves are gently slipping up the beach, and out across the bay the moonlight is turning the ripples to silver. 'If I'd known we needed violins I'd have organised a string quartet.' I always forget he's carrying the weight of all those medals around with him, plus the dedication it took to win them. There's no real wonder he's fun-deprived.

He tugs at the bow tie hanging undone around his neck. 'I know Nell was the one who insisted on the suit you may have missed, but dressing up *is* hanging loose for me. I've even done the teeth.'

'So you have.' I'm so determined to avoid the view he's offering and save my stomach I shut my eyes tight. A moment later my toe hits something solid, and as I snap my eyes open my feet are caught up in a branch and I'm sailing forwards through the air, out of control.

Then two strong hands grasp my shoulders. When I finally come to a standstill with my body realigned with my boots Ollie's holding me at arm's length staring down at me.

For a second the world stops. As I look up in the half light, the shadows are accentuating the strength of his jaw. His lips are parted enough for me to catch a glimpse of those damned teeth. As the world starts to spin, I hitch my breath in expectation. And then his grasp relaxes and I'm standing on my own.

'Steady, Snow White! You nearly fell there.'

I have to make this clear. 'I'm not drunk. Or off my face. Or trolleyed.'

There's a sardonic tone to his voice. 'Anyone can fall over driftwood in the dark.' We walk on in silence, then a hundred yards along the beach he turns to me again. 'If you're cold I can lend you my cape.'

'I'm not cold either!' As I shelled out fifteen quid on eBay for plain black tights with thigh bones painted on in what Ella says is cheap white emulsion paint, I'm not about to cover them up with a coat the size of a tepee. More so because in spite of the eye-watering bad value, the white lines add a good six inches to my very short legs. Not that I'd be wanting Ollie to notice. 'We're almost back now anyway.' We're actually nowhere near, but due to hurrying to get this over, I'm swiping sweat off my forehead.

Ollie gives a cough. 'I still need help with Stargazey House.'

That's random, even for him. 'We talked about this before.'

His sideways stare is so long he's lucky not to trip too. 'I still know you'd be the best person to do it.'

I give that the groan it deserves, for all the reasons. Last time my refusal was because I don't have the skills. This time I'm adding in the vampire-teeth shivers too. Even if I knew enough to advise on furniture and paint colour selection, I could hardly concentrate with my insides spinning round so fast I'd want to throw up. 'Unless something big has altered, the answer's still the same.'

As he pushes his hands into his pockets he sounds even more sure of himself than usual. 'The game-changing suggestion I've come up with *may* persuade you to reconsider.'

Office jargon like that makes me lose the will to live. 'I seriously doubt anything would.'

His eyebrows rise. 'How about a labour swap? I could lend you Jago for the cottage, and in return you could come and help me next door.'

That's enough of a surprise to make my feet freeze to the spot; there has to be a catch. I turn and give him a hard stare. 'How much of *our* labour shortage would that cover?'

His expression is inscrutable. 'All of it.'

He can't mean that. 'That's a lot more work for Jago to do at ours than for me zhooshing up yours.'

His head is tilted. 'Remind me what zhooshing is?'

It's one Ella saves for her snazziest clients. 'It means making things more lively or exciting. Bejewelling. Giving the place some real razzle-dazzle.' Embellishing the bum off it in other words.

He nods. 'Right. My side of the wall is a lot bigger than you'd imagine. And I owe it to the house to get it right.'

As someone whose last trick was doing a nosedive over a stick, upping my game this far might be beyond me. And I'd hate to short-change him. 'I'll talk it over with Ella.'

He blows out a sigh. 'At least think about it. Jago could start on yours in a couple of weeks.'

Put like that it's *so* tempting. But even with Ella's help I'd be in so much trouble on his side if I accepted.

He's still going. 'There's no pressure. I'm prepared to wait for the best.'

I'm dying out here. If he knew even half the truth he wouldn't be offering.

Before we start walking again he leans forward with his hand extended.

'If you know where to look you can actually see the terrace and the back of the house from here.' He slides his arm around my shoulders so I can see the exact place he's pointing. With his cheek grazing mine, and engulfed in his scent, I'm almost too dizzy to focus. But it makes sense. If we can see the bay from the Stargazeys, we can see his house from here.

And when I find what I'm supposed to be looking at I can't help but smile. 'You've put pumpkin lanterns all along the terrace?'

He nods. 'I told you I liked them.'

I'm half closing my eyes to see better. 'Our cottage is in darkness. Are there lights on at yours?'

He sighs. 'Whenever I'm here I light candles on the windowsills for Alex. He may not be with us any more, but when they shine out in the darkness it's like a promise that he'll live on in the house forever – along with all his crazy, over-blown schemes and ideas.'

I'm struggling to make sense. 'Alex is the friend who started the work on the house?' I'm kicking myself, because when we talked about him last time, I had no idea he'd left so permanently.

Ollie nods. 'The one with great taste in kitchens. At least he did have, until he died.' He takes a breath then answers the question I'm wanting to ask. 'When he put all that effort into the house, he didn't plan to fall off a yacht and get lost at sea.'

What the *actual* eff? At first I'm reeling as I take in what he's saying. Then my chest twangs for what he's been through.

I know enough from Ned not to skirt around this. 'And you're the one trying to carry on what he began?'

'Trying my best, and failing.' Ollie sighs. 'There's no other way I'd have ended up building a house like this, in an expensive place like St Aidan.'

'But you owe it to Alex to make the effort to finish?'

'Or kill myself in the process.' Ollie blows out his cheeks. 'It's not as bad as it sounds; Jago knows what he's doing with the bones of the job. All I need now is the right person to pull the whole thing together at the end.'

I'm nodding quietly to myself. 'Someone to help you make it into the amazing place Alex would have wanted it to be.' Bursting with pizzazz and polish, in other words.

'Exactly.'

That's definitely not me. 'I completely see why the hanging loose and kicking back aren't happening.'

This has flipped everything on its head. I was the one who managed to write Ollie off as miserable and ungrateful, when all the time he was grieving for his friend. Of all people, I shouldn't have made that particular mistake. I need to make amends and the least I can do is to be honest.

'I'm truly sorry for your loss, Ollie. But I don't have the background to give Stargazey House the shine it deserves.' It's sounding more like something Ella would say, but it's the closest I can get to telling the truth without admitting I know nothing at all. And I need to take a leaf out of Ella's book and turn a negative into a positive to finish. 'On the plus side, I may not be able to help you, but I have taken your idea to heart; I'll be lighting my own candle in the window next door as soon as I get back.'

Ollie draws in a breath. 'For your mum. That's cool.'

I can't believe I missed her out. 'I'll actually be lighting two.' Then I push on before he can ask any more. 'Shall we go home now before we get too cold?'

Everything I've heard here tells me I need to distance myself, and fast. And it's about so much more than me not being able to do justice to the interior. Mostly I succeed at keeping up my cheery facade and holding things together. But there's no knowing what will happen if I expose myself to Ollie's desolation too. I'll only add to his burden if my own grief leaks out.

It works for Ella and me to support each other because our problems are so different. But if we let two lots of hopeless sadness like Ollie's and mine collide, we'd both drown in despair. We really can't have that.

NOVEMBER

20

Bonfire Night at the beach and Seaspray Cottage
Big bangs and echoes around the bay
Saturday, a week later

'You said two.'

It's Bonfire Night, and I'm standing on the sand in the darkness, a little way back from the crackling fire, watching figures silhouetted in the bright orange glow from the flames. The incoming tide has moved up the beach and as the fire has burned from a huge pile of planks and branches to a heap of embers, I've been working my way around the groups from the singles club, bringing out the treats from Clemmie's kitchen. My last round is with a tray of toffee apples, and as the wind blows spark showers over my head, I'm pulling back the cellophane, sinking my teeth into the last one.

I'm so wrapped up with my puffer jacket hood pulled high over my scarf and bobble hat I'm not actually expecting anyone to recognise me. Being ambushed by Ollie was the last thing I wanted, especially as I've dedicated the whole of the last week to avoiding him. I don't even need to turn to look, I already know it's his voice.

'Two what?' I'm barely thinking about the question as my teeth crack through the delicious sweetness of the toffee to the tarter apple inside. 'If you're wanting toffee apples, they're well worth waiting for. I'll be bringing more out on my next trip.'

A lot of St Aidan have gone to a clifftop barbie and fireworks up at the school, but as Ella and I got the hot tip that we'd still get a great view of the fireworks from the smaller singles club meet-up, we've come along to that. Even from down here, with the rockets exploding over the bay, the bangs sound enormous.

Ollie's standing at my elbow now. 'I'm talking about candles, not toffee apples, Gwen. When we mentioned lighting them the other night, you said you'd be lighting two – one for your mum. But you didn't ever say who the other was for.'

Between the clouds the sky is dark and pricked with stars, but the moon is only a tiny slice tonight, and as I look up at Ollie's face above his dark roll-neck jumper, at least I'm saved from moon shadows on stubble. I give a long sigh as I get that he's waiting for my answer.

He flicks his scarf over his shoulder and starts again. 'When I looked up from the terrace the other night and saw the candles shining in your attic window, I wondered who I should be thinking about, that's all.'

Okay. He's got me. This last week I've found the flickering candles in jam jars on my bedroom windowsill a big comfort in the darkness. As he was the one who prompted me to light them, I'll break my rule and tell him. 'My brother Ned was caught in a freak avalanche four years ago.' It never gets any easier to say; every time it's like I'm reminding myself that it's real, all over again. 'As soon as anyone knows that, they simply don't know how to act or what to say. Mostly it's easier not to share.'

His arm comes around me, and he squeezes my elbow. 'I'm sorry, Gwen. Thank you for trusting me enough to tell me.'

Usually when I tell people, I end up having to reassure them I'm fine, because that's really all they want to hear. But for once I don't feel he's waiting for any more than I've given him.

He sighs. 'I know exactly what you mean about not telling people. Not that many young people have lost someone the same age. Nothing prepares you for how you're going to feel when you lose your best friend or a sibling. There's no one there to help either.'

His tone is so desolate, I'm replying before I realise. 'It's not a thing you get over. While we live on, the people we've lost come through life with us, reminding us over and over that they're not there. Ned's in my head a huge part of my waking hours, and in my sleep too. Way more than he ever would have been if he'd lived.'

Ollie squeezes my arm again. 'You with Ned, me with Alex, we're on parallel paths. I hate that you're going through this too, but it helps to know I'm not on my own.'

I pull a face. 'Paths that are parallel never meet; grief has a strange way of driving everyone and everything away.' That's one less thing for me to worry about then. Although I hate to think of anyone else falling apart or aching inside like I am; I wouldn't wish that on anyone. Just in time I remember to throw in a positive note. 'We're in the loneliest of places, but hiding it is the only way. Find your coping mechanism, hang on to it for all your worth and tell no one.'

'I'm pleased I told you.' He sighs. 'As for coping, finishing the house for Alex is what's getting me through. Throwing myself into that, there's less time to hurt.' He pauses for a second. 'How about you?'

I hesitate too, but I have to tell him. 'I have my cooking. At one time I thought I'd never be able to cook anything for anyone ever. But then I made some sandwiches with Nell's bacon, and everyone was so kind. Then there were breakfasts, then the work party. Now I've started to bake my favourite cakes again.' It's true what Clemmie said that first day in her kitchen. And just this last week she's been asking me to choose a different cake to make every day, and patiently listening to the stories behind them. 'Every single thing I cook feels like it's going to kill me with the pain of remembering, but each time after I've done it, it's as if another tiny part of me has healed.'

He smiles. 'Everyone in St Aidan loves what you make.'

I have to be honest. 'I get a lot of satisfaction looking after people. It's what I used to be good at.'

'You *are* good at it. And you will be again.'

'Thanks for believing that.' A smile in the dark brings this neatly to a close and there really is a warmth inside me that makes it easy to slip back to my brighter self again. 'If you'd like that toffee apple, I'm about to get some more.'

He's pushing his hands in his pockets, staring up at the sky. 'I'm probably okay for now. But thanks for the chat.'

Except we both know he's not okay, and he probably never will be again. But we also know there's very little anyone can do to help with that. Especially not me, now I've lost my strength. I'm in over my head with my own tragedy, but something makes me shout one last thing over my shoulder as I leave.

'Keep going, Ollie. And don't forget to hang on to those little wins.'

Then I hurry away across the dune path and head back through the garden at Seaspray Cottage. It's a relief when the warmth of Clemmie's downstairs kitchen hits me and draws me in.

I push my way through to where Clemmie is standing at the fridge and try to think about something different. 'The pumpkins in the garden are holding up well.'

She smiles and swaps Bud onto her other hip. 'Charlie reckons they'll still be here at Christmas.'

My stomach contracts at the word. That's another thing I'm trying to avoid that I haven't told anyone about yet, so I smile harder. 'Halloween until Easter sounds good to me.' Somehow I hadn't considered that a sunny-all-year seaside town would make anything much of the bit in between.

She looks down at Bud. 'This time last year Charlie and I were wearing the same fancy-dress outfits that Nell and George had on at the castle. Mine clashed with my hair hideously.' Her smile widens. 'It's funny to think that a year ago Bud was still a bump hidden underneath a pumpkin costume.'

My ears prick up. 'So was Nell hiding anything last weekend?'

Clemmie pulls a face. 'I'm afraid not. It's no secret, they've wanted a baby for a while. She's drastically cut back on her work hours to help, but it still hasn't happened for them yet.'

Babies aren't even on my horizon, but I can imagine. 'It must be very hard in that situation.'

Clemmie purses her lips. 'Don't we know it! Our little one only happened thanks to a wonderful clinic in Sweden. We went through so much to get her, she's going to be our one and only!' She smiles again. 'That's why it's so lovely to have the right person helping us here. We're so lucky to have found you, Gwen.'

I smile back. 'I'm lucky to have found you too. Not every baby would appreciate my taste in YouTube clips quite as much as Bud does.' Then before I start to over-think this and collapse in a pool of guilt, I get back to tonight. 'I think I over-catered on the toffee apples. Shall I take more out?'

She has a large container of milk in her free hand. 'They're pretty much wrapping up on the beach now, but we'll always have takers for the toffee apples if we leave them on the counter. If you fancy making a large pan of your pumpkin spiced drink, the besties said they'd call in for a warm-up on their way home. I've got the cream topping ready here.'

A few minutes later the door opens and Ella comes in followed by Nell, George and Charlie, then Ollie, Plum and Jago. They all peel off their coats and pull up high stools alongside the counter.

Clemmie calls through to them. 'Everyone up for warm spiced pumpkin drinks, and a slice of Gwen's ginger cake?'

Ella calls to me through the open kitchen door. 'You've no idea how good it is to taste your baking again, Gweneira.'

Clemmie laughs. 'Since she let me have a peep at her recipe lists, she's been treating us to lots. They're going down a storm in the bake boxes.'

It's a sign of Clemmie's warmth and understanding that I can bear to hear them being talked about so lightly and easily. 'They're already tried and tested. That's the secret.' There are still a few I haven't been able to face making yet. But I'm getting there.

Clemmie's calling to Ella. 'We're using her brioche buns in our afternoon teas now too.'

They were another random try-out that Clemmie loved.

'The sandwiches they make are so light, they're great if you want to tuck into more afterwards.' I put the milk on to heat up, and sprinkle sugar and pumpkin spice into the pan then turn to Clemmie. 'Shall I tidy round out there while you stir this?' I owe her so much, I'll happily start to clear up, so there's less for her to do at the end.

She nods, hands Bud to me, then takes over at the stove. As we go through the doorway Bud's rubbing her eyes. 'Who's a sleepy baby? Are you going to your daddy?' I slide her onto Charlie's knee, then make my way around the room, putting chairs back in their places, tweaking cushions, and centring the jars of flowers on the tables.

As I look across from the far side of the café the group at the counter are already warming their hands on their mugs and wiping away their whipped cream moustaches. Listening to them laughing and joking from a distance there's no hint of anyone's deeper problems: Ella with her broken marriage, and the others with their struggles to have families. As I glance over and see the lines and tension on Ollie's face, it's good to be reading it as anguish rather than arrogance. As I take in the dark circles under very beautiful eyes, and how forlorn he looks, I want to wrap my arms around him and never let go. As one human to another, my heart goes out to him; for this one moment in time, I'd give anything to be able to make him feel better.

At the end of the counter Ella's animated arm-waving as she talks to Charlie about eco paints tells me she's in full flow. She's the only person I know who could spend an evening wolfing down hot dogs as big as her head, survive three toffee apples *and* whipped cream and still have her lippy intact. When she turns to Jago on the next stool her smile is dazzling.

'A progress report for interested builders – I still haven't ordered the boring cream paint for the cottage yet. Just saying.'

Jago licks a lump of cream off the end of his finger and smiles at her. 'So it's still all to play for at yours?'

She leans forward and waves her cake slice at Ollie. 'We all thought Gwen would never bake again, and here we are eating her sticky ginger parkin.' The sideways stare she sends him is a thousand times more significant than any words. 'Call round later in the week and ask again about the skill swaps. See if you can persuade her to change her mind.'

My only answer to that is to shake my head as I join them with an empty tray.

'No chance.' I take a toffee apple off the pile, and hand it to Ollie. 'Life's too short not to enjoy these though.'

He takes the toffee apple and the tray too. 'Ella's offered to collect the mugs.'

Jago grins. 'Great idea, Ollie. People who start a foam fight and annihilate the opposition have to understand, there *will be* penalties down the line.'

I can't help laughing at the shock on Ella's face. 'Come on, Ells, I'll show you where the dishwasher is.'

In the end they all load their mugs onto the tray for her, and I swing open the dishwasher door and pull out the top rack as she arrives in the kitchen. 'There you go, are you going to load them in?'

She stares into the machine in front of her. 'I'm sorry, but I have no idea what to do.'

I frown. 'Seriously, Ella, you must have stacked a dishwasher before?'

She shrugs. 'No, I honestly haven't. Washing up has never been my thing.' She takes in my squeak of disbelief. 'Why would I? Merry always did it at home, everyone else did it at uni, then Taylor took over.'

'But Taylor did the cooking. Didn't you help clear up?'

She shrugs. 'I left him to it in the kitchen.' For a second a flicker of doubt crosses her face. 'I always assumed that was how he liked it.'

She's left everything in the kitchen to me since we've got here, but I assumed it was because she was worn out with her new job, and our arrangement with the bills. I had no idea it was a lifelong position. 'When Taylor wasn't there, who did it then?'

She pulls a face. 'I left my plates on the side and the cleaning lady dealt with them twice a week.'

I had no idea, but now I do I can't let it go. 'So almost thirty-five may seem too late to start, but let's do a fast-forward lesson. I'll start with the basics – this is the dishwasher, the plates slide in here, the cage is for cutlery, and the mugs go upside-down on the top shelf. Next time there's a singles event we'll have you on kitchen duty, but in the meantime, you can be in charge of washing up at home.'

Clemmie comes through, followed by Nell, who's chortling to herself. 'We need to brush up your skill set, Ella. We can't have guys like lovely Jago thinking you're a spoiled princess.'

Ella's grinning. 'The spoiled princess thing hasn't held me back this far, but I take your point – we women need to be multifaceted. Don't worry. I'm on it.'

Clemmie's laughing. 'This could only happen in St Aidan.'

We shouldn't judge other people's partnerships, but Taylor must have been a put-upon saint or a control freak. Either way, it wouldn't make for a particularly healthy relationship.

As for me, I'm not sure whether to be super-embarrassed by the gaping hole I've missed in my bestie's education, or pleased I'll be seeing more of her at the sink from now on. But after an evening full of surprises, the thing that's staying with me is Ollie.

I can't get over the feeling that he needs someone to rescue him. He's inadvertently swung in to help me so many times already, maybe this is my chance to even the score. To be less indebted. But do I have it in me to do it?

The other thing that strikes me is that when I arrived in St Aidan I was totally stuck and felt nothing could ever improve. The steps I've been taking during the last few weeks have been tiny, but all together they're mounting up. I'm never expecting to be properly healed, but maybe there is hope to improve where I thought there was none. Knowing it could be the same for Ollie, I just wish there was something I could do.

It's not even as if he particularly responds to sugar. I'm just so sad I don't have the expertise he needs for Stargazey House. But I'm the woman who had no idea my bestie had never been in a kitchen. Maybe if I dig deeper, I'll find a way with Ollie too.

21

At Stargazey Cottage
Sweet dreams and sticky fingers
Tuesday

'Ollie, have you got a second to come up for a chat?'

I have to say, those are not words I ever saw myself calling down the rock face outside our kitchen door, to the man himself on the terrace below, on a cold and blustery Tuesday afternoon. But since Saturday night when Ollie wrung my heart out, I've been racking my brain to find the best way to help him. And this morning I came up with the answer. In fact, it's so effing ground-breaking I've barely stopped grinning about it since.

'Two minutes.' There's a scraping sound, then a clunk, and moments later he's stepping gracefully off the top of a ladder and onto the broken concrete next to me. He pats the top rung. 'If we're going to be seeing more of each other, this is easier than climbing the north face of the Eiger every time.'

I ignore how much ahead of himself he is and push down

my alarm that the near-impossible ascent from his to ours has been slashed to a cosy short-cut.

I look for something positive to say. 'Ella loves a ladder.'

'She's very welcome to wash up at mine any time.' He rolls his eyes. 'I hope she's keeping her word on that at home?'

It wasn't what I'd planned for my opening remarks, but I'm wading in to defend her. 'To put that in context, her mum did put the hours in with kitchen tuition, but I was the one who got the benefit.' Merry, being the best kind of stand-in mum-next-door, started with toast making and egg scrambling so I could help Dad out, and went on from there. 'Once we'd got into the habit of cooking together, we never stopped.'

Ollie shakes his head. 'How come get-ahead Ella missed out then?'

I'm feeling wistful as I remember. 'Merry was brilliant, she ran me through every dish when I was learning my chalet host list, but Ned and Ella were more interested in other stuff.'

Ollie pulls a face. 'We all have to eat. There's not *always* a Maccy D's close by.'

In spite of myself, I grin. 'Especially not halfway up the Matterhorn.' My sigh is as despairing as it always is when Ned and a pan crop up together in a single thought bubble. 'Ned burned everything; his signature flavour was pure carbon.' I hesitate for a moment because this is something else I'm easing back into. 'Can I offer you a microwave mini-pudding? They're very quick and easy to whip up.' If Ollie needs persuading to accept my upcoming offer, sponge may help.

From the way he tenses he's interested. 'I heard you'd worked the ski resorts. Do *your* puddings come in flavours other than charcoal?'

I'll toss him a few that weren't Ned's go-to favourites.

'Steamed syrup sponge, could be with custard, but delish and more instant with ice cream…'

Ollie jumps in before I get any further. 'Perfect. I'll have the fast version.'

It's out before I think. 'I didn't know you went for sugar highs.'

He gives a guilty shrug. 'I do for the right ones.'

I take the flour and sugar off the shelves made from the stacked-up crates I transported my stuff in and help myself to a couple of Nell's smaller eggs from the tall red fridge that was Ella's third best in Islington. Then I scoop some butter into the bowl and start my mini hand whisk. When the mixture is made, I look at Ollie and hold up a spoon. 'If you need a scoop of mixture, now is the time.'

He takes the spoon from my hand and it's in his mouth in one movement. Then he lets out a long groan of pleasure. 'I'm sure it'll be great cooked, but there's just something about cake mix.'

I'm trying very hard not to look at his lips as the weight of the syrup tin in my hand jogs my mind again. 'Ned practically inhaled anything sweet, especially flapjacks.' I'm miles away as I dribble the golden syrup into the ramekins and put the sponge mix on top. 'Whenever he was working as a ski instructor in the same village, he'd always call in on his way back from the ski lifts, on the scrounge for leftover cake.'

Ollie nods. 'Skiing's like sailing, they both burn through the calories.' He raises an eyebrow at me as I put the puddings in the microwave. 'But so does building work, so we definitely need these.'

I pull out a stool from under the makeshift table and push it towards him. 'Have a seat. I have a suggestion to run past you.' The next bit is what I'm bursting to tell him. 'I've been wondering if I could help next door by doing the clean at the end of your building work?' I'm so pleased to have found something he needs that's a perfect match for my skills. 'Ski hosts are sizzling-hot cleaners. When I've finished polishing the butt off next door it'll be more shimmery than the sea.'

Instead of the delighted look I'm expecting he gives a grimace. 'That's very thoughtful, but Jago's sister's husband's cousin runs Dainty Dusters. I'm afraid the cleaning's already spoken for and partly done.' He pauses. 'At local rates too.'

Damn. Damn. Damn. I had no idea how much I was hoping for this, but my insides deflate like a popped balloon. And somehow, all Ollie's vulnerability from Saturday has gone too. I know he's the same guy, with the same tragic past, but after that knock-back and his local-rate swagger, he's suddenly back to Mr Invincible. All the more reason not to put myself in the firing line by accepting his offer of work I'm not capable of doing.

I'm going to have to woman up and come clean on this one, but the ping of the microwave means it'll be sweetened by the syrup sponge and the ice cream I'm pulling out of the freezer.

I rearrange the mini lanterns I've bought and had on the table since the work party, tweak the jam jar of pinks and the rosemary plant, put the puddings onto the wood plank table and pass him a paper napkin. I let the hot sweet syrupy sponge of my first spoonful merge with the freezing vanilla on my tongue. Then I swallow, and fire.

'The thing with the Star Sisters is, Ella's very much the real deal. But everything we led people to believe about me and my renovation skills – is all total bollocks.' I take in a breath because I'm throwing us both under the bus here. 'Which means, we actually got this house under total false pretences.'

He's looking a lot calmer and less horrified than he should be. 'There may have been other reasons you were chosen.'

I'm jumping down his throat. 'Like what? I'm a total fraud, but it wasn't malicious. We were just desperate to get the cottage so Ella could get her new start. But the end result is, I can't possibly come up with a super-duper interior for your house because I have no design skills and zero experience.'

He takes a breath. 'Gwen, I didn't come round here with the intention of taking "no" for an answer.'

There he goes again. He's actually round here because I invited him!

He pulls out a catalogue from his jacket pocket. 'I'm not looking for a design spectacular. What if all I'm asking for is someone to help me choose the furniture?' His eyebrows go up expectantly. 'You must have done that before?'

I'm shaking my head. 'It's a lot worse than you think. I haven't ever had a home of my own.' I look around the mottled walls of the kitchen. If he's looking down on me now, who knows what he'll think when he knows the next bit. 'This is my very first rental contract.'

'Wow.' He says that under his breath, then picks himself up off the floor. 'Well, at least this way I'll get honest, instinctive reactions.' He pushes the open catalogue towards me. 'So, tell me what you think of that sofa, there?'

I stare at him. 'That's all you want me to do?' When he nods, I can assess it in a second. 'I recognise that buttoned style from the chalets. They're way less comfy than they look.'

He flicks the pages and points to another. 'And this one?'

It takes another nanosecond. 'Avoid that suedette like the plague, it shows every grease mark and vacuum stroke.'

'Gwen Starkey, you're hired.'

My mouth drops open. 'Excuse me?'

199

He shrugs. 'You covered everything I wanted to be reminded of. You're exactly what I'm looking for.' He rubs his hands together. 'If you're free to carry on next door tomorrow afternoon, we'll sort out when Jago can start on yours.'

I can't let this go. 'That's not a good swap for you.'

'Hold my hand until I fill the house, and I'll be more than happy.'

I'm so shocked by that image I can't get my words out. 'S-s-so that's it? Are you going now?'

He gives me a sideways stare. 'I was hoping we could finish our puddings first.'

He wants me to tell it like it is, so I will. 'I'm too stressed to eat.' With the sawdust taste in my mouth right now, I may never eat again.

He's staring down at my dish. 'It's too delicious to waste. I don't want to sound like a scavenger, but if you're really not eating yours, I can give it a good home.'

Which leaves me flicking through the pictures of coffee tables in the catalogue, shaking my head in disbelief. Then I get to the beds, and slam it closed. How many episodes of Kirsty and Phil can I binge-watch between now and work in the morning? The saddest thing is, I could watch a thousand and still make a total fool of myself next door. By the time he finally puts his spoon down and pushes his stool back, I've practically lost the will to live and the ice cream is dangerously close to melting.

He taps the catalogue. 'I'll leave this with you, shall I?'

I've enough breath in me for one word. 'Fabulous.' I hope that's designer-y enough for him because it's the only work-word of Ella's I can think of with my brain this scrambled. And I hope he knows it's ironic.

He drops the dishes into the washing-up bowl. 'After

everything we've said about Ella, shall I take these next door to wash up?'

Somehow, I manage to shoo him out of the door without answering that and take two steps into the living room.

What kind of person bowls into your kitchen, takes exactly what they want, *on their terms*, then bowls out again? Why did I ever feel sorry for anyone so driven and self-interested? How the hell am I going to cope with what's to come?

I'm just about to collapse on a bean bag when the door opens again.

'What now?'

'Shhh…' Ollie puts his fingers to his lips and he's beckoning me.

I cross the kitchen and follow him out onto the collapsing concrete. Then I look to where his hand is pointing. Two rungs down the ladder there's a white bird.

Ollie's eyes are shining. 'Minty's coming up to see you. What a good thing we put the ladder here.'

I'm barely breathing. 'I came onto your terrace that time because I saw her and thought she was injured. By the time I got down there she'd gone.'

He's whisper is soft. 'She's a pigeon who has damaged her flight feathers. I'm looking after her until she can fly again.' It's as if every bit of his arrogance has been driven out and replaced by the same tenderness I'm feeling myself.

She's so small and delicate yet self-contained as she flutters up to the top rung of the ladder. 'She's beautiful. So that's why you asked about the cat?'

'She's got a box in the shed at the back, but I'd hate anything to happen to her.'

I let out a sigh and as she looks up at us my heart melts. 'How do you know she's a girl?'

'Her tail sticking up means she's female.' His voice is very low, as he reaches out and gently rubs the top of her head with his finger. 'She doesn't have a leg ring, but she must have been handled when she was young. She's been here nearly a month, so she trusts me now.'

'So what happened to her?'

He tilts his head on one side as he slides his fingers underneath her and gently lifts her up. 'The vet thinks she was attacked by a seagull, but the feathers should grow back. She'll be free to fly home again in a few weeks.' His eyes have softened and he's cradling her as if she's weightless. 'She's one of the good things you were talking about. I'll take her back down now, keep her safe.'

He climbs onto the ladder and a moment later he's gone and I'm swallowing back a lump in my throat.

Arrogant was so much easier to cope with.

Now I'm stuffed from every side.

22

At Stargazey Cottage
Hearts and flowers
Later on Tuesday

Even though Ella often grumbles about waiting for contractors, I could have done with at least six months longer to get used to the new arrangements for collaborating with next door. But within the hour Jago was striding off the ladder at the back, his tape and notebook at the ready. It took no time for us to go through the cottage from top to bottom, measuring up the changes and deciding on a running order for the work he's going to do. If he's as efficient with his knocking down as he is with his talking, we'll be done in no time!

As for keeping our side of the bargain, Jago brought round a set of plans showing the layout of next door, and Ella and I have been poring over them at the table this evening, after finishing our spag bol. And as we move on to the washing up, Ella is up to her elbows in bubbles, trying to calm my nerves.

'You can't do anything to mess things up, Gwen. Next door is already immaculate.'

I let out a moan. 'That's what I'm worried about.' Ella's helped me make a layout for every room, with suggestions for furniture and where to put it, but even so it's majorly scary.

She grins at me. 'That's the good thing about furnishings and paint – if you get them wrong, it's fixable.' She's rubbing the last plate so hard with the washing-up brush the stripes might come off. 'All you're really there for is to sprinkle your fairy dust and fill the place with your warmth and love.'

I let out a shriek. '*Love?* Any more talk like that, you'll be drying up as well as washing.'

She brushes away my protest. 'You know you adore making people comfortable. Admittedly you've never had a place of your own, but homemaking is definitely your thing. It's great you're finally going to get a chance to show us all how good at it you are.'

This is just more of Ella's bollocks, but I'm clinging on to everything she's just told me as I dry the forks. 'Hero pieces, layering up, artwork, taste not trends.'

She finally drops the plate onto the draining board. 'Any problems, I'm here for you. But there won't be.'

I dive and catch the falling plate an inch above the floor. 'Accessorise the arse off the place. And if in doubt, add plants.'

She smiles as she peels off her Marigolds. 'You're going to surprise yourself.' Then her smile widens to a grin. 'Design from the heart – with a guy like Ollie, you can't go wrong.'

That gets the towel-shake it deserves too. But I'm completely aware; Ella may be the shittest in the kitchen, and she may boss the hell out of everyone, but when I need her most, she truly has got my back. I'll settle for that in a best friend any day.

At two o clock on the dot the next afternoon, I'm on the doorstep of Stargazey House, shuddering as the pottery fish eyes on the doorstep stare up at me. If you asked me, on a scale of one to ten, how scared I am, I'd have to say fifteen. As for my appetite, I'd expected to be too nervous to eat at all, but it went the other way. If I'd been counting the nervous muffins I wolfed my way through this morning, that would be close to fifteen too.

I've been at Clemmie's since early, stayed on to do prep for her mums and bumps afternoon, then ran up the hill for a quick wash and change. As the freezing wind whooshes up the hill and straight through my newly washed dusky pink sweat-shirt, I do one knock on the door then glance down and take in a definite nipple situation. Before I knock again I'm desperately shuffling the pile of files I'm clutching, but before I get anywhere near covering my boobs, the door swings open.

'Gwen, great you're here on time. I was waiting for you.'

'Ollie!' It takes me by surprise that he has his hand on the doorknob, but I'm handling it. The only way I'm going to get through this is to act as confident as he is, so I take a giant step forward into the house. What I don't bank on is jumping so far that my Doc Martens somehow tangle with his size eleven deck shoes. I lurch forwards and save myself, but somehow the files and papers get away from me. They fly through the air, hit the floor, and fan out across the polished timber boards.

'Everything okay there?' Ollie's hand is clutching my elbow.

'Absolutely fabulous.' I'm lying, but I'm not beaten yet. I nod at the ground. 'As you can see, I've brought *all* the catalogues.'

He stoops and picks up some papers. 'Plans, too. You have been busy.'

I manage to scoop the rest up into an armour-plated chest shield, so at least that side of the embarrassment is covered. And the best bit is, I saved myself there without actually doing a full face plant. 'So, where would you like to begin?'

He wrinkles his nose. 'Shall we start at the top and work down?'

My voice is a shriek. '*Bedrooms? Absolutely not* – yet. Eventually, obviously.'

The corners of his lips are twitching. 'Downstairs, then?' He leads the way through to the part where we ate on the night of the work party, and nods over the glass balustrade. 'The main living room down there opens onto the terrace. Let's start with that.'

As I follow him down I know I need to take the lead here to survive. But at least I manage to make it down the full flight of open-tread metal stairs without falling, so that's a win.

I look around the enormous echoing space that's completely empty apart from one folding chair and try to think what Ella would say. 'If ever a room was crying out for a hero piece, it's this one!' I ignore Ollie's baffled frown and bash on. 'The plan is to build a framework of signature pieces for each room, and then to layer up with accessories and finish off with cheese plants.'

'Great.' His eyes suggest bewilderment more than happiness, but whatever.

I dare to put my papers down on the floor, pull out a magazine, and flip the pages. 'So what kind of look are we going for here? Have you thought about sofas at all?'

From the side, Ollie's jaw joint is visibly clenching and his cheeks are pale. 'Throughout the build I've tried to stick with Alex's vision for the house – the double-height windows with views of the bay, the steel, the huge expanses of white wall.'

I nod. 'Delivering perfectly executed detail with wonderful volumes.' That's pure Ella. Thank heavens she made me learn a list of phrases I could use to sound more like I had a clue. 'You've done a really beautiful job.' Even I can see that.

Ollie sighs. 'It's down to Jago and his team more than me.'

I'm curious to see what's coming next, but I'm clinging to my crib sheet. 'Every sofa needs space around it – there's plenty of *that*. Any ideas on colour, style or fabric?'

He nods and gets out his phone. 'Alex first saw the sofas he wanted at the Singapore Yacht Club. I'll send you the link. They may have to be imported.'

There's a ding in my file pile, and I slide out my own phone. 'Ventura Tropic, I'm sure Ella will have heard of that make.' I take in a minimalist bench as long as a runway with a low back that looks about as inviting to sit on as a concrete block. 'A fabulously big sofa with a price tag to match.'

Ollie blows out a breath. 'He'd planned three for down here and three more for upstairs.'

Even before transportation costs that approximately adds up to ten years' salary for a chalet host. I need to test the water here. 'Would Alex have ever considered a less expensive, locally made lookalike product?'

Ollie looks appalled. 'Alex wasn't about compromise.'

I'm desperately thinking ahead to my layering, and the pops of colour Ella swears by. 'So he probably wouldn't have wanted to add cushions to those?'

'What?'

The answer is in his incredulous tone. 'Just checking.' And

there's one other thought, too. 'So long as you like them, that's fine.'

'Like them? White leather wouldn't be my choice. But it's not my house, is it?'

I assume Ollie's the one who'll be sitting on them, but with the anguished lines on his face, I'm not about to go there either.

He gives a snort and spits out his words. 'Do you know what – I can't actually do this now.'

That's absolutely fine by me. I've pretty much exhausted my designer lines for the day anyway. 'Would you like me to leave tomorrow afternoon free instead? We can pick up where we've left off.'

'I had no idea it would be this difficult. Let's put it to one side indefinitely.' He glances at his phone. 'Sorry to rush away, but I've got places I need to be.'

Just when I thought I was holding my own too. My insides are deflating, with disappointment and guilt in equal measures.

Which bit shouldn't I have said? Where did this go so horribly wrong? I'm opening and closing my mouth, because it's not only myself I've let down here, it's Ella and the cottage too. 'I take it the build next door is off now too?'

If he's rejected the only swap I have to offer, it has to be.

His face is like a storm cloud as he heads for the stairs. 'That can go ahead. At least something good might come out of this.' He springs up to the next level and hangs over the rail. 'Thanks for coming, Gwen. This is not you, it's me.' As he disappears from view he's still shouting. 'Jago will give you a key. Feel free to use the shower here when he cuts off your water.'

I'm picking up my pile and murmuring as I see his jumper

hanging on a chair. 'Wherever it is you're off to in such a hurry, Ollie, you left without your hoodie.'

As a break-up phrase, 'it's not you, it's me' is pretty final, and there's no suggesting this will be any different. I have to face it – I had my chance, and for whatever reason, I blew it.

And then the front door slams, and he's gone.

23

It's as if Ollie has literally as well as metaphorically disappeared off the face of the earth. In other words, there's absolutely no sign of him here in St Aidan, which in some ways just goes to show how insular my little Cornish world has become these last few weeks. Ella gets out and about, but I rarely venture further than I can walk.

The good news is that Ella got the go-ahead from George to say all the required hoops have been jumped through now, so Jago is free to crack on with the cottage. He's starting with the attic first, so work began today at the top of the house, taking out the window with its own little roof that projects up above the slope of the tiles, and making it into a door with a Juliet balcony. From Jago's hand wave I get the impression it's a tiny job that should be over before it's begun, but Ella warned me builders have a habit of saying that about every job, large *and* small, so we'll get back to you on that one.

In the meantime, Ella and I are squashing into her room on the first floor, and once the attic is done and the plaster has been made good, we'll swap to sleeping upstairs.

On Friday afternoon, Jago is in the kitchen about to leave, with his kicking-back-for-the-weekend smile on his face and a Fat Max tool bag in his hand, when Ella arrives home from an uncharacteristically early finish. As she breezes in, he drops his bag again and leans his shoulder against the wall.

He raises an eyebrow to get our attention. 'A word about Ollie while you're both here.' He puts his palms together and screws up his face. 'Our Ollie's having a hard time lately, so make allowances and don't take offence. Whatever went wrong the other day, it's definitely him, not you.'

There's a familiar ring to that, but as Jago's brought the subject up, I may as well double-check. 'So it's nothing personal?'

Jago rubs his hands through his sandy hair and blows out his cheeks. 'Give him time. He'll sort himself out and come round. The poor lad gets in a terrible tangle with himself. Those shoulders of his are so broad they hardly fit through the door, but they're carrying the weight of some very big burdens.'

It's good to have reassurance. 'So long as you're sure.'

His serious expression softens to a smile as he dangles something from his fingers. 'He'd hardly have left you his key otherwise, would he?' He drops it onto the table. 'Take this as a peace offering. And no need to wait until your water's off either before you dive into his bathroom. Just help yourselves.'

'Thanks for this.' The key's already in Ella's hand and she turns her smile up to full dazzle.

'You're welcome.' Jago grins back at a similar wattage and picks up his bag again. 'If you'd like me to show you how the shower tower works, I'll be there for the next hour.'

As he disappears through the front door Ella wiggles her eyebrows. 'When did builders get so helpful?'

And when did interior designers sound this enthusiastic? I pull a face. 'I've cleaned so many showers, I can probably work that one out for myself.' I stare at Ella. 'All the showers you test at work…?' She should be at least as good as me.

She's frowning as if she's agonising over her decision. 'All the same, I might have to take him up on his offer. Just for the fun of it. So many weeks without a decent drench, I may go right away.'

She dashes off upstairs, but it's a full ten minutes before she reappears with her towels and sponge bag.

As she passes me I see her face. 'Ells, you've put make-up on!' Not just a bit of lippy either, there's foundation and she's gone to town with the contouring too. I roll my eyes. 'You're going for a shower; it'll wash straight off!'

She tosses her head and her plait flies over her shoulder as she reaches the door. 'I'm going out onto the lane first. You never know who I might bump into.'

I call after her as I close the door behind her. 'Have fun.'

If I'd known the promise of a good soaking was all she needed to put the bounce back in her step, we could have wrangled the use of the showers down at the harbourside.

24

At Daisy Hill Farm
Cake stands and blushing brides
Wednesday afternoon the next week

'**O**llie's loss is our gain! Who'd want to choose wardrobes and agonise over paint charts when you could be serving afternoon tea at a wedding?'

Put like that, I have to agree with Clemmie.

I can't resist teasing her and Nell, who's also come along to help. 'I think the wardrobes are mostly built in.'

We're near the village of Rose Hill, which is in rolling green countryside about twenty minutes inland from St Aidan, at Daisy Hill Farm Wedding Venue, serving one of Clemmie's special afternoon teas for forty at a wedding. The setting is a Georgian house in the middle of an authentic farmyard, with small-paned windows and stone flag floors and an orangery, where the tea is being served, that opens onto walled gardens. We've brought mismatched china plates, cake stands, and cups and saucers, although at the moment most of the guests are drinking fizz from champagne flutes rather than tea as they tuck into the sausage rolls, sandwiches, scones, and a delicious cake selection.

We're in the kitchen waiting while they enjoy the food we prepared earlier and brought here with us.

Nell's pulls up a chair and flops down onto it. 'So while we've got a two-minute breather, tell us how that builder of yours is getting on, Gwen?'

I'm smiling as I think about it. 'He's galloping through the cottage. We've already got the attic back in use again. And every morning when I get up I can stand at my little balcony and look straight across the bay.' The view from so high up is wonderful, although at this time of year I'm looking out as the sky is dark turning to dawn because on weekdays I'm up and on my way down to Clemmie's as the sun is rising.

Clemmie's folding her arms and leaning against the kitchen wall. 'And how's the legendary builders' dust?'

I laugh. 'Whatever you imagine, there's ten times more now they've brought in the knocking-down team to move the walls on the first floor. It's way too noisy to stay home in the day; that's why I was begging to come to the wedding.'

Nell laughs. 'And here we are thinking you just wanted a glimpse of the bride to get ideas.'

I smile. 'I'm not planning to have one myself any time soon if that's what you're thinking.'

Clemmie laughs. 'That's what they all say.'

Nell gives her a nudge. 'You can't talk, can you – you and Charlie eloped!'

Clemmie wrinkles her nose. 'They were special circumstances. Charlie lost his first fiancée weeks before their huge Cornish wedding, so we wanted to keep things small. And we wanted to be married in time for Bud to arrive, but again, we hardly dared to breathe the whole nine months we were waiting for her. We only went to Falmouth.'

'Ella had a massive wedding years ago, and she's on her own again now.' I'm sure she wouldn't mind me sharing that. Reflecting how often Ella's been next door for showers, I'm thinking of our building work again.

'We're both sleeping in the attic together while Jago does the middle floor, then he'll do the ground floor at the end. And then we'll paint from top to bottom once the dust goes.'

Clemmie laughs. 'You're going to be begging to come to any events we're doing.'

I nod. 'I can't tell you how exciting it is to know the cottage is changing. It's going to get a lot worse before it gets better though.'

Nell gives a sigh. 'We all thought you were going to be flat out for Ollie.'

I have to be honest. 'For a very short time – like a day – so did I.'

Clemmie's tidying her empty cake containers. 'Has he come back at all?'

I shrug. 'Not that I've seen.'

Nell's shaking the cake tins, searching for leftovers. 'When he does, you be ready to knock him out with your good ideas. You did it with the cottage, you can do the same with the house!' She looks up at me as if she's had a brainwave. 'Would it help if we did some Facebook polls again? Everybody loved joining in with those.'

I give a grimace. 'If Ollie's running scared, we'd better leave those for now.' I don't want to make things any worse. 'It just seems unfair that Ella and I are getting our work done and I'm not keeping my side of the bargain next door.'

Clemmie folds her arms. 'It's his choice. Let's just hope a break from St Aidan helps to clear his head.'

Nell's as adamant as Clemmie. 'And have your best game ready when he comes back.'

I appreciate the encouragement. 'I'll try.' I've no idea how I'm going to do it, but I'm not going to let any man get the better of me, especially not Ollie with this.

Nell shakes a tin, and when there's a dull thud she lets out a cry. 'Result! What's in here?'

I can tell from the sound. 'It's flapjacks.' I almost daren't say the words. 'I made them this morning when Clemmie was busy.'

Nell's eyes are almost popping. 'You made *flapjacks*? But that was on your never-can-never-will list!' She's up on her feet and pulling me into a hug. 'That's wonderful.'

I give a shamefaced grin. 'It was completely by accident. The bride sent a last-minute request through, and Clemmie was up to her elbows icing cupcakes. Next thing I knew, the pan was on the stove.'

Clemmie's hugging me too. 'It's so good.'

I sigh. 'I hadn't realised how much I missed the hot syrupy smell of it.' I smile. 'There's nothing like the taste of flapjack mix. Ella and I used to make it when we were kids and eat it straight from the pan instead of putting it in the oven.'

Nell gives me a hard stare. 'Really? Ella cooked?'

I laugh. 'No, you're right! I made it and we both ate it. It would be a good one to get her going with once we get our own stove to bake in.'

Clemmie's eyes go wide. 'You're *actually* teaching her to cook?'

I laugh at her in disbelief. 'Washing up is just the beginning. It's never too late for her to learn. She's going to be a changed woman once St Aidan's finished with her. Public opinion has helped to wake her up to her shortcomings – I'd never have managed it without everyone's help.'

Nell's got the top off the box. 'You don't mind if I have a piece?' As soon as she sees my nod she's sinking her teeth into a deep, sticky slice. 'I don't know what's wrong with me, I'm *so* hungry recently.'

Clemmie laughs. 'Me too. It must be winter coming on.'

Nell offers us the box, and we both take a slice. Nell's waving hers around. 'Make some of this for Ollie and I guarantee he'll do whatever you say.'

I laugh. 'Thanks for that suggestion, it might just work.' If ever he comes back, that is. I hold up my flapjack slice. 'I'm so pleased I made this. It's reminding me of Ned in the best way. He'd have hated me to have a life without flapjacks, wouldn't he?'

Clemmie smiles at me. 'He definitely would, sweetheart.'

There are tears in Clemmie's eyes as she comes and hugs me again, and Nell's snorting into a serviette. She lets out a shout. 'Listen to me, sounding like one of my dad's porkers as I blow my nose.'

And then a head comes round the kitchen door, and we all run off to clear the tables.

25

In the shed at Stargazey Cottage
New brooms and a sweet tooth
Friday afternoon

By Friday afternoon, two days later, it's been a week since Jago and his helpers started work on the cottage. Obviously, they're doing their best to be neat and tidy, but you can't smash a cottage into a million little pieces and not end up with lumps of grit in your eyes, nose, hair, pockets and cross-body bag. Honestly, if they'd had a wrecking ball in there followed by a crushing machine the first floor couldn't have been any worse.

I'm definitely not grumbling. But I am doing my darnedest to hurry the process along so it's over in the shortest time. Walls came out, the corner bath and washbasin went too – hooray! – floorboards came up, pipes are going in, and for now the old loo is still there until the new one is connected. What we're working towards is a new bathroom, on the lane side of the cottage, an open landing at the top of the stairs, and a spacious new bedroom over the kitchen where the bathroom was to begin with.

Despite the dirt, it's all looking very promising. And my energy-boosting mood-enhancer of choice to speed the builders to the finish is – fudge. For the last four years, just like all Ned's other high-calorie reach-for favourites, fudge has been on my *can't even think about it* list. But since making flap-jacks made me feel better not worse, and as the dust and rubble situation was so desperate, I was willing to give anything a go. And so far, it seems to be working. One large help-yourself boxful on the kitchen windowsill and we've got a cheery workforce of builders all very eager to come to work – which Ella assures me isn't always the case.

Obviously, with so many builders rushing up, down and around such a small house, they literally fall over me if I go in there too. So, when I've been at home during working hours, I've been taking refuge in the shed. Over the weekend I found a couple of red canvas director's chairs in the Cats' Protection shop, and some blue and orange flowery cushions. Ella hasn't yet joined me in my high-altitude refuge, but at least it's clean now with somewhere comfy to sit and read. I even tried lighting the little stove and it got so warm at one stage I ended up peeling my North Face padded duvet jacket off and sitting in my T-shirt.

The other thing that happened this week when I wasn't watching is that the ladder from next door's terrace to ours was replaced by some timber steps. Jago just gave me a wink and said it would be safer for me than wobbling on a ladder. I didn't like to say anything, but unless Ollie gets back from what is now being referred to as a work trip, and has a complete change of mind, Jago's probably wasted his time.

As for the fudge, it's ideal because I can make it in the

evenings in a large pan on the ring of the camping stove in the kitchen and it sets in no time in the fridge. So far, I've made salted caramel, chocolate, vanilla, and boozy Bailey's.

This afternoon, when I get home from Clemmie's, I'm sitting back in my chair in the shed doorway, a cup of tea in my hand, letting a lump of salted caramel fudge melt on my tongue. In the distance the sea across the bay is glistening pale turquoise with navy blue splodges as the sun bounces off the water and the stiff breeze whips the breakers up the beach. Then a flash of white on the top of the new staircase catches my eye.

'Minty!' I stand up and call, watching as the bird flutters off the steps and onto the concrete outside the kitchen. 'Have you come to see how the builders are doing? I hope they've left you some sandwich crumbs down there!'

A moment later Ollie comes up behind her and calls up to me. 'Can you tell she's been practising all week?' He turns to the bird and stoops to tickle her head. 'You think the stairs have been put in just for you, don't you, Mints?'

I'm leaning forward in my chair, calling down. 'And haven't they?' I ignore the tiny yet misguided bit of my brain that's telling me it might be nice to see him back again and move on to practicalities. 'I have fudge up here. Grab yourself a cup of tea from the kitchen if you want to have a taste.'

I feel a bit like the witch in Rapunzel, luring the prince up the tower with promises, when he could just as easily help himself from the box on the windowsill. But as he's here, I may as well find out where we stand on our deal.

When he arrives a few minutes later, carrying a mug, with Minty tucked in the crook of his arm, I smile at him. 'Hello, stranger, it's your lucky day, there's even a seat for you.'

He nods. 'Cool new chairs.'

223

I pull a face. 'Not quite Ventura Tropic, they're pre-owned, post-millennial vintage.' I can't help grinning at Ella's spin on beaten-up second-hand.

He sits down on the edge of the doorstep and lets the bird go. 'I'll be fine down here. I can keep a better eye on Minty.'

I promise myself *my* eyes will not be straying, however taut the denim is on his thighs as he crosses his legs in front of him, then I pass him the sweet box. 'There's salted caramel, or chocolate.'

He takes one of each, then looks up at me. 'And I owe you an apology. I'm sorry I rushed away last week.'

'It's not a problem.' Apart from totally destabilising the deal, he's completely free to do what he wants.

He ignores his fudge and blows out a breath. 'I wanted to do the house exactly as Alex intended, but when we got to ordering the sofas he wasn't ever going to sit on, I just couldn't hack it.'

I know exactly what he's talking about. 'One of those moments that come out of nowhere, and hits you like an express train?'

He nods. 'For weeks you can feel like you're almost managing. Then it all catches up with you and you're back where you started.' He sighs. 'The house is ready for the furniture, but apparently I'm not.' He gives a shrug. 'Maybe I never will be. I so wanted to do justice to Alex's plans.'

I can tell how hard he's trying. 'You're doing the place exactly as he would have?'

'He was obsessed from the day he bought it; he had every detail worked out.' Ollie's putting his hands together, staring at his fingers. 'Me finishing is like carrying out his legacy.'

I take a breath. 'You've taken on a lot.' For once I don't need Ella's expertise to see that either.

He's shaking his head, staring out across the bay. 'We made these crazy wills years ago, leaving everything to each other if we died, but we were never meant to have to use them.' He's clasping his fingers. 'Alex was well off, but there still wasn't enough cash to do all the work, so I've sold my place now, and I'll use the equity from that to finish. Or that's what I'd hoped until last week. I never thought I'd stall this close to the end.'

So many complications. At least with Ned, all I had to take care of was his van. My heart goes out to Ollie for the position he's in. 'At times when you're completely stuck it's often a sign you need to stop and take an overview of where you're going.' I'm watching his face. 'Making a memorial to Alex could be the wrong way to go?'

He tilts his head in query. 'Go on, Snow White.'

I'm looking at the box. 'I thought I'd never make fudge again, but Ned would be happy that I have.' I smile at Ollie. 'If you make next door into a place where *you* feel at home, I think Alex would be happy about that too. It has to be better than not finishing, doesn't it?'

'So shall we have a look?' Ollie's sounding tentative, but decided.

I grin at him because there's nothing to lose for either of us here. 'I can't let you get this far and give up.'

He reaches up and taps my knee with his fist. 'Thank you, Gwen.'

Now all I have to do is find a way to do it. No pressure there, then.

26

At Stargazey House
Ski lodges and wild ideas
Later on Friday afternoon

'It's a big house for one person.'

After we came down from the shed, I braved the builders next door to grab Ella's brochures. As I gaze around and take in how much there is to do to transform Ollie's huge spaces into a home, I'm tempted to make a run for the door.

I tap my pen on my teeth. 'My take will be more cosy than Alex's, and it's meant as a springboard.'

Ollie rubs his thumb over the stubble on his chin. 'You'll be used to big places if you worked in ski resorts.'

And that's the lifeline I was waiting for. If this were an alpine chalet, I could tell you what every room would contain pretty much down to the last coat hanger. 'A five-bedroomed ski lodge would sleep ten or twelve. Shall we size the dining table from that?'

Ollie's nodding. 'Alex wanted to commission a hammered steel table.'

I'm thinking of my favourite chalet of all time, which was the one I looked after the winter before I lost Ned. 'How about simple Scandi wood, with some side benches, and chairs for the table ends?'

Ollie's smiling. 'Definitely different – probably in a good way.'

The budget is another consideration. 'You can get good design and a great result without breaking the bank with every purchase.'

He sniffs. 'I can't argue with that. Any thoughts on the sofas?'

I'm remembering how I'd charge around to finish the cleaning so there was time to curl up on the favourite chalet's sofa for a chapter of my book. I never actually pretended I lived there; even staying in it for a night would have been way outside my reach. All the same I loved being there. 'The sofas will have to be the big squishy kind you sink into.' I'm already imagining how much they'll soften the plaster. 'Inky blue velvet, with cushions in shades of navy and aquamarine.'

Ollie's eyebrows go up. 'A big departure from Alex's mono-chrome, but I *am* mentally flopping down onto one.'

I ignore that in my head I've already flopped down next to him. 'I'm pleased you're buying into this.' I'm thinking of the deep midnight paint behind that favourite sofa in the chalet, the sheepskin throws on the chairs as I lit the fire and filled the log baskets. 'Accent shades could work on the walls, too.'

'More colour?'

I laugh at his surprise. 'Obviously it'll be less wild here than in the cottage.'

His eyes go wide. '*So what are you planning there?*'

'It's only small, we might as well have fun.'

'Keep going.'

I'm suddenly self-conscious about the pictures I've gathered on my Pinterest boards. 'Green cupboards, blue and pink chairs. Red fridge. Me spending so much time at the Little Cornish Kitchen, it had to rub off.' I'm surprised how much I'm looking forward to it all.

His lips are twitching. 'I'll remember my sunnies when I come to visit.'

He's caught me unawares. 'So when we're all done here, you'll still be coming round?'

'Of course.' Then he seems to regret his haste. 'We're neighbours. Why wouldn't I?'

Right now, I can't work out which I'd hate the most – him coming, or him not coming. But as neither of us are certain to be around, I hurry on to the next thing. 'We'll have coffee tables, side tables, accent lighting, and rugs. Any ideas on a theme for your artwork?'

He screws up his face. 'Anything *but* yachts.'

I shake my head at him. 'You with your boats, me with my mountains. What are we like?'

He sighs. 'Alex and I learned to sail when we were eleven, but when we were solo sailors competing, we hated each other. Then one day they threw us in a boat together, and no one could get near us. And we were never apart again.'

I smile at the image. 'So what made you so good?'

He shrugs. 'We were physically strong with wills of iron and a feel for the wind. But most of all we'd honed our tactics against each other.' He's smiling into the distance. 'Alex was naturally wilder and took more risks. As skipper I knew when to let him go and when to pull him back.'

I pull in a breath. 'It sounds like a dynamite combination.'

Ollie pulls a face. 'We were world-beating. We finally stopped competing because the opportunities were there to build up a consultancy business, and after that we spent our lives building and sailing multi-million-pound racing yachts all over the world. Then one awful tragic accident, and it was over forever.'

I'm sensing the door on life-as-he-knew-it closed for him exactly as it did for me.

He carries on. 'It's very hard to find a way forward when the ground you were standing on has disappeared. I only take on work I can sub-contract now.' He's lost a lot more than just his best friend. All the more reason to make this place work for him. 'It's a relief to find someone else who understands.'

'Same here.'

He gives a grimace. 'But should I be feeling guilty for going rogue?'

I'm going to help him out here. 'None of this is easy. You're simply finding your own way through, as best you can.'

He pulls down the corners of his mouth. 'I am, aren't I?'

I let out a very long sigh. 'That definitely rules out Plum's seascapes for pictures.' I'm thinking back to what else was at the gallery. 'She has some lovely vintage railway posters of Cornwall. They'd work well with the blue sofas.'

'And if it does end up as an Airbnb, they'll be great for the job.' He's blowing out his cheeks. 'Any thoughts on the bedrooms?'

My heart really shouldn't be skipping beats whenever he says the word 'bed'. 'It's very "now" to have a bed without a headboard and paint the rectangle of wall behind it. Keep it simple, just bedside tables and lamps, a couple of comfy chairs.'

He laughs. 'I definitely need somewhere to dump my clothes when I take them off.'

I scrub away the image of him unzipping and stepping out of his jeans and think back to that first day when Ella picked up his sweatshirt from the pile of clothes on the floor. 'Somewhere to stack your clothes other than the floor will be a real luxury.' I smile at that without meeting his eye. 'Use similar bedding right through the house and add variation with your throws and rugs.'

He gives a groan. 'Choosing duvet covers! This is exactly why I need an expert.'

I've seen Ella at work so often, there's one last thing to explain. 'We'll make a colour palette for the house, choose the main pieces, then we'll build up from there. That way it'll all look fabulous in the end.'

He pulls a face. 'I'll take your word for that.' Then he grins. 'I'm only joking, I'm sure it will.'

Not that I'm wanting to put him on the spot, but he's going to have to make a decision sooner or later. There's no point going through brochures until he's decided what he's doing. 'So are you up for taking the cosy route?'

He's got his thumbs tucked in his belt loops. 'Even if I can't live in it myself, at the end I'd have a finished place and cash left over.' He gives a grim smile. 'The other way I'd end up with a place I'd hate *and* spend all my money.'

'So that's a plan!' I pull out my emergency box by way of a goodbye. 'Shall we celebrate with more fudge before I go?'

I'm definitely not looking at the way his pupils dilate with pleasure as he pushes the chunk into his mouth. 'Do you ever make this to sell?'

'For now it's only to keep the builders on site.' From where I'm standing, I've got a view of the front door. Only a few more seconds now, and I can make my escape. 'If that's everything, I'll leave you to your Friday evening.'

'But you haven't had your tour of the house yet.' He's blinking at me expectantly. 'That *is* why you brought your clipboard – to make notes room by room?'

Damn. I'm going to have to do this sometime, it might as well be now. 'Fabulous.' Truly, it's not. 'Shall we take it from the top and work back to here?'

27

At Stargazey House
Small print and clean sweeps
Even later on Friday

Have you ever tried walking upstairs looking down instead of up? On balance, as I climb the stairs at Stargazey House it's less difficult dipping my eyes and risking a stumble than watching Ollie's rear view stretching up onto every winding landing. I kicked off my boots at the bottom of the stairs in case there are carpets, so standing in my socks I already feel pretty undressed.

A family bathroom, five bedrooms, five en suites and landings across two floors require quite a lot of notes, even when you're faking them, because my mind is anywhere *but* on the job.

By the time we're in the last bedroom along a little corridor at the end of the first floor I'm into my stride. 'If you're looking to keep the budget down and add character, we could buy second-hand chests and paint them?'

Ollie's nodding. 'Like all good professionals you're going to save me more than you cost me.' There's a brief moment of basking before the blow. 'We could look for those together.'

The only answer to that is to change the subject. 'Jago's got on so well with the bathrooms, you're practically finished upstairs.'

Ollie blinks but takes the bait. 'Only a couple more things left to do in the main kitchen, too.' He smiles. 'I'll show you as we go down. It should be ready in time for your next work party.'

I sniff. 'I seriously doubt there will be any more of those.' The last one was a disaster, and everyone who matters has forgotten about them anyway.

He frowns. 'Aren't they mentioned in your contract?'

Obviously I was too nervous and excited to read what I signed that afternoon we arrived, but I don't want to get caught out. 'In that case we might take you up on that.'

His face relaxes. 'You may want to do a cleaning party when the time comes. I'll suggest it to Nell.'

There's a strange feeling that he's saying my lines and I'm saying his, but before I can put that into words there's the distant sound of feet running on the stairs, then the slamming of a door. I turn to Ollie. 'What the hell was that?'

He looks at his watch. 'It might be Ella coming round for her shower.'

'Right.'

'Or Jago.'

I'm nodding. 'Of course.'

As Ollie hesitates for a moment there's another bump. 'Or both of them.'

'*Both of them?*' I'm silently mouthing the words as I move

out into the corridor. When I look for signs of alarm on Ollie's face at the next thump he's completely unbothered.

As he squeezes past me and makes his way back to the landing, he calls ahead. 'Hi, it's Ollie. Just to let you know, Gwen and I are *upstairs making notes!*'

I hiss at him. 'Why did you say that?'

'Say what?' He's come to a halt and he's laughing down at me.

'You made it sound like you were covering up for us pashing against the bedroom wall!'

His eyes go wide. 'Gwen Starkey, interior designers aren't allowed to take advantage of their clients!' He laughs. 'Or their workmen.'

We've got as far as the landing at the top of the stairs when a bedroom door swings open and Jago strolls out. Then the door moves again.

Ollie nods at his watch. 'Ella, I knew it was shower time.'

Jago's grinning. 'I was just showing Ella the grouting on the herringbone tiles in bathroom three.'

Ella smiles. 'He's made a lovely job.'

Ollie nods at me. 'We saw those earlier, remember, Gwen? The first en suite we visited.'

Ella's smiling at me indulgently. 'Look at you two, still busy making notes on a Friday afternoon, way after finishing time. And not remembering any of it.'

Jago laughs. 'Don't worry, your secret's safe with us.'

'There is no *secret!*' My protest is loud, but my cheeks are scarlet. I'm clutching my clipboard to my chest to hide that it doesn't contain a single sensible sentence.

Ollie's got his arm round my shoulders and is gently guiding me towards the stairs. 'We'll let these two get on and debrief in the hall.'

As for our word choices, no one's excelling themselves today. I'm still cringing at Ollie's as I start to head down, but what I see on the third step brings me to another sudden halt. The sequined thong I pick up is hardly big enough to cover a fingernail let alone any more.

I'm frowning at the scrap of red satin hanging from my hand and then at Ella. 'But I thought you always wore black Sloggi maxi pants?'

Ella's nodding. 'Ideally the whole of St Aidan *wouldn't* know my underwear of choice, but you're totally right. So, whatever you're holding in your hand doesn't belong to me!'

I'm puzzling. 'Surely I'd have noticed it earlier.'

Jago's grinning, but a second later Ollie leans across, whips it off my finger, and closes his hand around the satin. 'There's no mystery. This one's mine, I must have lost it on the way up. Sorry you tripped over it.'

Ella laughs. 'Health and Safety. Please avoid dropping panties in the workplace in future, Ollie.' She beams at me. 'We'll get back to our tiles, and let you get back to your briefs.'

I'm staggering down the rest of the stairs, shaking my head, as Ollie swings past me at the bottom.

He squeezes my shoulder. 'Don't worry, Gwen, that's St Aidan for you. Things like this happen all the time, there aren't always explanations.'

I can't tell if he's covering for someone or, worse still, if it's actually his. Except why would I even mind anyway? He's completely free to take thongs off and on whoever he likes. Any seasick feeling in my stomach is from eating too much fudge. It's nothing to do with the pictures of Ollie and a half-naked Madison flashing through my brain.

He rolls his eyes. 'On the plus side, I think *we* got away with it.'

'We weren't...' My mouth is open as he spins me around and I'm suddenly staring straight into his eyes. And for a terrible, horrible moment as I freeze, I feel like he's going to kiss me. And instead of hating it, I'm letting my eyelids flicker, staring at the way his lips are quivering as they come towards me a millimetre at a time.

And then suddenly he turns away, and next thing I know, he's leaning his shoulder on the door frame. 'Thanks for this afternoon, Gwen, it's been a life-saver for me. I'd never have got even close without you.'

'You're welcome.' Considering the most significant thing I mentioned was a favourite sofa I sat on in another lifetime, he's completely overstating. But whatever.

He gives a small cough. 'What I'm taking away from today is, firstly – you really should be making that fudge to sell.'

'What's that got to do with anything?' I roll my eyes. 'I'll talk to Clemmie and the girls; I don't want to step on anyone's toes. Plus, I might not have time, and people might not even want it.'

He looks straight at me. 'If you're taking orders, I'd like a box of salted caramel, please. Two if you have capacity.'

Over the sound of a power shower somewhere above us, I can hear laughter too. 'You said firstly, is there something more?'

He smiles. 'Secondly – we're going to be doing an awful lot of shopping together.' He falters. 'You are coming with me, right?'

I just almost kissed the guy. Or to put it another way, if he'd kissed me, I'd have definitely kissed him back. He should be a thousand per cent off limits for all the reasons. Add in that I can't ever bear to fall in love with anyone ever again – even for a second – how is spending time with him in the confines of commercial spaces any kind of a possibility? From where I'm standing, it's the worst idea in the world.

The fact I'm even considering it shows how desperately I want the cottage to be done. It's actually a long time since anything meant that much to me.

28

On the beach
Pistachios and bottomless pockets
Sunday lunchtime

'Okay, what flavour haven't I had yet?'

Ella's peering into the cross body bag filled with fudge that I've brought down to the beach to snack on while she has her run.

As the wind lashes my face, I retie my ponytail. 'You still haven't tried the raspberry and white chocolate.'

She licks her lips. 'I'll take another chunk of the pistachio too.'

'How many pieces is that?' It's not that I'm counting, but she has to be using up more calories chewing than jogging.

She rolls her eyes. 'When you exercise as much as I do numbers aren't important.'

'They are when it's my lunch you're swiping.'

But before I have time to get the words out, she turns and dashes away.

Her sprints between stops are getting shorter and shorter. It's as if every time she arrives back, she's trying to say something. But in the end, all she asks for is fudge, then we stare at the shine of the wet sand together, point at the white lines of breakers on the edge of the iron-grey sea, and the whole thing starts again.

It's ten days now since Thong Friday. Later that evening, Ella dismissed the incident with a 'what are guys like?' head shake and moved straight on to talk about the exact position of the freestanding bath. Obviously, anything that exciting blew teensy pieces of lost underwear out of the park, although when it came to it, there wasn't *that* much choice for the bath – it was literally one millimetre to the left, or half a mil to the right. But by the time we'd agonised for most of the weekend, any thoughts of sequins were long gone.

Ollie did another of his disappearing acts on the pretext of work the next day, which was fine by me. It means I can tiptoe round next door for showers without fear of bumping into him. And as he's left me with seed and pages of instructions for looking after Minty, I'm in and out all the time. She's taking food from my hand now, hops in through the open door at his, and flutters up to tap on our kitchen door too. Is it mean for me to hope her feathers don't grow back too quickly? When she's strutting around, dipping her beak to pick up crumbs, and cooing, I can't imagine her not being here.

Unless I've been helping Clemmie, I've spent most of the afternoons in a cosy chair, hooked up to the Little Cornish Kitchen's super-fast broadband, visiting Ella's go-to economy-with-style websites, and running the choices past Ollie by email. By the end of this week, a lot of my spreadsheets have ticks in the column showing the items are on order, awaiting dispatch. And a lot of the essential items like bedding have been ordered too.

I'm not sure if it's down to the sugar highs, the thought of Ella *not* wearing sequins, or a desire to finish in record time, but Jago is putting in the hours at ours, round the clock, seven days. On Thursday, I came home after lunch to find that they'd knocked through the kitchen wall to outside, put in the steels and already had the hole covered in a tarpaulin, with a makeshift door at the side, so the view we're going to get is still under wraps for now. And then yesterday they went on and made a hole between the front room and the kitchen.

'Right, is there any cappuccino flavour left? I might need a couple of rum and raisin while I'm here. And a vanilla too.'

Even for Ella that's a lot. 'Is everything okay?'

She snaps her eyes open. 'Why shouldn't it be?'

'Just a feeling.' I pull a face and wave the bag at her. 'You're eating your body weight in fudge when we're on our way to a fudge tasting afternoon where you'll likely eat even more fudge.'

She blows out a breath and taps into her watch. 'Am I really that transparent?' Then she lets out a shriek. 'Three thousand two hundred calories! What the actual eff?'

I totally sympathise. 'They're big pieces, but you'll soon run that off.'

Her eyes are blazing. 'That's six hours of solid exercise. All because of a bloody man who isn't worth it anyway.'

And there we have it. 'A man? You aren't seeing any men!'

She lets out a snort. 'It's not for the want of trying. It's Jago. *Jago!* I'd like to sit on his head and turn it to pulp.'

Oh my. 'What's he done?'

She closes her eyes and fans her fingers in front of her face. 'He's refusing to sleep with me until I learn to cook.'

'He's *what*?' I'm biting my lip, trying not to smile. Thinking of Ella's fledgling skills at the sink, they might be in for a long wait. 'Is that even legal?'

She's spitting out the words. 'Of course it's not, it's hugely discriminatory and anti-woman. Our grandmothers burned their bras to get out of the kitchen, and now it's come full bloody circle.'

If we're talking legality, there's something else niggling. 'What about keeping workplace relationships professional?'

Ella shuffles her feet and sniffs. 'That's not a problem; Jago's your builder, not mine.'

My smile's breaking out. 'I'm pleased we've cleared that one up.' There's another burning question. 'Do you even *want* to sleep with him?'

Ella's looking at me like she always does when she remembers I have no A-levels. 'You've seen the man's muscles, Gwen! Hot moving-on sex won't come any better, he's heaven-sent!'

I have to point it out. 'He's great at grouting too. But is he really worth *that* much trouble? Learning to cook is huge.'

She shakes her head. 'I know! That's why it's completely unreasonable.'

I can't wait to find out. 'So how have you left it?'

She's snorting. 'Neither of us are about to give in any time soon.'

'And in the meantime?'

She reaches for another piece of fudge and inhales it. 'Every time I go for a shower, he literally dangles what I can't have in front of my nose. It's hugely hot and steamy, the chemistry is electric. But he hasn't broken me yet.'

I've got a question. 'Has a guy ever turned you down before, Ells?'

Her eyebrows shoot up. 'Hell no! Me getting the knock back on sex is a huge shock. I'm not coping well.'

I have to say it. 'It could be good to have a partner who can stand up to you.'

She looks appalled. 'What's good about it? Taylor never said no in over fifteen years and that worked really well.'

I sense she's strong enough to hear this now when she hasn't been earlier. 'He left you for someone else, Ella. She might not have been as pretty as you, or as go-getting, but maybe – *just maybe* – she lets him do what *he* wants sometimes instead of always making up his mind for him.'

She's staring at the sand, kicking a seaweed covered rock. 'Gwen, that's low.'

Me standing my ground is for her own sake. 'It might not be what you want to hear, but I suspect it's the truth. I don't think it's healthy if one partner always gets their own way.'

She's got her appalled-of-St-Aidan face on and she's shouting again. 'So you're saying I should roll over and become a bloody kitchen goddess?'

'Not at all.' I sniff. 'What I'm saying is that it might be time to take on board that a relationship is better if there's give and take on both sides.'

She's blinking. 'Right. Thank you for your honesty, I'll give that some thought.' As she pulls out another chunk of fudge from the bag her lips twist. 'And have you thought about sleeping with Ollie? Because if we're talking about give and take, it couldn't be any more obvious that's what *he's* wanting.'

As I pat the bag and feel it's empty, I let out a wail. 'Ella, you've eaten all the fudge! This is what I'm talking about! You have to think of other people, too! You can't always expect to grab all the good bits for yourself. It's selfish.'

She's on to me. 'Stop changing the subject, Gwen.'

I grin at her. 'I'm working for him, Ella-bella. Once I've finished being Ollie's interior designer, *then* we'll review the sleeping-together sex situation.' We totally won't, but whatever.

'Great, I'm pleased.' She stops and looks down at me. 'I'm the one with the award-winning career and the legs that go on for ever, but you're the one everyone likes. You do know that, don't you?'

I blow out a breath. 'Now you're just being silly.'

She looks down at me. 'It's true, it's always been the same. And I *do* know I need to sort myself out. I didn't used to, but I do now. Thank you for being the friend who was honest enough to tell me.'

'You're so welcome.' I laugh.

'You might be small, Gwen, but you're so self-contained and self-sufficient and generous, it's just so reassuring being around you.' Her lips curve into a smile. 'However far off course I blow, you always know how to get me back on track. Of the two of us, you're by far the strongest. Not only that, you're funny too.'

Now she's being ridiculous. 'That's *not* true; I never remember a punchline.'

She grins. 'Being naturally hilarious isn't only about jokes. If you don't believe me, look at your outfit.'

I glance down at my T-shirt. 'What's to laugh at?'

She rolls her eyes. 'Most people would wear their Beach Run T-shirt under their puffer jacket, not over.'

I roll my eyes back. 'Most people don't have a bestie who's on their case as much as you and requiring public displays of solidarity.'

Ella smiles down at me and pulls me into a hug. 'It's so lovely you're getting your natural balance back.'

I blow out a breath. 'Who'd have thought I'd ever be making fudge.' As she pulls out another piece my jaw drops. 'Where did *that* come from?'

She wriggles. 'That's why I pay arms and legs for Sweaty Betty running leggings, the pockets are huge.' She gives me a squeeze. 'You pour your goodness into your food. You know Ollie wants you for your aura?'

I snort. 'That man will get more than he bargained for if he doesn't watch out. Cushions don't only come in shades of navy.'

She gives me a sideways grin. 'Gwen, you wouldn't?'

The more I think about it the better I like it. 'Zingy orange and pink might be exactly what Ollie needs to make him fall in love with the house.' I've got an answer for her wagging finger. 'I'd be designing with my heart, just like you told me to.'

She looks at her wrist again. 'You may have overlooked it, but in less than an hour lots of our other friends are coming to Clemmie's to taste your fudge. It might not be a biggie for you, but for me it's actually really important.' She does a couple of hamstring stretches and starts running backwards.

I know what she's getting at, and she's got a lot more to run off than I have. 'Shall I see you there?'

Ella might be a handful, but I couldn't love her any more. I just hope Jago knows how much she's worth the effort.

29

At the Little Cornish Kitchen
Authenticity and a big climb-down
Sunday afternoon

'Cookies and cream, white chocolate chip, cappuccino or hazelnut? How can I possibly choose a favourite to vote for when I love all four?' Plum groans, then her face brightens. 'I'll taste them all again, then I'll decide.'

My grand fudge tasting get-together at the Little Cornish Kitchen is underway and so far it's going okay. We've pulled the easy chairs into a wide circle in front of one pair of tall French windows that open towards the beach, and Sophie's children are handing out samples from platters while Bud watches them from her low bouncy chair, and Diesel the dog stands and wags his tail beside her. We're downstairs rather than upstairs due to what Nell called 'popular demand', and Clemmie called 'partners flatly refusing to stay home once they knew what we were tucking into'.

Clemmie waves her piece around. 'For me it's salted caramel all day every day.'

Nell lets out a splutter. 'I'm the same. I've promised myself I'll go back to pork when January comes, but I'm not even sure I will.' So much for Nell and her legendary bacon sandwich habit. Since fudge has been on offer, she and Clemmie have eaten very little else.

Sophie's sinking her teeth into her piece with her eyes closed. 'Dark chocolate and pistachio – two words: simply divine.'

Nell's sitting with her own personal box on her knee. 'Wouldn't this make a brilliant singles evening?' She looks round at everyone nodding in agreement. 'We'll get that in the calendar, if that's okay with you, Gwen?'

George's checked shirt matches Nell's, but other than that he looks very like he did the day we called in his office to sign up for the cottage. He's holding his selection on a plate and waving his hand to get a word in. 'A request on behalf of office workers – please can we have boxes of this on the counter at breakfast club to buy to take away? And if you had a clipboard for orders too, they'd make exceptional festive gifts for clients.'

I suppose it had to be too much to hope St Aidan would skip from November to January without any kind of celebrations in between, but my tummy clenches a little anyway. Ever since October began, I've been bracing myself for Santas and snowmen but so far there aren't any in the village. Christmas with all its resonances is something I want to avoid; if it wasn't for me working, and a house full of builders, I'd stay under the duvet and not come out now until New Year's was over.

Sophie's husband Nate is nodding too. 'And for those of us who don't get here for breakfast, can we please have fudge boxes on the Little Cornish Kitchen Facebook page, so we can drop in to collect them?'

Jago and Ollie have somehow blagged themselves an invitation and are sitting here too. Jago frowns at me. 'With so much demand, I hope you'll still have time to fill up our private supply on the windowsill, Gwen?'

I smile. 'The builders' box is top priority.' I turn to Clemmie. 'I may have to make a few batches here while my camping rings at the cottage are out of action.'

Clemmie smiles. 'Of course.'

Sophie's smiling too. 'There's fabulous year-round business potential here, Gwen. The St Aidan market for fudge is completely untapped.'

George joins in. 'Tasting like this, it's yours for the taking!'

Ollie catches my eye. 'Help yourself to the kitchens at mine any time.'

Ella's got a twinkle. 'You can talk to her about cushions while she's there, Ollie.' She turns to me. 'Do you have a recipe for a tangerine version?'

I turn back to her. 'Why, would you like me to show you how to make it while I'm there? Jago could be our chief taster.'

Ollie's sitting up straighter in his pink velvet chair, oblivious to our private jokes. 'If you need a kitchen assistant, count me in!'

Ella looks at Jago and tosses her head. 'And *count me out!*' Then she turns back to me, flops her arm over my shoulder and pulls me into a squeeze. 'You've done so well here, Gwen! It's wonderful that the Little Cornish Kitchen is working out so well for you.'

Sophie waves a chunk of raspberry fudge in front of her face. 'Gwen's working out pretty amazingly for the Little Cornish Kitchen, too!'

Clemmie's smiling. 'Breakfasts are booming. Bud and I couldn't be happier.'

Nell's straight in there to back her up. 'And takings are record-breaking.' She leans back and pats her tummy. 'They're growing almost as fast as our waistlines!'

Plum's eyes are shining as she smiles at me. 'So we'd like to say congratulations from all of us – if these are the tricks up your sleeve, keep them coming!'

As I mumble 'thank you' and 'you're welcome', my cheeks are so hot they must be as rosy as the velvet chair I'm sitting in. I'm fanning them with my fingers, but at the same time my heart is so full I feel like my chest is going to burst.

George gives a cough and turns to Nell. 'Don't forget, you haven't mentioned you-know-what yet.'

Nate leans forward. 'What's that?'

Nell's tutting at him, but George carries on, oblivious, his voice thick with the white chocolate chip fudge he's swallowing. 'The way Gwen's workload is mounting, you need to grab her quick! Before she gets a better offer!' He turns to Nate. 'I don't know why they've waited so long, I wanted to sort this back in September.'

Plum's laughing as she turns to me. 'What *George* is talking about, and what *we* were just about to come on to, is—'

Sophie jumps in. 'We'd love you to mastermind the decorations for the singles club Christmas events here at Seaspray Cottage.'

'*Christmas?*' My gulp is so huge, I feel like I've swallowed a balloon.

Plum's carrying on. 'Like you did for Halloween, but with festive shizzle instead.'

Sophie's nod is vigorous. 'But as Christmas is your own

huge speciality, you don't have to stop at decorations – we'd love you to roll out some fabulous themed events too.'

Clemmie reaches over and pats my knee. 'You've gone very pale. Are you okay?'

George is mumbling. 'I knew we should have told Gwen from the start.'

I'm stammering. 'B-b-but I don't understand. There's no sign of Christmas anywhere here.'

Clemmie's smiling. 'It's one of St Aidan's unspoken rules; we try to save Christmas until December.'

Nell nods. 'In a few more days, Christmas will explode. You'll be falling over fairy lights, there'll be festive pixies round every corner and mistletoe in every Roaring Waves beer delivery.' She gives a grimace. 'We even have a real-life Santa and his right-hand elf, who career around town in a pony and trap – but be warned, they are very full-on and in-character, and their quips can be very snipy.'

I'm shrinking into the chair as my insides implode. '*My speciality* – why do you think that?'

Plum's beaming. 'The dossier Ella sent though with your application – one look at all those Christmas photos and your file went straight to the top of the pile.'

George puts up a finger. 'It actually went on a pile all of its own as the Christmas market organisers had just pulled out and we were desperate for someone who could deliver serious sparkle.'

Nell's chortling. 'Ten years of Alpine chalet hosting, you're the closest thing to Mrs Christmas we've ever met! If anyone could guarantee us some extra-special Christmas magic it was going to be you!'

Ella's been very quiet, but she's speaking very thoughtfully now. 'So you chose us for our Christmas talents rather than our design ones?'

Clemmie's frowning. 'We definitely fell in love with the idea of the designers who could make the cottage beautiful, and the workshops too. And I was needing help here, so *I* was hoping Gwen would be free to spare a few hours for that too.' A smile spreads across her face. 'So if Gwen's up for delivering us Glühwein by the gallon and authentic apres-ski, it's starting to look like you've ticked *all* the boxes we were hoping for.'

Ella's beaming. 'Fabulous. Couldn't be better.'

I'm dying inside. In a second Ella's going to turn to me, just like she did with Halloween, and promise I can deliver. The difference is, every other time I haven't had a clue what to do, and I've faked it, saved us from getting found out and surprised myself with what I've done. This time everything she told them about me is true, nothing is a lie – I'm just not able to do it.

I swallow. When she turns to me, and tries to press-gang me into this, I'm just going to have to tell the truth. As she opens her mouth, I take a breath, and brace myself. But Ella's beam has gone, and instead of her usual radiant self, she's looking very small.

She gives a sniff, grasps my hand and turns to me. 'None of this is okay, is it?'

I give a tiny shake of my head in reply.

She sniffs again and turns to the circle of faces. 'I have a confession to make. It's not anything I'm proud of, and I hope you understand that I only did what I did because I was so desperate to get the cottage. But some of the photos and information in that file were sent by me without Gwen's knowledge or permission. I sent them because I picked up they'd be something else special and unique we could bring to St Aidan, and I wanted to help our case. But whatever impression I gave about Gwen and Christmas, that's not anything she will be able to fulfil.'

There are murmurings around the table, Clemmie bites her lip and sends me a grimace, and I just sit completely still, waiting, completely unable to say anything. This is so unlike Ella. She never explains, she never apologises, and she never admits she's in the wrong. And I may be mistaken but unless she stops now, it sounds as if she's about to do all three.

But Ella is carrying on. 'What I did wasn't only for selfish reasons. In my defence, I really did think that Gwen desperately needed a change. I had this feeling that time here in St Aidan would help her get out of the awful place she was in. That being by the sea, in a lovely cottage, in a little village where everyone knew her, would help her through, help her remember and reconnect with the person she used to be. That if she could spend time getting to know people, instead of constantly moving on, that would somehow be good for her. I'd watched my best friend falling apart with grief for four years, and I was ready to do anything to help her feel better.'

She's swallowing, rubbing her nose, scraping tears from under her eyes. And round the table everyone else is doing the same.

Ella shudders and starts again. 'The pictures are all genuine. But as most of you know already, Gwen lost her brother, Ned. He actually died in a tragic winter accident in the Alps, and since then she's distanced herself from anything that would remind her of that place or those traditions. When I sent those photos, I imagined that whatever the village needed us to do, we'd pull together somehow to deliver, as we have with every other challenge we've faced here.'

Nell blows out her cheeks. 'It's us too. We should have

known better. The pumpkins went so well, and after the photos we thought this would be right up your street too.'

Ella's shaking her head. 'It's not your fault, Nell, it's mine. I'm sorry, Gwen. I take full responsibility for this. I made the wrong call and it's put you in a terrible situation. I can see by your face how you feel about it.' She takes some tissues from Clemmie, hands one to me, blows her nose, then looks up at everyone. 'I'm truly sorry for the disappointment, everyone. I think we've all seen how Gwen's confidence has come back since we've been here, and that's all down to the love and care she's getting from all of you. But we can't ask Gwen to do Gluhwein. Or Christmas. It simply wouldn't be fair.'

My face is wet with tears, but for once I'm not crying for Ned. I'm crying because Ella has cared so much, I'm crying because she tried so hard and because she refused to give up on me, even when I must have felt like a complete lost cause. Because I'm so lucky to have a friend like her. And I'm crying because of all the anxious faces sitting round the room here. Because of all the help they've given me, although they didn't even know me. Because of all the things I can do now that I couldn't do when I first arrived – from bacon sandwiches to flapjacks.

With all those things I thought I couldn't do, when I actually did them, they made me feel better. Maybe I shouldn't be so quick to turn this down. All the people who've helped me up to now will still be here around me. Maybe if I find my own way through this, with their help too, there will be a way that works for all of us. The Gwen who came here back in September wouldn't have been able to do this. But the Gwen I am now should know to give it a go.

I sit back and look at Ella. 'Thank you for pushing me. And for pushing so hard for the cottage to bring me here.' I look around the room. 'I'm sorry if we misled you, but I feel so lucky that you chose us to come, because I truly feel like a different person from the one who arrived. I'm not completely mended, and I maybe never will be, but I'm so much less broken than I was, so much more like the person I used to be.' I force myself to smile at them all. 'After you've given me so much, it only feels right that I should dig deep and help you with this. There may not be Gluhwein, but there will be other ways to bring you Christmas magic. Leave it with me.'

There's a flutter of murmurings round the room, then Clemmie comes and gives me a hug, and the others follow behind her. We're all flopping back into our chairs, like wrung-out dishcloths, when Sophie gives a cough.

'Ahem, all this talk about Christmas, but there's so much to fit in before!' She wiggles her eyebrows. 'A little bird called Jago tells me he's almost ready for a cleaning party at the cottage…'

Nell's looking at me. 'Is Saturday okay for that, with supper after? Shall we get it up on the singles Facebook page?'

And Clemmie's holding her finger up. 'If it's almost time for decorating the cottage, I've got pots of paint in all the colours left over from here. You're welcome to take them to use as testers.'

As Sophie and Nate round up their kids, and Ella sidles over to Ollie and Jago, I look out from the French windows. The sea stretching around the bay is deep green, with patches of black, and seagulls are flying around a fishing boat coming into the harbour. I have no idea how I'm going to face designing Christmas, or what I'm going to do. But I do know the friends all around me deserve something wonderful. I just hope I can do that for them.

DECEMBER

30

At Stargazey Cottage
Being ironic
Friday afternoon, five days later

When Nell said St Aidan would explode into Christmas, she wasn't wrong. As December arrived, we woke up to windows all around the village that were twinkling. Now, when I pop into the mini market above Plum's gallery to buy sugar, the tills are ringing to a festive soundtrack, and the Hungry Shark is doing a roaring trade in hot cider. The assistants are in every kind of costume, from robin earrings to head-to-toe *Frozen* characters. Even Hardware Haven has its ladder stacks and brooms decked out with chaser-light icicles. I'm doing my best to embrace the festivities, but it's still hard to take when every festive fairy light makes my chest constrict all over again.

But right now, it's Friday afternoon, I'm back from a morning at Clemmie's, and I'm wandering round a cottage refreshingly free from decorations that's suddenly feeling very empty too. After three solid weeks of having the place bursting with noise and builders, Jago and his team have temporarily withdrawn so we can have our cleaning party tomorrow. They only have a few bits left to finish but as they're waiting for some extra narrow base units to be made and the French windows to be delivered it makes sense for us to clean so we can start on decorating the rest of the house.

So, for now, I'm here on my own again and it's eerily quiet as I go round picking up timber offcuts and sawdust piles that have appeared since this morning. The floors still have builder's dust caked into every crack, but I'm running my hands over newly fitted door frames, taking in the dusky pink of the newly plastered first-floor walls, breathing in the sharp scent of new wood. Marvelling at the bathroom with its free-standing bath, revelling in the luxury of having a toilet that flushes, and a bathroom door that closes. Smiling at the size of Ella's new bedroom over the kitchen with its view right across the bay.

All week, as I've watched the builders finishing their jobs, I've resisted looking in the boxes of leftover paint we brought back from Clemmie's. But as I've called in on Janice at Hardware Haven for supplies, I'm ready to move on to some colour try-outs. I actually went in for a paintbrush, but thanks to being dazzled by the all-over green sequins on Janice's elf outfit, I actually have a huge bag of stuff she assured me I'd need that I have no idea what to do with. I also have a big bag of St Aidan souvenirs with a Christmassy twist, because she assured me they'd make perfect gifts, were selling like hot cakes and it would be a shame to miss out. What else could I do but buy one of every kind?

Looking at the drips on the sides of Clemmie's paint tins I can see they're the same gorgeous jewel colours as the Little

Cornish Kitchen and the flat at Seaspray Cottage. I go for the ones I can easily get into with my butter knife, paint a little patch of colour on the wall, then wash my brush before making the next splodge.

An hour later, the landing wall is covered in patches of pinks and yellows and greens and blues and I'm standing at the top of the stairs staring down into an almost-full tin of vibrant poppy and an almost-empty tin of zingy kingfisher. By the time I've added the teal patch to the rest and I step back to see which I like best, the rainbow mix on the wall in front of me is more confusing than helpful. I'm just about to dip into the last container of red when there's a knock at the front door.

I call down the stairs, 'Come in, it's open.' Then I wait to see whose head appears. 'Ollie, nice of you to drop in. What can I help with?' He's taking tomorrow night's supper at his very seriously, i.e. doing a lot more worrying than he needs to. It's only veggie lasagne for twenty, followed by individual sticky toffee puddings, ice cream and a cheeseboard. As he's already got a table and most of the chairs there this time, and Plum brought her lanterns round yesterday, I'm not sure what the problem is.

He looks up the stairs at me. 'I was next door and I remembered how much there is to do before the work party and how small and helpless you are. So I thought I'd come round and offer you a big, fortifying hug.'

I let out a shriek. 'You *what?* How many times do I need to tell you? I don't need saving!'

He's biting his lip. 'No need to panic, I'm being ironic.'

He's dangling something in front of me in jest that I'll never be able to accept, from him, or anyone else. And I need to stick to that. Me jumping down his throat when the guy is only messing about is no good at all. I should be pleased he's smiling rather than serious.

'In that case, well done on the comedy.'

He lets his grin go. 'Looking at the horror on your face, it's worked too. It would be less prickly hugging a hedgehog!'

That's such an outrageous thing to say, I'm trying to give a huge Ella-type head-toss to show I don't give a damn, but I get a bit carried away. As my flounce ends up in an accidental foot stamp my toe hits something solid. By the time I realise it's the paint, the tin has already left the edge of the landing and is flying through the air.

I hear Ollie cry, 'Mind the paint, Gwen!' But he's way too late.

All I can do is to watch as the tin somersaults downwards to hit the steps, then spins and bounces off the wall, and back onto the stairs. And all the time it's flying downwards the gorgeous poppy coloured paint is whirling out in an endless moving arc of splashing red. It takes approximately ten seconds for the tin to make its descent and slide to a halt at the bottom of the stairs where it splatters the last of its contents over Ollie's Timberland boots.

Ollie leans down and tilts the tin upright. 'Best make sure we don't spill any more.' He's grinning. 'Little Greene must be great for coverage, it's everywhere!'

There's no way I can pass this off as something that was meant to happen. All I can do is to stand and gape at the mess. 'What the eff are we going to do now?'

He laughs. 'At least it missed the ceiling. Maybe you need that hug after all?'

'Absolutely not.' I jump back. 'What I need are hot decorator's tips on how to clean up.'

Ollie's grin widens. 'Do you or Ella *know* any *hot* decorators?'

I dismiss that with an eye roll. 'Before you say it, rookie tip number one, don't leave paint tins at the top of the stairs without a lid on. I've got that one now, thank you.'

He's still grinning. 'Throwing paint at me, I'm not sure I'll be passing on any tips at all.'

'Why are you in such a good mood?'

'That's what I came to tell you. Minty just flew off the table onto the floor.' He stops for a proud-parent smile. 'I thought she'd be hopping forever, but it looks like she might make it into the air again after all.'

'That's lovely news.' She's spending so much time with him inside the house these days, I'm not sure how either of them will take to her living in the wild again.

He's blinking. 'Before you ask, it *was* the dining table she fluttered down from. Obviously I'll clean it thoroughly before tomorrow.' He's looking at the paint. 'If you fill some buckets with warm water, I'll go and get some scrapers, cloths and newspaper. It's worse than it looks here, we'll clear it up in no time.'

I pull down the corners of my mouth. 'I'll assume that's another joke. In the interest of honesty, I might as well get this into the open now.' I pause and pluck up my courage for what's going to come. 'Yet another anomaly on our application; however much we *implied* I was a hot-shot decorator, I'm really not. I don't do Christmas *or* decorating.'

His lips are twisting into another smile. 'I'm with you on Christmas. But I already know about the rest. You gave the game away with the paper stripping and the YouTube videos.'

I thought I'd done such a good job on the work party. 'It was *that* obvious?'

He shrugs. 'No one else needs to know. I'll help you with the painting and prepping. A bit of tuition, you'll be rolling on paint like a pro. You stick to Christmas and leave the decorating to everyone else.'

'Shall I get the water?' It seems like the best answer and an ideal time to avoid any more awkward questions. He's bound to ask how my Christmas ideas are progressing, but after a whole week thinking about it my mind is still a blank.

Ollie's jokes might be dodgy, but when he comes back with all his kit his techniques for clearing up paint are excellent.

After half an hour of really good progress, I have to say, 'How come you're so good at this?'

He gives a low laugh. 'It's not the first time. Just be grateful it wasn't a bigger tub.' He gives a grimace. 'Decorators' dust sheets are for spills as much as dust, and they're always in the wash.'

Without Ollie, I might not have spilled the paint, but he's made the clearing easy. As we're bound to get to this before we finish, I might as well ask the question first. 'So you don't like Christmas either?'

He blows out a breath. 'It doesn't feel right to celebrate. I usually lock myself away and come out again when it's over.'

That sounds achingly familiar. 'I don't see that strategy working in St Aidan somehow.' There's another thought. His lovely new interior isn't unpacked yet, but every day more packages arrive. 'With Stargazey House fully zhooshed, it'd be a shame for so many cushions to go unused and unappreciated.'

He shakes his head. 'The trouble is, since Alex died I never feel comfortable enjoying myself.'

I'm frowning at him as I rub at the patch of floor on the step in front of me. 'You can't be sad forever. Surely Alex wouldn't have wanted that?'

He stops scraping and thinks. 'Alex would have hated me being miserable. He partied for England, and he'd be furious if he thought I'd missed a single drink. Three entire years of me not going out … he'd be appalled. I can't begin to think what he'd make of me not being able to sail.' He sighs. 'It's good to meet someone else similar. Seeing you is like looking in a mirror.'

I'm agonising. 'Ned would be the same. He lived life to the max; he'd have hated me to do anything less.' I shrug. 'It's such a contradiction – being without him has crushed me. If he knew how much I'd closed down he'd be so upset.'

Ollie's talking slowly. 'So how would Ned want you to be?'

I give that the thought it deserves. 'He'd want me to seize every opportunity. Live life for both of us.'

Ollie looks like he's discovering something for the first time. 'You're right. They'd want us to climb mountains and win round-the-world yacht races. They'd want us to celebrate being alive.'

I sit on the step, prop my chin in my hands, suddenly feeling dreamy because it's so different from the way I've been. 'They'd want us to live happily ever after, wouldn't they? Being miserable is a waste.' I blow out my cheeks. 'It's easy to say, but it's a lot harder to do.'

Ollie's narrowing his eyes. 'It's a different way of thinking, that's all. We owe it to them to start living again.' His voice goes softer. 'You've already begun – cooking the things you thought you never would. They don't always have to be big heroic acts; small can be just as effective.'

I bite my lip as I ponder. 'And to start with I need to find a way to decorate and do events at Seaspray Cottage that makes new happy memories rather than bringing back painful ones.'

'Exactly.' When Ollie's smiles like that it lights up his whole face.

I'm thinking of what might warm everyone's hearts. 'Hot chocolate! That was one of my real big things. I make it with melted dark chocolate and whipped cream.'

Ollie's straight in there. 'Stop, you're making me drool. But a hot chocolate evening would be brill.'

I'm thinking of the kids, too. 'We could make edible decorations. Gingerbread people, angel biscuits, stars.'

Ollie sighs. 'Stars are so much bigger and significant than just at Christmas. People have always used them to find their way.'

When it clicks it's like a lightbulb moment. 'We should make stars the theme. Like we did with the pumpkins.'

Ollie's laughing. 'Why would a Star sister from Stargazey Cottage choose anything else?'

The garden at Seaspray Cottage is coming to life in my head. 'I'm seeing tiny star lights on copper wires, stars hanging in the apple trees, metal stars, driftwood stars, glow-in-the-dark stars for inside.'

Ollie's rubbing at the last red patch on the wall. 'Gwen Starkey, you might have found the signpost for our happy endings.'

It's a relief he's acknowledged that they're separate. That we'll be getting one each. 'The decorations are as far ahead as I'm looking for now.'

Ollie's wringing out his cloth. 'At least you've inspired me to make plans for Christmas.'

I laugh. 'Every spilled paint pot has a silver lining.' It's completely ridiculous that I'm disappointed he got in first and won't be here.

He coughs. 'So, that's a date, then. For anyone who'd like to come, Christmas lunch is at Stargazey House! I'll do the cooking.'

I'm blinking, just in case I heard wrong. 'You're inviting *me?*'

He looks at me. 'As interior designer you're top of the list. You, Ella, Jago, Plum, Clemmie, Nell, George, Sophie – anyone who doesn't have a better invitation.'

My grin is a lot bigger than it needs to be. 'I'd better chase up those cushion orders.'

He laughs. 'And could you add Christmas deccies to your list for mine, too? The star theme will do nicely there.'

Then another thought hits me. 'You're cooking! That's usually my job. Would you like any help with that?'

He gives a shrug. 'You deserve a rest so I'll handle the starters and the main. But I'd love help with the puddings.'

'So now we've all got plans.' As I look down at the floor all that remains of the carnage is a few light-red stains.

Ollie looks down too. 'This is as good as it's going to get here. By the time we've painted the floors and the walls there'll be no trace left of your paintballing.'

I push last wraps of newspaper into a bin bag and pick up my bucket. I drop the bag by the front door and look out of the window into the dusk. As I see the Christmas trees nestling by every doorstep up the lane, I take a sharp intake of breath.

Ollie's frowns. 'Everything okay?'

I let out a low moan. 'It's the trees. The night Ned didn't come back the village was full of Christmas trees as I ran around trying to find him.' My insides feel as if they've turned to stone. 'There was even one in the office at the town hall when we went to sort out the paperwork.' I clasp my hands in front of me and try to suppress my shivers.

Ollie drops his bucket, and a moment later his arms close around me. For a second, I resist. Then I give in, and as I let myself lean into him, I'm enveloped in a sweet, deep warmth. I close my eyes, let my face press against the softness of his shirt, and as my breaths synchronise with his, his heat slowly penetrates through my body. And somehow with every breath we take together, the pain subsides and the hurt is ebbing away. I must be hugging him back too because his muscles are flexing under my fingers, but I don't even mind. All that matters is that as I'm breathing in his scent, for the first time since forever, I feel calm, and safe and wonderfully cared for. And as the rhythmic beat of his heart thuds against my cheek, I don't want it to end.

I'm there for so long that when I finally open my eyes again the light outside the window has faded to dusk. Long enough to lose all track of time and space. By the time I ease myself fully back into the here and now my left foot is going to sleep, and I know I'm letting this go on longer that I should. Reluctantly, and very slowly I release my fingers. Ease myself back. As the space between us widens I'm already regretting that it's gone.

And just as I'm about to step away he pulls me in again, the planes of his body hard and firm against mine. And as I'm crushing myself against him, my whole body is wide awake with wild thrums of excitement pulsing through me.

Then as his hold lightens and I stagger backwards, I have to make myself clear here. 'I really can't do…'

'Absolutely not, me neither.' He lets out a low whistle. 'Sorry. That was definitely a comfort hug. Human to human, nothing more.'

How can I be pleased and gutted at the same time? I smile. 'Or should that be hedgehog to hedgehog?' My smile widens to a grin. 'You have been known to be prickly too.'

He's still close enough that I can see the crinkles at the corners of his eyes as he laughs down at me. 'Thoughts like that are why no one minds that you can't decorate, Snow White.'

I pull a face. 'Thanks for helping me out earlier. Yet again, I'm so grateful I was rescued.'

He laughs. 'Back at you for your life advice. Who'd have thought I'd have turkey or fairy tale endings in my sights?' His smile fades. 'However hard things are over the next few weeks, we're in this together.'

I reach out and meet his fist-bump with my own. 'Keep on smiling, we've got this!'

As for the way my heart is pounding when I look at him, like the waves coming onto the shore in a storm … I'm not sure which will be harder to deal with, that or Christmas.

31

Stargazey House
Angel wings and over-reaching
Saturday evening

'So, Christmas *without* Christmas trees? What an original idea!' Plum enthuses.

Today's cleaning day has been so busy we're at the end of the meal at Ollie's by the time she gets a chance to talk about the festive details and ask if there's anything she can do to help.

I still found it hard to understand why anyone would want to come and scrub floors and clean skirting boards with us, but since they've been here, and everyone's complimented us on the work that Jago and his team have done, I can see how it might inspire people to try it at their own places. As Madison said, having wallpaper glue up to your elbows and a mop in your hand makes you feel way more real than simply poring over pictures on Instagram. Apparently, it also gives you as much of a workout as the ballet fusion class she's come straight on from, still wearing her one-piece leotard.

But leaving flippy dance skirts and leg warmers to one side, it's lovely for the village to be part of our journey. And going back to Plum, every time I talk about our theme, the more I love it.

'It's all about stars, Plum. And thanks to Nell's dad's willow and hazel plantations, we'll have twig bundles with star decorations too.' In St Aidan, the minute you float an idea, everyone jumps in to add their own take, and Nell ran away with that one. And it's a good thing too. I know everything in St Aidan is very immediate, but we can't hang around with these deccies. If they aren't done fast, they'll be going up in the New Year.

Plum looks as if she's going to burst. 'I can see the stars in the Seaspray garden! Large, thin ceramic ones, in unglazed white clay. I've got a kiln at the gallery; I'll make as many as you need. They'll show up wonderfully in the daytime and they'll be luminous in the moonlight.' She jumps forward. 'And the hazel will make really lovely twig stars. As soon as it arrives, we'll sort out some designs and have a crafting evening at the gallery.'

I laugh. 'At this rate we're going to have more events than there are days in December.'

Sophie comes into the kitchen with a tray of empty sticky toffee pudding ramekins. 'We'll have to combine! Hot chocolate with wreath making, hot chocolate while making festive biscuits...'

Plum rolls her eyes. 'Not that we'd guess that Sophie's chocolate obsessed.' She smiles again. 'We'll get Nell straight on to it as soon as she's up and running again.'

I'm actually without two of my right-hand women tonight.

Nell was here this morning but had to go home before lunch, and Clemmie lasted until six and then staggered off clutching a box of ginger fudge I'd made for her.

Sophie wrinkles her nose. 'Nell's got an iron constitution so whatever she had at the Yellow Canary last night that felled her, I'm pleased I didn't have the same.'

Plum laughs. 'It sounded more like the hangover of the century than anything on the menu.' She frowns. 'Did Clemmie have the same as Nell?'

I've really missed Clemmie in the kitchen, even though there's a lot of other people here too. 'Bud's teething so Clemmie was just totally sleep-deprived.' She's usually so energetic, but today she was so pale and shattered it was a relief when she stopped cleaning windows and went home for a hot bath and an early night.

Plum's chewing her thumb. 'Two mermaids down – I can't remember that ever happening before.'

Sophie unloads her dishes onto the side. 'Whatever's wrong, let's hope it isn't catching.'

Plum laughs. 'Said with feeling by a mum of four.'

As the kettles boil, I fill the cafetières and load the boxes of chocolate mints and a bottle of Baileys onto the tray of cups and glasses. In the distance, I can hear Ella entertaining everyone with the latest goss from the Cadenza Oak Luxury Lodge site she's working on nearby. It's not that she's dodging her other duties. She rolled her sleeves up, propped her clipboard on the windowsill, and mopped floors with the rest of us today, *and* kept up a non-stop stream of design tips for small cottages.

As Ollie comes in with a tray of plates and glasses, Sophie gives him a playful nudge. 'Showing off your lovely new dining table and benches, *and* your tame pigeon! No wonder you're looking happy, Mr Lancaster.'

Ollie's basking in reflected glory tonight. 'Minty's in her element out there, she's very sociable.'

Sophie's brows close together. 'You and Minty could hire yourselves out for children's parties; we're crying out for something new.'

Plum laughs. 'Or you could get her some friends and release them when Gwen helps Clemmie at weddings.'

As someone who did the same thing for years, they amaze me with their constant stream of new ideas. 'We're getting a bit ahead of ourselves; Minty still can't fly.' At first it was confusing, even panic-inducing having to consider every suggestion. But now I know they aren't all obligatory, it's fine to pick and choose.

Ollie raises his eyebrows. 'It won't be long before she does.'

There's a tightness in my chest whenever I think of Minty not being here. But more than that, at one time here any mention of the future made *me* desperate to leave, but lately that compulsion has gone too. The six-month lease renewal has lost its dread. In fact, I'm actually looking forward to it.

'I'll take these out.' I rub my hands and go to pick up my tray.

Ollie dips in and takes the coffee pots. 'Let me help.'

And yet again I surprise myself, because for once I don't feel as if he's trying to take over. And when he gives out the cups and moves on to pouring the coffee, I don't even mind.

Ella breaks off in the middle of an anecdote about tile adhesive. 'You two look as if you've always worked together.'

Ollie smiles. 'I'm getting in training, only twenty-two days to go.'

When I think how much we've got to fit in between now

and Christmas Day, I seriously doubt there'll be time to go to bed.

Jago grins at Ollie. 'Your place this year, mine next.'

Ollie laughs. 'Never. Yours is just a shell.'

Jago pulls a face. 'Haven't you noticed how fast I work?'

Ella laughs. 'Builders' houses are rarely finished; they're too busy working for clients.'

I look at Ollie and he answers my question. 'It's a boathouse, out towards Comet Cove. You could fit five Stargazey Houses into it.'

Jago grins. 'Vast and empty. Exactly how I like them.'

I'm watching Ella to see if her antennae are on full alert, but weirdly she barely seems to have noticed. In fact, more alarming still, she's loading up the tray I just brought through with used glasses as easily as I once would have done.

She looks at me. 'You two should do this full time.'

'Excuse me?'

Ella raises her eyebrows. 'Hosted holidays for exclusive groups at Stargazey House.'

Sophie's straight out of the kitchen, joining in. 'Boutique hotel meets B&B. That's *very* original with *huge* business potential.'

It's so unlikely, it's not even worth a head-shake. 'I work at Clemmie's, I couldn't do breakfasts in two places.' In any case, they're missing the main reason it's unworkable – Ollie actually lives here. Then my chest gets full of nervous butterflies as I think that may not always be the case. If he still decides he hates it even with the comfy sofas, he's likely to disappear over the horizon. And I'd hate to think how dull St Aidan would be without Ollie around to wind me up.

Madison sidles up to Ollie, slithers an arm around his neck and hauls him into a head lock. 'There *are* other cooks in town.'

As she scrapes her palm down his cheek, she's practically licking his ear. 'If you'd like to try out my breakfast skills, we could discuss team tactics and make a night of it?'

I've no idea why, but the back of my neck is prickling, and I'd like to flatten her. If only Nell and Clemmie were here, they'd have sorted her out.

But Ella's wading in, pointing to the beer bottles lined up by Madison's seat. 'Too many Kick Flips, Maddy? Put Ollie down.'

But Maddy isn't listening. As her Lycra-clad knee slides through the slit in her skirt and up to Ollie's waist, he shoots an appalled glance over his shoulder and hisses. 'Help me out here, someone, please!'

As I'm the only person behind him in earshot, 'someone' must mean me. And with how much I owe him for yesterday, I'm not waiting to be asked twice. I hurry across and slip my hand round his neck from his other side. 'Sorry, Maddy, this one's spoken for. Ollie and I have plans for later.'

Maddie's spluttering. 'Plans? *What plans?*'

Ella's jaw dropping open only spurs me on more. 'Colour schemes, mood boards, scorching sex…'

Maddie lets him go faster than a hot potato, and as Ollie grabs hold of my hand, welding it onto his shoulder, he murmurs, 'Nice one, Gwen. Shall we validate that detail?'

I'm so busy trying to work out what he means, I completely miss what he's doing. By the time I notice his face dipping towards me, we're fully committed. His lips hit mine and the kiss he pulls me into is long and hot and sweet and dizzying. And when I finally break away, it's only because we're in danger of becoming a public spectacle rather than making a point that's so distant I've forgotten what it was.

Ollie's still squeezing my waist as he gives a low laugh.

'Don't forget, we've clearing up to do as well as interior design, Gwen.'

Plum's laughing because she knows how much we're faking here. 'Sounds like you two might be up all night.'

Ella's standing up with a tray in her hand. 'Absolutely. I'll make a start now.' She turns to Madison with a growl. 'And stay away from Jago while I'm gone, he's off-limits for now, too.'

As Ella stacks the tray high with plates and rushes away with a wink and a grin, I'm walking round in the kind of daze where my feet don't quite feel as if they're on the ground. Knowing what happened was a complete one-off mistake, and yet wishing it could accidentally happen again. Like, immediately. Except it's totally not going to.

Ollie's lifting both thumbs up to me. 'Nice job, Snow White! Princess to the rescue, yet again!'

I manage to swallow back my heart, which is lurching into my throat with every beat. 'You're welcome. Any time.' Then I stagger back to the kitchen and start pushing dishes around the work surface. It's quite a while later when I come to my senses and notice I've filled the beer crate with ramekins instead of bottles.

Ella's swinging one of the dishwasher doors shut. 'Any more plates to go in before this goes on?'

I bob up from the floor with my hands full of dishes. 'One or two small ones here!' As she opens the door again, I'm looking into a perfectly stacked dishwasher. I frown at her. 'Who loaded this?' The last time I saw Ella next to a dishwasher at Clemmie's she didn't know what it was let alone how to stack it.

She's shaking her head at me. 'It's only a few plates, it's not rocket science, Gwen.'

But they're meticulously done. And weirdly, the cutlery is arranged exactly as Ollie insists it should be when he does the filling. I nod at her. 'Nice one, Ells.'

She laughs and wiggles her eyebrows to tease me. 'Any time, princess.'

I let that one go. I literally must have caught her loading the last spoon after Ollie did the rest, but I don't think any the less of her for it, because for the rest of the day she couldn't have been any more serious about helping. To be honest, it doesn't matter who's done what. Today has had its weird moments, some unexpected surprises, and brought some challenges. But everyone's surpassed themselves, Ella included.

She must be feeling happy because her eyebrows have gone into overdrive. 'You've worked miracles next door, Gwen, you've done the Star Sisters proud.' She pulls me into a hug. 'I can't wait to see it painted.'

'Me too!' I squeeze her back. 'You're sure you don't mind I won the Facebook votes and got my way?'

She smiles. 'You were right. Everyone else could see that. I'm so proud of you for sticking to your guns, fighting for what was right and delivering your dreams.'

'We're going to be so happy here, aren't we?'

She's blinking for a moment. 'Absolutely. We totally are.'

And with the day we've had I should be flying. Except there's a tiny doubt holding me back.

Much later as I'm lying in bed she texts me saying: *WTF?! Taylor's texted!*

I text her back: *WTAF??? What did he say?*

Great Christmas offers at Screwfix

A minute after that, she texts again: *Panic over – that has to be meant for someone else*

32

At Barnaby and Browne, The Barns, Saltings Lane
Close to the wind
Wednesday

With the cottage spotless except for the odd splash of pigeon poop, we turned our sights to Stargazey House. Jago's guys have left now, and the feature walls have been painted, so on Sunday we unpacked all the boxes that have been arriving, put the furniture into its places, then stood back to see how fabulously it all hung together.

'Don't worry, Gwen, homes always look bare at this stage' was how Ella broke the news that the job so far was good, but there were many miles further to go.

The living area works really well, with inky blue walls exactly the right shade to set off the most gorgeous navy velvet sofas. But now all the heroic pieces are in position, *apparently* we need more layering.

So, on Wednesday afternoon, Ollie and I head out to Barnaby and Browne's up on Saltings Lane, armed with the list

Ella and I made, entitled *Everything We Need to Fill the Gaps at Stargazey House*. As well as being where the shepherds' huts are made, The Barn Yard also sells vintage furniture prepped for painting. As we go through into the first lofty space the range of stylish accessories sets my heart racing.

I have to come clean – my excitement is not *all* down to the candles made by local crafters and the cute dogs wagging their tails by the sales desk. This is my first time alone with Ollie since our accidental snog, and every time he comes within a yard of me my pulse is skittering. But luckily for me he's turning out to be a super-decisive shopper. Mostly he's been racing out ahead, slapping 'reserved' stickers from our person-alised sheet onto items like there's no tomorrow.

By the time we're through to the third barn and I stop to swoon at compact sofas, which would be perfect for the cottage, my 'to buy' sheets are filling up with ticks. I set off again at a run, and barrel into Ollie as he comes to a stop in front of a display cabinet.

I read the label out loud. '*Glass and metal, IKEA 2015*. Very cool, but it's not on our list?'

Ollie slides a sticker onto the corner. 'It'll be perfect for my local memorabilia.' He sees my raised eyebrow and shakes his head. 'Every time I go into Hardware Haven for Minty's seed, Janice sells me souvenirs from St Aidan.'

'Not you too?' I can't believe we've both been buying. 'I've picked the miniature ones. I've even got a tiny fisherman's cottage with a lifting roof to keep my earrings in.'

'Janice is very persuasive.'

For once, I completely agree. 'I've even got a mini St Aidan ice-cream van that has carols for chimes.'

Ollie grins. 'Anything that kitsch can't stay in the shop.'

'Says the man who bought fifteen Ercol chairs in the last

barn.' I narrow my eyes at him because he can't blame the pushy salesperson here. 'If they gave medals for shopping, you'd win gold.'

He gives a shout of protest. 'They're very current, what's more they'll look great in the house.'

He's right, of course. I leap backwards so his elbow-nudge doesn't make contact and send my stomach into orbit, and come to a halt a metre further along, wedged against something ten times worse.

Ollie runs his hand over the black metal bed frame I'm sprawled against. 'This would go well in your attic. I've always fancied climbing up into one of these every night.'

I take a second to prise apart the images of us together in the bed and put us safely back in our own bedrooms. 'Something else you can't leave in the shop?'

He wrinkles his nose. 'It would look better in yours than mine.'

'If you're sure?' Once I shut out the awful image of Ollie in only his boxers sliding under my duvet, I'm loving the bed enough to add a sticker and take a photo. Then in the next aisle I spot another one identical.

I turn to Ollie. 'Look what I've found! You can have the bed of your dreams after all.'

He wrinkles his nose. 'Why not ask Ella if she'd like it?'

'Your loss.' I choose the best pictures and ping them off to her and follow Ollie through to a barn, its whitewashed walls hung with word art pictures. I'm reading the captions as we pass. '*Good morning sunshine!* That would make a great start to the day. *Winning* would suit you, Ollie. *Fly free* is Minty's.'

Ollie's staring up. 'What about you?'

I'm shrinking now the spotlight's on me. '*Footloose*, or perhaps *Wild like the wind.*' And then when I see it, I want to hug it to my chest. *'Give me the sea, and a little cottage just to be. That's mine for today.'* It's a surprise to me too, but that's the one that best expresses what's in my heart for now. It's probably just until I get the work at the cottage finished, then I'll be eager to be off again. *Won't I?* Once my little iron bed is up in the attic, I may want to stay forever.

Ollie nudges me. 'There's one up there saying *Let's make plans.* Weren't you making plans for *us* the other day?'

'What?' Damn. 'That was to help you out with Madison. End of.'

His grin is inscrutable. 'We still haven't talked about what happened there.'

My eyes flash open. 'Because there's nothing to say!'

'It was hot, though.' He's staring at me sideways. 'Scorching, even?'

Flaming is what my cheeks are now. I dash forwards, banging into a hat stand full of wind chimes as I go.

Ollie calls over the jangling. 'Watch out for those mood boards!'

If I don't react, hopefully he'll get bored and let it drop. It was a few seconds in a very full-on day. As this is the first time it's come up, I assume it was as much of a non-event for him as it was for me. I definitely *haven't* replayed it in my mind every hour since. It's actually been more like every five minutes. But that's nothing to do with Ollie. If it was the sweetest, most earth-shattering kiss of my life, it's probably only because it's so long since I had one. If I can't ever remember my heart galloping like that, or shivers zithering through my body, it's not because it hasn't ever happened. It's just that I've forgotten.

Except would you forget something that sent your insides into full spin and was still making you breathless five days later? I'm confused enough as it is. At the best of times there's something about Ollie that still makes my heart race. It started that very first day when we got in the wrong house, and it's been the same ever since. Him teasing me, as he is now, is making it all a hundred times worse.

'Look what I've found, Ollie!' I'm hoping the suspended fabric triangles I'm standing under, and a more professional tone, will push the reset button. 'One or two of these would work really well on your terrace.'

The label is spinning in the air above me. *Authentic and eco-friendly to use inside or out. You can still see the symbols, each number on these reclaimed sails is unique.*

Shit. As I read my blood turns icy. 'Are these sails – *off sailing boats?*'

Ollie looks up and rolls his eyes. 'What other kind are there?' He gives a shrug. 'They're the last thing I'd hang up at my house.'

I stare at his face, which is as white as the sailcloth. 'I'm so sorry. What a blunder! Let's go back to the village. I'll get you a sticky flapjack and a cappuccino. Extra-large fish and chips, and a double chocolate muffin. Then a walk on the beach. And hot cider at the Hungry Shark for the shock.'

He's running his fingers through his hair. 'It's okay, Gwen.'

I blurt it out. 'But it's not though. You're really upset and it's all my fault.' If I'd known, I'd have steered him to the next barn. Or even the next county. The sadness in his face is so deep and real, my heart is literally breaking for him.

He blows out a breath. 'The sail up there is from a Fireball. It's the first boat Alex and I crewed as a pair.' He hesitates then begins again. 'You might as well know. He died because of me – it was all my fault.'

My whole body tenses, because it's so much worse than I

thought. 'You blame yourself? What happened? Were you there?' The questions are flooding out before I stop myself. 'I understand if you'd rather not say.'

He pulls a face. 'It's better that you know – I wasn't there, but I should have been.' He rubs a hand across his temple. 'It was a prestigious sailing race and we'd been brought in to head up a team on a big corporate-owned yacht. The weather conditions were abominable and there was such a risk to the crew that as captain I made the very controversial decision to stay in port. But Alex convinced everyone he had the skills to outrun the storm and beat the opposition, and he went without me.'

He's shaking his head. 'The whole race was carnage; a lot of boats went down. If only I'd gone, my cool head might have prevailed when conditions became crazy. At the very least I'd have checked he was tied on. But Alex was lost at sea, the boat was badly damaged, and they were lucky to make it back without losing anyone else.' He gives a grimace. 'I'll always regret not being there for him. I should have read him better. When I stood down, I assumed he would too, I never dreamed he'd go it alone. But he did and I wasn't there to save him.'

'What an awful thing to live with.' I'm standing, watching him wipe the tears from his cheeks and rub his nose.

Then he thrusts his hands deep in the pockets of his jacket. 'I feel so guilty that I failed him. I always will.'

I'm in front of him and all I want to do is to make him feel better. Take some of his pain away. I reach up and slide my palm onto his shoulder, rest my cheek against his chest. As he eases towards me, I put my arms around his body, and hold him. Let his stubble tangle with my hair. As I drag in his scent, feel the bang of his heart against his chest wall, I'm hoping he gets as much from this as I did from his embrace at the cottage last week. I feel his chest heave as he sighs.

'Hedgehog to hedgehog, not a prickle in sight. Thanks for caring, Gwen Snow. When I say these things out loud, it always feels like a weight has been lifted off my shoulders.' He gives a rueful smile. 'As we've said before, we need to look forward not back. Sometimes it's hard. But it's helped a lot having you around.'

I ease myself away. Rub my cheek where it was resting on the soft cashmere of his sweater. Then as I look up at the wall beyond the awful sail, I jolt. 'Look, there are stars! Long strings of paper stars!' They're lovely – plain, white and simple, yet decorative too. Coming across them now, they feel like stars of hope, helping us find our way.

Ollie's face brightens. 'If they've got more of those, we could take a hundred strings.'

'Even for an Olympic-level shopper, that sounds a lot.'

He frowns. 'I'm seeing them on the wall over every bed, over the dining table, across the living room. And all over the Little Cornish Kitchen too.'

I think for a second. 'Maybe we could make our own?' Ella's mum, Merry, taught us to fold paper and cut out strings of people, and I loved making them.

There's a crease between Ollie's eyebrows as he thinks. 'I don't want to overload you, there's a lot to fit in between now and Christmas. But maybe next year?'

'Definitely. Maybe.' It's ages since I did that kind of forward planning. I try not to think how much I like the thought I might still be here next year. Daring to hope Ollie would be here too is too much of an ask. As it is, buying a bed of my own for a room of my own is so huge, that's the most I can get my head around for today. But every time I remember it, I get the warmest feeling inside.

As Ollie smiles he has crinkles at the corners of his eyes. 'So that's a hundred star strings. Anything else we can think of while we're here?'

'Let's go and talk to the assistant about what we've chosen so far.' I'm wishing my insides didn't pool to syrup every time he smiled. Then my phone pings, and I stop to look. 'It's a message from Ella.' My heart sinks. 'That's a shame. She says to hold off on the bed.'

It's a tiny thing. There are a thousand reasons why she would want to choose her own bed, so I don't know why this one small text has taken the light out of my late afternoon. But when you're learning to be happy all over again from scratch, the feelings can be very fragile. One minute they're there, and then just as fast they're gone again.

As for Ollie, when he's so sad and broken, the emotion I feel sweeps through my whole body like a tidal wave. At times like this the tenderness inside me is overwhelming; it would be hard for me to care any more. I want to wrap him up, make his hurt go away, and never let go. However engulfing the feelings are, I'm very careful to separate the inexplicable and desperate desire to rip his clothes off that's been there since the first day I saw him, from the compassion of an empathetic, caring person.

Ollie clears his throat. 'Cheer up! We still have the painting at yours to look forward to. I'll be helping Jago's guy with the preparation.'

I try to make my smile as bright as it should be. We're so lucky for all the help we're being given from all sides; we wouldn't be where we are without it. I'm just wishing my sudden nagging doubt would go away. It's only a bed frame, but that's how well I know Ella – there's definitely something else going on. I'm kicking myself too. Whenever we've been together lately, it's always been her helping me with my design struggles. I used to check in with her all the time to check how she was doing, but I can't actually remember our last proper girl chat. And I don't want to sound selfish, but I really don't want anything to derail the cottage, when we're so close to finishing.

33

At Stargazey Cottage
Home truths and panic rooms
Friday afternoon

'I t's funny how you dread things. I assumed Christmas
would finish me off, but now it's done I love the starry
garden at Seaspray Cottage.'

I'm talking to Ollie. It's Friday, ten days after our shopping
dash at Barnaby and Browne, and since then he's been as good
as his word. Every weekday since, he's been at the cottage with
his filler and his dust sheets, putting mist coats on the new
plaster, painting ceilings, and making sure the walls and
woodwork are prepped and ready for our upcoming
paintathon day.

Most of the decorations inside and out at Seaspray Cottage
went up a week ago, with a join-in event that stretched over
the entire weekend. I walk through the garden on my way to
work every morning, and I can't stop talking about how
wonderful the result is.

We're in Ella's newly created bedroom, and Ollie stops sanding and looks down at me from the top of the step ladder. 'The lights in the trees make the stars shine when it's dark.'

Madison did a great job for us there. She got in before the guys, and was up and down ladders stringing lights in all the right places. Then Jago's electrician oversaw the rest of the wiring in return for payment in fudge. And inside, the white paper star garlands strung across the ceiling show up really well against the colourful backdrop, and the seven-foot-tall willow twig bunches threaded through with tiny star lights look amazing too.

The last ten days we've barely stopped. I helped Clemmie do afternoon tea for a wedding at a gorgeous holiday home out along the coast road. We did decorate-your-own-gingerbread-people for the mums and bumps group and the people who came down from the care home, then all the breakfast regulars demanded they have a go, too. We've also had super-popular crafting evenings at Plum's gallery, with special hot chocolate and star biscuit snacks.

Ollie's disappeared back to his in the evenings, but whenever we've been at the gallery, he's dropped by right at the end, supposedly to help carry things home, but we all know he's around to eat any leftovers. And Ella's been similar, working late at the day job, then appearing to join in the last half-hour making origami or twig stars, or putting the final touches to gingerbread stars and people. As for that check-in chat about Taylor I've been wanting to have with her, Ollie always walks back up the hill with us, so I miss my chance there. And other times, the second I open my mouth to start a gentle interrogation, Ella seems to sense it and rushes away. She's never been one to have secrets, but if I didn't know better, I'd say she was avoiding that talk.

Some days animals are easier than people! Minty's been coming to work with Ollie at the cottage and he's training her to jump up and down the step ladder. When I've been out, he and Jago's painter have also managed to paint the floors with their special quick-drying paint.

After living here for almost four months, choosing paint colours happened easily. So, we're all set for tomorrow's painting party, with Ollie, Jago and Ella standing by to supervise. I've already made spag bol and melting chocolate puddings for the evening meal and my homemade vanilla ice cream is almost done, so all we need after that are the willing workers.

As I stare up at him sanding the last bits of filler, in the last corner of the last room, I can't express how grateful I feel. 'Thanks for this, Ollie. It's a million miles over and above the job swap.'

He hitches up his jeans and looks down at me. 'I *may* have an ulterior motive.'

The softness of his smile and the rips on the front of his thighs both have me biting my lip. Okay, I admit, my heart turned three complete cartwheels when he said that. Just in case he might – in even the teeniest kind of way – be expressing that he's hoping I'll be so happy here I'll stay on after February. But obviously it wouldn't be that, so I put it straight out of my mind.

He laughs down at me. 'You are allowed to ask what that reason is.'

So he's not letting it go. As my stomach just left the building again there, thinking it might be about me, I *definitely* can't.

'Did you and Alex have partners?' As a fast subject changer, I'm as shocked as he is that I came up with that.

He blinks. 'That wasn't quite what I was getting at. But it's no secret – of the two of us, Alex was the good-looking one.'

It takes a moment for that to sink in. 'Definitely not possible.' Then I readjust to a more appropriate reaction. 'I'm guessing he rocked the "wow" factor that goes with success?'

Ollie rubs at the wall. 'That was Alex – he played the field, without apology. There were supermodels waiting for him on every jetty, but none of them stayed around long enough to call it a relationship.'

'And what about you?'

Ella would be proud of how unflinchingly direct I'm being here.

He hesitates, smooths his fingers over the wall, then starts to rub with the sanding block again. 'Alex was the one they chased. I stayed behind and watched the dust clouds clear.'

'I'm not buying that.'

He shrugs. 'All that travelling and hard work, it wasn't the best scenario to find a mate for life. There was never anyone I wanted to be with enough to make the sacrifices.'

I look at Minty, perched on the bottom rung of the step ladder. 'Pigeons stay together forever. Someone in the village where we lived when I was young used to have a loft. That's the only thing I know about them though.' I smile at her. 'There's a husband waiting out there for you.'

Ollie frowns. 'If you're still here in spring, Minty, we'll ship you one in, don't worry.'

I tickle the top of her head. 'Or you may fly away and find your own.'

Ollie looks at her and shakes his head. 'With her current rate of progress, she'll be on our terrace forever.'

Which is sad in one way, but lovely in another.

'How about you?' He's looking straight at me.

'I always thought I'd want to fly away too, but I've surprised myself – I'm really looking forward to waking up in my new bed, seeing the dawn breaking beyond the balcony every morning.'

He rolls his eyes. 'I was talking about partners, not flight paths. Aren't chalet staff renowned for their partying?'

'Oh right.' I can feel my cheeks getting warm for that mistake. 'I chose the mountains for the wilderness, not the nightlife. We moved on every season, too; there was no one I wanted to hold on to.'

'So you've never had that special person who lit up your world? Who gave you butterflies every time they walked in?'

My stomach plummets. He can't possibly know about my somersaulting heart – can he? I'm desperately swallowing down the nausea. 'Is that *really* a thing?'

'So I'm told.' He laughs. 'You have to believe in the magic or you'll never find it.'

My heart rate has galloped every time I've been around Ollie. If I denied that, I'd be lying. If only Ella were here, she'd tell me straight. It's not that I haven't noticed every single time – because I absolutely have – it's just I never quite put it in a nice, neat, gift-wrapped box like he has done here.

The thing is, I went through this ages ago, when I fancied the pants off him but couldn't even stand to be near him. Since he's being kind as well as making my knees go weak, it's getting worse by the second. And when my heart aches for his pain, it's practically unbearable. But the more I like him, the more the reason I have to fight those feelings. Yet, working together so closely, it's hard to keep the distance I need.

I'm turning this back to him. 'So you're a tough guy with a soft centre?'

When he stares down at me it's as if he's looking straight

into my soul. 'Everyone hopes to fall in love one day – don't they?'

I give a cough. 'I couldn't cope with losing someone I cared about all over again. It's better for me never to go there at all.'

'Don't say that!' He's down the ladder, gently stepping over Minty, and across the room in two strides. He slides a finger under my chin, tilts my face to look into his. 'You can't be on your own forever. It's such a waste.'

I'm swallowing down the lump in my throat. 'There's no other option.'

'Come here.' As my face squeezes against his chest, his arms close around me. 'My snow goose, we have to make you better. Of everyone I know, you most deserve to be happy.'

I'm torn. Desperate to soak up the sweet heat, to feel the strength of his body pressing against mine. To never let go. But at the same time, I'm fighting. Desperately wanting *not* to start to like it so much I can't do without it.

'Don't give up, Gwen. Look at me – for eighteen months I couldn't even come here, let alone imagine I'd want to stay. Now I'm all about the lanterns and the word art.'

I sigh. 'I always told you the right interior changes everything for the better.'

He sighs too. 'Or it *could* be the interior designer?'

I didn't hear that. I smile down at Minty, pecking at my Converse. 'For my money, the white dove is the big pull.'

Ollie narrows one eye. 'And talking of local wildlife, what kind of hug are we having here. Hedgehog? Human?'

I pull a face. 'Zero-alcohol? Or sugar-free?' It *has* to be comfort-only.

'Other options are also available.' He stares down at me. 'We don't *have* to be fun-deprived *all the time*. Just saying.'

'I'm glad we sorted that out. Hedgehogs may not agree.'

Seeing his Adam's apple bobbing in his throat as he swallows now, I want to kiss him again so badly. But I can't.

He gives a grimace. 'I still haven't come clean about my ulterior motives.'

I put my finger to his lips. 'Save that for when the cottage is done.'

We won't have long to wait. Sixteen hours from now the painting crew will be arriving. All I have to do now is work out how to let go of Ollie.

He gives a sniff. 'One other thing – about the lighting up stuff…'

I'm on this. 'Bedside, free-standing angle-poise or under-unit?'

There are those crinkles at the corners of his eyes, as he smiles down at me again. 'I mean the bit where the whole room lights up – it's just that it happens for me when you walk in.'

'*What?*' Surely he can't be serious? I'm so close that when I look up, I can see every prickle of stubble on his chin.

He pulls down the corners of his mouth. 'Every time since the first time I saw you.'

'The day I stripped off?'

He smiles again. 'Long before I saw your bra. There was just this thunderbolt, and I knew.'

'Shit.' *Oh my, oh my, oh my!* I *can't* admit it was the same for me.

'If you don't feel it, that's fine.' He pauses, staring down at me through those long sooty lashes. 'If you do, it would be a shame to ignore it.'

'Right.' I can't even *start* to handle this.

'Let me know.'

'Lovely, I'll get back to you on that.' I *totally* won't. 'In the meantime, I *really* do need to go.' For the last time ever, I lean into his body and I let myself run my hand through his hair. Twirl a curl around my finger. Trail my palm across his face hoping to commit the feel of his skin stretched across his cheekbones to my memory. 'There's a load of homemade ice cream round at yours that needs a second beating.'

I let my hand fall and I step back. A moment later I'm out on the landing and clattering down the stairs.

34

Stargazey Cottage
Cliff hangers and straight talking
Late Saturday evening

'Our last night on the bean bags.'

As Ella goes through to the kitchen, I kick off my Converse, flop down in our newly gorgeous living room, stare around at the amazing plaster-pink walls, and soak it all in.

Twenty people in a tiny cottage – all running around with paint rollers – could have gone horribly wrong, but today's paint party helpers were our dedicated repeat-bookers, and somehow it all went okay. After supper and a final 'thank you' of gingerbread Martinis next door, Ella and I waved them all off to Christmas karaoke at the Hungry Shark, and now we're home again, taking it in. It already feels so cosy, I want to stay here forever and not even go to bed.

For anyone on the edge of their seats wanting to know how things went with Ollie after yesterday's clinch, I barely caught more than a glimpse of him all day. Then he sent a message with Jago to say he'd been called away which was a very 'Ollie' way of sidestepping any awkwardness. So that was the end of that. If it left me feeling flatter than a pancake that's been under a steam roller, I definitely won't be letting on.

As I hear the fridge door closing, I call to Ella, 'Do you need a hand through there?'

'No, I can manage.' When she comes through, she's hugging bottles to her chest and she's carrying glasses, and a punnet of raspberries.

I'm blinking. 'What's all this?'

She swishes back her plait and nods. 'Fever Tree tonic. And Cockle Shell Castle Star Shower gin with a hint of fruit.'

I'm blinking. 'The pink and silver stars on the label are a perfect match for the walls!'

She shakes her head. 'I took a paint sample along, because I couldn't risk a clash after all the effort you've put in. I really do appreciate what you've done here, Gwen, it's amazing.' Her face breaks into a grin as she unscrews the top. 'When we started the cottage, I knew I'd be busy, but I never imagined I'd be at work more than I was here. This is a little thank you, for pulling everything together.'

'Awww, that's nice.'

She puts the glasses onto the upturned wine box we're still using as a table, tosses a handful of raspberries in and stares at the bottle. 'How much of this do we need?'

I think I may be about to witness Ella mixing her first drink. 'Slosh in a couple of inches and then top up with the mixer.'

'That's all?' She frowns. 'So what's missing?'

I jump up. 'It's the ice. As you've bought the gin, I'll get that.' I tip the cubes into a bowl from the plastic bag in the freezer, come back and put it down in front of her. 'Two or three in each will do.'

As she drops the cubes into the glasses, she looks up ruefully. 'Taylor and I always had ice makers. Doesn't it feel like a lifetime ago now?'

'It really does.' I edge forward on my beanbag, take my G&T, and chink my glass against hers. 'Cheers!'

Ella grins. 'To an almost-finished cottage.'

I was just about to say the same, except I think I might have used the word 'home' instead of 'cottage'. But that's just me.

I lean back, sipping and listening to the sound of the fizz, but she's still sitting up straight, looking at me. 'I know why you're quiet. Ollie's told you, hasn't he? About liking you?'

My lurch is so big, I lose an ice cube and a raspberry.

Ella watches as I scoop them off my knee. 'I know from Jago. It's why Ollie skipped dinner.' Her voice is soft. 'It's only what we knew already. We all saw that kiss, don't forget.'

'That was totally fake.'

Behind her glass her lips twist into a smile. 'It might have been unscripted, but it was a thousand-volt snog.' Her eyebrows edge upwards. 'So how do you feel – honestly?'

This is Ells. There's no point trying to hide it. 'As if my stomach is a washing machine. Like I'm going to throw up.' I give a grimace. 'Every time I've seen him, ever since we got here, even when I *hated* him. What *the hell* is that about?'

Her smile softens, and she reaches out and squeezes my wrist. 'That's what it feels like when you're in love, Gwen.'

Oh frig. I slump down on my bean bag. 'You *are* joking me?'

She's shaking her head, but her eyes are shining as she pulls me into a hug. 'When it happens, you can't fight it.'

I turn on her. 'You just watch me! I can't deal with a relationship! Not now, not ever!'

She's eased back onto her seat. 'Not every love lasts a lifetime. Some burns so intensely it's over really fast.'

'So what are you saying?'

She purses her lips, swirls her ice round her glass. 'Feel lucky that love has found you at all. Give it a try!'

'Keep going. I know nothing about it, remember.'

'That didn't hold you back any with the cottage.' She gives me a nudge. 'Don't over-think it, Gwen, it's only like that moving-on sex you're always advocating for me. If ever the chance comes your way, just seize the moment and enjoy yourself. Worry about the rest later.'

This doesn't sound like anything I'd ever be able to do, but whatever. I tuck that thought away in my brain, and smile. 'Thanks for sorting that one out for me.'

Her brow furrows. 'You know to use a condom?'

I put my hands over my ears. 'Yes!'

Her eyebrows wiggle and she grins. 'I have some flavoured ones left over from a hen party, I'll pop them in your bag. You don't want to get caught without.'

I give a snort. 'Shouldn't you save them for Jago when he finally surrenders and lets you into his bed?'

She freezes with her glass halfway to her mouth, her eyes wide.

'What? Don't tell me he's given in already? I knew it! How did you manage that?'

She closes her eyes for a moment, then she takes a deep breath. 'It's nothing like that at all. It's much more of a surprise. One of those things that come right out of the blue and knocks you sideways. A complete shock. Earlier today.'

I have no idea what she's talking about. 'You're going to have to be clearer than that.'

Her nose wrinkles. 'I wanted you to be the first to know.'

She blows out a breath. 'Taylor rang me and asked me to take him back. He wants us to try again.'

It's a few seconds before I can even get any words out. 'So what happened to Head of Sport?'

She looks at the ceiling. 'It can't have been easy, Taylor moving in with her three kids. He wasn't always good at sharing the attention.' She allows herself a grimace. 'Anyway, that's all over now, and he says it was all just a terrible mistake.'

'So has this come out of nowhere?'

She rolls her eyes. 'He sent me that random text a couple of weeks ago, remember? I let him know he'd sent it to the wrong person, and he texted back to ask how Merry was. But I had no clue this was coming.'

'And what are you thinking?'

She blows out her cheeks. 'For so long I was desperate to have him back so we could carry on with the life we'd planned. If he'd done this four months ago, I wouldn't have hesitated.'

'And now?'

'Being here with you has made me see I wasn't always fair to Taylor. We'd be setting off from a better place this time, but maybe I've changed too much – I'm not the same person he left.'

'You're still the same people. You won't ever know if you don't give it a go.' Of all the days, just when the cottage is almost finished too. 'Is this why you didn't let me buy the bed?'

Her face falls. 'I hesitated on that because Jago likes his extra long.' She reads my mind. 'I haven't seen his in the flesh. He told me.' She lets a sigh go. 'It's all very complicated.'

My mind is buzzing. 'So where would you and Taylor live?'

Ella rolls her eyes. 'I haven't got that far.' Her head tilts. 'Definitely not London, so it would have to be Cornwall. A rental until we found somewhere to buy. St Aidan was always a favourite of ours. George could put in a good word for us at Hanson and Hanson.'

So much for not having thought about it; she's got it worked out, even as far as bribing the agents.

She and Taylor have so much shared history, but it's more than that. If she picked up where she left off, they'd be pooling their incomes; she'd be back to her ice-maker lifestyle within the week. And if you're Ella, that counts for a lot.

I'm looking round the room, knowing what I've probably known all along. That however it happens, Ella's future is somewhere else. Even with the minute rent here, there's no way I could afford to stay here and pay the bills on my own. So I probably felt completely secure in my lovely home for about three minutes before the dream was shattered. But I can't claim it's a complete shock; my gut was already warning me she'd be moving on. Taylor riding back into town to claim Ella makes it even more of a certainty. She might be pretending to waver, but we both know she loves the certainty that life with Taylor offers. She could have that set of monogrammed towels. They could get married all over again. She could settle straight down and have kids. In nine months' time they could be a family. That wouldn't happen with anyone else.

Ella swigs back her drink. 'I've got a lot of thinking to do. Don't worry, let's enjoy Christmas first and sweat the details later.'

'Enjoy Christmas – isn't that an oxymoron?'

Ella's staring at me. 'Bloody hell, Gwen, when did you start talking like Ollie?'

There's nowhere to hide on that one. For one time only

she's got me, and I can't wriggle, so I pick up the gin bottle. 'Shall I pour you another G&T?'

She nods. 'The day I've had, make that a double.'

And for all the wrong reasons I know exactly where she's coming from with that.

35

The Little Cornish Kitchen breakfast club
Stepping up
Tuesday afternoon

O n Sunday morning, when I wake to the sound of Ollie starting the last coat of the paint on the skirtings and doors out on the landing, it's so early the sky is still starry. As Barnaby and Browne's delivery is arriving later, for approximately five seconds I think about staying in bed until he's gone; and then I think again and get up and get on with the day. With me having to step over him every time I go to the bathroom we somehow move past the awkwardness of Friday and settle for brief mumbles about drying times instead. By the time he, Ella and I have had coffee and bakery-muffin bacon sandwiches I make at his, we're warming to the job and putting our personal problem to one side.

It's all thanks to Ollie's dawn start that by afternoon the paintwork is dry enough for us all to unload the furniture into the cottage. Then we put the beds together and my lovely metal one is beyond amazing. We roll out rugs and bring out the new duvet covers we've been saving. Mine is cornflower blue with tiny green stars, finished off with a green wool throw. With sofas to snuggle on, cushions to arrange, pillows to plump, fresh flowers to put in vases, and even a bedside table to rest my phone on, the cloud I'm floating on is so light and airy, I'm not going to allow anything to spoil it. Rather than thinking about Ella leaving, for today I'm just shutting it out. But deep down, I know – she's been desperate to forgive Taylor and take him back ever since he left. Looking back, she's just been biding her time here, waiting for him to decide he wants that too.

On a cheerier note, along with the delivery from the Barn Yard, the surprise cushions I've ordered for next door arrive too, in colours that pick out the highlights in the posters of St Aidan. (That's my excuse for my rainbow breakout and I'm sticking to it.) Once the cottage is straight, which, due to the size, doesn't take long, I rush off to buy bunches of flowers in purples and orange and yellow and pink to go with the cushions, and head to Ollie's. I arrange a scattering of bright cushions along the sofas in between the dark-blue ones, throw some in the easy chairs too, add vases of flowers on the downstairs coffee tables, and along the dining table upstairs. At a stroke it changes the place from grown up, yet reserved, to fun, popping and zingy. Between us, if Ollie can't be happy here, he's not going to be happy anywhere.

And cut to Tuesday...

This morning I've done the breakfast club while Clemmie's been prepping for an afternoon tea-dance wedding later today, and Charlie's been looking after Bud upstairs because she's been a bit grizzly. Nell's out on an audit, Sophie's got a board meeting, and Plum's at an Arts Council Christmas bash down in St Ives, but as this afternoon is only for thirty, with fizz and no tea, Clemmie and I have decided we'll be fine to do it on our own.

Clemmie's literally wrapping the last ham and cheese brioche sandwiches, the boxes of crockery and food are ready to load, we're changed into our flowery serving dresses, and our ballet flats are tucked into our bags. We're on the point of walking out of the door when Charlie rings down from upstairs. As Clemmie listens to what he's saying her smile freezes.

As she ends the call and looks at me her cheeks are white. 'Charlie's just spoken to the GP, they've said to take Bud to A&E.' Her face crumples. 'I knew we'd been maxing out the Calpol, but now she's got a rash too.'

I jump forward and look at the stacks of boxes. 'You go, leave this to me.'

'But it's a wedding…'

Clemmie needs to be with Bud, it's not as if there's a choice. 'I've done weddings before, and Poppy from the venue will keep me right.'

Clemmie lets out a whimper. 'I can't believe all the girls are out of town on the same day. Who's going to help you?'

There's an obvious person to call. However much I'd rather not see him, I already know he'll drop everything and run. 'Ollie won't mind.' I squeeze her hand, then push her towards the door. 'Give Bud a hug from me.'

Ollie picks up on the second ring. Five minutes later he's down with the keys to his Volvo and plenty of muscle in tow. Thanks to Jago having a job two doors along from Hardware Haven we move the whole afternoon tea from Seaspray Cottage to the harbour car park in one lift. A few minutes later, Ollie and I are bowling along the coast road and out towards Rose Hill, leaning back in the luxurious leather upholstery.

Ollie's tapping his fingers on the steering wheel. 'We could be in for some weather later, but Jago's all set to drop in on Minty if we don't make it back.'

Sometimes he's so over-dramatic. 'We're serving afternoon teas, not chasing storms.'

He gives me a sideways glance. 'Pure habit, I've always got one eye on the sky – I'm pretty sure this could be snow, but at least we have heated seats.'

I go rigid, then relax as I remember. 'Ha, you nearly had me there! Cornwall's a snow-free zone because of the gulf stream.'

Ollie's voice is high in disbelief. 'Who told you that?'

I'm blinking. 'Ella. At least I *think* that's what she said.'

Ollie's voice is tentative, but his fingers are tapping faster. 'So would snow be a problem?'

'Hell yes! Snow is…' I'm trying to describe the imploding sensation I have in my head when I imagine a white-out. 'For me snow would be an end-of-the-world situation.' It feels important to make him understand the enormity. 'Like Christmas, but ten million times worse.'

Ollie's eyebrows shoot upwards. 'In that case let's cross our fingers for warm air not icy blasts.' He sounds more upbeat. 'The weather office aren't always right. And Pirate Radio and Janice in Hardware Haven have both been known to exaggerate too. Forget I mentioned it.'

I've pretty much lost the thread of where this started. 'Who'd want a December wedding if it meant getting blown away?'

Now we've turned inland, he's easing the car round the bends on the narrow roads between the high hedges. 'Friends tell me the rates are better this time of year. And if you don't expect a sunny day, you won't be disappointed.'

There he goes again. This man is an expert in so many unexpected areas. His white shirt and dark suit are a perfect choice too, although seeing him in them is making my stomach disintegrate all over again with each sideways glance I risk. But it's just like the shivers from the fish on the Stargazey doorstep; the more I can't bear to look, the more I have to.

Now we're safely on our way, I'm feeling a flood of gratitude too. 'Thank you for coming, Ollie.'

'I couldn't have done anything else.' He turns and grins. 'You had *all* the builder princes fighting to come to your rescue there too. When they heard a Star Sister needed help, they wouldn't stay on the site.'

I'm not taking it for granted. 'It's great to know people have your back.' I've widened it out there; it's actually a huge comfort to know *he* cares enough to be there for *me*.

He laughs. 'You're never on your own in St Aidan. I used to hate that, but I'm more used to it now. Same as your orange and pink cushions – they're growing on me too.'

I smile back. 'They're meant to fill your world with sunshine and make you happy every day.' I need to say it. 'That's not ironic either, it's real.'

His smile widens. 'I'd say you pretty much got that right. Any other minor personal disappointments, I'm working through.'

I've got a feeling he's about to expand on that, but luckily he breaks off as I lean forward to direct him. 'Straight through the village, bear right, and then it's half a mile on the left.'

He raises his eyebrows as we trundle towards the entrance. 'With a sign saying "Daisy Hill Farm Wedding Venue"? That could be the giveaway.'

As we draw into the cobbled courtyard and pull up outside the elegant stone farmhouse I take in a huge eucalyptus wreath on the grey front door, and bay trees lit by fairy lights, and blow out a breath. 'First task completed. We got here.' I'm so wobbly I'm blurting. 'I couldn't be any more nervous if I was here to get married myself.' Not that I'd ever do that, so I'm talking even worse bollocks than Ella, which is another sign of my panic levels.

Ollie laughs. 'I've seen a few grooms-to-be in pieces in my time.' Then he leans over and squeezes my hand. 'Don't worry. We've got this, Gwen.'

As I get out of the car, the gale lashes my puffer jacket and the sky above is black. 'Clouds like that, they'll get some very dramatic wedding photos.' Hearing Nell and Clemmie's chatter has definitely rubbed off; I'm talking like a proper wedding veteran.

Ollie comes round and opens the boot. 'Let's get this lot inside before the squalls start.'

Then the house door opens and Poppy comes hurrying along the stone flagged path, her red dress flapping in the wind, and a big smile on her face. 'Come on in, Gwen. Clemmie rang and explained you're on your own. I'll show you where to set up.'

Once we've unloaded and Ollie's moved the car further up the yard to make way for the bridal party, the next few hours are a blur of pretty china plates and linen napkins, home-made mini sausage rolls and slices of Victoria sponge. The ceremony is in an orangery, but for the afternoon tea and dance the guests are going to be seated at tables in a room with a grand piano and a huge fireplace with a log fire. The sparkling chandeliers overhead fill the room with a yellow glow, and the light muslin curtains at the line of French windows shut out the gloom of the fading afternoon in the walled garden outside.

Between the table laying and putting out the food I'm hanging onto my phone in case there's news of Bud, but there isn't. Luckily, I've taken photos of the cake stands at the other weddings, so I have those as a guide. Ollie and I both have time to sigh at the wedding cake Poppy has made, with minia-ture bunting draped around every tier to match the jugs of country garden flowers.

Once the guests sit down and start to eat, I'm so busy making sure I don't spill as we pour champagne, there's barely time to notice the bride's satin tea dress with the swirliest skirt and long chiffon sleeves, or her hair caught into the prettiest messy braided up do, with pearls on the hairpins.

And then we're back to the kitchen, then doing another round of champagne refills, then we wait again until the speeches are over. As we go to start the clearing Clemmie messages to say they're all home and Bud's okay. I'm so busy doing silent cheers that when I see Ollie talking to Poppy in the hallway all I catch are the words 'made in Sweden, winter tyres' so I assume she's asking about his four-by-four. I'm focusing so hard on making sure the plates get into the right boxes and that no containers get forgotten, that when there's a whoop from a guest loud enough to reach the kitchen, I barely notice. When twenty people stampede down the hallway I'm looking for Ollie to tell him we're ready to load up. Then, as he reappears in the kitchen, the cries echo in from outside.

'Snow! It's snowing!'

I freeze and stare at him. Then I remember Clemmie and Nell's wedding stories and I relax. White doves are just the start. Every wedding now has to have some surprise to make it unique, and there's nothing more fitting for a white wedding in winter. 'They're talking about a snow machine, aren't they?' Even the ones in the mountains aren't that good. Unless you run banks of them for days, the most you get is a flurry of flakes. That's completely survivable.

Then I look at Ollie's face again. 'It isn't a machine, is it?'

Ollie pulls a face. 'I'm afraid not.'

As my chest constricts at the thought, my voice is a whisper. 'How bad is it?'

His hand closes around mine. 'First of all, I'm on this. I'm going to make things work for you. Can you trust me on that?'

'Mmmm.' For some reason I'm nodding.

His voice is very level. 'I'd hoped we could make it home, but the roads to the coast are already impassable. Everyone from the wedding is staying in the farm cottages, and Poppy has a small one spare that we can use tonight. The snowploughs will be out overnight so by morning the roads should be open again.'

'Right.'

He runs his fingers through his hair. 'It's a fully stocked cottage, there's Netflix, Wi-Fi, and a wood-burning stove. We'll put on back-to-back episodes of *Friends* and the time will soon pass.' He's holding my hand really tight now. 'If you close your eyes, I'll lead you up to the cottage so you don't have to look at what's on the ground.'

'How much is there?' It'll help if I know.

He hesitates. 'It's very white. A lot fell very fast.'

'Thank you, Ollie.'

He looks at the ceiling. 'I'm sorry I can't do better; it turns out Swedish traction control only takes you so far.' Then he leads me back into the kitchen. 'We'll load this lot tomorrow. While you tidy up in here, I'll go and put the fire on in the cottage.'

I close my eyes, release his hand, and let the relief ebb through me. As my numbed mind starts to come back to life again, I have a huge impulse to throw my arms around him. But when I blink again, he's already across the kitchen on his way out to the hall.

36

Cuckoo Cottage, Daisy Hill Farm
The biggest blizzards start with a single snowflake
Tuesday evening

Cheese and tomato toasties by a roaring fire, with a bottle of shiraz. Whitewashed walls, waxed floorboards, grey plaid sofas, soft wool throws. Air warmed with the scent of vanilla and cinnamon, and I'm not even halfway there to listing the home comforts.

By the time we got to walking up the yard, it had stopped snowing and the men from the farm had been down with shovels to clear a path for the guests between the farmhouse and the holiday lets, so we made it all the way to the grey plank front door without getting so much as an ice crystal on our boots. And Poppy's single-storey cottage in the converted stable block couldn't be any more lovely or welcoming.

We've eaten, and watched four episodes of *Episodes*, because in the end we decided that was less likely to have any accidental reminders to trip us up than *Friends*. When you're as tentative as we are with our recovery, you don't want to get ahead of yourselves by being rash. As I sit on the rug after supper watching the flames licking over the logs, the tension in my shoulders and the pent-up feeling in my chest are starting to ease.

I look at the little pine tree on the table, its gold and silver baubles shimmering in the firelight. 'All that effort I put in avoiding Christmas trees, and then I get hit by a snow bomb.'

Ollie stretches out his legs. 'They're rare in Cornwall.'

I take a breath and know I have to tell him. 'I only mind the snow because of what happened to my mum and Ned.' I pause and pluck up the courage to say it out loud. 'They were buried in freak avalanches in the Alps, thirty years apart, and both times they were trying to rescue other climbers when it happened. They were both so careful with their own climbing, but when someone else's life was at stake, the risk didn't matter; they went right ahead and broke all the rules about never putting themselves in danger.'

Ollie lets out a whistle. 'I'm so sorry, Gwen, I had no idea it was so awful.'

I sigh. 'Everyone knew Ned had the same brilliance as my mum on the rock faces and the ice, but we never dreamed we'd lose him in exactly the same way as her.'

Ollie's expression is pained. 'It must be very hard to live with.'

'It is. And it's not always nice.' It comes out in a rush. 'Sometimes it makes me feel really, really angry. Not with my mum, because I was so young when she died, that's just a blur, but at times I'm so cross with Ned for not taking care. For leaving me when I needed him so much. For making Dad go through the same thing twice.

'Those first minutes knowing he was missing. Waiting. At

first believing he had to come back. Then as the hours stretched to a day, refusing to give up on him. And then when they finally came to tell us they had found his body, having to take that information in. It took a long time to believe that he was actually gone.'

Ollie's stretching out his hands, looking at his fingers. 'Feeling angry is part of how we deal with tragic events.'

My fists are clenched. 'But it makes me feel so selfish. Then I'm angry with myself too.' I sigh. 'Of everyone in the world, Ned was the person I was closest to. He may have always been scaling some ridge or hanging off some overhang, but even at a distance, he always understood me and looked after me.

'It crept up on me without realising. As we got older, me watching over him took over my life, a bit like an obsession. I made myself believe so long as I was there, he'd be okay, that if I stayed close to him my presence would protect him. I didn't dare to go anywhere else.

'The more fearless Ned became, the more stressful the waiting was. All those years of worry, and in the end my worst fears happened anyway.'

Ollie swallows. 'You must miss him so much.'

'When I've centred my life around him for so long, I just feel so alone.' It's stark, but it's the truth. 'It's like I physically chopped off a part of myself because when I lost Ned a huge piece of me disappeared with him and I hate how weak and useless that makes me feel.' I open the door of the wood burning stove, and throw on another piece of wood. 'After so long I'd pretty much accepted that was how I would be forever. That's why I've liked being in St Aidan and doing the cottage. I'll never be the person I was, but making something new, surrounded by friends to help, has made me stronger again.' I watch as the flames ignite around the branch. 'It's surprising how much it helps to hear myself say that out loud.'

Ollie's staring at his wine glass. 'Talking is like making flapjacks. It's hard to understand why, but you feel better afterwards.' He's staring down at me and rubbing his thumb across his chin. As he takes a sip of his wine his throat moves above the collar of his shirt. 'There's the old saying: "you can run but you can't hide".'

I ignore the flutter under my sternum from watching his neck, pick up another log and throw it onto the flames. 'However hard you try to dodge what you fear the most, you have to face it in the end.'

Ollie nods. 'For so long I tried to distance myself from Stargazey House.' The corners of his lips twitch. 'Since you showed me a new way to think about it, it isn't dragging me down any more.'

'It was nothing, but you're welcome.'

In one fluid moment he's up on his feet. He crosses the room in three strides, parts the long curtains, and stares out of the French windows. 'Maybe you'd rather not know, but it's very beautiful out here.'

I sniff. 'Tell me what you can see.'

'There's a blanket of whiteness all the way up over the hills. The moon's nearly full and it's shining on the fields so brightly it's like daylight.' He stops and looks around at me.

'Go on.'

'The walls and hedges are black and the snow's sticking to them in clumps. I can see the bump of every stone, the shape of every field, the outline of an old barn up on the horizon. And it all looks so still.' He holds out his hand. 'It would be a shame to miss out?'

I catch hold of his fingers and he eases me to my feet. Then he pulls me in front of him and wraps his arms around me as we both stare out into the night.

His voice is low. 'There are stars, too. How often do you see starlight on snow?'

I'm quivering and my face is wet with tears, but I'm looking and seeing it too. 'It's nothing like the mountains. It's completely different. You're right, it's very special.' I let out a sigh. 'If you hadn't persuaded me, I'd never have seen it.'

His arms are holding me tighter. 'No one can ever take Ned's place, Gwen, but we're all here to look out for you and to help you.'

There's a lump in my throat as I remember; it's everything from Ella's talking at the fudge afternoon to Ollie dropping everything to be here. 'I know.'

I'm standing there, taking in the white expanse stretching all the way up the slope to meet the sky. This fear of snow that has defined me and limited my existence for four whole years as I tried to avoid it. But now it's a different time, a different place, and the snow isn't the same at all. Nothing's going to make Ned come back, but maybe I'm getting better at accepting that. This is my life as it is, and I'm learning to live it again. And with Ollie's arms around me, it's a warm place to be, not a cold one. And for this one fragile, fleeting moment in time I couldn't feel any more cared for.

I twist around to face Ollie. 'I promised Ella I'd try to grab every moment.' It wasn't quite that, but I'm running with this. As I slide my palm up onto his face the warmth of his skin comes through the roughness of his stubble. The folds of his jeans and his belt rub through the thin fabric of my flowery dress, and my heart is jolting. 'I may need to seize *you*. Just to check the last time wasn't a fluke.' *Just to satisfy this aching need inside me.*

Ollie raises an eyebrow. 'That's fine by me.'

My hands are closing on the back of his head, my fingers tangling in his hair as I swallow and lay down the ground rules. 'It might be for one more time only.'

His smile widens. 'I'll work with whatever makes you comfortable. Can I kiss you, now?'

'Yep.' I take a deep breath, part my lips and move in for what I've been longing for ever since the kiss at the work party.

As my mouth hits his, the taste is like dark chocolate and salted caramel, raspberry and hot coffee, all rolled into one heat-filled explosion. It's like every nerve in my body has been sleeping for a hundred years and has woken up jangling. As for stars, my head is spinning so hard, even though my eyes are tightly closed, I'm seeing those too. As our lips finally part, I'm fighting to get my breath back.

Ollie's looking down at me, slowly pushing a strand of hair out of my eyes. 'So was it a fluke, or have those fireworks happened again?'

I have to be honest. 'That was better than rockets exploding over St Aidan.'

'Same here.' He's biting back his smile. 'It's starting to snow again. I don't suppose you'd like to try that once more outside? Then afterwards I can kiss the snowflakes off your nose and make you happy again?'

I can't help laughing. 'Do you think that will help?'

He's nodding. 'I think it might.'

Which is how, after a quick scramble into our boots and coats, we're stepping out of the French windows into the snow-covered garden, clinging together, and staring up at gently floating snowflakes that look a lot like stars falling from the inky sky.

As Ollie pulls the hood of my puffer jacket around my face, his cheekbones are etched by the moon shadows. 'How about if I promise to kiss away every snowflake that ever falls on you?'

As he comes down to kiss me, I kiss him back, laughing. 'But first I'm going to take you back inside and seize you all over again.' I send a fleeting thank you through the airwaves to Ella. 'I *may* have strawberry condoms.'

His voice is very low. 'You don't say…'

I laugh again. 'There *might even* be scorching sex…'

'Better and better.' He laughs too. 'You have to love a princess who knows her own mind *and* comes prepared. But only if you're sure?'

I drag in a breath and fill my lungs. 'We have to start living again.'

His arms close even more tightly around me. 'A very brave decision, and I agree.'

As my hands find his and I squeeze his fingers, I'm trembling with anticipation. 'It doesn't need to be scary. We'll take it minute by minute. Hour by hour. One night at a time.'

His face is buried deep in my hair, and his words are muffled. 'Let's just try it and see how it goes.'

And as I lead him back inside, I can't remember when I was ever this sure about anything.

37

Stargazey Cottage, up at the garden shed
Big days and mackerel skies
Wednesday

We've had approximately twenty minutes of sleep when we wake up the next morning, and Ollie makes bacon sandwiches and coffee before we head back to St Aidan.

In the past, when people talked about mind-blowing sex, I never really knew what they meant – but now I do. And weirdly, rather than four times being enough to last me for the next decade, I feel like waiting until lunchtime for more would be too long.

The snow has all gone as fast as it came and by the time we're whizzing down the lanes on our way back to town the drifts that blocked every route last night have melted to streaks along the bottom of the hedges. And if we're talking about how important it is to grab opportunities – had the wedding had today's weather instead of yesterday's, we'd have been back home in St Aidan by late afternoon and last night would never have happened. That's how lucky I feel with this. And a big thank you to Ella for giving me the wake-up call that made me dare to go for it.

As we crawl back into the harbourside car park, I'm aching for Ollie to drive as slowly as he can to make it last. By the time we get out of the car and the freezing breeze whips off the navy-blue sea and straight through my coat, apart from Ollie and me having circles under our eyes dark enough to belong to zombies, it's already as if last night never happened. As we unload the boxes and take them along the beach and back to the Little Cornish Kitchen we find Bud is upstairs, taking it easy with Charlie, and Clemmie's doing a breakfast club that's slightly depleted after the white-out of the night before.

Obviously after all the excitement I have the kind of calorie deficit Ella would kill for, so I wolf down four gingerbread people without them touching the sides. I hoover up most of the leftover sausage rolls, three iced cupcakes and a box of fudge and then I start to feel more like myself again.

We'd set this afternoon aside to put up decorations at Ollie's, and at midday Jago messages to say he and the guys are ready to give us a hand with that. As they've almost finished putting the glass in the big kitchen window at the cottage, they want to have a reveal for that too. Obviously, we couldn't have a moment that momentous without Ella, so she's juggled her site visits and is calling in later.

Since we're surrounded by so many people, public displays of affection are right off the table for Ollie and me now we're back in the village again. As we fix miles of star strings across Ollie's reception and dining areas, and twirl lengths of star lights around two-metre-high twig bunches in tall zinc florist's buckets, I'm back to admiring him from a distance.

Sneaking a peek at Ollie's thighs straining against the

denim of his jeans, and going dizzy thinking about how it was being naked and completely entangled with them, is too much even for me so I escape upstairs, taking star strings to fix above the beds and copper tubing stars to hang on the en suite and the bedroom door handles. By the time I've hung a larger version on the front door, the guys have come back in from stringing lights around the terrace edge, and they're all waiting in a group in the dining area. As Ollie looks up at the paper stars gently swinging on the strings criss-crossing through the air above our heads, I can't help thinking about the stars last night.

He rubs his hands together. 'Another great job here, guys. Thanks for hanging up Christmas so quickly, looking forward to seeing some of you on Christmas Day for lunch.'

Jago sidles up to me. 'Nice work with Mr Lancaster too, Gwen.'

My jaw drops open, and my mouth is so dry I can only manage a rasp. '*What?*'

Jago wiggles his eyebrows. 'You've certainly put him back on the right track.'

Ollie catches my eye. 'In case you're having a heart attack over there, Gwen, this is *old news* from last weekend rather than anything more current. I'll tell you about it later.'

I'm staggering back against the wall. 'Lovely, pleased to hear that, Jago.' I glance at my phone, wanting to push things on as fast as I can. 'Are we ready to move next door for the reveal? Ella should be arriving soon, and she can't stay long.'

As if on cue, there's a tap on the front door, and Ella strides in. 'Thank you so much for waiting, I wouldn't have missed this for the world.' She holds up her fingers. 'I have ten minutes before I need to head to Falmouth.'

If there's no time to come clean about last night, that's one less dilemma for me; I'm not ready to share that yet, even with Ella.

Jago gives a scarf to Ollie and holds out another one to her. 'In that case, let's crack on. Ready for your blindfold, Ella Bella?'

I stand as Ollie comes in close and ties mine around my eyes. 'Everything okay, Snow White?'

'Fine.' That's fine, *apart* from my stomach doing so many somersaults, after all those cupcakes I may be about to throw up.

As Ella grasps my hand, Jago calls to the guys in front of us, 'Okay, lead the way.'

It's not far to go. Jago guides us through the two front doors, squares our shoulders up, then I feel a cushion arrive in my hands. 'Hold these in front of your eyes while we take the scarves off, then we'll tell you when you can both look.'

After what seems like weeks of the view from the kitchen being completely obscured by a tarpaulin with a temporary wooden door at the side, anything would be an improvement.

'One two three – *look!*'

As I drop the cushion, I'm completely unprepared for what I'm about to see. I'm standing by the sofas, looking through the recently made gap in the wall between the kitchen and the living room. The whole place is flooded with light, which makes the newly painted walls come to life even more. And the tall double doors that open from the kitchen to the terrace do exactly what I saw that day at Clemmie's little flat.

I let out a gasp. 'Look at that view! It feels as if the cottage is as big as St Aidan Bay.' I'm wiping away my tears, grabbing a tissue and blowing my nose. 'Who cries because their house is so beautiful?'

Ella's arm is around my neck. 'It couldn't be any better, Gwen.'

Jago laughs. 'Even as hardened builders, we're pretty chuffed with how this one's turned out, ladies.' He grasps our hands. 'Welcome to your very own little cottage by the sea.'

I'm so thrilled I could burst. 'It feels so much bigger than it used to. And so much lighter.'

Ella pulls me into a proper hug. 'Well done for holding out and following your heart. Just think, I'll be able to see all the way out to sea when I'm washing up!'

I squeeze her back. 'Look, there's a fishing boat coming in now, with seagulls trailing after it!' I let Ella go and throw my arms round Jago's neck. 'Thank you for all the work.' Then I throw my arms round Ollie's neck and try to make it casual. 'Between you, you've given us the best cottage in the world.'

And when I suddenly remember that I might not be able to stay here after all, I start crying all over again.

Someone's got a bottle, and there's a bang as a cork pops and hits the wall. 'Who's got the glasses?'

One of the other guys appears with a tray of plastic flutes and catches the frothing liquid.

Ella's laughing. 'Mind that ceiling with the next bottle, we don't want any dents.'

Jago passes us our glasses then waves his own. 'Here's wishing you many happy years in your lovely new home, Gwen and Ella.' He has no idea how poignant that is.

I wave my glass too and try to ignore that my heart feels like it's being ripped out of my chest at the thought of leaving. 'A home of our own! If I live here forever, it won't be too long.' I go round giving all the guys a teary hug and a kiss on the cheek, and Ella follows me. 'Thank you all so much!'

Jago raises an eyebrow. 'The Star Sisters will be in big demand when the village gets a look in here.'

Ella winks at me. 'It's no secret which one of us was the powerhouse behind this place! You've got a great eye, Gwen. With Jago and Ollie on board we could be looking at a dream team?'

It's best that I don't reply to that. As a beginner who lucked out, I know to quit while I'm ahead. I'm fanning my face to get rid of the heat and to try to dry the tears which won't seem to stop when Ella murmurs in my ear.

'How was your unscheduled stopover at the wedding venue?'

For now I'm avoiding specifics. 'Starry.'

'*That good?*' She raises an eyebrow. 'Ring me if you need a debrief.'

'Defo.'

Then she dashes off again, leaving the rest of us milling. We're all admiring how smart the deep green painted units look in the sunlight, how the green and pink chairs pop against the red fridge, when Jago gives Ollie a nudge and points up to the top of the garden. 'Hey, Minty's off again. She was up there yesterday.'

Ollie laughs. 'She's after Gwen's cake crumbs.'

I swallow hard and manage to laugh too so they don't guess I'm breaking inside. 'Double chocolate muffins are her favourite.'

Jago grins. 'She's never going to take off at this rate, her wings won't be big enough to hold her.'

Ollie laughs. 'I keep telling you, Minty's not going anywhere, she's too happy here.' He turns to me. 'Shall we go and see what she's up to?'

'Why not?' The blood's rushing to my cheeks like a tidal

wave as we dive through the doors and out onto the cracked concrete.

Ollie takes the steps two at a time, so I'm running to keep up. By the time we reach Minty in front of the shed, my lungs are bursting and I'm aware someone could glimpse us from the windows, so I'm keeping a space between us.

Ollie squats down and tickles Minty's head. 'How are you doing, Araminta?'

I push open the shed door, and she hops inside. 'No cake today, but you can both tell me what colours you think for the little hideaway in the sky.'

Now the cottage is done, I want to carry on up here to stave off the worry about Ella. In my heart I know – it's not going to be *if* she goes to be with Taylor, it's just a matter of when. It's breaking my heart that the best I can hope for is a few more weeks at the cottage. When we signed that first lease with a get-out clause after six months, I had no real thought that Ella would use it. But at least I've been lucky enough to be here at all. Not everyone has lived anywhere they've loved as much as I love this place.

Ollie peers in. 'So what are you thinking?' He flips through the squares of coloured paper I've painted with samples that are fanned out across the floor. 'I like this blue. And the deep green.'

'My project for the new year – I'm determined to learn to paint.' Whatever else happens, there should be time to fit that in. Is it too much to hope Ollie might offer to give me a bit of tuition?

But he skips right over it. 'You must be wondering what Jago was talking about earlier?'

I go pink all over again. 'Which nice work are *you* talking about, Mr Lancaster?'

Ollie gives me a grin. 'You're not the only one to overcome your demons, Snow White. I've started sailing again.'

I'm blinking. 'You've *what?*'

He smiles. 'Three years off the water, and all thanks to you I'm back in a boat again.'

'Really?' It's a whimper.

'I took a single-hander out on Sunday. There were a few wobbles at first, but by Monday I was out putting a forty-footer through her paces.' He punches the air. 'That whole area of my life had closed down, and now I'm back in the game again. Isn't it fantastic? If that's the healing powers of St Aidan, bring them on!'

Somehow, I ignore that my stomach has dropped through the floor, and find something good to say. 'Fabulous! How brilliant is that?'

I have to be pleased for him, but it hasn't escaped me – the Ollie my heart went out to was the broken one. It's great for him if he's bouncing back, but he'll have no need for someone like me once he's back to his hard-shelled, confident self again.

I have to be honest with myself here. We've had one night together and however amazing that was I can't cope with waiting at home while Ollie goes off on races round the world risking his life. Even more crucial, I can't let my fears hold him back; it wouldn't be fair for me to constrain him.

And even as all this flashes through my head, I know this barely begun relationship of ours is over. As for Ollie reinventing himself as a sailing legend, I did *not* see that coming. *I'm sailing again…* For me that one short sentence means the end of whatever we had. However much I love him, I am out of here.

Love. From the crushing sensation in my chest when I think of never burying my face in his chest again, Ella might have been right about that part too.

I screw up every bit of my courage. 'Fabulous news from you, Ollie. Well done for that. And I have some of my own.'

He's still smiling. 'Yes?'

I'm biting my lip. 'Thanks for looking after me yesterday. I had a wonderful night ... but I have to leave it there.'

His face falls. 'Please don't say that.'

I'm pulling my coat around me like a tourniquet, biting back the tears as I push through the door. 'I'm sorry, I just can't do this...'

And then, as I slip out onto the ledge in front of the shed, I almost fall over Minty. She jumps away with a flutter, but she's so close to the edge. Just like I did all those weeks ago when I almost fell in the same place, the ground under her feet runs to nothing. She's flapping frantically and I'm watching for her to flutter to the ground further down the hillside. There's a moment when she hangs in the air almost motionless. And then her wings open wider. And she begins to flap harder.

I let out a cry. 'Ollie, it's Minty! Minty's flying!'

He arrives on the ledge in time to see her circle a first time. And then another. Then she accelerates, and we both watch open-mouthed and silent as she picks up speed and merges with the blue-grey above the horizon.

I sink back against the shed. 'Oh my. She's flown away!' I look across at Ollie. 'I'm so sorry. It's my fault for startling her.'

He's staring back, his face as white as Minty's feathers. 'She's only done what she was always meant to do.'

There's a gaping hole where my heart should be as we both stare upwards. 'Do you think she'll come back?'

Ollie's shading his eyes with his hand. 'Looking at that empty sky, she's probably miles away already.'

All I can do is to stare at the clouds and murmur. 'Fly safe, Minty, I hope you find your way home.'

Ollie clears his throat. 'I'll stay up here for a few minutes, if that's okay with you.'

I'm still breathless with the shock, but I take the hint because there's no point doing anything else. 'Totally. I was leaving anyway.'

I'm halfway down the first flight of steps when he calls.

'If you could stay off the area outside the kitchen? Just until Jago's laid the flags.'

'Fine.' With a whole house down below, it'll be good to have a few days to get used to being without Minty.

And I also know that Christmas is one of those times that crystallises feelings for couples. If Ella and Taylor get a sprinkling of festive fairy dust, by the time I get to see the shed again, my life may well be spinning off again in a whole new direction. And I can't express how much my heart aches when I start to think about that.

38

Stargazey Cottage
Duck down duvets and straight talking
Wednesday evening

'Just tell me what's going on.'

Ella's supposed to be at the works Christmas do at The Esplanade in Falmouth, which has five stars, and is tipped to go Michelin very soon, so I have no idea why she's phoning me when she should be at dinner.

'With the lights around the bay the French windows are as amazing tonight as they were this afternoon. Jago's moving straight onto the paving. And this evening's roller disco down at the harbour was explosive.' What else is there?

She huffs at the end of the phone. 'What the hell's happened – *with Ollie?*'

'Oh, *that*.' I let out a groan.

'You'll be asleep by the time I get in and I'm between courses so tell me in a sentence – but don't miss anything out.'

I snuggle further under the quilt. 'When Ollie and I were

stuck at the farm because of the snow, I seized the moment… And it was bloody amazing. Then today he told me he's sailing again, so I had to end it.'

'Gwen!'

I'm protesting at her shout. 'Someone driven and successful who does extreme sports? It's like Ned all over again. How can I cope with that?' I'm talking over her so I can get to the end. 'Then Minty flew away. And you were definitely right about the love thing. How the hell did *that* happen? That's all of it.'

'Minty's *gone?*' Even from across the county I can sense her disbelief and her horror.

I pull the covers further up under my chin and rub the bruises on my knees. 'It's been one of those days. You were well out of the roller skating too. I will *not* be suggesting that again next year, it was brutal.'

She gives a sigh. 'Don't worry, Gwen, I'll sort this out.'

'What are you going to do?' After all we've been through, I can't believe Ella still thinks she can fix things by throwing money at them. 'Even if you buy a new pigeon, she won't do the same tricks. And she definitely won't sit on Ollie's elbow and peck his nose.'

She sighs down the phone. 'Sleep tight, Little Gwen. I'll see you tomorrow and I promise I'll make this right.' And then she ends the call.

And I'm left in bed kicking the sheets. Kicking myself.

Next year? What was I even thinking? I won't even be around next year.

And I know I'm used to hurting inside. But when I think of never holding Ollie again, or being somewhere where he *isn't* just the other side of the wall, that's a different kind of pain altogether.

39

Stargazey House
Trolleys and a missing hostess
Sunday morning, Christmas Day

There is no point moping around, especially when my problem is so private. So, I'm back to my old tactics, smiling wildly, making sure I show everyone how happy I am. I know from experience that the only way to get through my crisis is by hurling myself into Christmas, and so that's what I do.

The next few days there are carols and hot chocolate for the over-sixties and a singles club Christmas cocktail party at the Little Cornish Kitchen. There's an Eve of Christmas Eve fancy-dress Christmas party and disco at Plum's gallery, and when Sophie offers to lend me a Snow White costume from their dressing-up box, I go for it. I've helped Clemmie make desserts for Christmas Day at hers. I even have a ride in the pony and trap decked out with so many fairy lights I can only think they hit Janice from Hardware Haven on a pushy day. Santa's elf was wearing more eyeliner than a zombie and was as toxic as I'd been warned. He gave me a piece of his mind about me and Ollie, which left me so gobsmacked I didn't even manage a reply. I mean, who told *him*? We were over before we began. I barely knew about it myself.

As for the man himself, Ollie seems to have done another one of his disappearing acts, so I haven't even had the chance to test how I feel when I see him.

As always, plans in St Aidan are constantly evolving. As soon any arrangement is made, it's like a challenge for someone else to come up with a better one. But now we've got as far as Christmas morning, I'm assuming the running order is final. The plan is to have Buck's Fizz and canapé starters at Stargazey Cottage, the main at Stargazey House, cheese at Plum's, puddings at Seaspray Cottage, and then to move on for the evening at Sophie's castle. For someone who didn't intend to celebrate at all, it's going to be a bumper day.

I've barely seen Ella for the whole week. She must have been off her face when she phoned from Falmouth because she hasn't mentioned any of what we talked about as we've passed each other rushing around the cottage. And however much I've stared at the clouds, it hasn't brought Minty back either.

I'm still scanning the sky for her this morning as I tuck into a light Christmas morning breakfast in the kitchen. And just to show how much effort I'm making to be in the mood, I have a Christmas-songs-you've-never-heard-of playlist playing in the background, which means I'm listening to Amy Winehouse singing 'I Saw Mommy Kissing Santa Claus'. I'm also dunking donuts into my coffee, looking past a pile of bags of sand on the newly levelled patio area Jago's made, out onto an ocean streaked with dark turquoise.

Then Ella clatters down the stairs and I look up as she

bursts through the gap in the living room wall. 'Can I get you a tea or a donut?'

She tosses a posh paper carrier on the table. 'Just open this quickly. It's an early present, I want you to put it on.'

'But there won't be any surprises later if I do.'

She gives me a sideways stare. 'There are plenty more in store for you today, believe me!'

'Meaning what?' If she's already got back together with Taylor, I'd rather hear that now.

'Nothing.' She's definitely back-tracking. 'That's just the kind of day Christmas is.'

I let it go because the sweatshirt I shake out is soft and the same colour pink as my favourite velvet cushions on the sofa. I push my arms into it, drop a kiss on her cheek for getting this so right, and read the logo on the front. '*Love will save the day!*'

She raises an eyebrow. 'Let's hope it does.' She smooths down her Sweaty Betty leggings and slips on her second-best trainers. 'Is there any fudge left? I'm nipping out for a run.'

As I pass the box of salted caramel over to her, I'm kicking myself for being so wrapped up in my to-do list that I've completely overlooked our usual Sunday morning outing. 'Would you like me to come?'

She gives a shout. 'Absolutely not!' Then she back-pedals and smiles. 'Much better for you to stay and get the Buck's Fizz chilling.' She gives me a little wave. 'Enjoy your sweatshirt. Back soon!'

When did Ella ever think about putting *anything* in the fridge? But whatever. If she hadn't been in such a rush I'd have checked if she's seen Ollie. I know he's only two steps down the hill, but somehow it's easier getting news of him than searching him out myself. As he's doing the main course today, I'm guessing he'll be flat out in his own kitchens, but I've got him a tiny gift from Janice's cabinet. After the way we left things on Wednesday I'd rather give it to him here than in public at the scheduled present opening down at Clemmie's later. But for now I put that in the 'too difficult' pile and move on to my own preparations for when we start off the celebrations.

First, I use up the very last of the hanging star strings, zigzagging them across the kitchen and living room, and then I move on to the canapés. I've finished some tiny veggie vol au vents and I'm just putting the mini smoked salmon tarts onto the cooling rack when Ella bursts through again and flings open the fridge door.

'Anything I can help with?'

She's staring at the contents of the shelves with wild eyes. 'I was on my way for a shower, but Ollie needs more eggs.'

I pass her an egg box. 'Take a dozen to be sure.' Then I frown. 'We have our own bathroom now. Have you forgotten?'

I'm the one whose face is usually scarlet, but Ella's pale cheeks get a definite rosy tint. 'The jets in en suite number three are too stupendous to give up.'

She's almost out the door, and I call, 'Sponge bag! Towel!'

She carries on running. 'I'll borrow Ollie's. See you later.'

And then the front door slams and I'm on my own again.

All that's left for me to do now is to make a few tomato and feta skewers, along with some maple-glazed sausage blinis, and then put out some glasses and some extra nibbles. It's hardly anything. And I definitely wasn't expecting any help from Ella. I'd just somehow hoped she might be here to keep me company with her non-stop anecdotes and site gossip while I worked. Instead, she's probably smoothing her hair to perfection and using Ollie's superior Wi-Fi to FaceTime Merry in Spain and get back with Taylor. Let's face it – my sweatshirt has Simpson-Ramsay-Christmas-morning-reunion written all over it. If I'm reading Ella's not-so-hidden messages, it can't mean anything else!

In fact, as my phone ticks round to half-past eleven, she's still not back. And then the door bursts open, and Nell, George, Plum, Sophie, Nate, and all their kids pile into the living room, all crying out at how beautiful the finished cottage is. And two minutes later they're followed by Jago, Charlie, Clemmie, Bud and Diesel, which means all the guests are here except for Ella and Ollie.

At one time I'd have been totally reliant on Ella to do the welcoming, but they've all been here so often, it's practically home-from-home for them anyway. George comes through and pops the fizz, Nell's taken charge of the jugs of freshly squeezed orange juice, and while I hand out the glasses, hugs and air kisses, Clemmie is telling everyone what's on each plate.

We're all milling around when Ella rushes in again. Her hair's even more all over the place, her cheeks are definitely crimson, and she's still in the same clothes.

She calls, 'Happy Christmas everyone, I'm running very late, I'll leave you with Gwen.' Then she swoops in for a pea and almond bruschetta, and rushes back out again.

If she had Jago waiting, warming the water in en suite number three, I'd understand what was going on. But he's by our twinkly twig tree, chatting to George about patio pavers and garden offices.

Clemmie pushes a mini mushroom-sausage roll into her mouth and gives my arm a squeeze. 'Totes delish! I'm sure Ella will be back soon.'

I roll my eyes. 'I know how long she takes to get ready! I'm pretty certain she won't be.'

And she isn't! But it really doesn't matter because there are so many other friends to chat to, we don't actually miss her.

She isn't even back when Ollie texts Jago to say he's ready for us next door. And when we get there, she's nowhere to be seen either. Instead, Ollie's in smart black trousers, which show his bum off to the max, and a crisp white shirt that sets off his stubble and cheekbones. He hands us more drinks, and shows us to the dining table, where we all sit down.

I knew it would have been better to get the 'how I feel about Ollie' test out of the way earlier. As it is, I fail on every count, and end up feeling sick *and* sad. But I'll have to woman up because there's no way I'm going to give myself away by letting it show.

Charlie hooks Bud's highchair onto the table edge and slides her into it, and Clemmie sits next to me.

Plum is calling through the door to the second-best kitchen, which seems to be where the action is, pulling an apron over her dungarees, ready to help with the serving. 'So what are we having, Ollie?'

Ollie comes out, and hands everyone a little card. 'It's all on here, just in case anyone wants to pick and choose.'

The lanterns down the table centre are flickering as I read. 'Nut roast, turkey, pork, sausage meat stuffing, apricot stuffing, sprouts and chestnuts, forcemeat balls, Yorkshire puddings, peas, cauliflower, red cabbage, carrots, Stilton sausages, chipolatas, homemade cranberry sauce, crispy potatoes, creamed potatoes, veggie gravy, real gravy…'

As Plum and Ollie start to carry things to the table, everyone is murmuring because it all looks so delicious. Then it suddenly hits me.

I give Clemmie a nudge. 'That small, neat handwriting is Ella's! That's where she's been – writing menus!'

There's a laugh from Ollie as he comes out of the kitchen. 'Good guess, but she actually wrote those last week.'

We're all staring at each other because she's still not here. 'So where is she?'

Ollie laughs. 'Look this way, you might be about to find out.'

Sure enough, as we look to where his finger is pointing, the first huge platter of meat from the kitchen comes into view, carried by Plum. And following behind her with an even bigger tray, laden with more meat, is Ella.

Her ponytail is skew-whiff, she's got a smudge of gravy browning on her forehead, she's still in her leggings and second-best trainers, and her T-shirt is streaked with sweat. As she collapses next to me into her usual chair at the head of the table, she rubs her nose with her fist. 'A few weeks ago somebody challenged me to learn to cook.' She's staring at Jago on her other side, then she turns to the rest of the table. 'So here you go everyone! Christmas dinner! I have no idea how it's going to taste, and I'd never have done it without Ollie, his four ovens and his tower steamer, but dig in, I hope you enjoy!'

There's a huge round of applause around the table, and a chorus of shouts of 'Well done, Ella.'

When the noise calms down she turns to Jago. 'I seriously hope you're worth the effort!'

Jago looks as if he's about to burst as he stares at the table groaning under the weight of the food. 'You've put me under a lot of pressure here, Ella-Bella!'

I pull her into a hug, and whisper in her ear. 'Would you like me to get you some lippy?'

She laughs. 'Stuff that, I'm having my lunch first. Jago said learn to cook. He can't have Maris Pipers crisped to perfection *and* flawless make-up.'

As I pile my plate high and start my meal, I can't help asking her. 'So how on earth did you do it, Ells? In running terms this is the equivalent of couch to round the world!'

Ella shrugs. 'Ollie offered to teach me, and you know how much I like my spreadsheets. Once he explained I could use them for my timings I didn't look back.' She wiggles her eyebrows. 'And I *was* highly motivated. Objectification aside, Jago is a total peach.'

I have to ask. 'And where does Taylor fit into all this?'

Ella's eyebrows arch as she chews, then she takes a swig of her wine. 'I told you to be brave, and you were, so I decided it was time I chose that hard route too, rather than always taking the easy one – I'm putting my faith in the future not the past.'

I'm shaking my head. 'Well done with that.'

She lowers her eyes. 'Taylor's a lovely guy. When he meets the right person, I'm sure he'll be very happy.'

After all my worries too. If this is what Ella meant by surprises, she wasn't wrong. But I'm never one to count my chickens, so it's always best to check before I make any assumptions. I lean forward to Ella. 'So have you and Jago made any plans, or do you have to check if the Christmas dinner's up to scratch first?' It is. A thousand per cent.

Ella laughs. 'You know me.'

'I do,' I say. 'That's why I asked.'

Her eyebrows are wiggling. 'I've already made a hundred spreadsheets for his boathouse conversion.' Her face goes more serious. 'When you're my age, time can run out on you. Not that we'll rush, but it might make sense for me to move into his rented place before too long.'

'Fab.' It's fine. I'm only back where I thought I was. Nothing's been lost.

She's squeezing my hand. 'It is, isn't it?'

And yes, it really is. I'm so happy for her. Hell, I know how hard Ella worked for this. I wouldn't begrudge her for a minute. Everything on the plate is delicious. I know how much it takes for a seasoned cook to pull that off; for Ella, it's remarkable. It's so yummy that when we're finished, we go in for seconds and do it all again.

And afterwards we're all sitting rubbing our stomachs when George gets to his feet and chinks his fork on his glass.

As he clears his throat, we all look up to listen. 'When the Star Sisters came to Stargazey Cottage, they promised to bring many things to St Aidan, though Christmas dinner wasn't actually on that list. But thank you for surprising and astonishing us all with this wonderful lunch, Ella. And congratulations to you and Jago. You're both very talented and deserve the best.'

There's a cheer, and everyone raises their glasses, and Jago squeezes Ella as tightly as their adjoining chairs will allow. But after all the clapping dies down, George stays standing, and begins again. 'I know no one can compete with Ella's surprise, but Nell and I have a little one of our own.'

We're all looking at each other around the table, raising our eyebrows expectantly. I've already got a lump in my throat as I think what it might be, but at the same time I can hardly dare to hope in case it's not.

George goes on. 'It's no secret Nell and I have been wanting a baby for what feels like a very long time.'

As Clemmie and I exchange glances, we both have drops on the end of our noses because we're already crying.

George goes on. 'A little while ago Nell had what we thought were some bouts of food poisoning, but we've recently found out that the reason Nell can't fit into her trousers any more isn't because of all the cake she's been eating...'

Nell's sitting beside him, and as she stands and stares down at her tummy there are tears rolling down both their faces. 'It's because we're expecting a baby! Who'd have thought? I'm four months along and had no idea!'

There's a roar and then everyone mobs them.

Sophie's eyes are shining. 'We knew Gwen's fudge was special.' She laughs. 'I'm tempted to do it all over again myself if it's an excuse to eat fudge all day like you were doing, Nell.'

Sophie's kids are calling to her. 'Four's enough, Mum, we've already run out of seats in the car.'

Sophie looks at them and claps her hands. 'Right, you lot. Time to help us clear the table. Start stacking those plates. Now!'

I turn to Ella. 'You're excused washing up today.' Then I remember what I haven't asked. 'So how did you fit in your cooking tuition?'

Ella's smile widens. 'Ever since the fudge tasting day I've come home and cooked tea here at Ollie's. I'm not a one-trick pony either. I can do mac and cheese, pasta and chorizo, beans on toast, chilli con carne, and homemade burgers and salads too.'

Jago winks at Ella. 'Sounds like Ollie found out my favourites and taught you those. At this rate you'll be parachuting straight into my penthouse.'

Ella's grinning. 'Ollie's a very wise guy. He is also excused from washing up.' She looks down at her T-shirt, then grins at Jago. 'If we're done here, maybe we can move up to en suite three, and I'll get cleaned up.'

I watch as they get up. 'We'll see you down at Plum's in a bit.'

Ella's hand is round Jago's neck and she's holding on very

tightly. 'Or we might give Plum's a miss and catch up with you all at Clemmie's.'

I wink at Ella. 'After a lunch like this, Plum will forgive you anything.'

After keeping my distance from Ollie since I arrived it's a shock to find that as I spin around on the bench to go to the kitchen my way is blocked by a white shirt and a black belt buckle. I drag my eyes away from his trouser zip and make my smile extra bright. 'Thanks for a lovely lunch, Ollie. Sophie's taken charge of the clearing but I'll go and help her.'

Ollie's biting his lip. 'You're excused washing up today too.'

I laugh much too loudly. 'I know my way around the kitchen. Unless there's anything better to do?'

He's tilting his head, looking down at me. 'It won't take long. There's something I'd like to show you at the top of the garden.'

I stiffen as his hand reaches towards me, thinking of the last time we went up there. 'Do I need a blindfold?'

After how that day ended, I completely understand why my feet feel like they're rooted to the spot.

His lips twist. 'You're probably okay without.'

I think it must have been the smile. But something inside me gives way, and I'm not resisting any more. I stop fighting. And without even realising I've done it, his hand is closing around mine and I'm letting him lead me out into the hall. We pass Ella and Jago on the way to the door, and Ella stops me and puts her hand on my arm. 'You've proved to all of *us* that you can be brave, Gwen. Now go and prove it to yourself.'

I'm still asking myself what the hell she's talking about as I follow Ollie out onto the lane.

40

Up in the shed
Make-overs and happy landings
Christmas Day

As Ollie and I climb the steps to the top of the cottage garden I can't help but think that the last time we raced up here our world was poised to explode with happiness – and within seconds it came crashing down.

This time we're going up more tentatively, and I'm back to being picky.

'I thought Jago said not to walk on the terrace?'

Ollie looks over his shoulder at me. 'That was my way of keeping you out of the garden.'

When we finally reach the shed, I sit down on the step and hug my knees to my chest. 'Remind me why we're here?'

His Adam's apple bobs. 'There are things I need to clear up. I'm sorry I upset you when I told you I'd been sailing again.'

I'm straight onto him. 'You spoke to Ella, didn't you?'

His eyelids flicker. 'We've spent hours together at the hob;

we were bound to talk.' He takes a breath then he looks straight at me. 'Okay, you got me – after you ran down from here the other day, I rang her at the Esplanade and told her everything.'

I'm staring past him out to sea. 'What I told you both on Wednesday still stands. I'm delighted you're mended, but I can't cope with the new version. And I'd rather die than limit you.'

The last few days I've shut him out of my mind to numb what I'm feeling. Now he's standing here in front of me, his hazel eyes brimming with a mix of concern and pain, I can't bear to see him hurting all over again. When it hits me there could be a time soon when I don't see him at all, it feels like an axe is cleaving my chest in two.

He takes a breath in then exhales very slowly. 'Okay, I completely understand that. But look at it from the other side. When you conquered your demons and stood out in the snow, you were really happy to have done that. But does it mean you'll be signing up for the next ski season? Are you desperate to go and live in the mountains again?'

It takes me no time to reply. 'I'd actually prefer to stay here. I like it by the sea. These last few months I've made friends, I've made a life and I've made a home. And if I had any choice at all, that's what I'd be holding on to.'

It's ironic that when I completely decide I want to stay, the possibility has been taken away from me.

Ollie's thumping the air with his fist. 'That's my whole point! When I was able to get back in a boat again, it was a life-changing moment. But that's not how I want to live any more. I'm a whole different person now.' He's staring at me. 'For the first time ever I've fallen in love. When I think of spending every day with you, Gwen, I feel so excited about the future. What matters to me now is making that happen.'

'You're right. That does change everything.' I'm swallowing back a mouthful of sour saliva because it's all come too late. 'But I'm not even going to be here.'

Ollie's forehead creases. 'But why not?'

I stare past his legs at the iron-grey clouds lined up across the sky. 'Ella's a heartbeat away from moving in with Jago and I can't afford the cottage on my own. Cornwall's a really expensive place – St Aidan especially – so I won't be able to afford to stay.'

As Ollie comes to sit on the step beside me, his hip and arm wedge against mine. 'Before we go any further, there's something I need to explain.' He's staring hard at his outstretched fingers. 'St Aidan was always too expensive for me too, I'd never have come here if I hadn't inherited Alex's place. But along with the main house I also inherited the adjoining cottage. When George saw me struggling, he suggested we could let the cottage at a low rent and get the tenants to do the work.'

My eyes are popping. '*So you have the cottage down the hill too?*'

Ollie's face creases as he laughs. 'No, Gwen. I'm talking about Stargazey Cottage. Stargazey Cottage and Stargazey House are both mine.'

'All this time, *and you didn't say?*'

He catches hold of my hand. 'I couldn't risk wrecking things. But I could see that what you wanted to do to the cottage would transform it. When the sale of my own place went through, I had cash to spare, so it made sense all round to pay Jago to do the work next door too.'

I'm shaking my head. 'This is unbelievable; you'll need to give me a minute to take it in.'

Ollie's nodding. 'George is the only one who knows. But the best part is, it means you can carry on living at the cottage. You *have* to stay, Gwen! You can stay rent-free. Just please say you aren't going to leave.'

It's such a shock that I'm blurting, 'Rent-free doesn't sound right. How would I ever pay you back?'

He lets out a sigh. 'Money isn't important if you have enough. I'd be more than happy if you paid me in fudge.'

It's slowly sinking in that I might not have to go after all. I'm so grateful that I'll be able to keep my little home forever, I barely know what to say. 'Well, thank you, Ollie. Is that it?'

He blows out a breath. 'One more confession. Maybe two.'

It's only fair to let him finish. 'I'm not sure how many more shocks I can take.'

Threading his fingers through mine, he holds on to me tightly. 'Nell put up the Facebook advert for the cottage and they all helped sort through the applications but I had the final say. I don't want to sound like a stalker, but I saw the photos of you in the file Ella sent and that was it.'

I'm picking my jaw up off the floor. 'So it wasn't our design pizazz, or the workshops, or our ability to pebbledash St Aidan with Christmas glitter?'

'I'm afraid not.' He gives a grimace. 'And then when I found you in my bedroom the day you arrived, my heart literally jumped out of the building, and I've loved you ever since.'

'Oh my.' I'm shaking my head again as he continues.

'I used to loathe coming here – I hated everything about the house – so your arrival was bittersweet. Because once you were here, I couldn't stay away. All I want to do now is to be with you and make you happy. But I know it's got to be right for you too.' He blows out a breath. 'Right, shall I show you what I brought you to see?'

'Okay. But first I have to tell you, I did feel it too. The same thing. That first day.'

He smiles. 'I'm so pleased you told me that.' He's up on his feet and pulling me up too.

'So what next?'

He's smiling again. 'Have a look inside the shed.'

As I push the door it swings freely as if it's been recently oiled. As I step inside, I'm hit by the smell of fresh paint, and engulfed in warmth from the stove.

Ollie's beside me. 'So, what do you think?'

I'm staring around at the plank walls painted the lovely green we chose together, the roof is dark blue with tiny white stars on, there's a stripy wool rug on the floor and sheepskins draped over the comfy new armchairs. There's a table and chairs too, painted in darker blue, and a red chest of drawers and bookcase.

My voice is a squeak. 'Oh my days! You zhooshed it!'

When I see the two little stars made out of bicycle chain resting on the bookshelf, I'm biting back the tears.

'I did. I have.' He's laughing. 'I used all the pointers you gave me on mine. And Ella helped too.'

I clasp my hand to my mouth. 'The metal display cabinet!'

He's looks guilty. 'I'm hoping I'm not getting ahead of myself, putting all my souvenirs in here too. But they just seemed to fit in so well.'

'This shed was made for Janice's kitsch.' I pick up one of Barnaby and Browne's pictures from the table. '*Fill every day with colour!* I like that too.'

He shrugs. 'It feels like that's what you've done for me.'

Then he frowns. 'I hope I'm not treading on your toes too much. I haven't bought cushions yet.'

I smile. 'There are still plenty of gaps to fill.' It would be lovely to do those together, but there's a long way to go yet before we get to that.

He's resting his shoulder on the wall, silhouetted in the doorway. 'I understand how scared you are to lose someone close to you again, Gwen. But more than anyone else I know, you deserve someone to love and care for you, and no one could care more than I do.'

However much I'd love this, I have to weigh it up. 'After a lifetime of adrenalin rushes sailing over oceans, are you really ready to settle for a cosy armchair by the wood burner and a view of the bay?'

That makes him smile again. 'I could if I were here with you.' Then his smile fades. 'The point is, I wouldn't need to go and push the limits on my own. If we wanted to take risks, we could take them together.'

I'm taking this all in, and it's huge. 'So you'd be looking at a total career change?'

He's nodding. 'We could work on that. My consultancy has been shore-based lately anyway. But with my painting and your eye, we could always do home makeovers.'

That makes me laugh. 'Move over, Star Sisters, here come Stargazey Interiors.' Then I hitch my breath. 'Or you could move into the cottage with me and we could open Stargazey House as that hosted hotel we talked about?' Then I realise what I've said and retract. 'That was totally random, off the top of my head. Forget I said it.'

'I'd go for that.' Ollie raises an eyebrow. 'I've always been more comfortable at your place than mine.'

I ran out on this once already, so I have to be certain, or it isn't fair to Ollie. 'I need to get this straight in my head.'

He hesitates. 'We all know you're strong enough to be on your own, Gwen, but we'd be stronger together. And don't overlook how happy we'd make each other.' A smile spreads across his face. 'And there's our explosive chemistry too.'

I'm agonising. 'This was easier when I wasn't in love with you. Right now, I'm weighing up the real-life pain I'll feel if I let go of you, with the imagined pain I might feel if I lost you in future.'

Ollie gives a low laugh. 'Put like that, there's no contest.'

I'm shaking my head because I'm so surprised. 'Ella implied I'd need my courage. But you know what, Ollie Lancaster? I love you so much, I don't have a choice, I *have* to be with you!'

He's still standing by the door. 'Are you sure about that?'

'I totally am.' I'm nodding madly. 'So do I get to have my Christmas kiss now?' I hurl myself into his arms and bury myself in an embrace that makes my whole body ache with pure lust.

When my lips finally leave his, my heart is pounding, but I push him down into a chair and go straight back in for more of the same. By the time we venture out onto the terrace again it's a long time later and there are lights coming on around the bay.

Ollie nuzzles my ear. 'Is there time to go upstairs at yours and do that all over again?'

I look at my phone. 'We've already missed Plum's cheese board. If I'm going to help Clemmie serve the puddings I spent all of yesterday making, we may have to save bed for later?'

His breath is warm on my neck. 'Clemmie's it is, then. What are you looking at?'

I'm squinting as a shaft of sunlight breaks through the clouds, watching a dot like I have done a million times since Wednesday. 'There's a bird in the distance. Probably just a seagull.'

Ollie stiffens beside me. 'But it's white.'

'It's the seaside, Ollie, a lot of birds are.' I've lost count of the times my hopes have been dashed.

'Well, whatever it is, it's heading straight for us!'

A moment later, there's a fluttering of feathers, and Ollie lets out a shout.

'Minty! Minty, you're back!'

I can't hold back my tears. 'Our snowbird has come home again. Isn't that the best Christmas present ever?' Then I realise what I've said, because I think it might be a tie for first place with me and Ollie getting together at long last.

Ollie laughs. 'It's been a day of good surprises.'

I watch as he scratches Minty's head. A moment later she springs onto his shoulder and starts pecking his ear. 'However exciting the presents are, I think we've had more than our share of happiness.'

I mean, Ollie and I love each other and we're officially an item, and our lost bird just flew back to us. They don't come any happier than that.

But as we go down to settle Minty back into her box and give her some seed, it's not quite over yet.

41

At Seaspray Cottage for puddings
Not quite wrapped up
Christmas Day

'When I think what you were like the first day you came in, Gwen, all quiet and shy. And now look at you! Happy, confident, and ready to take on the world again,' Clemmie says.

We're all sitting around a long table downstairs at the Little Cornish Kitchen, wearing paper hats and drinking yet more fizz. Beyond the French windows that open towards the sea we can still make out the lines of the breakers as they move towards the shore in the darkness and hear the gentle whoosh as they rush up the beach.

The remnants of the puddings we've demolished are up on the counter behind us. In the last hour we've eaten our way through a profiterole stack, a Baileys tiramisu, a Malteser covered ice-cream bombe, meringues, Christmas Eton mess, next-level chocolate log, ginger cheesecake, amaretto Bakewell tart and a retro trifle. And just for now, I feel like I couldn't eat another thing.

As I move Bud from one knee to another, I have to point out to Clemmie, 'It's not only me that's changed. Ollie's all smiles, and Ella's all helpful and hands-on. And Jago's beaming like a builder who's just been told he'll never have to make his own tea again.'

Ella coughs. 'Excuse me, Jago will be cooking half the time.'

Plum laughs at us all as we sit in a row. 'With your arms around each other like you've been superglued together, you four are a great advert for the singles club.'

Nell's leaning back in her chair. 'There's nothing we like better than the challenge of hard-bitten solo-and-staying-that-ways.'

Ella laughs. 'My mum, Merry, is heading here in January. Your work isn't over yet!'

Sophie's resting her chin on her hands. 'With all these couples getting together, St Aidan is crying out for its own baby shop.' She looks across to George. 'We should definitely flag that up at the next Chamber of Commerce meeting.'

Clemmie's laughing. 'Not wanting to take anything away from Nell and George's announcement, but Charlie and I might be needing one of those, too.'

Plum's narrowing her eyes. 'Why would you need that? Bud's already got two of everything!'

Clemmie's smile widens. 'For when we have our *new baby*.'

There are some puzzled frowns around the table, and it's Sophie who says what we're all thinking. 'But you go to Sweden to make your babies – *don't you?*'

Charlie's grinning. 'We did for Bud, but the next one has come along all by itself. It's our very own Christmas surprise!'

Clemmie's nodding. 'I was seeing the midwife for Bud's

check-up this week, and when I told her I was feeling a bit off, she did a test there and then. And we're definitely pregnant too!'

Nell lets out a shout. 'Another one who stopped their morning sickness with Gwen's fudge! What a pair we are!'

Sophie's already up and giving her a hug. 'Two mermaid babies arriving together! It's going to be a busy summer!'

We're all hugging Clemmie when Plum chimes in. 'Just as well some more mermaids will be getting their tails soon. They're hanging up at Sophie's ready for later.'

I'm smiling, looking at Sophie's youngest girls. 'Maisie and Tilly?'

Nell lets out a laugh. 'No, but as we mermaids brought you here, and seeing how well you've fitted in, we were hoping the Star Sisters from Stargazey Cottage would agree to become honorary mermaids?'

I'm flapping my fingers in front of my face, blinking away my tears. 'I don't know why I'm crying, but yes, thank you so much.'

Ella's frowning. 'So remind me what do we have to do if we're mermaids?'

Sometimes she has so little idea.

Clemmie laughs as she looks at me. 'I reckon Gwen's got the hang of it already. Let Bud eat your crown on a daily basis, wear your tails whenever Sophie has a party at the castle, lay down your lives for St Aidan and the crew. That kind of thing.'

Plum gives Ella a nudge. 'Cockle shell bikini tops are completely optional. Mostly we wear our tails with T-shirts.'

Ella gives a nod. 'In that case I'd be honoured and delighted.' She pulls a face. 'I promise I'll re-do my make-up too before we get to the castle. If I'm going to do my mermaid tail justice, I can't have smudges on my lippy.'

Ollie leans in to murmur in my ear. 'If I have my way, you'll always have smudges on your lippy.'

I lean over and wipe a pink smudge off his jaw. 'If that's how much you're promising to kiss me, it might just be best to leave it off for the next thirty years.'

He gives a low laugh and pulls me towards him. 'Fine by me.' Then he comes in closer. 'Just checking ahead – how about Christmas lunch at mine again next year? And maybe a summer wedding?'

I'm laughing back at him. 'With white doves? And our very own happy ending?'

And as Sophie's crew begin to clear away the plates, and we move on to the presents, I feel like I'm the luckiest woman in the world, because in St Aidan I haven't only fallen in love and made so many friends and met my life partner – I've finally found my home.

PS

Just in case you're wondering, my bed is every bit as comfy as I'd always hoped. More so for having Ollie in it. We wake in the mornings to the pink light of dawn coming through the balcony door, polyanthus in the window box, the sound of the sea in the distance, and Minty sitting on the balcony rail, tapping on the window. We never really got to try sleeping at Ollie's – Stargazey Cottage wrapped itself around us, and so that's where we always stay.

Ella slid into Jago's place down by the harbour in the same way Ollie moved into the cottage. It wasn't a proper decision; one day we just woke up and realised it had happened. Ella's not one to stand still either. She's already chosen the kitchen appliances for Jago's boathouse, and we often meet her down on the quayside at dusk at the weekends, covered in dust after a day helping on site there. Jago's still doing amazing work in St Aidan, with his double scale of prices. And Ella's still zhooshing those top-price holiday homes right across Cornwall, but she's also working for Charlie on his eco-housing schemes too.

When Ella's mum, Merry, comes to visit in January she stays with us in Ella's room at the cottage, but she enjoys the St Aidan social whirl so much that when a studio flat comes vacant in Jago's building down on the quayside, she moves in there.

As for Ollie and me, as the months have gone by, we have become true citizens of St Aidan. We do a bit of this and a bit of that, we have impetuous ideas and follow our hearts on the spur of the moment. He takes me sailing, and I'm amazed to find how huge the skies are, and the sense of freedom when we're totally surrounded by the ocean. And when the snows melt in spring I take him to the mountains, and we jump off the edges of cliffs and hang in the air under parafoils, just like I used to do with Ned and Dad. Only this time I'm doing it because I want to, rather than because they wanted me to, and I'm soaking up the exhilaration and adrenalin rush more that I'd ever have thought possible. We're even planning a visit to Dad in New Zealand next year.

As spring turns to summer, Nell and Clemmie's bumps are growing. Bud's scooting round the floor on her bottom, but still likes watching decorating videos when she's kicking in her highchair. I'm helping out more at Clemmie's, but, yes, we're also letting Stargazey House to groups, where Ollie's on break-fasts and we do the evening meals together. It's early days, but it's going well. And when Ollie goes out for supplies, Minty flies along above the car, and then follows him back home again. And Janice's partner's cousin kindly finds Minty a husband, so our pigeon flock grows and so does our seed consumption.

Since Ollie and I have been in St Aidan we've both redis-covered our brave sides. And obviously we've fallen in love, but most of all we've learned how to live again. We still light our candles in the window every evening. But these days life is about everything we've got to look forward to together.

And if you ever happen to be in St Aidan and look up to see a flock of white pigeons circling in the sky, it might just be Minty and her family, flying home to Stargazey Cottage. And Ollie and I will be sitting at the top of the garden in our little shed in the sky, making plans for our next adventure, as we drink our gin and tonics and watch the sun go down across the bay.

GWEN'S RECIPES

In case your mouth is watering after reading the book here are a few of Gwen's recipes to give you your own taste of St Aidan.

Microwave Golden syrup sponge in a mug

One of the first times Gwen invites Ollie into the kitchen at Stargazey Cottage she makes him a quick syrup sponge – in the microwave, because it's the only cooker she has. It's so delish he ends up eating hers as well as his! This version only takes a couple of minutes to prepare, and the same to cook; with the light and fluffy sponge and the molten golden syrup, it's instant heaven in a mug. Gwen made hers in ramekin dishes, and added vanilla ice cream too.

Make sure whichever dishes or mugs you choose are safe to use in a microwave.

Cooking time may vary depending on the power of your microwave, and the size of your dish.

Serves one, in a large mug (or you can do smaller versions, and split the mixture and the syrup into two ramekin dishes instead – for this the cooking time will be shorter)

3 tablespoons self raising flour
1 tablespoon caster sugar
1 medium egg
A few scrapes of lemon zest (if you're not going for the gourmet version, you can miss this out)
2 tablespoons milk
1 tablespoon vegetable oil
1 tablespoon golden syrup

Put the flour, sugar, egg, milk, oil and (optional) lemon zest into a large deep mug and beat with a fork until the batter is smooth.
Without stinting, take a tablespoon of syrup, and drop it into the centre of the batter.
Cook on high for three to four minutes, until the sponge is firm to the touch.
Let it stand for a minute before eating, as the syrup will be very hot!

Serve with vanilla ice cream. If you're feeling extra indulgent add a drizzle of golden syrup too. Totally yummy!

Easy Fudge

Gwen's secret to persuading Jago's team of builders to get the job done at Stargazey Cottage is to keep them supplied with fudge.

This is a very easy recipe for melt-in-the-mouth British-style fudge, and it's still one of my favourites.

397g tin of condensed milk
450g soft light brown sugar
120g butter, cut into cubes
125ml milk
Pinch of salt

Have a bottle of pre-chilled water in the fridge.
Grease an 8 inch square baking tin. (If you have baking parchment to hand, you could line the tin instead, as this helps if you want to move the finished fudge to cut into pieces on a chopping board.)
Now for the action! Place all the ingredients except the salt in a large dry saucepan. Stir continuously over a low heat until the butter has melted and the sugar has completely dissolved. Increase the heat gradually to bring the mixture slowly to the boil, then keep at a rolling boil for ten minutes. Stir thoroughly and continuously at this stage, and take special care around the edges, to make sure the mixture doesn't catch or burn on the bottom of the pan. Also take care not to splash the mixture, as it is very hot.
After ten minutes at a rolling boil the mixture should be darker and thicker.
Take the pan off the heat, and fill a mug with chilled water from the fridge. Then scoop some fudge mixture

onto a teaspoon and drop a little of the fudge mix off the spoon and into the water.

If the fudge has reached its setting point, the dropped mixture will form a soft ball as it hits the cool water. After a couple of minutes in the water, the ball should be hard enough not to stick to your fingers or the mug side when it touches. If this happens you are ready to move to the next stage. If the mixture hasn't reached its setting point, the drop of fudge may stay soft and sticky, or it may just mix with the water. If this happens you need to return to pan to the heat. Bring the mixture to the boil again and stir for a couple more minutes, then try to drop a blob into the water again. Repeat this process, testing the fudge mixture every two to three minutes. Once the fudge forms a firm ball in the water, the fudge is cooked and you can move onto the next stage.

Now you are ready to add that pinch of salt! Then beat the mixture well with a wooden spoon.

Leave to cool in the pan for ten minutes, then beat again.

Leave for another five minutes, then beat again.

(For these stages, you'll need to break through the set surface each time before you beat.)

Pour the mixture into the tin, and level it out using the back of a spoon.

Put into the fridge and leave there for at least three hours, or until it's completely firm and you can cut through it with a knife without the knife getting stuck.

Slice up into thirty six equal pieces. Then share!

In the unlikely event you don't eat it all immediately, the fudge will keep in an air-tight container.

If you want to vary the flavour, and add chocolate, coffee, vanilla, nuts etc, you can do it as you add the salt.

As George pointed out at Gwen's fudge tasting afternoon, a batch of fudge, nicely wrapped makes a wonderful gift – so long as Ella's not around to eat it first!

Delicious Golden Syrup Flapjacks

The day Gwen finally made flapjacks, it really was a milestone on her journey back to happiness. As kids she and Ella had made flapjack mixture and eaten it raw from the pan – and I have to come clean and say that when I made flapjack as a teenager it was so I could lick the pan out, rather than because I loved the flapjack itself. Happily, I have changed my mind on that now, but the recipe here will let you do either! With only four ingredients, they're wonderfully easy to make, and ready in half an hour.

Some people like their flapjack dry, while others like a stickier version. If you are like me and enjoy yours on the sticky side, cut down the cooking time slightly until you find your preferred consistency. Adding more syrup than the recipe says gives a stickier result too.

250g porridge oats (jumbo ones will give you a slightly coarser consistency)
125g butter (plus whatever it takes to grease the tin)
125g light brown sugar

367

2-3 tablespoons of syrup (depending on how sticky you'd like it)

Pre-heat the oven to 200C/180C fan/Gas 6.
Lightly grease an eight inch by eight inch baking tin.
Put the sugar, butter and syrup into a heavy bottomed saucepan.
Stir the ingredients over a low heat, until the sugar is dissolved.
Then add the oats and mix.

(An alternative method is to put all the ingredients in a food processor and pulse until mixed. For this you need the jumbo oats, and will need to be careful not to over-mix or the texture will be too smooth.)

Transfer the mixture to the baking tin, pushing the mixture into the corners.
Bake for around fifteen mins or until golden brown (see note on baking times above)
Leave to cool slightly, and cut into twelve equal-sized rectangles while still warm.

Then enjoy.

Love, Jane xx

AUTHOR'S NOTE

To my readers...

Thank you for choosing A Winter Warmer at the Little Cornish Kitchen. These books are all for you, I'm so grateful to you for enjoying them – it's your hearts and imaginations that truly bring the stories to life. I love hearing from you on Facebook and Instagram, and I'm so looking forward to the time when book events are like they used to be, so we can have more opportunity to meet up in person again.

St Aidan is a fictitious place, but I feel as if I live there, and some readers feel the same. If you've enjoyed your time in St Aidan, you may like to visit again. All my St Aidan stories are standalone reads. The books run chronologically, some characters appear in several books, but not everyone is in every story. For anyone who'd rather avoid accidental spoilers, this is the order they were written in:

The Little Wedding Shop by the Sea
Christmas at the Little Wedding Shop
Summer at the Little Wedding Shop

Christmas Promises at the Little Wedding Shop
The Little Cornish Kitchen
A Cornish Cottage by the Sea (aka Edie Browne's Cottage by the Sea)
A Cosy Christmas in Cornwall
Love at the Little Wedding Shop by the Sea
Tea for Two at the Little Cornish Kitchen
A Winter Warmer at the Little Cornish Kitchen

Happy reading and lots of love, Jane xx

ACKNOWLEDGMENTS

A book is so much more than just the words, and lots of people helped to make this one. Back in 2012 Charlotte Ledger pulled my first manuscript out of her e-submissions pile, and signed me to Harper Collins' brand new digital fiction line. It's been an amazing personal journey for me since then, from the slush pile to over half a million book sales worldwide. And wonderful Charlotte has been there all the way, with her amazing warmth, friendship and professional brilliance, making all of that happen. There are no thank you's big enough, or enough words to describe my love and admiration for you, Charlotte. You are – quite simply – a legend! And the team you've drawn around you at One More Chapter are truly amazing. Their covers, production, promotion, creativity, collaboration and support are awesome.

Huge thanks and love too, for Amanda Preston, my agent. I couldn't do this without you. Whatever I need, you are there with it, I love how much fun we have alongside the serious stuff. I couldn't wish for anyone better to share the excitement.

Thanks to Kimberly Young and the fabulous team behind the scenes at Harper Collins. To my lovely friend, Emily Yolland. To the fab foreign rights team, not forgetting the team at Harper Collins Germany who work their own magic with my books over there. To my writing friends especially Zara Stoneley and Debbie Johnson who keep me sane on a daily basis. To my wonderful Facebook friends who constantly support me, especially Wendy McClaren in Australia. To the fabulous book bloggers who spread the word, especially Rachel Gilby who delivers the most amazing Blog Tours.

Jess Cushway began lockdown as someone who made great brownies and ended it with a fully fledged baking business. Congratulations on creating Cushway Cakes, Jess, and thanks for all the baking inspiration and advice you give me along the way.

And last of all, huge hugs to my family for cheering me on all the way. And big love to my own hero, Phil.

YOUR NUMBER ONE STOP

ONE MORE CHAPTER

FOR PAGETURNING BOOKS

One More Chapter is an
award-winning global
division of HarperCollins.

Sign up to our newsletter to get our
latest eBook deals and stay up to date
with our weekly Book Club!
<u>Subscribe here.</u>

Meet the team at
<u>www.onemorechapter.com</u>

Follow us!

 @OneMoreChapter_

 @OneMoreChapter

 @onemorechapterhc

Do you write unputdownable fiction?
We love to hear from new voices.
Find out how to submit your novel at
<u>www.onemorechapter.com/submissions</u>